DEATH AFTER DISHONOR

A DICKIE FLOYD DETECTIVE NOVEL

DANNY R. SMITH

COPYRIGHT

Cover by Jon Schuler

www.schulercreativelab.com

ISBN-13: 978-1-7322809-8-4

ACKNOWLEDGMENTS

I would like to offer a special thanks to my beta readers, whose eyes for detail have helped me polish this novel: Scott Anderson, Ernie Banuelos, Michele Carey, Teresa Collins, Andrea Hill-Self, Henry "Bud" Johnson, Phil Jonas, Ann Litts, William "Moon" Mullen, Dennis Slocumb, David Stothers, and Heather Wamboldt. Also my wonderful wife, Lesli, and daughters Jami and Randi Jo. I am beyond grateful for this wonderful team of all-stars!

As always, a big thanks to my very good friend, Patricia Barrick Brennan, whose scrutinizing eyes are the first to peruse all of my writing.

And to my editor, Ms. Robin J. Samuels (Shadowcat Editing), thank you for the great job you did polishing this book.

There was a special case and it happened in a place of otherwise breathtaking beauty, and that place, one special in my heart—but not mine alone—is mentioned in this novel. That story—that heartbreaking, wretched story—is one that is best left untold, for its memory is both sacred and burdensome—but not to me alone.

This is in her loving memory.

The truth was, some victims really did matter more than others. When a hardcore gangster—a known shooter—got himself killed one week, and the next week you picked up a murdered child case, that's when you grasped the reality of homicide work. You came to terms with choosing one victim over another, and you accepted the fact that not all cases were equal.

1

IT WAS OUR TURN IN THE BARREL.

The lights were dimmed now that the phones had stopped ringing, and the vast office—home to eighty-some homicide detectives—had emptied of its final night owls. Josie and I, however, were there to man the phones on the graveyard shift.

I had just finished updating the on-call schedule on the grease board that hung on the wall above my head. I sat as reclined as I could be in an office chair, my feet propped on the desk. Josie's heels clicked across the tile floor. I looked up to meet her gaze as she stopped at the counter between us, a cup of coffee in her hand.

"How is it we get early mornings in the barrel *and* we're first up for murders at six?"

She was looking past me toward the board where I had just changed our position in the rotation for murders.

"Apparently Martinez and Castro have a meeting with the sheriff at nine, so *your* lieutenant said to pull them out of the rotation until it's finished. He doesn't want them getting hung up on anything and not making it downtown."

"A meeting with the sheriff?"

I nodded. "And his entourage. They should be done by noon and we'll be back to sitting third in the rotation."

"If we haven't caught," she said, offering a slight smile to let me know she wasn't complaining.

"We'll be good."

She pushed a lock of hair behind her ear and lightly blew on her steaming coffee.

"I look forward to a new case," she said, "but I hope we can get a few hours of sleep before it comes in. I'm ready to get back into the swing of things around here. You know?"

Detective Josefina Sanchez had been off for six months recovering from a broken leg and a fractured hip, while dealing with some psychological issues that remained after being held captive in the mountains for nearly a week. Cops were the world's worst victims of violent crime; we were wired to overcome and conquer. When that didn't happen, the scars ran deep. I knew.

"I'm glad you're back, Josie. It's been a long six months running solo around here, getting paired with different partners every rotation."

"Anything good?" she asked.

I watched her sip her coffee as I told her about a case Rich Farris and I had picked up together in her absence.

The victim, Jackie Melvin Lowe, was a Blood gang member and up-and-coming rapper. In the neighborhood he was known as "J-Lowe." When he first broke into the music industry, he had taken the name "D.J. Low Boy." He didn't want to use "J-Lowe" and be compared to the singer/actress Jennifer Lopez. But "D.J." sounded like the titles of *players* and *hustlers*, not gangsters whose lyrics were harsh and dark and told of life in the ghettos and prisons of the white man's America. So when he cut his first album, *Riding Low with Killer B's,* he dropped the "D.J." and the E and had quickly gained fame as "Low Boy," a hardcore gangster rap artist.

But fame had its drawbacks. When *the hood* was the most important part of one's life—which was the case with hardcore gangsters—homies came first, family second, and "bitches" were way down the list. The homeboys demanded that it remain so, that they ride together no matter where "the car" went: music videos, award ceremonies, trips to Vegas and

New York. They expected to be rolling together, high and hard, each getting a piece of the action. And Low Boy and his entourage did roll hard, but only for a year.

The night Low Boy was killed, the entourage was curiously nowhere to be found, and he didn't die in the glow of his name in lights. No, he had been unceremoniously gunned down in the darkness of a perilous street in the city of Compton, in his own neighborhood.

The murder had originally appeared to be a random gang killing— something that is all too common on the streets of Compton and South Los Angeles—but the victim's status had given me and Rich Farris pause. We had wondered if the murder was an "in-house" hit, a case of his being killed by fellow gang members. If not that, maybe it was related to the rap industry, wherein the dynamics were similar to traditional organized crime syndicates; players would get whacked by people they had known their whole lives and with whom they may have just shared a meal or a drink. But in the rap industry, there were no warehouses or garages where the dead would fall neatly onto a plastic sheet and be disposed of in the harbor or woods. Rappers were gangsters, and when they killed, they killed gang-ster style. Our victim had been sitting in a Cadillac in front of his home-boy's house, smoking a blunt, when someone had walked up and filled his red-clad, gold-laden, obese body full of lead.

I finished telling Josie about the gangster rap case as she drained the remainder of her coffee and then stared at the cup as if contemplating a refill.

It was almost three now and we were both tired, having come in for barrel duty on the early morning shift after being in court all day yester-day. Neither of us had been able to get more than a short nap before relieving the PM desk crew. Now we only had a couple of hours left until we'd both be able to go to our homes and get some much-needed sleep— unless we got called out.

"You can relax," I assured her. "It's a cold and rainy Wednesday morn-ing. Nobody's going to die before noon."

She regarded the board once more and then looked over her shoulder at the muted TV on the wall showing a local news station covering the weather. Her soft, brown eyes came back to me.

"What's the meeting about?"

"Martinez and Castro?"

She nodded.

"One of those dog and pony shows for the executives, briefing them on their case and answering their stupid questions."

"What'd they have that's got the old man interested?"

By "old man" I knew she meant Sheriff Rolando Guzman, though he was far from being a senior citizen. In fact, I had more time on the job than he had and was probably older too. But he had been elected sheriff of Los Angeles County and now sat behind a big desk with fancy furnishings and a view of the city that I still tromped through night and day with scuffed wingtips and worn-out fedoras.

"The woman that went off the balcony in West Hollywood," I said.

"That wasn't a suicide? I saw it on the news. A couple weeks ago, right?"

"Just before you came back," I said. "And whether or not it was a suicide remains to be seen. Martinez and Castro don't think so. The sheriff was made aware of it because it has political overtones. Apparently, there was a conference at the hotel where this happened, and several city officials were partying in the bar after. I think maybe the girl was seen there too, but I don't know all the circs."

Josie shook her head and rolled her eyes, showing her disgust. I wondered if it was directed toward the councilmen or the dead woman who had apparently entered the danger zone by rubbing elbows with politicians, even if unwittingly. Josie started to leave, then stopped. "Do you need anything? Cup of coffee?"

"Not for me, partner. I'm going to try to get some sleep while it's quiet. No reason not to; you never know when the big one will come in and we'll be back to running full speed ahead."

"It's Wednesday, remember?"

I smiled. "Touché."

"I'll be at my desk if you need anything. I want to look at some old cases while the phones are quiet."

What she would actually be doing was stalking a game warden named Jacob Spencer. He was the man who had been credited with saving her after she was taken, but a shroud of doubt hung over the case. Josie and I, in particular, were skeptical about what had really happened on the mountain, and we were determined to discover the truth. Josie had somehow—*magically*—managed to procure background investigation reports from several law enforcement agencies to which Spencer had applied. She had obtained personnel records from his current employer, the Department of Fish and Wildlife—what most of us still called Fish and Game—and reports from every arrest he had ever made and every citation he had ever written. How she had gotten it all, I had no idea. She sifted through these files whenever she had time, and she scoured social media where Spencer had established a presence but not much more. Josefina Sanchez had set her teeth into the case in traditional bulldog fashion.

"Suit yourself," I said.

I lowered my fedora to cover my face. As I listened to her heels click away, I could see her in my mind, walking away with the slight limp her ordeal had left her with. The footfalls faded and I knew she had entered the carpeted squad room. I pictured her approaching her desk, the way she looked in those gray and white checked slacks, her shapely, athletic figure; these were things that couldn't be ignored in a testosterone-driven environment like law enforcement—limp or no limp. Though much had changed over the decades and generations, there were no policies ever written that could change what a man naturally thought about when he saw such things. Most of us had learned to keep our mouths shut and our flies zipped to avoid being caught up in workplace harassment drama, but that didn't mean that nature had somehow been neutralized in the office.

My eyes grew heavy and I didn't fight the beckoning sleep. The next thing I knew, I was jolted from my slumber by the loud ringing of the desk phone. I sat up, shook myself awake, and glanced at the clock on the wall. It was almost five in the morning, nearly time for our relief to arrive, and about time for Josie and me to be up in the rotation for murders. I punched the blinking line and answered the call, trying to sound as if I hadn't been sleeping.

"Sheriff's Homicide, Jones."

Josie rounded the corner and our eyes met while a female on the other end of the line began telling me she was a deputy sheriff and that they had a death to report in Palos Verdes. I frowned at the phone. I frowned at

5

Josie. I frowned at the muted TV that now showed an infomercial about some type of diet or nutrition scam.

Palos Verdes was within the jurisdiction of Lomita Sheriff's Station, but it was not a place we often went to investigate murder cases. There were accidental deaths, recreational deaths—boating or diving accidents— and the occasional suicide, someone jumping from one of the high cliffs into the Pacific Ocean. But seldom a murder. Nonetheless, it was more than likely that one of us—me or Josie—would now be tasked with driving from Monterey Park to Palos Verdes to have a look.

"I'm sorry," I said, now fully awake, "I missed your name."

"Jessica Lambert, Lomita Station."

"Okay, Jessica, what do you have?"

Josie passed behind me and sat down in the adjacent chair, pulling a Dead Sheet from the file tray, something that would be required no matter the type of death being reported. She readied a pencil over the sheet and watched me, waiting. Probably, like me, hoping it would be a natural death and that the deputy had already located a treating physician who would agree to sign a death certificate. That would allow Josie and me to drive to our homes and crawl into our beds rather than fight traffic to the coast after being up all night. Well, most of the night.

Deputy Lambert said, "We have a murder to report, sir."

I cupped one hand over the mouthpiece and reached toward Josie with the other, indicating the Dead Sheet. "She's calling in a murder."

Josie handed it to me and glanced at the grease board, then checked her watch. As my gaze moved to the paperwork before me, I was left with the image of Josie smiling widely as she settled back into her seat.

The Dead Sheet is a living document that is started with the first call to Homicide and would be updated throughout the investigation as facts and details came to light. For now, I wrote down the date, the time of notif- ication, the person making the notification, her employee number and assignment, and then I hovered my pencil over the empty line where the victim's name would be memorialized once it was known for certain. Sometimes that day never came, and John or Jane Doe would be assigned a file number along with a coroner's case number. Other times, the person is known, but not yet positively identified; there was a reason these forms were completed in pencil and not pen.

"Do we have a name yet, Jessica?"

"Yes sir. Edward Robert Bellovich."

"Jesus Christ, not—"

"Yes," Deputy Lambert interrupted, "it's the mayor's kid."

2

It was an unwritten rule that you didn't send a team out in their last hour of their on-call rotation. They would have just covered murders for thirty-six or forty-eight hours—depending on if it was during the week or on the weekend—and they would be worn down from either catching cases or lying awake in their beds wondering when they would, whereas the next team up would be fresh and ready to go. In most cases. Of course, Josie and I were far from fresh, and the two teams that should have been up for murders ahead of us had been pulled from the rotation for the time being. I knew we had no option but to take the Lomita callout ourselves. Handle our mud. Carry our water.

When I hung up with Deputy Lambert, I swiveled my chair to face Josie.

"What are you smiling about?"

She pushed out of her seat. "We have a new case, and it sounds like an interesting one, not the usual gang or drug killing. You ready?" Josie clapped a hand on my shoulder as she passed behind me. She started for the squad room but stopped and looked back at me. "Come on, Dickie. Let's get crackin'."

"Jesus, what are you, a miniature Floyd?"

"Hurry up," she said, disappearing around the corner.

We cleaned up whatever we had going from a night in the barrel and made a fresh pot of coffee, something I desperately needed and that would also be appreciated by our relief. By the time we were both ready to go, our relief had arrived, freeing us from desk duties. It was time to go work our fresh murder case.

We opted to take one car and leave the other at the office so we could keep each other awake as we drove to and from Palos Verdes, an impossible drive at any time of the day or night. Josie had beat me to the parking lot and was waiting behind the wheel of her car as I marched across the parking lot, avoiding puddles and ducking against the light rain.

"You're driving?" I said, now at the side of her car.

She raised her face to speak through the window, which was open only a few inches. "Yeah, come on. Besides, you look worn out, even after your nap."

I felt worn out but wasn't about to admit it—to Josie or anyone else. I went to my Crown Vic, which was parked just beyond where Josie waited, and retrieved my suit jacket and raincoat from the back seat. I opened the rear door of Josie's blue Ford Taurus, folded my raincoat onto the back seat, hung my jacket on the hook, and set my briefcase on the floorboard. I settled into the front seat with Josie watching me.

"Let's go," I said.

"Buckle up, partner."

I thought I caught a look of sadness in her eyes after she said it, and I wondered if she was thinking of her ex-boyfriend. Tommy Zimmerman had been killed six months earlier while riding in Josie's car, when they were forced off a mountain road. Tommy hadn't been wearing his seatbelt and was ejected from the vehicle and killed. Josie survived the crash, only to be taken and held captive for nearly a week. The ordeal would have a lasting impact on her and those around her. It was a delicate situation. I belted up and avoided her eyes.

She turned out of the lot and we headed toward the freeway in silence.

Traffic was already heavy at six, the result of Angeleños staggering their work schedules in desperate efforts to avoid spending their lives looking through windshields. It hadn't worked, and it especially didn't help on rainy mornings. We had been in the car for ten minutes and neither of us had spoken since the seatbelt conversation. I was thinking about that week when Josie was missing, and she was likely thinking of it also while trying hard not to.

I broke the ice. "So you were all excited to be getting a case, but now you seem melancholy. Is everything okay? Are you sure you're ready to be back at it?"

She glanced at me, and then turned her attention back to the road. "I'm ready. I need this."

I nodded, but she didn't see me, her eyes back on the traffic ahead of her.

"If anything changes—"

Josie drew in a deep breath and I worried that I had irritated her with my questioning. After a long moment, she glanced at me again, then back to the road before replying.

"Did you and Farris talk about my case much while I was off? You guys must've spent a lot of time together working the new case you picked up."

The traffic slowed to a crawl as we approached the 105 freeway, south-bound on the 710. I wondered if it would be faster to take the 105 or continue down to the 91. Either would get us over to the 110, which we would take south to Pacific Coast Highway and then head west to Palos Verdes. To Rolling Hills Estates, to be precise. I wondered why Josie hadn't turned on the radio for up-to-the-minute traffic reports on KFWB. *Traffic on the ones*, every ten minutes. The station was perma-tuned in my Crown Vic.

"You want to check the traffic?" I asked, indicating the radio.

She reached between her legs and picked up her cell phone, flashing it my direction to show me a mapping application that was running on the screen. She set it back on her seat and said, "This is better than the radio. Right now, the 91's the fastest route. Now answer my question."

I crossed my legs and leaned back into my seat. "Sure, me and Rich talked about it."

"And?"

"And what?"

She glanced over again, riding the brake as we crept along in the burgeoning daylight, wipers lazily swiping at the raindrops pattering against the windshield. "I want to know what he thinks about Spencer. I told you about my vision, or dream—whatever you want to call it—where I saw the warden's smiling face. If the vision is a sign, it was Spencer who dragged me to that shed and tied me up. But we'll never know for sure, since he killed the Watkins kid, will we?"

I shrugged. "I don't know, Josie. I mean, I have dreams too, and on a few occasions I've found answers to questions I had about cases. I think it's similar to being under hypnosis, where your mind reaches deeper levels of memory when you're in a deep sleep. So I'm certainly not going to dismiss the idea that Spencer had something to do with it, but I can't for the life of me figure out how or why. And if he did, why was the Watkins kid taking care of you?"

"I don't have an answer for that. Maybe he was slow; that was an impression I had of him. He treated me like a found pet, but something he couldn't take home. You know? He never did anything bad to me. He never even tried. He fed me, brought me fresh water, allowed me to relieve myself outside of his presence. He was almost a gentleman about it, or maybe just a bashful boy. But—and I've been thinking about this a lot—that night, the night he was killed and that creepy warden 'rescued' me, the kid had cut the ropes from my hands and said he was going to help me. Other nights, he untied the ropes and then refastened them before he left, after I finished everything. Then the warden blows him away. How did the warden find me that night? And why did he have to kill the boy?"

"He said Junior came at him with the knife. You saw the knife on the ground."

"But Junior also had a gun, right?" she said. "Why didn't he pull his pistol on the warden if the intent was to kill him?"

I was gazing out the window, aware of the traffic and our location and the length of time it would take us to get to the coast at this rate. The topic wasn't one I would have brought up on the way to a new case, if for no other reason than I liked to concentrate on what awaited us and go through a mental checklist of the possibilities. It occurred to me I could shift gears on her easily enough as soon as I felt it necessary; I didn't want to spend much more time on the topic of Josie's having been kidnapped. Not today.

"That bothered me too," I said.

"What did Farris tell you about the interview? That's what I want to know."

11

I pondered my answer for a long moment. Maybe too long.

"Well?" Josie prompted.

"He had a bad feel for the guy. He told me so from the beginning, but I was—well, I was certain he had saved you. To be honest about it, that night, when I went back up the mountain to check the shed, I had a strong pull to return, like a real gut feeling you were there. Why it didn't come to me sooner, I don't know. Then I get there, and I see the warden's truck, and the rope going down toward the shed, and I think, thank God, he had the same feeling as I had. See, I kind of liked Spencer from the start, when we met a few days earlier. He seemed like a good guy to me, and I usually have good instincts. I mean, we're all wrong at times—and I'm no exception—but there was no bad vibe from him for me. Not then, anyway."

Josie's gazed remained straight ahead, and I could see the reflection of brake lights in her eyes. She waited, wanting more. Knowing there was more.

"Then, when I was headed down the mountainside, the gunshot rang out. I…I about lost my mind. I tumbled half way down, trying to get there faster, tripping over brush and rocks and whatnot. When I saw Spencer with the gun, he looked at me, and said, 'It's your partner. She's inside. She's going to be okay.' Those words blinded me, Josie. You have no idea—it was an emotional experience."

I looked out my window with moist eyes but all I could see was a scene in my mind, a dim light glowing in the dark mountains, a game warden directing its beam into a dingy shed where my partner had been tied to the floor. A young man lay dead on the ground next to her, his clouded eyes fixed in her direction.

After a moment, I continued. "That next day, when I gave my statement to Farris and Marchesano, I actually argued with them about it. I left the interview room thinking the two of them had missed the mark. I guess emotions were still getting the best of me. Then, since the hospital—after he visited you and you felt creeped out, and you sent me the text saying you didn't trust him, and that you had had that dream about him being the one who first took you—I haven't been able to stop thinking about it. About him. And now I see that scene play out slightly differently in my head, but I don't know if it's real or imagined. If I'm being biased now."

"What do you see?"

"His first reaction. He was startled—almost panicked when I called out his name as I approached him. And there was a slight pause before he directed my attention to you in the shed. Like he wasn't sure what to do next. I remember seeing the gun in his hand, and back then, it didn't concern me in the slightest, because I knew him, and because he's a cop—"

"Well, a fish cop—"

"—and he was no threat. I mean, I didn't reach for my gun or anything the way I would have with any citizen holding a gun."

Josie shot me an inquisitive look. I wondered if she was questioning my judgment, my actions that night on the mountain, or whether I was telling her everything.

"And now?" She paused. "How do you see that part now, Richard?"

We were finally on the 110 south. Traffic was lighter and the rain had nearly stopped, only sprinkles remained. The northbound lanes were packed with the vehicles of people commuting toward downtown, but relatively few were headed to the coast, or to San Pedro, at least not this early in the day.

"Now I think he might have considered for a moment what to do next, like whether or not to shoot me. I've thought about it long and hard—believe me—and I have just about convinced myself of it."

"Okay, but to be devil's advocate," she said, "why wouldn't he have just killed you at that point? He had the drop on you."

I shrugged again. "I don't know. I guess because then he'd have to kill you, too. Why—if he is the one who took you—had he not killed you already? Or done other things? Why would he have done any of it? None of this makes sense."

"All I can think of is that he killed Brown. He's good for the murder. He caught William Brown out poaching and backed him against the tree and pulled the trigger. Then he sees me and Tom up at the scene, and he panics. He wouldn't have known we were cops, but for whatever reason, he runs us off the road on the way out. Maybe to keep us from reporting the crime, if he didn't know that the body had been discovered by then."

"Why would he execute the kid for poaching? That seems a little extreme."

"Maybe it was an accident. Maybe he tried to scare him, or whatever, and he didn't mean for his gun to go off."

I thought about that for a moment. "That makes more sense when you question why he didn't finish the job with you. He's not a killer at heart."

"And why he didn't finish the job with you, either. He didn't have it in him to murder either of us. He sees himself as a good guy. He killed two poachers, but he's not going to kill cops. So he took his chances that nobody would put it together. He knew I was unconscious after the wreck and wouldn't be able to ID him. I think he didn't know what to do with me, but he knew he needed to keep me from coming down off that mountain."

"I wonder if he thinks you saw something *before* he ran you off the road. Like maybe he was up at the scene when you guys drove up."

"Then he would have known that the body had been discovered," she said. "I don't think that's it."

"You're probably right. Well, we'd better talk a little about this case before we get there. There'll be plenty of time to contemplate the mountain ordeal." And that was how I referred to it from then on: the mountain ordeal. It was my way of watering it down, like saying you put your pet to sleep.

"We *are* going to solve it," she said.

"I hope so. We'll definitely have a lot of pressure from the sheriff, the mayor's kid getting whacked."

"I mean the mountain. Spencer. Watkins. William Brown. We're going to figure it all out. We have to. And we'll solve the goddam mayor's kid case too, because that's how badass we are."

And for the first time during the drive, Josie's smile reappeared.

3

───

Two black-and-white sheriff's radio cars stood parked on the street at the bottom of a sloping brick driveway that was bounded by neatly manicured hedges outlining a kidney-shaped lawn. The grass was cut tight as a putting green, and I imagined on a sunny day there might be a crew of four or five laborers arriving in their pickups, trailers full of equipment, invisible to the residents and leaving no trace of their visit other than the always-perfect landscape. At the end of the brick drive and beyond the lush landscaping rose a contemporary Mediterranean two-story, a single-family residence with a red tile roof and shutters of the same color against a pale stucco finish. The street was named Crenshaw, but this community was very different from that which surrounded L.A.'s Crenshaw Boulevard.

Josie came to a stop on the wet street behind the second black-and-white radio car, a Ford Explorer I presumed was assigned to a sergeant. A uniformed deputy began walking down the driveway, her tan uniform shirt speckled by raindrops. I popped out of the car before Josie had turned off its motor.

"Good morning."

The deputy who made the call had sounded young, and I had imagined her to be a petite blonde with a nice smile. The lady coming toward me

15

was tall, her legs were long and her shoulders broad. Her dark hair was pulled into a bun on her head, accentuating her pasty complexion. She appeared strong, an athletic type who may have used those legs for running long distances or leaping over hurdles, maybe both. I pictured her running down a crook and driving him into the turf like a lawn dart.

She proffered a pleasant but professional smile, and as she drew closer, presented a clipboard without explanation.

"Good morning, sir," she replied.

I offered her my free hand. "Richard Jones, Homicide."

Her grip was firm, and she looked me in the eyes while shaking my hand. "I'm Jessica Lambert, the one who called it in."

"Nice to meet you," I said.

Josie came around the front of the car. Deputy Lambert turned to greet her. "Good morn—hey, Josie."

The clipboard held a soggy crime scene log. I scribbled our last names on it, noting our arrival time as 0705 hours—*7:05 a.m.*—and indicating that we were from Homicide. A quick glance above our names showed that few people had entered the crime scene before us: Deputy Lambert, Sergeant Taylor, Lieutenant Okamoto, and a paramedic from L.A. County Fire Station 83.

I looked up to see Josie and Lambert embracing quickly, in the way that women sometimes do with other women with whom they may have shared experiences but not intimate secrets.

"Jess, how are you? It's been a while."

The two of them held a comfortable gaze while exchanging pleasant smiles for a long moment. Lambert glanced over to see I was offering to return the clipboard, and she stepped away from Josie to take it from me.

"This is it?" I asked, indicating the crime scene log. "Nobody else came and went? No looky-loos?"

"None," she said, confidently. "There were a couple of other units that arrived, but it was after the house was cleared and we knew what we had —and who it was that had been killed. There was no way I was letting anyone else into that house. Other than the lieutenant, who insisted on entering."

"For what purpose?" I asked.

Lambert shrugged and rolled her eyes.

"I'll handle that," I said.

There were few things homicide detectives detested more than looky-loo deputies at crime scenes, but one of them was looky-loo brass. They contributed nothing, but somehow felt their rank entitled them to take a look at any time, regardless of how many times they had been told otherwise. Homicide detectives were known for their intolerance of such matters, and it was not uncommon for the offending administrators to be subpoenaed to court as witnesses. On one occasion, a detective had tried to keep a commander from entering a crime scene, but the commander had insisted and had made it clear he would not be stopped. Privilege of rank. When the commander exited the home, the detective told him he now had to seize his shoes as evidence because shoe impressions had been left by the suspect. Anyone who had entered the crime scene without protective booties would have to submit their shoes to be examined and compared by a forensics team. The truth was, they could have photographed his shoes there at the scene, which is what was often done with paramedics when necessary. However, the commander didn't know that because he had never been a detective, and he hadn't had much patrol experience either. He refused to provide his shoes, and the detective pulled out his notebook and stared at the commander's name tag for a long moment, saying, "No problem, sir. You'll just have to appear as a witness in the trial and explain why you entered the crime scene. Better hold on to those shoes, too, and bring them with you." The commander left the scene in his socks, and he likely never again pulled rank on a Homicide detective.

Lambert had turned back to Josie. "You're at Homicide now. Wow, nice. I'm happy for you. Do you like it?"

"It's a good job," Josie said, "for the most part. It has its moments though, some longer than others."

I wondered if Deputy Lambert knew of Josie's ordeal on the mountain and thought to alter the direction of conversation to be sure the subject didn't come up—at least for now. I indicated the front of the residence with a wave of my hand. "Where's your crime scene tape, Deputy Lambert? I thought we had a murder here." I grinned after saying it to let her know I was mostly kidding.

I didn't really care if there was tape or not, as long as the scene was contained and controlled. Some scenes required tape, some required tape and blockades, some required armed skirmish lines to maintain order and protect those trying to investigate the crime. But nobody had gathered in the streets of Palos Verdes on this quiet and peaceful morning as the sun broke through the clouds and cast long shadows toward the ocean. It was close enough for a person to smell and almost taste the briny, cool air that flowed inland from it. I knew that yellow tape here would only draw unwanted attention.

I had once driven a hundred miles to the high desert, where nothing other than lizards and vultures were within miles of a site of found human remains, yet the handling deputy had strung yellow tape across a few trees and cacti because he followed the book down to the last detail. I appreciated a deputy who could think outside of the box.

"Well, sir," she started, "I didn't want to draw more attention to our presence here and announce that a death had occurred before we absolutely had to. With it being the mayor's kid and all—"

"Makes sense, though the radio cars will likely create a spectacle once people start coming out for their morning walks." I glanced up to the sky. "Now that the weather's broke."

"Maybe not," she replied. "The neighbors are used to our presence."

I raised my brows. "Oh?"

Lambert nodded. "For a couple of reasons. One, he had a little problem with domestic violence. His girlfriend has called nine-one-one on more than one occasion to say he was drunk and putting his hands on her. He was smarter than to mark her up—if he had actually put his hands on her—and most times she'd recant her statement after we got here. He was only arrested once, and it was because the handling deputy saw scratches on his neck and the girlfriend said they had been choking each other. They both went to jail, but the case never went anywhere. I think they were given some type of diversion, mandatory counseling and anger management classes or something. Being the mayor's kid comes with privileges."

"Well that's interesting," Josie said.

I glanced at her while thinking about what Lambert had just told us, wondering if our murder case was a domestic case.

Lambert continued, "He was also a mixed martial artist and instructor. There's a studio in his garage and there have been a few deputies over the years who have trained with him. He always offered a discount for guys at the station—guys or gals—trying to stay on our good side."

"So he trained deputies here?" I asked, cringing at the thought of deputies being involved with a guy who was murdered.

"Some did, but usually not for very long. I never did. I thought he was an asshole and couldn't stand to be around him. But he was apparently very accomplished in the martial arts."

Josie had pulled out a notebook and was jotting notes, so I waited a moment until it appeared that she had caught up.

"So what's the story on this? How'd the call come in, and what'd you find when you got here?"

Lambert referred to her notebook to cite the time she had received the call, the nature of the call, the tag number—a method by which all calls for service are cataloged—and her time of arrival.

"The sergeant and I arrived together to find the informant—his girl-friend—sitting on the front steps. She was wearing jeans and a hoodie and tennis shoes, and she was soaked. Like she had been out there for more than a couple minutes. Her eyes were red and watery, and her face had streaks of mascara. She had a cell phone in one hand and a burning cigarette in the other."

"What's the girlfriend's name?"

"Veronica Steele. Female, white, twenty-four."

I held up a finger, indicating for Lambert to wait while Josie caught up with her notes. A moment later, Josie looked up and nodded.

I looked back to Lambert. "What did she tell you?"

"Not much. She seemed to be in shock and wasn't responsive to questions. All she said was that she came home and found him dead. She said over and over, 'They killed him.'"

"They."

Lambert nodded. "I couldn't get anything else out of her. We put her in the back of my car and cleared the house, and when I came back to the car, she was curled in a fetal position on the seat, wailing."

"Where is she now?" Josie asked.

"At the station. I had her transported as a witness, although she might be your suspect. I don't know. She has a little blood on her, but she's also the one who found him and called it in."

"What'd she say when she called in? Do you know?" I asked.

"Just that she came home and found him dead. I guess she was hysterical on the phone."

"And that's all you got from her? She didn't say anything on the way to the station?"

"I told the transporting unit not to ask her any questions, just in case. Before she left, I explained to her we'd need her to wait at the station for the detectives to talk to her. She went without any objection. They have her sitting in an interview room with a cup of coffee. Video's running and we allowed her to keep her phone."

I nodded, pleased with how everything had been handled up to this point. Some cases were better than others when you arrived on scene. Some were nightmares.

Josie, still keeping notes, said, "Who pronounced?"

Lambert referred to her notebook. "Paramedic Lawson out of eighty-threes, under the command of Captain Dee. He was the only one we allowed inside. I escorted him in and directed him to the body so he could pronounce him dead. Death was obvious."

I smiled at the firehouse way of referring to their stations as plural. *Eighty-threes, sixteens, nines,* et cetera. Ask any fireman where they work and they will give you the station number, and inexplicably refer to it plurally. Many residents in South Los Angeles refer to their driver's license in a similar manner: *Sir, I need to see your license. They at home.* Or, *I don't gots none.* Or, *They be suspended.* I never could wrap my mind around either phenomenon.

"How'd he die?" I asked.

"Bludgeoned by a stick, like a club. It's in there next to him."

"Well that's interesting." I looked over at my partner. "Shall we have a look?"

As we started up the driveway, Josie said, "Didn't you go to dope, Jess?"

Jessica Lambert was leading the way up the drive; Josie and I were trailing behind her, side by side.

She glanced over her shoulder to answer. "I did, for a while. I was working station Narco here at Lomita for a while, and then I went to Majors. Well, that had me working long hours—most of which you're

20

never paid for—and spending a lot of time driving. I live right over here in Redondo," she said, waving her hand to the north, "and decided I'd be happier working close to home. I've got two kids now and my husband is a sergeant here at Lomita. He works days and I work nights, so someone's always there for the kids. It wasn't that way when I worked dope. Besides, I love working patrol. If that ever changes—if I get tired of pushing a radio car—I've got my two years of investigative experience for the resume."

We had reached the front door and paused there while she finished telling us about her detective career. I indicated the door with a nod of my head. "This the way you guys have been in and out?"

She nodded. "Yes. It was standing open when I arrived with my sergeant, and we made contact with the girlfriend who was sitting here on the porch."

We all looked down as if we could see her sitting there the way Lambert had when she arrived.

"Just inside, and to the left, is a hallway that leads to the garage. That's where the victim is, inside his studio."

"So what's your gut on this, Lambert? Is the girlfriend good for it?"

She shrugged and raised her brows. "I don't know. She acted like she was in shock. Was it an act? Who knows?"

We stepped inside and paused. The interior was decorated in dark leather, chrome, and glass, tile floors littered with Persian rugs and runners. On the walls hung paintings that I assumed were valuable but to me looked like angry spatterings of a drug-crazed, unemployed hippie. A door stood open at the end of the hall. I could tell from where we stood that it led to the garage studio where the victim had reportedly been killed. Still, I stood in place and visually examined the rest of the interior from the front doorway before moving. Josie and Jessica Lambert stood on either side of me.

The sound of a chair scraping against the floor came from my right, somewhere beyond my view, and each of us swiveled our heads in response.

Lambert said, "My sergeant. He's in the dining room writing a supp on his laptop."

As she finished saying it, a short man with a thin comb-over job and a thick, dark mustache rounded the corner from that direction and greeted us with a nod.

Jessica said, "Sarge, Detectives Jones and Sanchez from Homicide."

Josie and I each shook hands with the sergeant.

"I was just writing a supplemental report. I'm sure she told you," he said, indicating Lambert, "that it was the two of us who responded, contacted the informant, cleared the house, and found the victim. I'm just writing my part out for you."

"Thanks, Sarge."

He smiled and nodded as a way to say I was welcome, and then he indicated the door to the studio. "Are you ready to go have a look?"

"No other areas of interest here?" I asked.

"No sir," Lambert answered. "We didn't see any signs of evidence anywhere else in the home, and all points of entry—other than the front door—were secure."

"Which lights were on when you arrived? Did you guys turn anything on or off?"

Lambert and her sergeant looked at each other.

"I know there was light inside the front door," the sergeant started, "and in the studio—"

"I think everything is just as we found it," Lambert added.

"Other than in there," Sergeant Taylor said, apologetically motioning toward the room he had exited. "I did turn the dining room light on when I sat down to type my report."

I acknowledged his statement with a nod that did not give him a pass on the altering of my crime scene, nor did it chastise him for what would probably have no bearing on the case. However, he could have sat out in his car to write his reports, the way most deputies would. The less disruption to a crime scene, the better, and a sergeant should have known that.

"Before we go any further, I think we'd better get a warrant."

Josie was on the same page. "You want me to write a Mincey real quick?"

Since we were in her car, Josie would have a box full of forms and paperwork in her trunk, which would include the standard crime scene warrant—a Mincey warrant, as it is called. It was used whenever there was any question as to whether or not the suspect might have legal standing within a crime scene. Since the girlfriend would be considered a suspect until it was determined she wasn't, we needed to use all precautions during our investigation.

I pushed back the sleeve of my suit coat to check the time: 7:22 a.m. "You've got the fill-in-the-blanks Mincey forms in your trunk?"

"And I've got my laptop with the template, whichever."

"How about you get me a paper copy and I'll scratch out an affidavit while you drive us to Torrance Court. It's only a few miles up the road from here, and I'm sure there's someplace along the way where we can get a cup of coffee." I checked the time again. "That'll put us there about the time Judge Arnesen is strapping a shoulder holster under his black robe, preparing to take the bench. With him, we'll be in and out in ten minutes if we time it right. No stress, no mess."

"Sounds good, partner." Josie turned and started out the door.

"Hold up. I do want to take a peek at our scene before we go, get a visual for my affidavit."

I turned to head toward the studio and Lambert stepped out of the way, gesturing with her hand for me to go first. I led the four of us to the doorway of the studio and stopped there to take in the scene. We had a problem.

4

THE GARAGE-TURNED-MARTIAL ARTS TRAINING STUDIO OF EDWARD Bellovich was a no-frills setup with two hundred-pound Muay Thai heavy bags hanging from the ceiling on one side of the gym, a speed bag mounted on the wall near them, and the entire floor covered by blue padded mats. There were also mats affixed to the lower halves of the three interior walls, all of which were covered by drywall and likely insulated. The ceiling was finished, though two large holes had been cut in order to hang chains from the rafters for the heavy bags. The rafters were likely reinforced to withstand the weight of both the bags and the energy that would be generated by heavy Muay Thai kicks and punches. On the same wall there was a wooden cubby storage unit containing sets of boxing gloves, protective headgear, sets of focus mitts, and various protective body pads designed to be worn over the bellies, thighs, and knees of trainers. A row of coat hooks was mounted near the cubby box where jump ropes of various lengths hung, waiting to be whirled. This was no aerobics kickboxing gym; this was where you learned to fight.

The garage door featured a row of narrow windows near the top, at about eye level, and I could see the sky growing lighter as the morning progressed and the clouds continued breaking up.

Near the center of the studio the mayor's kid lay sprawled on a bloodstained blue mat, belly down, head turned to the side, allowing us to see him from where we stood in the doorway. I could see multiple marks and abrasions about his face and head, from which he had bled profusely. His dark hair was a sticky mass of reddish-black matter, and blood encrusted the skin of his ear, cheek, and neck. A pool of coagulating blood encircled his head and shoulders. A bloodstained wooden stick lay several feet away from the decedent, offering a clue as to the violent manner of his death. The remainder of the studio appeared unremarkable from where I stood.

"What do you think?"

I didn't look at my partner when, after a long moment of consideration, I answered her. "I think we have a problem."

"Oh?"

"If our boy here, Bellovich, is an accomplished martial artist, imagine who it was that beat him to death. Assuming that's how he died."

"I would guess you're right," Josie said, "on both accounts."

I turned and motioned toward the front of the house with a jerk of my head. "Let's get out of here, get a warrant, and we need to have someone make notification to the father."

Lambert turned and led us toward the door, glancing over her shoulder as she said, "Do you want me to have that handled by the station? Maybe the watch commander?"

I knew that would be the lieutenant who had been at the scene. "No, he's done enough damage for one murder. I'm going to call our lieutenant, see what his ETA is here, and have him take care of it. We just need someone who can handle the heat to make the next of kin notification and be prepared to deal with the media."

We had reached the front door. A cool draft of ocean air flowed into the deathly quiet home. I continued, "Jessica, you might as well pitch a big striped tent because the circus is coming to town."

Josie rummaged in her trunk while I settled into the passenger seat. Before she pulled away from the curb, she handed me a posse box with a fill-in-the-blanks Mincey warrant clipped to the top. I sat it on my lap and pulled my cell phone from my pocket.

"Who are you calling?"

"My martial arts expert."

I looked to see Josie roll her eyes. "Anything to get Floyd involved."

He picked up. "What's up, Dickie?"

"What are you doing?"

"Just got back from a run, going to take Cody to school and then hit the shower, head in to the office after. Why are you irritating me so early in the day?"

"What are those sticks called?"

"Sticks. I don't know, dickhead, pixie sticks? Walking sticks? Sticks my old lady gets up her ass when I come home smelling like whiskey and telling her you kept me out working late? What the hell are you talking about, exactly?"

"The fighting sticks. The ones you homos dance around with when you're doing all of that ninja shit."

"Oh, a staff?"

"I don't know; is that what you call them?"

We were out of the neighborhood and headed north toward Torrance Court, Josie glancing from the road to the map on her phone as she drove.

Floyd said, "Yeah, a staff, or a baton. I think the longer ones are more commonly called staffs, and the shorter ones batons, if you're talking about a single stick, not nunchucks."

"Right, a stick, about three feet long."

"Okay, that's your typical fighting stick, usually called a staff, or a kali. What the hell are you up to anyway?"

"Josie and I picked up an interesting case in RPV, a dude who teaches martial arts out of his house was found beaten to death, or so it appears."

"Hmph."

"Yeah, that's what I thought too. Must've been a bad mamma jamma who did it to him."

We were stopped at a light, surrounded by morning commuters. The sidewalks were nearly free of traffic, with the exception of the occasional pedestrian or bicyclist. I wondered if anybody walked to school or work in this area, or even to the bus stop to catch their ride.

After a moment, Floyd said, "Well, that or he just had the drop on him. It doesn't really matter what a badass you are if someone el-kabongs you when you're not expecting it. Where'd this happen? On the streets?"

"No, in his studio."

Josie said, "Tell him who it is."

"And it's the mayor's kid, Bellovich," I said, while looking at the Mincey warrant form on my lap, pondering just how much of that I wanted to put into my affidavit. Probably none of it, I quickly decided; there was no reason to complicate an otherwise simple warrant: *I came. I saw a dead guy. He's in a house and we don't know who killed him, and whether or not the person who did would have legal standing at said residence.* Done. A couple paragraphs of my expertise: *Deputy sheriff twenty years, homicide detective seven, investigated a hundred homicides and thousands of other crimes, attended a shitload*—scratch that—*numerous schools, training courses, and seminars related to death investigation.* Et cetera.

"Oh Jesus," Floyd said. "Good luck with that. That's not only an interesting case, it's a cluster."

"Tell me about it."

"I can talk to some of the guys I know who train over in that direction, see if anyone knows him. I'm surprised to hear the mayor had a son, to be honest. He seems a little...I don't know, metro?"

I chuckled into the phone, glancing at Josie, who shot me a sideways look.

"You remember him from the Morrison case, a pain in the ass."

"Yeah, that one and another I had just a few weeks or so ago, a suicide off of Inspiration Point. Little chubby-cheeked asshole with the gold pinky ring and bracelet. The dude thinks he's mafioso in Palos Verdes, for Christ's sake. But his son getting killed, I don't wish that on anyone."

I couldn't imagine, even though I didn't have children. I had sat with plenty of parents who had lost theirs and couldn't imagine a more dreadful situation.

Floyd said, "Well, Dickie, you're starting to bore me. I'll be in the office later if you need anything, or I'll let you know if I find out anything after I make a few calls."

"Thanks," I said, and disconnected.

I slid my phone into my breast pocket and settled back in my seat, crossing one leg over the other in the cramped sedan. "Find me a place that serves black coffee and isn't filled with hipsters."

Josie had turned onto Torrance Boulevard, so I knew we were close to the courthouse. I glanced at my watch. "Or maybe we can get the warrant signed and grab something on the way back."

"Let's get the warrant signed," Josie said. "That's the priority. I'll buy my princess a coffee on the way back."

I smiled at her. "Your princess?"

"You best get cracking on that warrant, Jones; we've got shit to do."

WE FLASHED OUR BADGES AND BYPASSED A LINE OF PEOPLE WAITING TO BE screened by security, crossed the polished tile floor to a bank of elevators, and stepped into one that stood waiting for its next passengers. When the doors closed, I punched the button for the third floor and backed against the wall. Josie did the same on the opposite side. Neither of us spoke, and when the capsule settled and the doors slid open, I motioned for Josie to go first.

"Department M," I said to the back of her head.

She gave me a thumbs up and we turned the corner into a hallway lined with benches that would soon be filled with reluctant civilians holding subpoenas in their hands or shirt pockets, unenthused would-be jurors who had responded to summonses of their own, and bored cops who spent a lifetime riding the pine in these hallways and hundreds just like them throughout the county.

Josie veered left, stopped, then tugged one at a time at the double doors marked *Dept. M*. Both were locked. I peered through small windows embedded in the doors, catching glimpses of the courtroom through a second set of windows set in the inner pair of doors. I could see the bench was empty—I had expected it would be—but I had hoped to see the clerk at her desk.

I glanced at my watch. "We'll give it ten minutes and start knocking. I'm going to finish the affidavit."

I found the nearest bench and went back to writing. Josie came and sat next to me, her familiar flowery scent wafting beneath my nose. She didn't wear perfume—at least not to work—so I assumed it was her shampoo or body wash that was so pleasantly fragrant. Even after a long night of working the desk, she smelled as fresh as a daisy. That was one nice change from working with Floyd.

"So what are your thoughts on this," she asked.

I continued writing. "As far as?"

"Who could have done it. I don't think that's the girlfriend's work."

I shook my head. "Not likely. We'll take her clothes to be safe, make sure any blood is transfer, not spatter."

"Another martial artist? I mean, the dude would have to be strong, fast, and capable. Not to mention big-balled."

I stopped my pen mid-sentence and looked up at her, smiling. "'Big-balled'?"

Josie crossed one leg over the other and began bouncing her foot in the air, her shoe dangling from her toes. "I'm just saying, it'd be better to shoot a guy like that. Don't ya think?"

I went back to the affidavit. "Probably. If it was planned. My sense of it—with what little we know at this point—is that the victim was familiar with his killer, and comfortable in his or her presence. Not threatened. Not defensive. *Bam!*, he gets whacked across the head, unexpectedly. Takes a few more blows on the ground. But why? That's the question."

"*Who* is the question," Josie wisely countered. "We can't do much with the *why*, if we don't know the *who*."

I didn't reply, now more focused on the last few sentences that would finish up the warrant and affidavit. "Hey, go knock on that door while I finish up, would you?"

Josie rose without speaking and went to the doors. She knocked, and after a moment, said, "The bailiff's coming."

I tucked the papers under the clip and joined Josie at the door. She had pulled her badge and its holder from her belt and had it pressed against the glass. When the bailiff came through the inside set of doors and approached the ones behind which we stood, Josie lowered her badge, and each of us took a step back.

The bailiff was a tall man, six and a half feet or better, a man who had outgrown his hair line the way mountains surpass the trees, bald and pointy at the top. His mustache was black and thick, and his pinched face pockmarked and aged.

He keyed the door and opened it slightly, poking his head into the hallway.

"How're you?" I asked. "We're Sheriff's Homicide, here to see about getting the judge to sign a warrant. We're on a fresh case down the road in Palos Verdes."

The thin-faced man's gaze darted between us. "Was he expecting you?"

"Not unless he has ESPN," I said.

The man didn't smile. I wondered if he had no sense of humor, or if my smart-assed comment had sailed over his head, which would be no small feat.

Josie said, "We just got called out a short time ago, and we need to get into a crime scene. We were hoping Judge Arnesen would be available. If not, we can try some of the other departments."

He pushed the door open wide and gestured for us to come in. As I walked past him, I noticed the name tag on his chest because it was at my eye level, or not far from it. *Bailiff.*

"Thank you, Bailiff Bailiff," I said.

His deep voice thundered from behind me as Josie and I led the way into the courtroom. "If I had a dollar for every smart-aleck who threw that out there, I'd retire."

I had thought it was only somewhat clever, not an out-of-the-park slam or anything, but I had said it with a wide and friendly grin. To be called a smart-aleck gnawed at me, especially when he made his living calling court to session and told his neighbors he was a policeman. So, I couldn't resist another swing. "I thought you already had."

Judge Arnesen, seated in a high-backed leather chair behind an imposingly heavy and ornate cherry wood desk, glanced up from his work, peering over black-framed reading glasses as he motioned us to come in. His crisp white shirt, the cufflinks, gold bracelet, and watch seemed a contradiction to his leathery face, thick, gray mustache, and piercing blue eyes.

As Josie and I seated ourselves across from him, the judge set down his pen, gathered the papers he had been working on, and placed them to the side of his desk. He leaned back and his gaze wandered over the two of us.

His greeting was succinct. "Detectives."

"Thank you for seeing us, Your Honor," I said, leaning forward in my seat, offering the warrant and affidavit.

He accepted the papers and began to thumb through them, asking without looking up, "What have you got?"

"We're on a fresh murder down in Palos Verdes, a man found bludgeoned to death in his home studio, a place he teaches martial arts. The girlfriend found him, and, quite frankly, we have no idea at this stage who murdered him. We wanted to secure a Mincey before moving forward."

The judge grunted but didn't look up, still flipping through the pages. I had appeared before him on other occasions, and he likely would only skim the statement of my expertise and affidavit to hit the highlights. He knew who I was and what my assignment entailed, having been both a deputy sheriff and a prosecutor for the Los Angeles County District Attorney's office prior to becoming a judge.

"Sounds interesting," he said, while scribbling his signature, the date, and time on the warrant. He arranged the papers back in order and handed them across to me.

I stood to accept the papers, and Josie followed suit. "Thank you, Your Honor."

Judge Arnesen pushed out of his plush chair. "Not a problem. Let me know if you need anything else. I have a trial going, but I'll let the clerk know that if either of you comes in, I'll see you immediately." He turned to a coat tree behind him and took a black robe from its hanger.

As he punched his arms through one sleeve and then the other, and started to zip the robe closed, I said, "I had heard you wore a gun under that robe, carried it in a shoulder rig."

He smiled. "Rumors."

I nodded. "Thanks again, Your Honor."

As Josie and I started for the door, Judge Arnesen called out. "Detective."

I turned to face him.

He smiled and patted the front of his right hip. "Thirty-eight special, right front pocket. Shoulder rigs are a bit audacious, even for an old hanging judge."

5

On the way back to the crime scene I phoned our lieutenant, Joe Black, but the call went to his voicemail. When I put my phone away, Josie took her eyes off the road to look at me. "No answer?"

"He might still be with the mayor. This is going to be a mess."

We stopped for coffee along the way at a yuppie coffee house with a drive-through that had ten cars in line, and a walk-up window with one customer waiting. It amazed me how lazy people could be. We walked up and Josie ordered a latte and I asked for black coffee, something strong.

"Burning Down the House is our darkest roast," the young girl with spiked black hair and a tinge of purple in the front replied. She had a ring through her nose and another through her upper lip, multiple piercings in both ears and eyebrows, and a tattoo on her neck, a black rose with a banner beneath it and the letters *FTW*. There was an assortment of meanings it might have. Bikers displayed it to say, "*fuck the world.*" A Hell's Angel once famously said, when asked, that it meant "*forever two wheels,*" and apparently that became a thing also. The millennials used the acronym to say, "*for the win.*" I had even heard that the Greenpeace crowd used it for "*free the whales.*" With this young woman, I realized, the tattoo could have meant anything—any of those uses or others with which I was unfamiliar. Maybe she changed the meaning depending on her audience.

Spike said it would be nine-fifty and I handed her a ten. That seemed high to me, for two coffees, but I went ahead and dropped the fifty cents change into her tip cup.

It seemed her job was to take the orders, collect the money, and then entertain the customers while someone behind her made the drinks. She leaned through the open window, bored. "So, what do you two have going on today? Anything cool?"

"Just work," I said, hoping that would satisfy her curiosity.

"That's cool," she said. "Same here. It's been a stressful morning, you wouldn't even believe it. This job has more pressure than you could imagine. What do you do?"

"Oh, mostly just drive around, visit different people at different places."

"That's cool, man…no stress. Right on, dude."

We bumped fists and I pictured the dead martial artist chilling in his studio. It took every ounce of restraint I had to keep from describing it to her. *Yeah, we're getting ready to drive back to a little job we're working on now, this thing where a man is lying with his brains oozing onto the floor from where his skull was crushed sometime during the night, probably by someone he knew. We needed some coffee, but we also should probably get back to the poor bastard before too much longer, before rigor mortis fully sets and the maggots begin crawling out of his mouth, nose, and ears. Oh, and get this, the little asshole was the son of the mayor, so we'll have that to deal with too. Anyway, hope your day's not too stressful, hon.*

Spike handed us our coffees through the walk-up window. I thanked her and turned to walk away, feeling slightly dumber and a little less hopeful for the future of America.

When Josie turned onto Crenshaw, I had my face down, looking at emails on my phone.

"Jesus Christ," she said.

I looked up to see a line of news vans, along with throngs of onlookers crowding the property that was now properly lined with yellow tape. Deputy Lambert stood at the bottom of the driveway, facing them all down. Nobody was getting past her.

Josie pulled her sedan to a stop just feet from where Lambert stood.

We got out, ducked beneath the yellow tape, and walked quickly toward the front door, avoiding the questions that were hurled at us from the gathering of reporters. As we entered the house, I heard someone say, "Was that Homicide?"

We paused inside the doorway. "Let's have the desk get us an ETA on the crime lab and coroner."

Josie pulled her phone from a jacket pocket.

As she thumbed her way to the number for the office, I said, "And ask them if they've heard from your lieutenant."

She nodded, then averted her eyes as she spoke into the phone. I moved past her and went back into the studio, moving slowly and scanning my surroundings again as I did. I stopped again at the threshold and went through the same routine of studying the scene from the outside parameters, working my way visually to the focal point. Eddie Bellovich. The talented tough guy taken out by someone tougher. Or craftier.

I imagined the girlfriend as the killer, but only for a moment. I'd have a better idea after we spoke with her, and I would know for sure once the blood spatter analysis came back. The pattern of blood spatter on the ceiling above the victim immediately told me two things: the murder had occurred right where the victim lay, and he had been struck more than once. Castoff blood occurs in subsequent blows as a weapon is hurled rearward and then thrust forward again. We would have experts document and analyze the pattern. During the autopsy, we would learn the exact locations of blunt force traumas. That information might provide us with the parameters of the suspect's height, and we would almost certainly be able to determine if the suspect was right- or left-handed. The fighting stick—or baton, staff, or kali—would be examined for latent prints and then sent to Serology where samples of blood would be typed and compared to that of our victim. Samples of blood at the scene would go through the same process to determine if there was any blood that was attributed to someone other than our victim. Though I doubted that would be the case, if it were, it would be the best way to determine our suspect's identity. My instincts told me the victim had sustained a crippling blow without anticipating it, and therefore never had a chance to fight back. I would expect the scene to appear much differently had it been a case of mutual combat, with blood throughout the studio or at least not confined to the immediate area of where the victim lay.

"Crime lab's an hour out, coroner's at least that, maybe more. Nobody knows where Joe's at."

Josie was at my side, but I didn't look at her when she spoke. I was focused now on the center of the crime scene, replaying the possibilities in my mind. I only nodded and stayed in my zone.

I pictured the suspect and victim standing together in the center of the studio. What would they have been doing? Casual conversation? Training? Preparing to spar or fight?

The victim was dressed in a traditional white jiu jitsu gi which was fastened around his waist by a black belt. The belt had a single, solid red stripe on one end. He was barefoot. I wondered if the killer had been dressed in similar fashion. I retrieved my flashlight from my inside coat pocket and squatted to shine its beam across the floor. Lights had come a long way since I first began my career, when we carried large metal rechargeable flashlights that were heavy and could be used as a weapon when necessary. Now most detectives carried pocket-sized lights with lithium batteries that were brighter and more reliable than the lights of old. Casting a beam, I could see the impressions of feet scattered across the blue mats.

I looked over my shoulder and saw the light switch just inside the doorway where we had gathered. "Josie, can you kill the lights for a minute?"

She did, and I illuminated the floor once again, the beam of my light washing over it at an oblique angle. I could see a path of pedestrian traffic between the doorway and the body, and additional impressions in the immediate vicinity of the victim. There were other impressions throughout the studio, but the bulk of traffic had come and gone in the most direct route.

I knew that if Lambert said she approached the body once, that meant she had likely gone back and forth several times. A paramedic had been brought in to pronounce the victim dead. I had no doubt that the sergeant and Lieutenant Okamoto had ventured at least partway into the room.

"We need to have the crime lab lift shoe impressions before we do anything else," I said as I stood up and looked Josie in the eyes. "Let's put a hold on the coroner and make sure the lab is sending someone with the expertise to handle it."

Josie lifted her phone and paused before making the call. "Who handles that, Latent Prints?"

I nodded. "Yes, and we'll need them to photograph the soles of the shoes belonging to everyone who has entered our scene—Lambert, her sergeant, the paramedic. Some will likely claim they didn't, like the lieutenant. I can see shoe impressions across there," I waved a hand across the direct route to the victim, "and I would venture to say that most of the people who normally enter this studio, do so barefooted."

"Definitely," Josie replied. "Where I trained, you'd get your ass kicked if you walked on the mats in street shoes."

I flipped the light switch back on, returning it to the state in which we found it, and started toward the front door. Josie stopped a few feet shy of me and walked in a small circle, her head down, while speaking into her phone. I motioned for Lambert—who still manned the property line that was now cordoned off by yellow tape—to come up to the door. I didn't want our conversation being picked up by reporters.

"Yes sir," she said as she took her final few steps toward me.

"Eddie's going to continue chilling for a bit. We need to get shoe impressions off of those mats before we do anything else. Nobody enters this house again without my permission, other than the crime lab. Got it?"

"Yes sir."

"While they're doing their thing in there, Josie and I are going to get over to the station and interview the girlfriend. If you need anything, call me directly on my cell."

"I'll need your number, sir."

"I guess you might," I said, and smiled. From the back of my notebook I removed a business card with my office and cell numbers printed in the bottom corner. *Detective Richard Jones* was displayed in the center, *Los Angeles County Sheriff's Homicide Bureau* beneath it. The protocol for business cards was that the sheriff's star be emblazoned on the card, along with the name of the current sheriff. But we also had to buy our own cards. Mine had the star but not the sheriff's name. My position on the matter was that until he paid for them, his name wouldn't be on them.

Josie came up next to me. "Okay, we're good with the coroner and the crime lab."

My gaze traveled to the street below us where a crowd of gawkers and reporters had gathered, and beyond them to the rooflines of spacious homes with tile roofs and manicured lawns. Sporadic palms protruded high into the clouded sky, their fronds hanging heavily in the damp coastal air. The sounds of distant seagulls conjured images of the not-so-distant shores, a place where I imagined small waves gently collapsing onto wet sandy beaches, depositing clusters of seaweed and scattering fragments of shells before retreating back into the sea.

But not all coastlines featured sandy beaches with rolling waves and refreshing ocean spray cooling children who stood lathered in sunscreen, plastic pails and shovels in hand. At the bottom of Inspiration Point, not far from where we stood, violent waves crashed mercilessly against mountains of jagged rocks before breaking and rolling into dark caverns of deep, inescapable pools. Places where human remains sometimes floated, broken bodies beating against moss-covered boulders until spotted by fishermen or hikers above. Those bodies would be retrieved by dive-trained deputies while detectives stood on the rocks, writing in their notebooks, and crime lab technicians—bulky bags slung over their shoulders—carefully maneuvered along the rocks to capture it on film. The sounds of their clattering shutters would be masked by the powerful roar of waves, and the ocean spray would be neither refreshing nor welcome.

"Did I hear you say we were going to interview the girlfriend?"

My mind slowly closed the door to a particular scene I would never forget: the broken body of a small child in the recesses of a rocky cliff not far from where we stood. As I turned to answer Josie, I could see in her face that my expression had grown dark and my eyes distant. I took a deep breath and released it slowly, letting it drive away the tension that had engulfed me.

"Yes," I finally responded. "Let's do that." I forced a smile.

Josie smiled back. "Okay then, let's get crackin'."

6

LOMITA STATION WAS A THREE-MILE DRIVE FROM OUR CRIME SCENE.

Josie wheeled her sedan into the rear parking lot that was crowded with radio cars and the POVs (privately owned vehicles) of the station's employees. I helped her find a place to park, pointing out one and then another spot, and she pulled in with a huff. "This must be what it's like to be married," she said.

I smiled. "Why, thank you, partner. That's very sweet of you to say."

We exited her car and walked toward the back door of the station, elbow to elbow. I looked straight ahead as I continued, "That might be the nicest thing you've ever said to me. That and when you said I was the most *alpha* male you've ever known."

She didn't respond.

"Or when you told me I was the most *un-politically correct* person you have ever met. But I think we should keep this relationship professional, as difficult as it must be for you."

She stopped. I stopped a step later and turned back to face her.

"What?"

She grinned and shook her head. "You really are nuts, you know? They're not kidding when they say it."

She began walking again and I joined her. "Who says that?"

"Everyone. Floyd, Lopes, your captain. From what I've heard, the shrink."

I stopped her with a hand on her arm. "Wait a minute, that's not fair. The shrink wanted me to have her babies, so I had to fire her. She's biased. A little uppity too if I'm going to be honest about it."

"I think you just proved my point."

"Whatever."

We joined an employee at the back door, showed her our badges, and walked in with her. She was dressed in civilian attire, but was clearly a deputy, coming in wearing shorts and flip-flops, a gym bag over her shoulder. She asked if we needed help finding anything. I told her no, we would check in with the watch commander first, and that I knew where to find his office. If there were three places I could find in just about any station in the county, they were the watch commanders' offices, the jails, and the kitchens where I could get coffee.

Josie and I had just started down the hall when someone called out from behind.

"Hey, you guys Homicide?"

I turned to see a uniformed lieutenant. He was tall, dark, and clean-shaven, a distinguished sort whom I recognized immediately: Lieutenant Dennis Slocumb. His friends mostly called him "Deac." I had worked for him as a young patrol deputy at Firestone Station, and again when I was promoted to Detective Division and assigned to Metro. He had still been there when I left to go to Homicide.

"Yes sir," I said. "How're you doing, Deac?"

"Jesus Christ," he said, walking toward us. "I can't see down the hallway without my goddam glasses nowadays, didn't even recognize you." He indicated my hat. "I thought you were Louie, with the fedora."

"I'm his protégé," I said, referring to a veteran Homicide detective named Louie Van Vossen, who was also known as *Louie the Hat*. Deac and I shook hands. I said, "He even took me downtown to his favorite hat store. Did you know there was such a thing?"

Deac shook his head.

"Fifth and Main. Great place, if you like hats."

"I'll be damned," he said.

"You just might be. Hey, do you know my partner, Josie Sanchez?"

"Of course I do," he said, meeting her gaze with a wide smile. "We borrowed Josie a few times years ago when I was running the vice team, used her as a decoy on prostitution stings. You didn't know she used to be a hooker, did you?"

I grinned and glanced at Josie. She shrugged.

"I can tell you stories, buddy," Deac continued.

"Please don't," Josie said, teasingly. "These guys at Homicide are relentless; they don't need any more ammunition."

He grinned at her and then looked back at me. "Ask her, sometime, about the operation we did over at Lennox Station when she chased away a potential customer."

Josie said, "Don't even go there."

Deac chuckled. "So you know, your lieutenant is in with our captain right now, and I think they're waiting for the two of you to join them. I just talked to Deputy Lambert who said you were headed this way."

I didn't know where the captain's office was located. "Can you point us that direction?"

"Better yet," he said, "I'll escort you. I'm the Operations lieutenant and I'll be joining you there, I'm sure."

We started down the hall. "So how'd you end up as an Ops lieutenant at Lomita?"

He looked over and grimaced. "Stepped on my dick with the chief."

"I thought she loved you."

We paused at the door to the Operations office, and Deac lowered his voice. "There's only so much they can do for you when a peer files a complaint, says you threatened to kick his ass. I'll fill you in later, come on."

We stepped through the front part of Operations, then into the captain's office where Joe Black sat across from a woman in business attire whom I presumed to be the captain. She was an unattractive, heavyset lady whose hair was short and styled like a man's, and who wore a scowl which I figured to be her natural RBF—*resting bitch face*. Her name plate identified her as Captain Pat Russell.

Lieutenant Black gestured toward the two empty seats in the room. Deac stationed himself by the door. The captain, who didn't bother to introduce herself or greet us, told him to close the door behind him.

Once the door closed, Captain Russell leaned back in her chair and folded her stubby fingers across her rotund stomach. She took a long look at Josie, a quick glance at me, and then resettled her gaze on Josie.

"Tell me about your investigation."

Josie and I exchanged a glance, and I nodded to give her the go-ahead. She would have normally deferred to me in this situation due to my being more experienced in such settings. However, the captain clearly wanted to hear it from Josie.

"We don't know much at this point, Captain. The scene is being documented as we speak, crime lab techs searching for evidence. It is a significant undertaking, a long and methodical process. My partner and I came in to interview the victim's girlfriend who found him dead and called it in. We'll do that as soon as we're finished here with you, and then we'll return to the scene.

"All we know about the victim at this point is what we learned from your deputy, Jessica Lambert. Mayor's kid, martial artist, lessons out of his house, et cetera. We hope to learn a lot more from the girlfriend."

The captain nodded, seemingly pleased that Lambert was part of the equation. As was I, but likely for different reasons. She said, "Is the girlfriend a suspect?"

Josie shrugged. "Everyone's a suspect until we eliminate them. All we know right now is that someone was able to get the drop on him and crack his melon open. That tells us the victim was familiar—if not comfortable—with his killer."

The captain tugged at her top as she adjusted herself in her chair. "Cracked his melon?"

"It appears that he was hit in the head with a fighting stick," Josie said. "It was left at the scene."

The captain fussed with the blotter on her desk, arranging photographs beneath it. After a moment, she spoke. "The mayor—this kid's father—is a son of a bitch, and a pain in my balls."

I chuckled, and she shot me a stern look. It was all I could do not to burst into laughter.

"The whole fucking city," she continued, "to be honest about it. I've never worked in a city with so many whiny bitches involved in its politics. And I thought Lakewood was a pain in the balls!"

She was killing me with the male genitalia references. But I had to admit, I liked this woman. I pictured having drinks with her, talking shit about crooked politicians and ignorant administrators, downing a few beers and maybe arm wrestling her for the tab.

"I don't want any surprises. You two—" she wagged a fat finger back and forth between me and Josie "—will keep me apprised of every development. Got it?"

I wanted to stand and salute her, but instead I just grinned.

Josie said, "Yes ma'am."

The captain turned to Lt. Joe Black, who sat quietly taking it all in. "That'll be all, Lieutenant."

"Yes ma'am," he said, and rose from his chair.

I pushed out of mine and hurried through the door and into the hallway where I stopped and waited for my team. Josie led the way with Lieutenant Black behind her. When we gathered, I said, "She seemed nice."

Josie rolled her eyes.

Joe said, "This place is a political hotbed, a make-it-or-break-it for captains. She does well here, she gets promoted. If she leaves here in a cloud of controversy, she transfers to custody division or gets demoted. That's just how it is. RPV is a rich city and a nice contract for our department."

"Well, I've got a stiff waiting for me a couple miles across town, Joe. We'll leave the politics to you and the captain."

Black smiled. "That's what I'm here for."

"How'd the notification go?" Josie asked.

Lieutenant Black began to answer, but paused as a pair of civilian employees walked past us in the hallway carrying cups of steaming coffee. I visualized a fresh pot down the hall and decided that would be my next stop.

"It was interesting," Joe said. "I don't know if he was in a state of shock, or if maybe he and the kid just weren't close. I didn't see the emotional response I had prepared myself for."

"That is interesting," Josie agreed.

I pondered it a moment and wondered if the father might be on our list of suspects. "What does he do for a real job? I know that the mayor deal here is a part-time gig."

Joe Black shrugged. "I didn't know that. I assumed that was his job, being mayor."

I shook my head. "A lot of these smaller cities, the mayor gets minimal pay and puts in few hours. City managers run them."

"I apologize; I didn't think to ask."

"It's okay," Josie said. "We'll need to interview him anyway. Right?" She was looking at me now.

I nodded. "No doubt. We need to interview the girlfriend right away and then get back to the scene. But first, coffee." With that I started down the hall. Josie and Joe Black followed along.

"Anything I can do for you two?" Black asked.

We turned into an empty break room. A wall-mounted television showed a breaking news report, a conglomeration of news vans and trucks and onlookers. It was our crime scene. I watched it for a moment before answering.

"Yes," I said, turning to face him. I was looking up at his round face and thick mustache, the lieutenant being a few inches taller than I am, a decade or so older, and thirty pounds heavier. "We'll need to feed the fish"—I indicated the action on TV—"give them something to report before they start making shit up. It appears it's no longer a secret that the mayor's kid is dead, but they shouldn't have any idea how or why. And they're hungry."

"How much do you want to tell them?" he asked.

"The next of kin has been told, so you might as well confirm we're investigating his death as a homicide. No additional details—where the body was found, how he's dressed, the possible weapon—nothing. But if you give them a standup, it will help keep them off our asses for a while."

"You've got it. Anything else?"

"I don't think so, Joe. We're going to grab some coffee and then go talk to the girlfriend. Can I buy you a cup?"

He shook his head. "I'll see you back at the scene."

Lieutenant Black disappeared into the hallway as Josie and I filled our cups. I said, "The girlfriend is all yours; I'll take the notes."

Josie placed the carafe back on its warmer. "Works for me."

"You're not going to tell me the hooker story, are you?"

"Never."

7

THE INTERVIEW ROOM AT LOMITA STATION LOOKED LIKE EVERY OTHER interview room in the county: four dreary walls, a two-way mirror, and a bare rectangular table in the middle with two chairs on one side and one on the other. It didn't matter how many classes were given on proper interview techniques, investigators everywhere still preferred having a table between them and the subject of their interview. Everyone grew up watching the same setup on cop shows and couldn't seem to break from the tradition.

A lady stood in front of the mirror, either looking at her reflection or maybe trying to see through it. Her eyes shifted to watch our entrance, but she didn't turn around. Josie walked toward her and said her name as if questioning her identity. "Miss Steele?"

The woman turned toward her slowly. Josie introduced herself as I pulled one of the chairs away from the table. I pushed the table from the center of the small room until it was against one wall. I arranged two of the chairs along the long side of the table so that they faced each other, and the third chair at the end of the table. I set my notebook, pen, and coffee there to mark my spot, and then stepped over to the two women, removed my fedora, and introduced myself.

"Miss Steele, I'm Richard Jones. We're very sorry for your loss."

The three of us took our seats. Josie and Veronica Steele were seated facing each other, their knees nearly touching. I planned this. It was how I always sat with anyone I was going to speak with, no matter if they were a witness or someone who had just hacked a priest to death with a machete. A table acted like a barrier and offered a level of protection. To remove it created vulnerabilities—for both parties. We could get used to it; they couldn't.

Josie began, "Miss Steele—may I call you Veronica?"

She nodded, her gaze fixed on her lap.

Josie leaned down, trying to see her face. "Veronica, as my partner said, we are very sorry for your loss. Richard and I are the detectives assigned to the case, and we're going to need to get a statement from you. Can you do that for us?"

Veronica nodded once more and lifted her head just enough to look up at Josie, though she quickly looked down after. She seemed to be looking at the stains on her hands, the blood of her dead boyfriend.

Josie began with the basics: name, date of birth, home address, phone. Veronica lived with her boyfriend at the location of the crime scene. The revelation did not surprise me; it only reinforced the need for a Mincey warrant, and I was glad we had obtained one before the process of collecting evidence began. The statistics would indicate that she was a prime suspect; most murder victims are killed by someone they know. Furthermore, she was the one who reported the death, and as far as we knew at this point, the last to see him alive other than the killer, if the killer was someone else.

"We were told you came home to find Eddie dead. When had you last seen him alive?"

Veronica kept her head down and spoke softly. "We had an argument yesterday afternoon, so I left."

Josie waited a moment, but that was all Veronica had to say without further prompting.

"What time was that?"

"About two, three. I don't know. Sometime in the afternoon."

"What was the argument about?"

"No big deal. He was just being an asshole. He's always grumpy now —was. He was giving me shit about something and I got mad and left.

That's what I do. Go to a friend's or over to my mom's for a few hours, or days."

"Did you fight often?"

She shook her head. "Not really."

"Any violence?"

"No. Never."

Josie waited a long moment before continuing. "What was Eddie wearing the last time you saw him?"

She shrugged. "I don't know. Same thing he always wears, probably. Shorts and a tank top, maybe a Hawaiian shirt."

"He wasn't wearing his gi?"

"Not when I left. Nobody was there. He wasn't training."

"Did Eddie keep a written schedule for training?"

Veronica said, "He has a planner."

"Okay, we'll need that. Is it at the house?"

"I'm sure it is."

"You said nobody was there when you left. Nobody other than Eddie."

Veronica nodded.

"Do you know if he had any plans for company, or if he had any lessons lined up for yesterday afternoon or evening?"

She tucked a lock of hair behind her ear. "I don't know. I'm sure he did. Almost every night someone was there."

"Were his lessons one-on-one, or did he train several people at a time?"

"Both."

I could tell Josie was waiting for me to catch up on my notes during the pause. "Go ahead," I said without looking up.

"When you came home, Veronica, how did you find the front door?"

Veronica looked up and lowered her brows, contemplating the question.

"Was it locked, unlocked? Open or closed?"

Veronica looked across the room, likely reflecting. "I think it was unlocked. It wasn't open, but I don't think it was locked either."

"Was anyone else there when you arrived?"

"No, of course not."

"Do you know if Eddie left during the day?"

Veronica shrugged.

"So you don't know?" Josie asked, prodding for an audible answer to her question. She knew the interview was being audio *and* video recorded, but the audio recording was most important if the interview ever needed to be transcribed.

"No," Veronica said.

"My partner might not catch a nod of the head while he's taking notes," Josie explained. It was a brilliant way to ask her to answer with audible responses without telling her she was being recorded.

"Does Eddie have a cell phone?"

"Of course."

"Do you know where it is?"

She shook her head. "Probably in the studio, in one of the cubby holes."

"Did he train at night?"

"He trained all the time. If he wasn't giving lessons, he would train with his buddies."

"Who are some of his closest friends?"

"Todd, Sean, Steve—"

Josie glanced over at me. I knew she would be checking to see if I was getting all of it, or if she needed to slow down. A method I liked to use—one I had taught to Josie—was to hit rewind every once in a while, go back over their answers. That would allow the partner time to catch up on his or her notes, and it would also reaffirm the information a witness or suspect provided. I nodded to indicate I was fine, and Josie continued.

"We need last names, Veronica."

As time went on, Veronica seemed to become more comfortable. She was now looking up most of the time, making eye contact with Josie as she answered her questions. Her dark, shoulder-length hair framed her thin face, now painted by tears and mascara.

"Todd Bailey, Sean Bailey—they're brothers—Steve Morelli... That's about it. Todd died not long ago."

I looked up. Josie gave me a sideways glance and continued.

"What happened to Todd?" Josie asked.

"They say it was suicide. Eddie didn't believe it."

I underlined the name Todd Bailey in my notebook and put two stars to the side of it.

"What did he tell you about that?"

"Who, Eddie?"

"Yes, Eddie. Did he tell you why he didn't think it was a suicide?"

Veronica shook her head. "No, but something really bothered him about it. He wouldn't talk about it though. Not really, anyway. I thought maybe it was an accident, like he fell."

"He fell? That's how Todd died?"

Veronica shrugged. "That or he was pushed. I think Eddie thought he was pushed."

"Where did this happen?" Josie asked.

Veronica looked to her left and jutted her chin as if to indicate the direction. "Right over here, Inspiration Point."

I circled Todd's name and added two exclamation marks. I wondered if that was the recent case that Floyd had handled, a suicide that he wasn't quite comfortable with.

Josie let a long moment pass before catching my attention. "Do you have any questions, partner?"

I leaned back, loosened the knot of my tie and unbuttoned my collar while I thought about it. "Yeah, maybe just a couple."

I looked Veronica in the eye. "Do you recall seeing a stick near Eddie's body?"

She looked up and to the left. I remembered some training we had received back in the nineties which held that the direction of one's gaze would indicate whether or not they were being truthful. The theory was later debunked by scientific studies, though the idea of it remained in my head—and in those of many others.

She said, "Yes, I remember."

"Have you seen that stick before?"

She shrugged. "I'm not sure."

"Did Eddie often train with sticks?"

"Yes, I think so."

"So he has sticks there at his studio. That's not something you would be surprised to see."

Veronica nodded and then shook her head. "Yes, I mean, no, I wouldn't be surprised. I've seen him work with the sticks, and there are usually a couple around. I think he keeps one in his car, too."

We hadn't seen his vehicle yet, and I had assumed it was in the garage. The Mincey warrant would cover that because I had included any vehicles on the property as areas to be searched. It was common verbiage on the warrant.

"Did you handle the stick today when you found him?"

She paused for a moment and then slowly shook her head.

"Is that a no?"

"No, I didn't."

"Have you handled the sticks before—ever?"

Veronica shrugged. "Maybe. I don't know. What's this about?"

"What did you do when you found Eddie in his studio? Did you go to him, back off and call, what?"

Her brows furrowed as she answered. "I ran in there, grabbed him, saw that he was—"

Veronica took a moment.

"—saw that he was dead. I screamed. I cried."

"When did you call it in? Was that right then, or later?"

She looked at Josie. It gave me the feeling she thought I was being hard on her, and she was hoping Josie would retake control of the interview.

"Do you remember?" I prodded.

"A minute or so later. I got up, ran to the front door, looked all over for my phone—it was in my purse on the kitchen counter—and when I found it, I called nine-one-one."

Veronica dropped her head and began crying softly. Josie looked over at me, and I shrugged and shook my head, letting her know we could wrap it up.

Josie put her hand on Veronica's knee. "We're very sorry for your loss, Veronica. Thank you for being patient with us."

She looked up, tears in her eyes. "Are you through with me? Can I go?"

"We're going to have to take your clothes. I'll send someone for a change of clothes if you'd like, or we can get you some jail clothes to wear for now."

"Why do you need my clothes?"

Josie's eyes scanned her. "The blood, Veronica. It's all evidence, and we have to send it to the lab. I'm sorry."

Veronica slouched in her chair, accepting the situation.

Josie and I left her there and walked to our car without speaking.

In the car, Josie said, "She didn't do it."

I reached over to turn the air conditioner on. "Nope, I don't think she did."

"What's up with his buddy being killed?"

"We're going to find out," I told her. "That's next on the agenda, a call to Floyd."

8

I CALLED FLOYD'S PHONE TWICE; BOTH TIMES IT WENT TO VOICEMAIL. I didn't bother leaving a message. In a few minutes, we were back at the house. Lambert had wisely asked for additional deputies to help at the scene, as the crowd of onlookers had grown. The press and gawkers were all moved back so that those of us who needed to be there had a path in and out. The entire street in front of the house was now cordoned off, from property line to property line, and to the sidewalk on the opposite side. Josie slowed at the perimeter and a uniformed deputy hustled over, lifted the tape, and waved us through. We must have looked like homicide detectives.

Inside the Bellovich home a team of criminalists dressed in protective booties and gloves was hard at work identifying, tagging, and documenting evidence. Plastic markers created a path between the doorway and the decedent. Butcher paper had been laid on either side of this path and was being used as walkways for the bootie-wearing workers. The room had been darkened and auxiliary lights were positioned near the doorway, low to the floor. Their powerful beams of light shone across the mat, highlighting various impressions of footwear and bare feet.

Josie and I stood shoulder to shoulder near the doorway, silently watching the criminalists measure and photograph evidence. They were using a process known as electrostatic dust print lifting. It allowed them to enhance, collect, and preserve shoe and foot impressions from surfaces such as the flooring in the studio by electronically charging a plastic film and placing it where prints might be found. Electrostatic adhesions would draw the film to their surfaces, and due to the electronic charge, the impressions would adhere to the film.

Ten minutes after we arrived, the process seemed to be wrapping up. A woman who had been down on her hands and knees, with her back to us, stood and turned to face the door. It was Karen Provost, PhD, our department's most senior criminalist and the supervisor of the forensic narcotics unit. She had been very helpful to me and Floyd on a case where one of our suspects had inadvertently ingested Ketamine Hydrochloride—or GHB, as it's more commonly called—the result of a careless jailer.

She held a clipboard in one hand and a pen in the other. Her black hair was pulled back tightly into a bun, showing tiny beads of sweat gathering on her forehead. A pair of narrow, black-framed glasses hung at the end of her nose.

"Detectives," she said, nodding as a way of greeting us.

"Doc, how are you?"

"I've been well, thank you. You?"

"If I was any better, I'd be twins. Have you met my partner, Josie?"

"I don't think I have," she said.

Doc glanced down to watch her step and took two careful strides to reach us. She and Josie shook hands and exchanged smiles and greetings.

"What brings you out in the field?" I asked, unaccustomed to seeing her at scenes.

"Luck of the draw. We have such a backlog all of us are picking up field work. I don't mind, to be honest; I miss working the scenes." She glanced behind her as she finished saying it, maybe admiring the finished product.

"What did you come up with here? Anything good?" I asked.

"Several shoe and bare foot impressions good enough for comparison. Do you have a suspect?"

"Not yet," I said, "but I suspect those shoe impressions will be matched rather quickly to the girlfriend who found him, a paramedic, and a watch commander who should have known better than to come into my scene."

Provost shook her head, turned to face the interior of the studio, and pointed toward the ceiling. "There's a pattern of castoff on the ceiling. We won't mess with it until the body is removed and you guys are finished with everything else. Then we'll run some strings for the angles, get some more photos, and collect samples of the blood."

"Thanks, Doc."

Josie said, "Can they compare bare feet?"

"Just like fingerprints," Doctor Provost said. "Remember when they took footprints on newborns?"

"Uh-huh," Josie said.

"That was for identification. Same thing. If you can have the coroner print his feet at the autopsy, we'll eliminate those prints we lifted that belong to him. Hopefully, you don't end up with a dozen sets of others' prints."

"I don't think we will," Josie said. "The mats looked pretty clean. I was looking at them earlier and it reminded me of a gym where I used to train, and the mats were wiped clean daily with antibacterial soap and warm water. You had to be barefoot to be on the mats, and some people's feet can be funky."

"If that's the case, you could be in luck," Doc said.

I pondered it a moment. "We need to talk to Veronica again and see if we can establish a pattern or practice Eddie had for cleaning."

"That's Eddie?" Doc asked, indicating the dead man with a nod of her head.

"That's Eddie."

"Damn shame. Any ideas why?"

"Not yet, Doc, but we're just sinking our teeth into it now."

"Well, we all know how you Bulldogs are with your murder cases, and I know you're one of the good ones."

"Thanks, Doc. I appreciate that, but honestly, I'm about average. There are some damn good detectives at Homicide."

She brushed past us and stopped to remove her booties and gloves. A fragrance that reminded me of cocoa butter wafted from her. When she straightened, she looked me in the eyes. "I can tell you one thing: anything ever happens to me or any of my loved ones, I hope it's you who's standing in my living room with a blue notebook in your hand."

It was a reference to the Homicide Bureau–issued notebooks, blue with our bulldog mascot printed on the cover. You began every case with a fresh notebook. Some investigations used up several of them.

Then she smiled and put a soft hand on Josie's shoulder. "It was nice meeting you, honey."

I said, "Wait, what about the ceiling?"

"Call me, we'll come back. We have a Lennox murder they're sending us to next, I guess since Lennox isn't far from Lomita. There's another one over in Century's area, but they have someone else rolling out to it. Anyway, we won't be long there, I don't think. It's a gangster thing."

When Provost cleared the door, I turned to see Josie smiling. "What?" I demanded.

"There won't be any murders, not on a rainy Wednesday morning."

"Call for the coroner now, smarty pants."

The remaining crime lab personnel were two who were often teamed together, a man named Jack and a woman named Heidi. Behind their backs, Floyd and I referred to them as Doctor Jekyll and Mr. Hyde. They were packing their equipment into catalog cases, portable file folders that are wider and sturdier than briefcases, and are often used by lawyers, salespeople, and patrol deputies, among others. After they packed away their equipment, clipboards, notes, and documents, they each gathered their cases and the debris left from their work and started for their van that was parked out front. I thanked them, wished them luck at their Lennox case, and said we'd be seeing them back here soon.

I watched them walk down the drive toward the gathered news crews who appeared bored, standing around in small groups drinking coffee while waiting for bits of information. With my appearance in the doorway, some of them became energized, gripping their cameras or microphones, hopeful that I would come out to speak with them. I turned and retreated into the house.

Josie led us down the short hallway to the door of the studio and stopped there. I stopped behind her. Without looking back, she said, "I'll do the scene."

She took out her notebook and began writing. I knew she would be preparing the scene description which would include generalities of the home's location, a physical description of the home itself, and then a detailed description of the studio to include items of evidence and the position and condition of the victim's body. All of it would later be dictated into our investigation report, along with details of our notifications and responses to the scene, Lambert's statement, and the involvement of other parties such as the crime lab and the coroner. They would all prepare their own reports as well, which would ultimately be forwarded to us and be included in our murder book. The first report would also include a summary of the statement by Veronica Steele, who at this point—and likely forever, in my estimation—would be listed as a witness/informant.

While Josie documented the scene, I began a thorough search of the residence. I hoped to find a daily planner or any handwritten notes with information about any lessons he might have had planned for last evening. I also hoped to locate his cellular phone, though any information that might be contained in it would be slow coming. With all phones now being password protected, the best we could do would be to seize the phone as evidence and submit it to HOMCAST, a section of our bureau created by one of our own detectives so we would no longer have to go outside for forensic examination of phones. HOM, for Homicide, CAST for Cellular Analysis Surveillance Team. All of the data from the phone—including call logs, text messages, photos, videos, et cetera—would be downloaded, preserved as evidence, and provided to us for whatever evidentiary value it might contain. The last dozen contacts—voice calls or texts—always interested me most. However, until I delivered the phone to HOMCAST, I would monitor the activity. Fortunately, most phones—even when locked—showed current calls or texts coming in. Those were worth noting as well.

I found the victim's phone in one of the cubby boxes in the studio. The ringer was silenced. That told me two things: the victim had either been in his studio for a period of time, or had planned to be, and that he wasn't expecting any calls or didn't want to be disturbed while he trained or gave a lesson. But his planner was nowhere to be found. If a lesson had been scheduled, there was nothing to identify the student. Not yet, anyway.

"Hello?" a voice called from the front doorway.

I moved to the doorway of the studio and saw Nick Stewart at the door. "Come on in, Nick. Scene's back here."

The coroner's investigator made his way to me. "Busy day, for a rainy Wednesday. This is my third case—"—he glanced at his watch—"in the three hours I've been on."

"Murders?" I asked.

"Just another slow, rainy day," Josie said behind me.

"The other two were both suicides. Any chance yours is?"

I shook my head. "Not unless he beat himself to death." I stepped out of the way and gestured toward the body. "Have a look, but I'm pretty confident that's your cause of death."

Stewart approached the body and stood near it for a moment, studying it from head to toe while tucking his tie between two buttons on his white short-sleeved shirt. Then he squatted and studied it for a few moments longer. Before doing anything else, he pulled a pair of gloves over his hands. He then reached into his attaché case and brought out the temperature probe, essentially a meat thermometer for dead people. I hoped it was only used for dead people, anyway, but with these coroner's people you never knew. He set the thermometer on top of his attaché case, stood and began jotting notes onto a clipboard while again checking his watch. I knew he would be recording the ambient temperature in five minutes, once the thermometer had reached room temperature, and then he would stick it into the victim's liver and wait again before recording that reading. Then simple mathematics would provide us an approximate time of death. In temperate conditions, the body experiences heat loss of approximately 1.5 degrees per hour. So the body's temperature subtracted from 98.6 provides a number, which, when divided by 1.5, is an indication of the approximate time of death, absent extenuating circumstances.

Before he probed the body though, Stewart lifted, pulled, and tugged the leg, arm, fingers, and jaw of the decedent. Full rigor was set; the victim had died between eight and twelve hours prior. That gave us a ballpark. I glanced at my watch to see it was ten o'clock, so between ten last night and two this morning. The liver temperature would narrow the time frame.

Stewart stabbed the thermometer into Eddie Bellovich's cooling body, checked the time again, and noted it on his report. He then retrieved a

Sharpie and drew a black circle around the puncture wound so that the medical examiner would have no question as to the origin of that particular postmortem incision. Five minutes later, Stewart checked his watch, noted the temperature on the dial, and wrote it on his report. "Seventy-nine point six," he said.

I did the math in my head. The fact it was "point six" made it easier, but had it been anything other, I would have rounded it anyway. His body had cooled nineteen degrees, which told me he had been dead approximately twelve hours.

"He's been dead twelve hours or so," I said, and glanced at my watch. "Around ten last night."

Stewart removed the thermometer, packed it away, stood up and took a long look around the room. "Interesting case. Any clues?"

"There was a fighting stick with blood on it about a foot to your right. It was most likely the murder weapon. According to the girlfriend, he kept a planner with training sessions and students' schedules. It's nowhere to be found. I think those are pretty good clues. Likely someone he trained with, and maybe had a beef with. That's all we have so far, but this one is solvable, unlike the random gang shootings we always seem to get."

"Okay, I better get to it. My meat wagon is on its way and I don't want to hold you two up."

Josie said, "I'll let the crime lab know we're ready for their return."

I nodded, then looked to Stewart. "Don't rush on our account. We have to get the lab back out for the ceiling after you take Eddie away."

He glanced at the ceiling. "So I see."

Josie moved away, talking into her cell.

"Before I forget," I said to Stewart, "we'll need his feet printed once you get him cleaned up."

As I said it, something occurred to me. There had been no mention of handprints on the mats. In jiu jitsu, much of the training is on the ground, grappling. Yet no hand prints, only bare feet and shoes. Eddie Bellovich hadn't been training when he was killed. He hadn't trained since the last time he scrubbed the mats. Why was he on the mat, in his gi, and getting clobbered over the head?

This case might not be as black-and-white as I had hoped.

9

Doc Provost and the other crime lab personnel returned, documented the pattern of castoff blood spatter on the ceiling, took additional photographs, and collected samples. As they were finishing up, Floyd returned my call.

I stood in the doorway of the residence, taking in the late morning coastal tranquility that had settled over the bored reporters like a blanket of fog. The neighbors had all gone about their days: some were out for midmorning walks, others jogged past. A pair of ladies pushing strollers, clad in scanty workout clothes that showcased their fit, tanned bodies, peered at the spectacle through their oversized sunglasses as they passed by.

"Where the hell have you been?"

"What do you mean, Dickie?"

"Are you in the office?"

"No, change of plans."

I watched the reporters move about on the street, jockeying for positions as close to the yellow tape as possible, hoping for new information to report. Something seemed off with Floyd, but I had no idea what it might be.

"Everything okay?"

"Not really," he said.

I pictured his wife, Cindy, standing nearby, hands on hips, watching him. His tone suggested there might have been a little domestic quarrel taking place. "Okay, well do you have just a minute? I've got some questions for you."

His tone was low, calm, unrevealing. "I can't really talk right now."

I turned my back to the gathering media. You never knew when they'd have a lip reader among them. I also lowered my voice, knowing they used special equipment to home in on distant conversations. "Everything okay?"

"Gotta go, I'll call you back. Maybe."

I stared at my phone for a moment, then Josie came up to me. "What's wrong?"

I shook my head and frowned. "I have no idea. My ex-wife is pissing me off."

"Your ex-wife?"

My gaze drifted from the phone to meet hers. "Floyd."

She frowned and went back toward the studio. Over her shoulder, she said, "Just once I'd like to work with a group of sane deputies."

"Well, you came to the wrong bureau for that, Detective."

She shook her head, continuing down the hallway.

I meandered that direction but kept my phone in my hand, checking it every few seconds for any messages from Floyd. I hoped it was nothing serious, but with Floyd, you just never knew.

Doc Provost was telling Josie what they had collected in the way of evidence, what she intended to do with said evidence, and that she would forward their reports to us when they were completed. With that, the crime lab personnel filed out with hands full of equipment and evidence, and they departed in two separate vehicles without acknowledging the questioning crowd of reporters.

Lambert walked up to meet us in the driveway, the sun now glistening off the six-point star pinned on her uniform and the brass nameplate on the opposite side. I looked up to see a few clouds left in the sky where faraway seagulls circled, the sounds of their subdued caws setting the tone for our latest mystery by the sea.

"Anything else?" Lambert asked.

I glanced at Josie and then looked past Lambert toward the eager reporters. "Did you guys do a canvass?"

She pulled out her notebook and began flipping pages. "Yes, done. There was nobody home in the house directly across the street"—she paused to look over her shoulder toward the home—"but all the other residents in the immediate vicinity were contacted."

Lambert checked her notebook again. "Two homes have surveillance cameras, but neither has a view that extends beyond the ends of their driveways. Nobody saw or heard anything unusual last night." She looked up. "Nobody comes out in the rain."

I nodded. "Good job, Jessica."

"I'll write a supp with all the details."

"Good," I said, pleased again at Lambert's performance. On murder cases, the assigned patrol deputy would write a "first" report, which would be limited to very few details: *We came, we saw, someone pronounced the victim dead, Homicide was notified and arrived at some point later* (hopefully sober). No identification or detail of the killing would be included. Then the same deputy would write a supplemental report with more detail. This is where the position and condition of the body would be generally described, the victim might be identified, and where details of the patrol deputies' actions would be documented. Those actions might include additional notifications, a neighborhood canvas, transporting witnesses, detaining suspects, and so on. But the first report is what would be made available as a public record as long as the investigation remained active, and it would generally reveal nothing other than that a death had occurred.

"I think we can break it down now," I continued. "I was hoping my lieutenant would be back here to give something to the reporters by now, but it looks like we're out of luck."

Josie said, "Do you want me to give them a statement?"

I looked at her. "Do you want to?"

"Why not? I kind of enjoy it. Maybe I'll be discovered someday if I keep showing my mug on TV."

"Yeah, well, good for you," I said. "I've got a mug made for radio, so have at it."

She smiled, straightened her posture and adjusted her suit jacket, then pushed past me, headed for the crowd. Her movement stirred the waiting reporters, all of whom began preparing for what they likely saw coming: a standup with an attractive homicide detective—this was the type of thing that rocked their worlds.

Lambert and I stayed in the doorway, out of view of the filming. She said, "That Josie's quite a character."

I smiled. "She's pretty awesome; I'm not going to lie."

WHILE JOSIE FED A FEW DETAILS OF OUR CASE TO THE REPORTERS, Lambert and I pulled the yellow tape down from the front of the house, across the road, and everywhere else except where it still held back the camera- and microphone-wielding masses. We each tossed handfuls of crime scene tape into the trunk of her patrol vehicle so it could be disposed of at her station.

"You've got my card," I said, recalling that I had given it to her before Josie and I had left to go interview the girlfriend. "Anything comes up on this, let us know."

She closed the trunk lid and leaned against it. "You can get ahold of me through the station if you need anything done out here, or if I can be of any further assistance to you."

I nodded and watched Josie approach with her wide grin. "How'd it go?"

She waited until she was closer, and then glanced over her shoulder to make sure the reporters were out of earshot before answering. "It's always easier to sell them some shit than it is to tell them the truth."

I laughed. "I have a friend who was a rodeo clown and cowboy poet, and he tells a poem with that exact line in it. And *he's* a master bullshitter."

"Well there you have it then."

"What'd you give up?"

"Not much," she said, "just confirmed who the victim is and told them we didn't have any suspects yet, that we didn't consider the girlfriend a suspect, and that we were not willing to reveal the cause of death or any other details this early in our investigation."

"Perfect. You ready to hit it?"

She turned to Lambert and gave her a quick hug. "Nice seeing you, Jess."

"Same. Take care."

We walked toward Josie's car and she said, "Where to, partner?"

I thought about it for a moment as I watched her over the top of the car, each of us pausing at our respective doors. "Well, we've got three things to do in the very near future, as in A-S-A-P today: talk to the mayor, talk to Floyd about his cliff case—if he's not in a Tijuana prison—and find our victim's planner."

Josie opened her door and ducked into the driver's seat. I hung my suit jacket in the back and then joined her up front. She pulled away from the curb, watching her side-view mirror.

"How are we going to do that? If it's not here, don't you think the killer took it?"

She had a point, and it was something that had been bothering me. "That would mean the killer's name was in the book, and also that the killer knew our boy kept a planner."

"Maybe when he made his appointment, the victim said, 'Okay, I've got you down in my book.' Or, 'I've scheduled you in my planner.'"

I allowed the scene to unfold in my mind, me playing the part of the killer. It was one of the occupational hazards, getting into the twisted minds of sociopaths. I saw myself with a phone to my ear, looking out my window—but at what, the ocean? The city? And I saw the victim with his cell propped on his shoulder as he wrote down my name, and possibly my phone number, in his planner. But where was he at that moment? Was he in the studio, or some other part of his home? Or was he in his car? How sure could I be that the planner was missing? We had searched the house and searched the car, but we had come up empty.

Josie continued, "And what's going on with your partner?"

"I have no idea," I said. "Right now, I'm more concerned with that planner. Let's go talk to Dad next and see if he knows anything about it, how Junior kept his schedule."

She pulled over. "Where do we find Dad? Do you know?"

I readied my phone and took my notebook out of my pocket. "I'll call Joe and get a phone number for him, and we'll call first, make an appointment." Before I hit the send button, I paused and looked at Josie, who was watching me. "What if he kept his planner on his phone, like on the calendar. Isn't that what a lot of you millennials do? Everything's on your phone?"

"I'm no millennial, Grandpa. But yes, a lot of *young* people do just that. Maybe we'll get lucky with his phone."

"I'm no grandpa either," I retorted.

Josie rolled her eyes and looked away. I hit send and waited for Joe Black to answer his phone.

"Lieutenant Joe Black speaking."

The idea to prank him crossed my mind, but I quickly dismissed the thought. There were more important matters at hand. "Joe, Dickie here. Do you have a number for our victim's dad? We need to go see him."

"Sure, hold on. Are you guys finished at the scene?"

I told him we were.

"I'm sorry I didn't make it back there, I got hung up at Lomita with Captain Russell and her Ops lieutenant, Slocumb. You knew him from Metro, right?"

"Yeah, I worked for him there and at Firestone too. What's the deal, are they sweating this case?"

"No," Lieutenant Black said, "Russell began asking me about a deputy-involved shooting from a couple of months ago, wanting to know the outcome of our investigation, but I didn't recognize the case. She had Slocumb bring me their file, and I checked with our office and saw it was handled by Team One. So I explained that to her, and told her she should probably just call Stover and discuss it captain to captain, but while doing so I was thumbing through her so-called file on the case, and I saw she's got all these handwritten notes from interviews she's done. I asked her about that, and she said she likes to have all the information about these things, so she's not caught off guard."

I pulled the phone away from my ear and put it on speaker, and then asked my lieutenant to repeat what he had just said. "Wait, the captain is doing her own interviews on a DIS?"

Josie frowned.

"Yes," he said, and then repeated much of what he had already told me about the deputy-involved shooting case.

I said, "Did you explain to her that that can create a problem for us?"

"Well, I tried," he said. "That's why I was there so long. Slocumb just sat and looked at me as if to say, 'Don't even bother, she's on another planet.'"

I could tell by the look on Josie's face that she shared my concerns about the current case. I said, "Boss, I sure hope she doesn't inject herself into our murder, start interviewing our witnesses."

Josie said quietly, "As if we had any."

"Anyway," Joe said, "are you ready for the number?"

I had almost forgotten why I'd called. I steadied my pen over my notebook and said, "Yeah, the dad. Shoot, Joe."

We disconnected and I called the number and spoke to a woman who identified herself as Sue, the personal assistant for Max Bellovich. I told her who I was and that my partner and I would like to interview Mr. Bellovich about his son's death. She said he had taken a Valium and had gone to lie down; he wasn't available. I left my name and number and asked that she have him call as soon as possible.

"What now?" Josie asked.

"How about you find us somewhere to grab lunch, and I'll try Floyd again. He's killing me."

"Your boy, Russell, is killing me," Josie said of the woman captain.

JOSIE WHEELED THE SEDAN INTO AN APPLEBEE'S AS FLOYD'S PHONE WENT unanswered again. I didn't bother leaving a voicemail. She parked, but left the car idling and sat watching me for a moment.

"What?"

"That look on your face. You're worried about him."

"I just have no idea what the hell he's gotten himself into."

"Should we head back to the office, see if we can learn something there?"

I shook my head and popped my door open. "No, let's go have lunch. We have a case to work, and I don't want to get too far away from here before we talk to the dad."

She shut the car off and we met at the front of it.

"Plus, you can tell me your hooker story over lunch."

"Not a chance," she said. "And you're buying."

The restaurant was nearly empty, as it was closer to the dinner hour than it was to lunch. The hostess started to seat us near the door, but I asked for a booth farther away, preferably in the far corner. She grudgingly obliged.

A waitress appeared with two glasses of water. As she set them down, I ordered a BLT, fries, and an iced tea with lemon. Josie asked for a house salad with Italian on the side, and told the waitress that the water would do. We waited for our lunches in relative silence, each alone in our thoughts. I was thinking about our case and that if our victim kept his schedule on his phone's calendar, it might come together nicely. That would be a good change of pace. A man came through the door with a woman and kid, presumably his family. He was large and black, so my mind drifted back to the case of Jackie Melvin Lowe, the dead gangster rapper that Farris and I were working on. I thought about Lowe's mother, who mourned the loss of her son irrespective of the lifestyle he had chosen. She had always made time for us whenever we called on her with questions, and usually offered us food and drink, which we had always declined. I thought about the mayor who had taken a Valium—had probably washed it down with scotch—and had gone to sleep. Unavailable for an interview, his personal assistant presumably handling his business for him the rest of the day, cancelling meetings, taking messages, and answering emails.

The waitress brought our food and topped off our drinks. After she left, I watched Josie pick at her salad, moving pieces of lettuce and vegetables around with no apparent purpose. I figured she was also thinking about the case.

"What are you thinking?"

She looked up and locked her eyes on mine. She seemed distant, as if her mind was farther away, beyond the boundaries of Rancho Palos Verdes and Lomita Station.

After a long moment, she said, "Nothing."

I chuckled.

"What?"

"The one thing about spending all your time with other detectives is you don't get away with bullshitting very often. Now, if you'd like, I can ask the waitress to come back over, and you can tell her whatever story you'd like, and I'm sure she'd believe it. But you bullshit me, I'm going to call you on it, every time."

She looked down at her salad, moved her fork around until it was positioned over a cherry tomato, and stabbed it.

"Well?"

She ate the tomato slowly, obviously contemplating her response.

After she finished it, she set the fork down and leaned back in her seat. "I want to see about getting a wire up on Spencer."

Here we sat having lunch, and before our latest victim had even achieved room temperature, both of us were thinking about other cases. This was the burden of every homicide investigator: the accumulation of death. The body count. Murders stacked up faster than we could work them, so most of us had learned to triage our cases, sorting them by degrees of urgency, societal orders of importance. Dead cops and kids to the front, dead gangsters to the back. Unless there was a good lead on the dead gangster case, something you could handle quickly and take another gangster off the streets for *twenty-five to life*. We called those twofers. Twofer the price of one. Two birds with one bullet.

"I don't think we have enough probable cause for a wiretap on the game warden, partner. I wish we did."

"I'm recalling more and more about those days on the mountain— those *nights* on the mountain. And I am certain now that it was Spencer who moved me into that shed. I see his face clearly now; it comes in my dreams."

I had taken a bite of my sandwich and chewed slowly while I chose my words. "I don't doubt it, Josie. I really don't. But I don't think that's enough. We need corroborating evidence, something more than that. All wiretaps go through the presiding judge, and the applications are very closely scrutinized. One of the criteria is that all other investigative efforts have to be exhausted before they'll even consider it. Then, we have to have a reason to believe that there is something to be gleaned from listening to his phone calls. My impression is the dude's a loner. Who's he going to call and talk about this with?"

She lowered her gaze and her shoulders slumped, showing her disappointment.

"But like I told you before," I continued, "we can get back on that case anytime you want. We can make time for it. We can work it on our days off, if you want. Hell, we can do our own surveillance of him for all I care. I've got nothing else to do."

She looked up, her brown eyes sad. "You've got your fed now."

"I'm about to fire her."

"Jesus, Dickie. Do you ever keep a woman around? I think you have relationship issues. Besides, how are we going to do surveillance in the woods?"

"I don't know, put you in a deer suit, make you a little doe with those big brown eyes of yours."

Josie rolled her eyes and said, "That's all I need, to get shot out of season by one of those clansmen."

"I don't think they were actually clansmen."

"Whatever, you know what I mean. Anyway, seriously, we have to figure out a way to break him. I was even thinking about playing him, getting close to him and letting him make a mistake, let something slip."

The waitress walked toward us with a pitcher of tea. I shook my head to say I was okay, and she retreated.

"Too dangerous, Josie. You can't go near him. If he ever thinks we're on to him, he might panic. And who knows what would happen."

"Good, let him panic. Let him do something, give me the chance to put a cap in his ass."

I checked my phone to see if I had missed anything. Too often I would forget to take my phone off silent after doing an interview, attending a meeting, or entering court, all of which I had done in the last few hours. There were no missed calls and no text messages.

"Anything from Floyd?" she asked.

"Nothing."

"Can we get a rush on the cell phone? It seems like that might be our best lead."

It took me a moment to shift gears back to our current case. At first, I thought she was still talking about the game warden, but then I realized she was back to being focused on what we had in front of us. Triage.

"Yeah, that might not be a bad idea."

I checked the time on my watch out of habit, even though I had just seen the time on my phone. "Interviewing the dad today is probably out. We're both beat, and we'll probably have the autopsy in the morning. I say we head back to the office, get that cell phone over to HOMCAST so they can get going with it, and then you and I can each go home and get some sleep."

Josie stretched and pushed her plate away. It had hardly been touched, a few bites of lettuce and the tomatoes were all she had eaten.

"Okay, that sounds good to me. I'm getting tired now that we've slowed down."

I stood up and went to the cashier. After I paid, I turned to see Josie waiting for me at the door. She held it open and insisted I walk through, showing we were equals. As we walked toward her car, Josie said, "So are you going to tell me about Red the Fed? What's going on there? Are you still worried she's a plant of some sort, there to take you down or something?"

"Are you going to tell me the hooker story?"

"No."

"Then no."

At six thirty my alarm went off and I awoke feeling fresh and ready to go, having hit the rack at about nine with a couple of beers that helped me relax. The fact we had skipped a night of sleep may have also been a reason for my sound slumber.

As I showered, I began making plans for the day, an agenda that would no doubt be altered several times before noon. The mayor was still high on my list, but the first priority would be checking on Floyd. After that I could check the status of the cell phone examination, and then—depending on what information we got from it—start interviewing Bellovich's friends and associates. Of course, we could have an autopsy that pulled us away from everything else. It was only Thursday, and our team still had until tomorrow morning to cover murders. It was always possible we could be called out again and everything would take a back seat. Triage.

My cell phone rang as I was wrapping my tie into a Windsor knot. The display showed it was the office. "Autopsy," I guessed. I picked it up and answered. "Jones."

"Hello, Richard." It was my lieutenant, Joe Black.

"Good morning, sir."

"Another interesting murder has come in."

I assumed he was assigning it to us, and I could almost feel my blood pressure shoot up. There was nothing more stressful to me than when cases were stacked on cases. "Wait, what? Are we getting it, me and Josie?"

"No, Farris and Marchesano are handling it, but you might be interested in taking a look."

I frowned into the mirror, my blue striped tie now draping loosely against my white dress shirt. "Why is that?"

"It's another martial arts guy."

That gave me pause. "How was he killed? Beaten?"

"Gunshot."

Okay, maybe not related. Or was it? "When did it go out?"

"A couple of hours ago. I just got off the phone with Farris. He was giving me some details for the murder memo, and I thought, well that's interesting. I told him about your case, and he asked if I would let you know, see if you wanted to roll out there."

My mind raced with the possibilities: serial killer. Revenge killing. Coincidence. I didn't believe in coincidences. I glanced at my watch: 7:11 a.m. Traffic was going to be horrible. "Okay, Joe, tell him I'm rolling, but it's going to be a long one. I'll be on the cell."

"Thanks, Richard," Lieutenant Black said, and disconnected.

I called Josie and gave her the Reader's Digest version and asked her how long it would take her to get to the office. She was already there, she said. I told her we would meet there and go together. Then I said, "Have you seen Floyd this morning?"

"No."

I said okay and hung up, and then tried my former partner's cell phone again.

There was no answer.

11

JOSIE LOADED HER GEAR INTO MY CAR. I HAD CALLED WHEN I WAS FIVE
out and told her I'd be there in a minute, and suggested we take my car
today. The advantage to the Crown Vic was that it actually looked like a
cop car—unlike her county-issued Taurus—and it had a red light facing
forward in the center of its windshield, and blue- and amber-colored
excuse me lights on the rear deck. I fully intended to use both, if necessary,
to get through morning traffic. The red light to make people move, the rear
deck lights to keep the chippies off my ass.

She got in wearing a black pantsuit with a turquoise blouse, her hair
pulled back tight into a ponytail, glistening in the morning sun. A sweet
scent of vanilla filled the cabin as she closed the door behind her and
adjusted the belongings she kept with her up front: a leather binder that
held her case notebooks and pens, a clutch, which I knew contained her
pistol, extra magazines, her badge, and handcuffs—all of which she would
later thread onto a manly sized belt that could carry such weight, and
fasten it around her waist over her otherwise ladylike wardrobe. She set a
Starbucks cup on the dash and said, "Hold on," while she fastened her
seatbelt. She retrieved the cup and said, "Okay, let's go."

I idled through the parking lot, looking around for Floyd's car.

Josie noticed. "He's not here. I told you."

71

"I'm having déjà vu all over again." It was a reference to when Josie was missing, and right after I said it, I regretted doing so. I glanced over to see her eyes narrowed, her expression hardened, if only for a moment.

"Sorry, I—"

"Don't worry about it," she said, "I get it. But I'm sure nothing bad has happened to Floyd. Didn't you say he was taking some time off?"

"Not until next week, the way I understood it. The last time I spoke with him—actually, the second to the last time—he said he would be in the office later."

"Did you call his wife?"

We were cruising along Pomona Boulevard, paralleling the freeway we were about to take. I rolled my window up and turned the air conditioner on. "Hell no, I didn't call his wife. They haven't been getting along very well, and she seems to blame me most of the time. Or so it seems."

"You remember all that shit he talked when I was missing, that I'd probably run off with someone, was off to Catalina or whatever?"

I grunted an "Uh-huh."

"Well, that's because it's what he would have done. I'm honestly not worried about it; the boy is just plain squirrelly."

We were on the freeway now and nearly stopped in traffic. I drew in a breath and blew it out like I was trying to extinguish a dozen candles. I looked at the time on the dash, checked my watch, crosschecked my phone. It was a quarter past eight just about everywhere.

"Jesus, this traffic," I complained. "Shouldn't all these assholes be somewhere by now?"

Josie had dropped her visor and was checking her face in the mirror. "You'd think. But hey, it's L.A., baby." She flipped the visor back up and reached for her notebook. "How much do you know about Farris's case?"

"Not much, just that it's another martial artist. I doubt it has anything to do with ours. This one's in the marina—which is what, thirty miles from Palos Verdes? Their guy was shot, not beaten. I mean, martial arts have become a big deal the last couple of decades. Everyone does it. It would be like having two hookers killed a hundred miles apart and thinking they're related."

"Okay, well, I don't follow you with the hooker thing—"

"Speaking of—"

"No, I'm not telling you the story. Anyway, there's more to it than the martial arts connection. I did a little poking around while I was waiting for you to show up at the office, and their victim is friends with ours on Facebook."

"Was."

"Whatever, you know what I mean."

I glanced at my watch again, checked it against the dash clock. "I'm tempted to jump off the freeway and take surface streets, Slauson all the way over."

"Also, they were about the same age, both were into Jiu Jitsu and Muay Thai."

"Yeah, that's common though for mixed martial artists, a good ground game mixed with stand-up. Those are about the two most common."

"Are you grumpy this morning? Have you eaten?"

We were creeping south on the Long Beach Freeway making little to no progress. "The off-ramp isn't far. I'm going to do it, head across Slauson. And no, I'm not grumpy, it's just this traffic is pissing me off."

The Marina del Rey Sheriff's jurisdiction comprises the marina itself, both on- and off-shore, as well as unincorporated districts farther inland including Windsor Hills, Ladera Heights, and View Park. I followed the directions of my phone's mapping program to an address on West Sixty-second Street in the Ladera Heights community, an upscale enclave of well-kept custom homes that were erected in the fifties and sixties, most of which had been refreshed over the last couple of decades. Centered near Slauson Avenue and La Cienega Boulevard, the community is bordered by Culver City to the west, Baldwin Hills to the north, and Westchester to its south and southwest. It is also fewer than ten miles from the coast.

We arrived to find two sheriff's radio cars, two unmarked detective cars, and a coroner's van parked in front of a modest single-story, single-family residence on the north side of the street. Its small, manicured lawn sat elevated three feet from the sidewalk, held in place by a block retaining wall. The property sloped gently up from there to the home. The door on the attached two-car garage was up. Several detectives stood at its threshold, including Rich Farris, Lizzy Marchesano, and, of all people, my recently unaccounted for, former partner, ex-wife, and friend, Floyd.

Had a coroner's investigator not accompanied the three detectives, I might have been less cordial when I asked Floyd where the hell he had been.

Floyd, dressed in slacks and a white shirt unbuttoned at the collar beneath a relaxed tie, turned with a wide grin. "Hey, Dickie, I was just talking about you." He looked at Josie and batted his eyes. "Hello, gorgeous."

"Like my partner said, where the hell have you been?" she snapped. "You had him all stressed out yesterday, and I'm sure you remember what it's like working with this guy when he's even a little uptight."

Rich Farris wisely interrupted. "Hey guys, thanks for coming out. Lizzy and I picked this case up early this morning. Our dead guy there"— he turned and indicated a body lying on the floor inside the garage, on his back spread-eagled as if he were making a snow angel—"was found by his roommate who came home about three this morning. The roommate was out clubbing and should be easy enough to clear."

"This is the martial artist, I take it, and the reason we're here," I said, stating the obvious. Then I locked my gaze on Floyd. "What are you doing out here?"

"Wait till you get a load of this, Dickie. Tell him, Rich."

Rich Farris rubbed his hand over his short-cropped natural hair that seemed to be graying by the day. His thin mustache remained free of the aging process, but I wasn't sure it did so unassisted. A gold bracelet dangled from his wrist, and he wore a gold pinky ring on his left hand. The ring finger had been unadorned for several years now.

Farris said, "We thought the roommate was coked out of his mind, though his pupils didn't show it. But he was scared to the point of paranoia, saying he had to blow this town, 'Everyone's dying.'"

"Think he knows who did it?" Josie asked.

Farris shook his head. "He says he doesn't, but—"

Lizzy Marchesano, dressed today in a cream-colored pantsuit with a chocolate brown blouse and multi-colored checked scarf, chimed in, "I'm not so sure."

"Here's the thing," Farris continued, indicating the victim again, "this guy's brother went off a cliff a few weeks back—"

"Inspiration Point, Dickie," Floyd said. "And now you know why I'm here."

74

"That was the suicide you had some concerns about."

He nodded. "Yeah, like I told you on the phone yesterday—"

"Oh, did we speak yesterday? I couldn't remember."

Floyd chuckled. "I never liked that case for a jumper from the beginning, and then your case pops up, and now this, my so-called jumper's brother getting a bullet between the lanterns. Imagine the odds."

I turned and studied the interior of the garage. There was a heavy bag hanging in one corner, a speed bag mounted near it. There were miscellaneous weights and exercise equipment along two walls, and the floor was half-covered by mats similar to those found in our victim's studio—grappling mats. There were mirrors on two of the walls, interspersed with posters of scantily clad female bodybuilders and deeply tanned, hairless, muscular men.

The victim was dressed in shorts and a tank top with a powerlifter and the name of a gym printed on the front. He was white, in his late twenties or so, lean and muscular, and dead as disco.

I addressed Farris and Marchesano. "Mind if I have a look?"

Lizzy said, "Crime lab is done and gone. Jared was about to haul him out of here. Have at it."

Jared was the coroner's investigator, a short, stocky blond who spoke softly on the rare occasions he had something to say. Out of respect, I sought his approval as well. "Jared, you mind?"

He shook his head.

I moved slowly into the garage, being careful of where I stepped. When I arrived near the victim's bare feet, I stopped and again studied my surroundings—*his* surroundings. He could have been wearing a gi and lying on the blue mats in Rancho Palos Verdes alongside Bellovich, for all it mattered. Other than the mechanisms of death, the two cases were eerily similar: the victim had not been concerned with death until the instant it came. Neither this victim nor the last one—each exceptionally capable— had attempted to defend themselves or flee.

I squatted, and moments later the vanilla fragrance revealed my partner's presence behind me. Josie leaned down, bracing her hands on her knees, and the two of us studied the young man silently for several moments.

"Now we've got ourselves a murder investigation, I'd say."

I didn't look back at her when I replied. "You're right about that, partner. This just got interesting."

Outside the garage, Farris said, "The kid lived here with his grandmother until she passed a few years back. She had owned the house since the sixties, and our victim had apparently moved in with her at least a decade ago. No word yet on the parental situation."

"I can tell you about that," Floyd said, "if they are in fact biological brothers. The dad is an attorney here in L.A., and the mom is a washed-up fashion model who starts her days with bloody marys and goes downhill from there. By noon, she's loaded, and usually naked by the pool, hoping the pool boy or a neighbor or a pair of visiting homicide detectives might notice. And it isn't a pretty sight."

"Why's Floyd always find the naked women?" Farris asked, rhetorically.

"It's a curse," he replied.

"What's your boy's name?" I asked.

Farris opened his notebook as Josie said, "I have all that. We just need the info on Floyd's case."

Floyd stepped closer to Josie as he flipped his notebook open. "Here's all the horsepower. I'll get you guys copies of the reports when we get back to the office."

Lizzy said, "Rich and I were going to go make the notifications, hopefully get there before mom gets naked by the pool. Should we all get together at the office later?"

"Let's make it tonight, or tomorrow," I said. "I just got a text that we have a post at eleven on our guy, and we need to go talk to the dad this morning too—or at least try."

"Post at eleven?" Floyd said. "Who waits till eleven to start an autopsy?"

"Dr. Salazar, apparently," I answered.

"Oh dude, she's hot."

1 2

As we drove away from the house, Josie observed that the neighborhood was mostly black. "I mean, other than the dead guy," she said.

"I worked here for about a month a long time ago, on loan from Firestone. It was a lot different, very slow-paced. These are all working-class to upper middle-class families who take pride in their properties and the community. My guess is that most of the few white people who live here have been here since the sixties. Or at least their families have been, like in Bailey's case."

"Coming over here from Firestone must've seemed like a vacation."

An elderly man wearing his robe and house shoes reached the end of his driveway just as we drove past. As he bent to pick up his paper, I waved. His gaze followed as we passed.

"The thing is, there's still crime. Burglaries, dope, the occasional robbery or assault. I made a few good arrests. I also met some interesting people. O.C. Smith, an R&B singer, lived not far from here, just a few blocks over as I recall. He was a cool dude."

"Never heard of him."

"That's because you've got no soul, Josie, no taste for the R&B oldies.

Ever hear 'Little Green Apples'?" I sang her a line: *"God didn't make little green apples, and it don't rain in Indianapolis in the summertime."*

"Don't quit your day job, partner."

"Oh, and 'The Son of Hickory Holler's Tramp.'" I didn't even try humming that one. "You've never heard those songs?"

I looked over to see Josie shake her head. "How'd you meet him? Radio call?"

We had turned out of the neighborhood and were on La Cienega, which would get us to the parking lot known as the 405 freeway, which we would take south to Palos Verdes. "No," I said. "You want to hear the long version?"

"Sure, why not. We've got nothing but time, now."

"My dad met him first, a long time before. He always liked jazz, R&B, and the like. He had Smith's records, and I had grown up hearing the music. Then—and I was still little—he and my mom went and saw O.C. play somewhere. Well, my dad is the furthest thing from shy that you could imagine, and he went up to the stage during a break and said, 'Hey, brother, I dig your music, man.'

"Apparently, my parents were the only two white people in the place, and when my dad called him 'brother' it got his attention. Smith stepped off stage and they chatted for about fifteen minutes before the break was over and he had to get back to entertaining.

"Then, a few years later—now I'm a young deputy, working the jail— my dad calls and tells me he's going to go see O.C. Smith play somewhere in L.A. I look the place up, and I was like, 'Dad, that's not a great area.' He says maybe I should come along then, since I have a gun and badge.

"Well, I was both intrigued and concerned about my parents going down there, so I got myself a date and went along with them. Again, we're the only white people there, and we are definitely getting some looks. But O.C. takes the stage and my dad yells out, 'Sing your song, brother.'"

I looked over to see Josie smiling widely and shaking her head.

"Yeah, he's a little nuts like that. But O.C., he shields his eyes from the stage lights and looks over at our table, and he goes, 'Is that my brother, Jimmy Jones?' I couldn't believe it—"

"That's your dad, Jimmy Jones?"

"Jim, James, Jimmy—it depends on where he is and who he's with.

But he was the youngest of seven kids, raised in the deep south, so he's used to being called 'Jimmy' or even 'Little Jimmy.' Oh, and that was another thing that kind of connected them—my dad was raised in North Carolina, and O.C. was from South Carolina. They were both in the service around the same time, during Korea."

"That's where he got that soul from, huh, living down south?"

"He grew up with a black nanny, so yeah, probably. Anyway, now everyone in the club relaxes. I mean, if O.C. calls you his brother, all the other brothers are going to respect that, right?"

"Sounds about right."

"Well, I met him that night, briefly. But when I was working the area a few years later, my dad told me O.C. lived down there."

"Wait, what? What's your dad, a stalker?"

I chuckled. "No, not exactly, but kind of. See, my dad had told O.C. how he used to play in bands himself, and that he still played in a little group for their church. O.C. was like, 'No kidding, I'm actually a pastor, too.' He tells my dad that his group should come play at his church some-time. So, they did. And they became friends. Then my sister gets married, and my dad asks O.C. to sing at her wedding. And he did.

"So I didn't really meet O.C. Smith down here, but I got to know him when I was here. I had met him briefly that night at the club, and talked to him briefly at my sister's wedding, and since we were—after all—family, according to O.C. and Jimmy, I went by his house when I first got assigned to work the area, and O.C. was happy to have me visit. Very nice people, him and his wife. So anyway, I made it somewhat of a routine. He had nothing going on in the mornings during the week, so I'd go by and sit and visit with him and his wife over coffee."

"You amaze me at times," Josie said.

I looked over and grinned. "How's that?"

She shook her head. "You just do. There's more to you than what you allow most people to see."

I thought about that a moment. "Maybe."

"So do you stay in touch with him?"

"O.C.? He passed away a few years back, heart attack. He was a good man. Unlike this asshole we're getting ready to go talk to. Hey, to change the subject," I said, knowing we were close to our next destination and would only have a few minutes to discuss it, "after we talked about the Spencer deal, I've been thinking about some things, trying to come up with some angles we can work on that case."

Josie became rigid and serious at the mention of the game warden. "Yeah?"

"Well, it occurred to me, we never did get the ballistics back on the bullet we pulled out of that tree on the Willie Brown murder. I never did follow up with the lab on that case, and I think everyone was looking at that murder and your kidnapping as having been solved by the death of the Watkins kid."

"Okay, so what are you thinking?"

I looked over at her while coming to a stop again on the freeway, five lanes of traffic bottled up as far as you could see ahead and behind us. "I think the way we figure out your ordeal is to prove he killed Brown."

"You think he did."

I glanced from the road again. "I think if Spencer's good for your case, he's good for Brown too. I think they go hand in hand, and that's why your deal happened in the first place. You weren't a random target. If you and Tommy hadn't been up there at the scene, it wouldn't have happened. I think if Spencer is responsible for it, he must have seen you at the scene and panicked, not knowing who you were. It makes more sense as to why he smoked the Watkins kid so quickly that night. Not only to cover his tracks on your kidnapping, but to give us a dead suspect on the Brown case. Remember how he offered that up in the interview to Farris? All the mountain mysteries solved at once. That's a handy way to make everything go away."

We were finally at the off-ramp and just moments from the home of Palos Verdes mayor Max Bellovich.

Josie said, "So what are you thinking?"

"We get Firearms to give us the details on that bullet, and then we figure out a way to see if it came from Spencer's rifle."

"Yeah, easy enough. Do we just ask him?"

Her sarcasm came from frustration, I knew. "We can come up with something better than that. Give me some time to think about it. Hell, maybe we'll take him shooting."

"What about qualifications? Maybe Fish and Game makes them

qualify at certain times and we can set it up so that we are there to get his expended bullets when he's finished."

"Brilliant! Let's look into that. We've got a lot going on now but keep that on a back burner. Let's put some time in on it whenever we can."

"You know I'm all for that. I'm going to nail the son of a bitch sooner or later, one way or another."

We pulled to the curb in front of a mountaintop custom home with a view of the Pacific. I shut the car off but paused before stepping out. "Josie, if he did it, we'll figure out a way to prove it. It might not be the bullet—that may or may not work—but we won't give up. Enough time has gone by that we need to go through all of the files again, your case and William Brown's, and see what we've missed. Work it like a cold case. We won't ever walk away from it. I promise."

Josie had removed her sunglasses and set them on the dash when we stopped, and now I could see her eyes were watering slightly. I looked away and stepped out to break the mood. When Josie met me outside of our car, she had put her glasses back on.

INSIDE THE HOME WE WERE SERVED TEA AND COFFEE BY AN ASSISTANT named Katrina, who the mayor—Mayor Max—called Kat. I had no doubt she assisted him in many ways unrelated to his public service and whatever private work he did as well.

After offering our condolences, Josie got to the interview while I sat in an elegant Queen Anne chair near a wall of tinted glass that showcased their ocean view. I could see part of Inspiration Point, and my thoughts went to the bigger picture of our case. Three young men, all martial artists, dead within a short period of time. Two were brothers. What might have possibly gotten them killed?

Their parents were rich. Sometimes that led to trouble for the trust fund, silver spoon babies that they, or more likely someone else, had raised. Maybe they had gotten involved in trafficking drugs. It wouldn't be the first time. I thought about a pair of burglars in the Brentwood area who finally killed someone when they were cornered by a homeowner. Two young men who had never gone without anything they wanted or desired, two boys lavished with everything other than attention and discipline. Yet they stole and then they killed.

Drugs were the first thing that came to mind because for boys like these, the drug world offered big cash, status, and excitement. Until it didn't. Until something didn't go right and they learned that some little Columbian who weighed in at a buck-forty and couldn't lift their warmup weights was the deadliest opponent they would ever know.

The mayor was telling Josie that his wife of thirty-eight years stayed in New York most of the year due to business, and that she wouldn't be back until summer. *Hence the personal assistant,* I thought. They both were in real estate, but he prefers the west coast and she—a born and bred east coaster—specialized in Manhattan apartments. "I wouldn't care to ever visit the place again, personally," he said.

"Your son, what did he do for a living, Mr. Bellovich?"

"He gave lessons and trained martial artists," he replied.

Josie paused a moment, and the mayor saw where this was leading.

"The kid doesn't have to work. *Didn't.* The house was a gift from his mother and me, and he had a trust fund that paid him a generous stipend. The martial arts was his hobby and he found a way to make money doing it, teaching and coaching. It kept him busy, out of trouble."

"Had he been in trouble much?"

The mayor waved a hand to dismiss the notion. "Nothing other than just being a boy—a little drinking here and there, a fight or two. Why are you asking about him and not the son of a bitch who killed him?"

I sat quietly, enjoying the match, and knew that the mayor would be in over his head if it turned into an adversarial one. There were few notes in my notebook so far, which meant we weren't making much progress. Oftentimes, that was the case. Regardless, all family and close friends of any victim needed to be interviewed. Start close and work your way out.

"Most of the time, we have to know how a person lived in order to figure out why he died."

"Well maybe you should start then by looking at the tramp who lived with him—or maybe I should say *off* him. Does she have an alibi? Was she there when it happened? What does she know?"

He got up from his chair and shuffled over to the window, where he stood silently for a long moment staring off toward the sea.

82

"She's the one who found your son dead, Mr. Bellovich, and called it in. We've interviewed her and we are checking her alibis, but we don't think she's involved."

He grunted but maintained his position, his back to us.

"Is there a reason she would want him killed?" Josie asked. "I mean, if they aren't married, and she was enjoying her lifestyle, it seems—"

Bellovich turned to her, scowling. "Who knows, the stupid bitch. Maybe she found a new sugar daddy, or maybe she had some other scheme planned out."

"You didn't care for her."

He huffed and turned away.

"What about his friends, Mr. Bellovich? Can you tell us about his closest friends?"

The mayor turned again to face us, started to speak, but stopped, and checked the time on his watch. He walked over to the bar and poured himself a drink. As he did, he said, "I don't imagine either of you care for a scotch?"

"Not until later," I said.

He returned to his seat, a twin to the chair in which I sat, sipped his drink and waited for another moment before speaking.

"The Bailey boys were his best friends. They're two brothers who are also into the martial arts. One of the boys—Todd—sadly killed himself a while back. I don't know about the other—Sean—but they're both fine young men, just like my boy. I couldn't tell you about any other friends he might have. The list of women he has been through might require a task force to track down. Eddie was a player and the girls went crazy for him."

Josie shot me a glance that seemed to question whether we should tell the mayor about Sean Bailey being killed sometime during the night. I gave a slight shake of my head, and she returned the signal with a slight nod. She took a business card from her notebook and handed it to the mayor.

"We'll probably be in touch, but if you think of anything or have any questions about the case, don't hesitate to call."

I stood up and prepared to leave but paused to drink in the view one more time. I wondered how someone could get a guy like Todd Bailey out to that cliff and off of it. That's the part that bothered me most. Eddie's and Sean's murders could be explained easily enough if you just imagined that their killers had been a person or persons that they were comfortable with, or at least not threatened by.

"Mr. Bellovich, I have a question."

He had been looking down at the card with a sheriff's star and Josie's name and number on it. His eyes slowly shifted to me.

I pointed toward the ocean. "Is that Inspiration Point out there?"

"You can see part of it, yes."

"And that's where Todd committed suicide, right?"

"Yes," he said flatly. "Many others have as well. They ought to fence it off."

"Did you know him to visit that point?"

"Yes, as a matter of fact. He lived across the highway from there. There are miles of trails from one point to another, and down to a park. He was quite the swimmer also, and he would run the trails and then swim in the ocean. He was an exceptional athlete."

"And did you know this firsthand, or because Eddie had told you, or what?"

Bellovich frowned slightly and I had the feeling he was wondering why I was asking about Todd Bailey's suicide.

"I've known the Bailey boys most of their lives. Eddie has always been friends with them, since at least grade school."

I nodded and turned to leave, and Josie followed my lead.

The mayor called out to us as we reached the front door. "How do I get him back—for the services I mean? The man I talked to yesterday said the coroner would take his remains for an autopsy."

"Yes sir," I answered. I didn't tell him we would be heading to the coroner's office once we left his home, and that we would stand tableside while a medical examiner dissected his son's remains. "You just need to select a mortuary and provide them with the coroner's case number. Did anyone give that to you yet?"

He shook his head, and Josie returned to him and wrote it on the back of her business card. She said, "Just give your mortuary this number and they will take care of all the arrangements. You don't have to deal with the coroner's office at all."

He stared at the card as we let ourselves out.

13

WE DIDN'T LEARN MUCH FROM THE AUTOPSY, AS IT TURNED OUT. EDWARD Robert Bellovich had died as a result of blunt force trauma to the head. Manner of death: homicide. There was no way to determine with certainty the height, weight, or strength of our suspect, beyond that he or she would have been approximately the same height as the victim—give or take six to twelve inches—and that he or she would have been strong enough to swing a club with significant force to crack a skull.

The ambiguity was discouraging, but such is the case in blunt force trauma wounds. Gunshot wounds often allowed for calculations of trajectory, and, in the case of a knife wound, such measurements can provide insight as to the height of a perpetrator. But the skull was too badly damaged to determine the physical attributes of the killer.

Josie and I left the coroner's office and drove the short distance to Philippe's near Chinatown for a couple of French dip sandwiches, chips, and iced teas. I had suggested Yee Mee Loo's around the corner, but Josie wisely declined. "I'll have to see about a hundred more autopsies before I start drinking my lunch like some of you guys."

"That was pretty judgy," I told her.

She shrugged, unconcerned.

"I'm not even sure they're open this early," I lied, glancing at my watch. It was nearly one, and three things were certain: one, that at least four people would be bellied up to the bar at Yee Mee Loo's by now; two, that they would be public servants from the nearby Criminal Courts Building, Hall of Justice, City Hall, or LAPD's Police Administrative Building; and three, that Philippe's would have a line stretching from the front door to the counter where you ordered and collected your food before squeezing yourself into one of the long communal tables.

After lunch we drove back to the office in Monterey Park, where we would check with HOMCAST about Eddie's cell phone to see if any valuable information had been gleaned. I was mostly hoping for calendar notes of Eddie's appointments or training schedule, but we were equally interested in all of his recent communications—calls and texts. We had agreed that as far as interviewing Eddie's friends, associates, and contacts went, we would put together a list, research those we intended to interview, and then prioritize them. That alone could take the remainder of the day, then we would meet with Farris, Marchesano, and Floyd later that evening. We were in for a long stretch in the office once we got back, which was never where I preferred to be. Maybe I should have insisted on Yee Mee Loo's after all.

Josie checked messages on her phone while firing up her computer, and I had just returned from the bathroom and coffee urn and sat down at my desk when Stover appeared. He liked to roam the squad room, or *the floor*, as most called it, the warehouse-sized, carpeted room with six columns of desks that was home to nearly eighty detectives. Sometimes, when Captain Stover roamed, it was to visit with various detectives and see firsthand what was going on with different cases. The majority of cases that came through the bureau meant little to the captain beyond the statistics they represented. *Did you solve that case yet?* In a bureau that processed between three hundred fifty and five hundred homicide cases each year, and several hundred more cases of suicide, accidental, industrial, and recreational deaths, there would always be a handful of cases that mattered even to the administrators. Those were usually cases of social importance that garnered the most media attention.

Stover plopped down in an empty seat next to my desk. "What's the deal with your Palos Verdes case?"

"The mayor's kid?"

"Do you have more than one case in Palos Verdes? Yes, the mayor's kid. The one that's been all over the news and making my phone ring with questions from the top. That one."

Captain Stover and I were like two scrappy dogs circling, each about to pounce or expecting the other to. Lately, there had been much less tension between us. I believe this was because Stover had been passed up for a promotion to commander, and now he was mostly just looking to do his last year or two and pull the pin. Lieutenant Black had also played a part in defusing our contentious relationship by acting as a mediator to keep Stover off my ass and me out of his thick blond hair.

"Well, that is the question du jour."

He crossed one leg over the other and leaned back. "Am I going to need a cup of coffee or a stiff drink for this?"

I glanced at my watch. "I'd go for the drink, if I were the skipper of this boat."

"That's probably why you're not."

I shrugged. "Could be. Anyway, we might have a mess with this one."

"Of course."

"Farris and Marchesano picked up a murder over in Ladera Heights this morning that might be related, and Floyd handled a suicide—"

"Well if you and he are involved, I'm sure it's a mess."

"—or, I should say, it was meant to look like a suicide, and it turns out Floyd's dead guy and Farris's dead guy are brothers."

Stover frowned, not yet having the whole picture.

I continued, "My victim was best friends with those two. All of them were martial artists, pretty-boys, and rich kids. There's little chance the killings aren't related, and almost no doubt now that Floyd's so-called suicide is anything but that. We're all getting together this evening to go over the cases and see what we can come up with. Most likely, we'll be working them together."

"Didn't I split you and Floyd up a couple years ago?"

"No, Skipper, we're still partners. You must be thinking of two other assholes."

He thought about that for a long moment and then his eyes shifted, looking over my shoulder. I scooted my chair out of the way so that Josie could join the discussion. I hadn't realized that she had finished on the phone and was taking in our conversation with a slight grin on her face.

"How'd you end up stuck with this guy, Sanchez?"

She smiled. "Luck of the draw, I guess, Captain."

Stover got up from his chair and looked around the squad room while straightening his tie, likely trying to think of something clever to add. Finally, without meeting her gaze, he said, "Yeah, well, with luck like that I'd stay away from Vegas."

He started to walk away, then paused, looked back, and said, "Keep me posted on these cases, and have your lieutenant come see me when he gets in. Where the hell is he, anyway?"

I shrugged. "I have a hard enough time keeping track of Floyd, sir."

With that, Stover shuffled off, making small talk with other detectives he passed along the way. I turned to Josie. "I love that guy."

"I can tell."

Floyd burst through the back door, which was a short distance from where Josie and I sat. "Dickhead, have you seen my Mongo?"

His tie had been loosened even more since we had seen him a few hours earlier, and his sleeves were rolled up now too. If you didn't know otherwise, you'd think he had been hard at work all day. He was like the politicians who went to town hall meetings and scrapped the jackets and rolled up the sleeves as if they were about to grab a shovel and build a new road right after getting your vote. It was all bullshit, in politics and in Floyd's world. Not that he wasn't a worker, but he was an actor as well.

"Been a rough day, partner?"

He came over and sat in the seat Stover had just abandoned, pushed his sunglasses up onto his head and sighed. "Jesus, dude, it's always something."

"You've been busy?"

"Well hell yeah, Dickie. What do you think?"

"I think you should show me your notebooks and tell me all about your rough couple of days. I'm still trying to figure out how you go M.I.A. for twenty-four hours and have no explanation. I wouldn't be surprised if you've put in for overtime for it."

"Oh shit, that reminds me. I've got to get ahold of Mongo, have him go through that suicide file and get up to speed before the meeting tonight."

"He didn't work it with you?"

"No, it was a suicide, one-man response."

That was the standard, anything other than a homicide case was a one-man response. The purpose of our presence at any other death scene was only to make sure that it wasn't a cleverly disguised murder. But when Floyd and I were partners, we still worked them together, though most partners didn't. We were funny that way.

"Right," I said. Sometimes talking to Floyd about his new partner was like talking to your ex about their new spouse—awkward. "Anyway, where were you yesterday?"

He spun his chair around and popped out of it as if a fire alarm had sounded. "Dude, I've got shit to do. See you later." And he was gone.

Josie said, "He's up to something."

He probably was, but before I could guess what that might be, my phone rang. I picked it up and said, "Jones."

"Dickie, it's Ty."

I wasn't sure I caught that right.

"Who?"

"Ty Couture, HOMCAST, you dumb son of a—let me ask you somethin', how many white boys you know named Tyrone?"

I chuckled into the phone. "Sorry, brother, I couldn't hear you. What have you got for me, anything good?"

"Shitloads of text messages between him and some babe named Veronica. Do you know who that is?"

"Girlfriend," I said. "She's the one who found him dead."

"It seems they might have been arguing. He wanted to know where she was, and she said she'd be home later. These were all in the late evening. I'll get you copies of everything with my report."

"Who was the last person to call or text him?"

"There were several missed calls from your girl, Veronica, and the last connected call is from a number that appears to be a burner phone. That was just before nine."

"Interesting. What can we get from that, anything?"

"Dude, I'm on the road right now. Are you going to be in the office later?"

"I'm in the office now, and we're going to have a meeting in a couple hours. Looks like Farris and Marchesano just picked up a related case, and Floyd has a suicide that wasn't. I'm pretty sure you'll be looking at more phones."

"Floyd owes me a steak already, so this is going to cost him double. You guys are killing me."

"See ya later, Ty-*rone*."

"Later, Dickie."

14

THE CONFERENCE ROOM COULD BE COLD, UNINVITING, STUFFY, AND WORST of all, lacking in alcoholic beverages. At Homicide Bureau we had constructed a patio for barbecues and gatherings that we had declared to be apart from the business of solving murders, though much mayhem was discussed among those who gathered there, their business attire intact but modified for comfort. The department had regulations against drinking during business hours and at county facilities, but quite frankly nobody at Homicide cared. That was for everyone else, not for those of us who stood over dead children for a living. There should have been a hosted bar in the squad room, as far as most of us were concerned.

So as it was, on late Thursday afternoon when the bureau had mostly emptied for the day, our small, select group escaped the confines of the conference room and gathered around a picnic table that was set on a concrete slab. Half of the patio was sheltered by a free-standing wood-framed cover with a metal roof. The rain had moved out and the Southern California spring afternoon was perfect for a cocktail and business meeting.

Floyd pulled a patio chair from the covered area and positioned it in the direct sunlight, untucked his dress shirt, and pulled it off. Josie joked that she might join him. He looked up at her, the sun glistening off his Ray-Bans, and smiled. "No balls, you won't."

Lizzy Marchesano took a seat at the table, her notebook in front of her, all business. Josie, apparently rethinking the idea of sunbathing with Floyd, joined her. Mongo took an available seat with no regard for shade or sun, or so it seemed, as half of his body was shaded, and half was not.

Farris and I sat in a corner where we were shielded from the harsh rays of the late afternoon sun. Farris said, "You don't dig the sun either, huh?"

I had already loosened my tie, unbuttoned my collar, and turned my cuffs over twice. I pushed one sleeve up and displayed a pale, freckled arm. "I'm one of those fair-skinned white boys, Rich. Can't be in the sun without slathering on the peckerwood ninety-nine. What's your excuse, man?"

Rich chuckled, his smile a brilliant white against his light brown skin. "It'd be one thing if we were poolside and dressed for the occasion. I'm not about sweating in my Brooks Brothers Milano."

"That's what we need for the patio, Rich," Floyd chimed in, "a swimming pool."

Lizzy said, "Let's get this handled and get going. I've been up since three."

Rich took the lead. "Okay, let's do it. I say we go in order of the cases, so Floyd, Mongo, you two can lead off."

Floyd lifted his head from the back of the chair and slowly sat up. It was as if he had fallen asleep under the sun, or at least had allowed his mind to drift. After a long pause, he began.

"Six weeks ago, I get a jumper at Inspiration Point down in Palos Verdes. There have been more than a couple of suicides there over the years and at least one homicide—maybe one *other* homicide. Our guy is Todd Bailey, a thirty-four-year-old surfer boy who was a struggling actor and part-time stuntman. As we all know now, he was the older brother of Sean Bailey, Rich and Lizzy's victim from last night. What was he, Rich, a couple years younger?"

"Sean was twenty-nine."

"Same as my victim," I said.

"Anyway, there's almost no way to prove a murder out there on that cliff unless you have an eyewitness—which, of course, we don't. So we were looking at accidental or suicide, leaning toward the latter. The coroner has held off on a determination for us because I've never been comfortable with calling it a suicide. There wasn't a note, he'd never threatened suicide before, and by all outward appearances, he seemed well-adjusted. The only thing at all that I could come up with as a reason he might have jumped, is that whole struggling actor thing. You know how that shit goes. But he was also a trust fund baby and didn't necessarily need the work. That's about all I've got. Oh, and his mom is a trampy old broad who was probably pretty hot back in the day."

"Good thing we have that tidbit," Marchesano said.

"You're welcome," Floyd said, easing his head back and looking up toward the sun again.

Farris said, "Dickie, Josie, what've you guys got?"

Josie glanced at me and then addressed Farris. "Our guy, Eddie Bellovich, was a martial artist—"

"Oh, I forgot, same with Todd Bailey," Floyd interrupted. "Mixed martial arts."

"—who gave lessons and trained out of a studio in his home in Palos Verdes. His girlfriend, Veronica Steele, lived there with him. He and the girlfriend had a fight the day of his murder, and she split. When she came home late that night, she found him dead in the studio. He died from blunt force trauma to the head."

Josie flipped through a few pages of her notebook before continuing.

"His dad, the mayor of RPV, says Eddie and the Bailey brothers were tight, best of friends. When we spoke to him, he didn't know about Sean's murder, but he did bring up Todd's death. The mom is mostly in New York, and daddy has himself a personal assistant to take care of things on the home front."

"I bet he does," said Floyd, his Ray-Bans still pointed skyward.

"What else?" Farris prompted.

"That's about it, really. We feel confident the girlfriend isn't involved, but we have nowhere else to go yet. She said he would write appointments in a planner, but that's gone. It's likely the killer took it because his name was written in it. Our victim was wearing his gi in the studio and was barefoot, so we think the killer was scheduled for a lesson that night. The mats were relatively clean, so he hadn't been training before our killer arrived."

"What about the phone, Josie?" I asked.

"Oh, yeah. Couture has our victim's phone and we were hoping he might join us here before we're done. The bottom line is, so far there's nothing helpful other than that his last call came from a burner phone. We gave Ty a bit of information about these cases maybe being linked, and told him you guys would probably be giving him phones to go through also."

Mongo spoke for the first time. "We don't have a phone."

We were all silent for a moment as we waited for more, but it never came. Finally, I said, "Your dead guy didn't have a phone?"

"Yes, he had a phone," Floyd said, irritably. "We just can't find the damn thing. Probably somewhere in the Pacific, maybe in the belly of a shark. We have his number and can get records from the phone company. We had thought about doing that but haven't gotten around to it yet. We've caught two other murders since then."

"The timing is interesting," I said. "If all of these are related, why did Todd Bailey go first, six weeks ago, and then our guy, Eddie boy, gets whacked two nights ago, and their buddy—Todd's brother—the next night? Also, why three different ways of killing?"

"It appears to be an escalation," Farris said. "The first guy is tossed off a cliff. That's as clean as you can get it, as far as not being gruesome, violent, personal. Maybe that wasn't satisfying enough, so the next guy he beats to death with a stick. That had to feel good, if you're out for revenge."

"Revenge?" I pondered aloud. "That's interesting."

"I'm just saying," Farris continued, "if that's what this is."

"What do you guys think about a dope connection?" Lizzy asked.

"We didn't have any evidence of it," Josie said.

I shook my head. "I wouldn't dismiss it though."

Farris said, "I don't like it."

He pushed out of his chair and paced the length of the patio, his eyes on the ground. We all watched him for a moment. Even Floyd had sat up and seemed to be paying attention. Farris stopped at the far side of the patio and turned to face us, his eyes scanning his audience.

"Dope would indicate pros were involved. I don't see these killings as professional. On the one hand, you wonder how someone could get a tough guy like Todd Bailey out to the edge of a cliff, and then over the edge without going with him. And then you'd think maybe there was more than one of them. Or maybe he was dead or at least unconscious before he went over. If that was the case, there'd have to be more than one person involved. I take it there were no signs of someone being dragged out to the edge of Inspiration Point."

Floyd said, "None. But that's the bitch of it too, we didn't even find tracks leading out there. I mean, there are plenty of shoe prints on the paths, but to get to where our guy went off, you have to get way off the path onto the hard-shell ground where there aren't any tracks."

"Okay, so there are other possibilities," Farris continued. "Let's stick with one killer, for now. If it's one guy, he is either a stone badass, or he's smart. He sucks these guys in and they have absolutely no way of knowing what's coming, or no sense that they're in any danger. We know he has a gun, so you have to wonder if he had it with him the first time. Maybe took Bailey out to the edge at gunpoint and made him jump."

"I'd make him shoot me before I'd jump," Floyd said.

"Back to your escalation, Rich," I said. "Why do you think he would use the gun for your guy?"

Farris shrugged. "Maybe he was surprised by how hard it was to kill a guy with a club and decided to make the third one less messy. That's an easy in and out—*Hey how's it going? Bam!*—and he walks away."

"Your guy could have been walked up on, right?" I said.

"That's how it appears," Lizzy said. "If the garage door was open as it was when he was found, then the killer walked up the driveway, into the garage, and our victim turned to face him. To greet him, or whatever. Tell him to get the hell out, we don't know. But there's no indication that anything else transpired other than the shooting. No struggle, I mean."

"Nothing taken that we know of, right?" I said. "I mean, in our case, we're missing a planner, but that's easy to figure."

"Phone," Mongo said.

"We don't know of anything at all that was missing from our guy," Lizzy said. "His wallet and phone were on a shelf in the garage—along with a bottle of water—next to a stereo."

"Was the stereo on?" I asked.

Farris and Marchesano exchanged glances, and then Lizzy picked up her notebook and wrote something down. "That's a good question for Justin Martin," she said, "the roommate."

Floyd was digging cold beers from an ice chest and passing them around. "Well, yeah, I say we beat his balls about all of these cases. He knows something. He has to."

I nodded, considering the possibilities. Josie silently watched me. Lizzy closed her notebook. Farris walked back to his seat next to me, a cold beer in his hand. Mongo sat stretching his triceps, pushing one arm and then the other behind his head, his face anguished with the movement.

I said, "Okay, let's make this Martin kid a priority. The phones, and Martin. We see if the same burner phone was used in each case, just to remove any doubt. I say go back several weeks on each line, looking for that number. See if Martin gives us any idea about motive. Have any of you run your victims yet to see what their backgrounds look like?"

Marchesano shook her head as her partner answered. "No, we haven't gotten that far yet."

Floyd said, "My guy has nothing as an adult, and a sealed juvie record."

"Interesting," I said. "What's that about?"

He shrugged. "I don't know, didn't give it a lot of thought. Lot of juvie records get sealed, especially for people who can afford attorneys. Plus, it was a suicide, we weren't—"

"Yeah, I get it," I interrupted. "But now maybe that record gets some priority. We still have to run our guy. The dad said they had had their normal boy troubles, fights, drinking, things like that. I won't be surprised to find something on him. By the way, Floyd, your guy apparently jogged those trails out there all the time."

"Yeah, so we heard."

"Okay, didn't know if you knew that. Eddie's old man told us. You can see the point from the old man's living room, at least part of it."

"He lived just across the highway from there," Floyd said.

"Yeah, that's what Mayor Max said," I told him.

After a long moment of silence, Floyd said, "Now we just have to convince the captain that we need to work these together, like a task force, with unlimited overtime."

I pushed out of my chair, feeling stiff and sore from too much time sitting and no time for exercise during the previous several days. "Alright, let's meet again in a day or two, keep everyone up to speed with what we're doing. I'm ready to get out of here, get home at a decent hour for a change."

"How's Red the Fed?" Floyd asked. "You seeing her tonight?"

"I doubt it. I don't know."

He chuckled. "You kill me, so predictable."

"What can I say? I like traveling light, moving fast. Plus, the fed makes me nervous; I'm not so sure I trust her."

"Now see," Farris joined in, "that's just what you need, a professional woman who has a good income and has plenty to keep her mind occupied while you're putting in long hours. That's where I messed up—well, that's one of the ways I messed up. But next time—*if* there's a next time—it'll be a woman who makes as much as me or more. I'm not trying to see how many more times I can divide my retirement."

Lizzy swung her legs from beneath the picnic table and stood up. She looked at Josie. "Well, you and I might as well go now; this has turned into the Homicide swingers club meeting."

The ladies walked away, their heels clicking against the sidewalk. We watched until they were out of view. Mongo said, "We need more beer."

15

When I left for work Friday morning, I closed my door quietly and tiptoed away as if I were a kid sneaking out of the house. How pathetic it was didn't escape me. But I had been intentionally avoiding my neighbor, Miss Emily. Red the Fed. Maybe Floyd was right, that I was afraid of commitment, or maybe my instincts about her were not to be ignored. Something didn't seem right about her, and she made me nervous. Nervous enough that even though she was hot, conveniently located next door, and available, I had pulled back after a couple of casual get-togethers.

I even closed my car door quietly and then wasted no time speeding away.

Traffic would be lighter since I was hitting the road at six. I had fallen asleep early and slept soundly. When my eyes popped open in the predawn hours, I found that my mind was already awake and demanded that the rest of my body follow suit. I was thinking about our latest case and the stepchild cases of which I would now be a part, analyzing the data and planning strategies. I stopped at the 7-Eleven for a cup of coffee and a bagel to go.

As I negotiated traffic on the southbound Golden State Freeway, I thought about the day ahead of me. Josie and I were going to meet at the office, though she wouldn't be in until a little later, maybe eight or nine. We needed to run a background check on Eddie Bellovich and see what minor indiscretions he might have committed. We knew from Deputy Lambert that the local deputies had been called to his home on a few occasions for domestic violence, and that on at least one such occasion, he had been arrested. Though no charges were filed, I expected to find a record of his arrest on his criminal history report. There may have been other arrests of which Lambert was unaware, and I was particularly interested in finding out if Bellovich had a juvenile record. And if he did, whether or not that record was sealed.

I thought about Todd Bailey's juvenile record and how Floyd said it had been sealed. *Typical,* I thought. *The rich white boys and all of their layers of protection.* Well, a lot of good it had done them in the end.

But why were they each killed? There had to be something significant in their backgrounds that we had yet to discover, unless there was a serial killer taking out martial artists. The odds of that seemed astronomical. I thought about what Cappy—the senior-most investigator in the bureau— had said: *Throw out the impossible, brush aside the improbable, and usually you'll find the answer in what you have left before you.* Or something to that effect.

In my mind, the impossible at this point was that it was a coincidence that two brothers and a close friend had all been killed in a relatively short time span. The improbable was that the killings were professional hits, caused by drug dealing or the like. The reason I viewed that as improbable was primarily the lack of organization in the murders. Each one was different, as if the killer was experimenting or learning as he went. A drug hit is usually clean and crisp—no muss, no fuss—unless torture is involved for the purpose of sending a message. None of these cases had any of those telltale signs.

But what did that leave us?

Revenge killing. That was the first and most logical idea that was mentioned by Farris during our meeting. A tight group of three young men who have all been murdered screams of vengeance. But for what? Maybe the records check would give us some ideas.

The Benjamin Franklin line crossed my mind: *Three can keep a secret if two of them are dead.* The Hell's Angels had embraced this theory as well, and likely practiced it also. But simple mathematics would suggest that if that were the case, the same could be applied to four keeping a secret if three were dead. What secret could the three—or possibly four—have? It occurred to me that we would have to go back to Veronica at some point and press her harder. There would be time for that once we had more information.

As Veronica crossed my mind, I knew I had to consider the possibility that the murderer was a woman. Not that I actually believed a woman could have been responsible for the three killings—though I would never completely dismiss the idea either—but perhaps one was part of the equation. There were many men who had become guests of the coroner's office or of prisons who might have otherwise avoided those fates had it not been for a woman in the mix.

The regular interval of traffic reports were the only disruptions I allowed to distract me from my thoughts. Negotiating L.A. traffic was an art. I preferred the old-school method of listening to the reporters in helicopters, though I would occasionally use an application on my smartphone just to prove I wasn't a dinosaur. So far, reports on my route into the office were favorable, which meant I should be able to average thirty miles per hour on this early Friday morning.

As I neared the East L.A. interchange, my mind drifted back to the idea of revenge. What might these three boys have done that would get them killed? It had to be something extreme, something that destroyed another person's life—or *persons' lives*—for such a severe level of revenge to be exacted. If that were the case, the killer would likely have to be willing to lose his life—or at least his freedom—if he was unable to pull it off, or if he got caught. That's a significant gamble, requiring careful consideration.

Unless the person was deranged.

Speaking of deranged, I had never gotten an answer from Floyd about his unexplained absence, and I hadn't yet heard the story of Josie working as a hooker. I was surrounded by derangement.

Still a good ten, fifteen minutes out from the office, I gave Floyd a call.

"What's up, Dickie?"

"I'm still waiting to hear about your disappearing act."

"Well good morning to you, too, asshole."

"Good morning. Now, let's hear it."

"Dude, I'm literally stepping into the shower. I'll see you at the office later."

"You ass—"

He had disconnected.

I phoned Josie.

"Well good morning, partner," she greeted.

"Hey, how's it going?"

"Good. What's up?"

"Just headed into the office—"

"Aren't you an early bird today."

"Had a good night's sleep for a change, woke up with a little spring in my step."

"Good deal. I'm not far behind you, probably on the road in fifteen. What's up, anyway?"

"I wanted to hear the hooker story."

"Are you bored?"

"Yes."

"Well, call Floyd. I'm too busy to talk at the moment. I'll see you in a bit."

I set my phone back in its cradle and frowned at it. I'd have to get the story from Slocumb, I decided. I'd make it a point to see him the next time we were back on the mean streets of Rancho Palos Verdes, that affluent locale of our latest murder investigation. Deac was always up for telling a good story. I'd only need to get him away from the manly woman captain he served.

Shortly after being ignored by my partner and my ex, I was easing off the freeway in a steady flow of commuters in Monterey Park. I pulled into the office parking lot and backed into one of the many empty spaces. In a couple of hours, the place would resemble a Ford dealership that specialized in family sedans and tightly-wound sales-persons.

Inside, a few other early birds were at their desks staring at their computers and sipping coffee. Lieutenant Black looked at me over the glasses at the end of his nose as I set my briefcase on my desk.

"Good morning, Richard."

I returned his greeting with a nod. "Mornin', boss."

"When you have a moment," he said, "I'd like to have an update on your Palos Verdes case."

"Let me grab a cup, Joe, I'll be right back."

Walking to the kitchen, it occurred to me that he might have been briefed about the cases likely being related. Farris wasn't the type to go out of his way to inform a lieutenant about new developments in a case, any more than I was. Floyd and Mongo were on a different team, and they reported to a different lieutenant. But they, too, were unlikely to have mentioned the possible reclassification of their suicide case to their boss, not at this early stage of our collective investigation. But yesterday, when Captain Stover had dropped by my desk to ask about the case, I had mentioned the possibility that the cases might be related. When a mayor's kid is killed, it's suddenly more than a stat on the board for the administrators. Maybe Stover had said something to my lieutenant. If so, Black might not be too happy with me for not keeping him apprised of the developments on a newsworthy case.

I poured a cup of coffee and headed back to the squad room, greeting the few detectives I passed along the way to my lieutenant's desk. I pulled a chair from a nearby unoccupied desk and wheeled it over next to Joe. "I was going to update you yesterday, but I think you slid out of here before we decided to have a meeting."

Joe clicked out of a program on his computer and swiveled his chair to face me, giving me his undivided attention. He removed his reading glasses and set them on his desk, and then proffered his grandfatherly smile as his kind gaze settled on me. "You know me, Richard, I like to beat the traffic—coming in and getting out. Unless there's a reason to stay, I don't want to be here much past three."

It seemed he had not heard about the cases being connected after all. I relaxed, took a sip of my coffee, and crossed a leg.

"So the case that Farris and Marchesano picked up yesterday is likely related to the Bellovich case. The two were friends."

His smile dissipated while his forehead wrinkled in concentration, or perhaps consternation. "Oh, my."

"And Farris's dead guy is the brother of a case Floyd had a few weeks ago, a case they were looking at as a suicide, but never really felt comfortable with that."

"So you might have three murders connected?"

"It seems very likely, Joe. We got together last night and compared notes and came up with some ideas for going forward. Farris's victim was found by his roommate, who apparently was not only distraught, but unreasonably fearful as well. He made some comment about everyone dying. He's going to be one of our first focuses. We all feel like he might know what's behind all of this, so the plan is to put his nuts in a vise until he sings a pretty soprano song for us."

Joe cringed. I didn't know if it was at the thought of the vise, or my vulgarity.

I told him about some of our other plans, which included obtaining the cell phone records and doing thorough background investigations of all three victims. In the end, Joe assured me we had his support, and asked that we keep him apprised of any new developments. He said, "You know Captain Stover is going to pay close attention to this one, he and probably someone up in the sheriff's office."

My attention was drawn toward the sound of the door closing. I turned to see Josie with her arms full of case files, a purse slung over one shoulder, an attaché case with a long strap over the other, and a travel mug and a set of keys in one hand.

"Well, there's my partner," I said, standing up and returning my borrowed chair. "I better get to work. She'll crack the whip on me if she catches me lollygagging."

Joe smiled and returned to his computer.

"What's up, partner?" I asked as the two of us met near our desks.

I waited while she set her coffee and keys on her desk, along with a few of the files she had carried in. She then placed other files on the floor by her seat, along with her bag. She tucked her purse in the large desk drawer and plopped into her chair. "Nothing. What's up with you? What'd the lieutenant have to say, anything?"

"I was bringing him up to speed on the related cases, keeping him in the loop."

The folder that Josie had placed on the floor had no identifiers marked on the outside, yet it was heavy and full. All homicide cases were to be stored in expandable "poor-boy" file folders, each clearly marked in a specified manner to include the file number, the victim's name, suspect names if they were known, coroner's case number, date and time of murder—if known—and the investigators' names. The uniform identifiers were necessary for the eventual cataloging in our library, a warehouse of murder cases investigated by the Los Angeles County Sheriff's Department's homicide bureau, going back to 1927. I indicated Josie's blank file. "What case is that?"

Her gaze followed mine to the folder on the floor, but she paused a moment before answering. "That's just some stuff I'm working on."

"Spencer?"

She nodded. "Yes."

I walked around to my desk without saying anything more about it. I had promised we would make time to work on it, to try to shake something loose on a case that had, at first, seemed simple and solved. And we would. And we wouldn't wait until we had nothing else going on, because that day never came at the homicide bureau.

"Have you come up with anything?" I asked.

"Not yet, but something struck me, and it's bothering me."

I pulled my chair out and had a seat, keeping my gaze glued on my partner. "What's that?"

"If the Watkins kid *wasn't* the one who put me in that shed—if it was, in fact, Spencer—how did Watkins know I was there? And then why did he not free me when he first found me?"

"You're having doubts."

She looked down at her desk and shuffled some papers and file folders around with seemingly no purpose. After a moment, she looked up. "Yeah, maybe. I don't know. If the kid did it, it's over, and I can move on. If he didn't, then it had to have been Spencer, and how would we ever prove it?"

I drew in a deep breath and let it out slowly as I considered my response. "Josie, you have good instincts. I think you figured out something we all missed. We can't leave it as is, not knowing for certain. We'll keep working on it. It might take a while, but we aren't walking away from it. Got it?"

"Okay," she said, holding my gaze. "Got it."

"Now, let's figure out who's whacking fighters on the west side."

16

DETECTIVE TYRONE COUTURE CAME INTO THE OFFICE SHORTLY AFTER Josie and I had begun searching databases for background information on our victim, Eddie Bellovich. He approached with a file folder tucked under his arm and a wide grin on his face. Dressed in jeans and a short-sleeve button-up shirt, untucked, Ty sipped from a large fast-food soda cup and then tossed it into a trash can.

"Wussup, my brotha?" He glanced at Josie. "And sista."

We both stopped what we were doing and turned to face him. His longer-than-regulation hair was slicked back, a pair of dark shades resting on top. His mustache drooped past the corners of his mouth, another department grooming no-no.

"Hey, did you transfer to Narco?" Josie teased.

He dropped his file on an unoccupied desk and plopped into the chair next to it. "Dude, this is a sweet gig I've got going with the phones. Between the wiretap room and the HOMCAST gig, I haven't been in the rotation, or had to put on a suit or pull an all-nighter in the barrel for two years. Don't be hatin' on me."

I chuckled. "What'd you do, convince the captain you needed to go undercover?"

Ty glanced over his shoulder. "Shit, bruh, he thinks this shit I'm doin's magic. Have you seen the van they gave me? I spent about a hundred K of your overtime budget outfitting that bad boy with high-tech cool-ass shit. What do you want to know?"

"If you can identify a burner. Can part of my hundred K get me that much?"

"Nah, bruh, it's not that simple. I mean, it ain't just info sitting there waiting for the sick, lame, and lazy. You've got to work it, see? That's why you're paying me the big bucks."

"Explain," Josie said, her eyes showing skepticism.

Ty leaned back in his chair and crossed a leg, relaxed. "So what we do, we track the phone by its signal, develop a pattern. See, we don't have to know who owns the phone to know what its owner's up to and where he's at. It's called advanced tracking. The shit in my rig—and a handheld device I have also—will let me track a phone and put it right in the asshole's hand, or house. I can walk right up to Haji at the Coliseum and say, 'Come with me, motherfucker.'"

"Are you tracking terrorists?"

"Yeah, shit, bruh, Intelligence is using me more than Homicide lately. I don't know why nobody's tracking phones here, but over at Majors they always have me looking for burners, tracking these tangos. But Homicide gets priority, or Stover pulls me back. So let me know what you want on this burner phone and I'll get after it—track him to a location, get a history and put him at your scene, whatever."

I glanced at Josie and back at Ty. "What if he's gotten rid of it?"

"That's a problem, obviously. We can still get a history for you, tell us we're looking in the right direction. Might be able to triangulate his history to show a residence or place of business, if he works, which he probably doesn't."

The idea of it seemed too good to be true, and I pictured the burner at the bottom of the ocean or in a trash can at the beach. Josie and I exchanged several glances and I assumed she was on the same track, but she surprised me with another thought.

"Why couldn't we do this with Spencer, too?"

My eyes narrowed as I thought of the possibilities. Tyrone was saying, "Who's that?" while Josie continued addressing me. "We see if his signal puts him at that shed or up at the tree where Brown was murdered."

I shook my head. "There are no cell signals up there, or at least almost none."

She considered it for a moment.

Ty said, "Who the hell is Spencer?"

Josie, still speaking directly to me, said, "Well if there's no signal, then at least we know he could have been there. I mean, let's at least make sure his cell phone wasn't at Gorman Station, or out in Palmdale or whatever, the night I was taken."

"That makes sense," I said, "and it gives me another idea."

She tossed her head back as if to say, *Let's hear it.*

"Well, the idea of tracking his cell was a good one, until I remembered he likely wouldn't have a signal up there. See, I was thinking that with tracking him live, we might even see him revisiting the shed or the tree. But since there's no signal to see him do that, how about cameras? Why don't we get the tech crew to wire those two locations and see if he ever visits them, and if he does, see how he behaves."

"What he says."

"Well, for that we'd have to get a court order. But for video only, we don't need anything—not on public land."

She seemed to be considering the idea.

Ty, becoming impatient, said, "Are either of you going to fill me in on this?"

I looked at him. "When Josie was taken, up on the mountain—"

"Ahhhh," he began.

"—there was this game warden, and, well, we're not so sure he isn't our suspect, both in Josie's ordeal and also in a murder we were handling up there, the reason we were on the mountain to begin with."

"Wow," he said.

"Uh-huh," I said. "And it's not widely known, so let's just keep that between us girls."

"I like it. Get me a number for him and dates—the murder and also Josie's thing, the night that happened. I'll see what I can come up with."

"Will do, brother. Thank you."

Ty left the two of us sitting in silence, our gazes connected but our thoughts far apart. As was often the case, I was organizing tasks in my mind, trying to prioritize the various needs of competing investigations.

Triage. Josie's eyes grew dark and I could see that her thoughts had taken her back to the cold nights on the dark and lonely mountain. She would never be the same after what she had lived through. Nobody would be.

"Have you had breakfast?" I asked, trying to pull her from the darkness.

I watched for a long moment as her eyes, previously distant and dark, softened, and soon I could see we were once again connected. Without any emotion, she said, "Yes, feed me."

"Yes, you've had breakfast, but you want more?"

"Yes. No. No, I haven't had breakfast. Let's get out of here."

"Okay, where to?"

"You can buy me breakfast," she said, "on the way to STARS Center."

I frowned. "What do we have to do at STARS?"

"Tech crew. Let's talk to them about getting cameras wired up there on the mountain. I like that idea. Besides, there's nowhere around here to get breakfast, not anything good."

Levity and dark humor were two of the mechanisms by which cops shielded themselves from early onset of insanity, relatively speaking of course. They were two of the least damaging methods and you didn't have to pour them from a bottle. On the way to breakfast, I said, "While you were vacationing in your mountain cabin and Floyd and I were traipsing around up there looking for you, I took him to see the tree."

She shot me a long, threatening look but didn't respond. We were in heavy traffic, stopped at a light, Josie behind the wheel.

"One of the things we talked about was why Willie Brown didn't go for his rifle when it was within his reach, leaned up against the tree."

She glanced over again, curious now. I indicated the traffic moving ahead of us, redirecting her attention.

I continued, "What I had assumed was that someone surprised him, came up on him when he was taking a break, maybe he had stopped to have a leak. I pictured Brown being backed up against the tree, surrendering."

"Surrendering," she repeated, staring straight ahead. We were now moving along with the flow of traffic, nobody in a hurry.

"I think we even said that, 'surrendering,' when we were discussing it, me and Floyd. But I never thought about that beyond someone pointing a gun at him. I guess, in part, I was pretty hung up on Brown getting killed behind the rape charge. You know, the dad or uncle of that girl, Joanna what's-her-ass."

"Harding."

"Yeah, right, Harding. While I was thinking about putting the cameras up, and picturing what they might catch, maybe Spencer up there at the crime scene with his creepy fucking smile while reliving the kill, it occurred to me the gravity of that word. *Surrender. Hands up, don't move.* You surrender to authority."

Josie slowed to a stop at another red light and looked over. "Authority or force, either one."

"Yeah, but—"

"I see your point, and deep down inside I think you're right. I'm just very conflicted on it now. I mean—"

The light had turned, and traffic was moving. "Green."

She looked ahead and the car lunged forward. "I guess it's just like picking an old wound. I've been terrified that it was Spencer, because that means he's free and we have to prove that he did it, and there's a chance he gets away with it. It also means those wounds are opened up, and that's not something I'm interested in either. I dread the idea of it. All along I've been working on parts of the case, reviewing files and studying Spencer. And all along, I've told myself to let it lie. Walk away. Accept that Watkins did it and he's dead and get on with life." She looked at me. "I'm a coward, I guess."

I could see behind her sunglasses that her eyes were damp.

"You're no coward, Josie—you're anything but that."

She didn't respond.

"Look, we can drop it if you want, but I don't think that will work for you."

She glanced over and cocked her head.

"You're too much like me, Josie. You won't let it rest. Let's go after it. Let's figure it out."

Josie wheeled us into the Original House of Pancakes and backed into a spot by the door. She shut the ignition off and paused to look at me. "Come on, I need a stack of blueberry pancakes drowned in syrup."

I smiled. "Whatever you want, partner."

An hour later we walked through the campus setting of STARS Center, a high-school-turned-sheriff's-training-facility, and the home offices to various Detective Division assignments. One room was dedicated to the tech crew, men and women who were experts with the high-tech equipment often required for covert operations.

At the counter we were greeted by Paul Brady, a short, bald, bearded sergeant with close-set eyes. Brady supervised the crew and managed most of the requests that came through their office.

"Homicide is in the house," he said.

"What's new, right?" I said.

He smiled. "You're our best customers. How can we help you today?"

I told him what we wanted to do without mentioning Josie as part of the story. "There was a murder in the woods and there are two places we think the killer may revisit. It's a longshot, but we think it's worth a try."

The leprechaun-like cop tugged at his beard for a moment and then rubbed his hand over his head, fluorescent light reflecting off it. "Two choices," he said. "We can do something with battery-powered cameras that are motion-activated and should last for a long while unless you have a lot of traffic through there, bear or deer or killers or whatever. The second idea would be more elaborate and would take some real time and effort, but the quality of video would be much better and overall more reliable."

I nodded. "What's that?"

"Hardwired gear with a power source concealed a safe distance from your location."

"The two locs are not close."

He tugged at his beard and frowned. "That'd double the trouble."

Josie said, "Look, I think the battery-powered cameras are fine. We have a suspect in mind and would be able to identify him even from grainy video. That seems to be the more reasonable option."

"What do we have to conceal the cameras? Trees, shrubbery?"

"The first location is heavily treed. The second location, not so much, but there's a shack that we think he might visit. How big are your cameras?"

Brady whipped a pen out of his shirt pocket and clicked the point through its end, holding it up between us. "'bout that big. We can hide it pretty much anywhere."

"When can you do it?" Josie asked, excitement in her voice.

The sergeant opened a laptop on the counter and hemmed and hawed and hummed while his beady eyes scoured the screen. "Three o'clock."

My eyes popped open in surprise. "Today?"

He smiled. "It's today or next Friday, a week from now. Where are we going?"

17

JOSIE AND I DEPARTED THE STARS CENTER AND HEADED BACK TOWARD Monterey Park, riding in silence for the first several minutes. I was thinking of our tight schedule and wondering how we were going to be able to take care of the cameras this afternoon, while also running with a fresh case that now appeared to be one in a series of three. Well, three that we knew of, anyway. It occurred to me that the killer of Bellovich and company might not be finished, and we hadn't yet given much thought to that. I glanced at my watch and silently wished there were more hours in a day.

As I considered the logistics of having cameras installed on the mountain, I had a troubling thought: *What are the chances of running into Jacob Spencer while we're up there?* I thought about calling his office to check his schedule, but I didn't want to tip our hand.

"How are we going to pull this off, make sure Spencer isn't up on the mountain when we go up there?"

Josie glanced over at me but didn't answer.

After a moment, I asked, "Are you good with going back up there by yourself?"

She shrugged. "Yeah, why not."

"I can send Floyd with you, or maybe Rich Farris."

Josie's gaze flicked back and forth from me to the road. "Where are you planning to be? Do you have something else going this afternoon?"

"I'm just thinking that maybe I could set up an interview with Spencer so that we know for sure where he'll be. Have him meet me at the Gorman Station, maybe. Actually, maybe I'll have Farris come along with me, now that I think about it. He seemed to have a good read on Spencer, and he'd like nothing more than to rake him over the coals. What do you think, can you and Floyd take Brady and his crew up there, show them both locations?"

She nodded, her gaze now glued straight ahead, one hand on the wheel, the other propped against the door and apparently supporting her head. I sensed a darkness coming over her, and I knew she was starting to go back to the time and place that haunted her.

"It will look different to you after all this time, but Floyd and I crawled around those mountains for several days. Between the two of you, you can find both locations."

"It hasn't been that long."

"Well, six months—wait, you haven't—"

Still she stared straight ahead. "I've been back."

"You went back up there?" I shouted. "Josie!"

She glanced over. "I don't want to hear it."

I realized that once again I was treating her differently because she was a woman. I wouldn't have shouted at Floyd for the same thing. I would have called him a dumbass, maybe laughed, asked him what the hell was he thinking. After a long moment, I said, "I'm sorry. I shouldn't have reacted that way. It's just, I wouldn't have thought—never mind, I'm going to make it worse."

Josie's voice was low, her tone soft. "Floyd and I will handle it. What are your plans with Spencer?"

That was it, no further discussion. I got the message loud and clear.

"I don't know," I said, my tone now matching hers. It was quiet inside the car with the windows up and the air conditioner softly humming in the background. "I'll think of something. Maybe I'll ask him some questions about that night again, see if any of his answers have changed after six months, tell him we're wrapping the case up and just needed to confirm some things. Or, maybe I'll come up with something to say that will trigger him, see what type of reaction we get. If I can think of something that might drive him back to the shed, or to the tree, maybe suggest there was something the killer hadn't thought of, or whatever, maybe that would be good too. But more than anything, I want to draw him off the mountain for the afternoon and make sure he doesn't stumble across you guys."

"Call Floyd," she said. "See if he's available."

"Him and Mongo," I said, trying to lighten the mood, "in case you need someone to wrestle a bear."

But I got nothing in return. Josie stared through the windshield, likely looking far beyond the traffic in front of us.

First, I called Floyd, who agreed to accompany Josie and the tech crew up to the mountain that afternoon. He was in the office and would see us there. Then I got Farris on the phone and said, "How'd you like to take another shot at the game warden?"

I could almost see his smiling face as Rich Farris chuckled and said, "Say when, my brother."

"Let me make a call and I'll get back to you," I said. "But leave your dance card open for this afternoon, buddy."

I hung up, muttering, and thumbed through the applications on my phone, searching for the one that allowed me to access the Internet; I never could remember what it was called or what the icon looked like.

Josie said, "What're you looking for?"

"I need to find a number for Fish and Game, see if I can get in touch with Spencer."

She unlocked her phone and handed it to me. "It's in Contacts under Creepy Asshole."

"'Creepy Asshole'?"

"Yeah, there's a few assholes programmed in there. His is Creepy."

"What's mine?"

The corners of her mouth turned up in a grin. "Just 'Dickie.' That says it all, I think."

When we arrived back at the office, the lot was about half full of sedans, which reminded me it was Friday. A third of the bureau would be on their first of three days off, having come off a ten-day stretch. Another third would be gearing up for the weekend duty, and the third I belonged to, Teams Five and Six, had just come off our on-call period. Those of us who had caught murders would be in the field following leads, at the coroner's office watching butcher jobs, or in the office catching up on paperwork, using the computer databases, or working the phones.

Josie swung into a spot and parked. "Must be Friday."

I popped my door open and stepped out. When Josie met me at the front of her car, I said, "Indeed it is. The beginning of a lovely weekend we'll no doubt work straight through."

When we opened the office door, we nearly collided with Floyd and Mongo, who were rushing out.

"What's up with you guys?" I asked.

Floyd glanced at his watch and then looked at Josie. "What time do you want to leave here this afternoon?"

"Tech crew is meeting us here at three, and they're going to follow us up."

"Okay, cool," he said. Mongo was outside now, holding the door. Floyd dropped his glasses over his eyes while backing out of the office and finishing his conversation. "We have to run down to Torrance to see about unsealing a couple of juvie records on the Bailey brothers."

"No shit?"

"I'll fill you in later," he said, spinning through the door.

"Call me, asshole," I said to his back. He flipped me the bird in response.

I turned and followed Josie to our desks. Lieutenant Black looked around his computer monitor and over his glasses toward us. "Richard, Josefina," he said, beckoning us to come see him. We arrived at his desk and stood next to it, neither of us looking to get comfortable there.

"What's up, LT?" Josie asked.

He leaned back in his chair. "Captain Stover wants an update on the status of these three cases that might be linked, before he leaves this afternoon. Is there anything good I can tell him?"

Josie looked at me and raised her brows, signaling me to answer.

Oftentimes I would treat the brass in the same manner I'd handle the press: give them something to make them happy and go away so we could focus on our jobs. "Yeah, a few things that will probably have us working through the weekend. Floyd and Mongo have discovered sealed juvie records on the Bailey brothers and they're on their way to Torrance now to see if we can get those unsealed. That's a crapshoot. If it doesn't pan out, we're going to have to go back to their parents to try to find out what those records are about."

"Maybe the mayor knows," Josie suggested.

I shrugged. "Maybe. In fact, are we certain Bellovich doesn't also have a sealed or expunged record?"

She shook her head.

"Anyway," I said, readdressing the lieutenant, "we're working with the assumption that all three murders are related, and we don't think our killer is a pro. For one, we wouldn't expect a pro to use three different methods."

Lt. Joe Black held up a finger to stop me. "That actually brings up a good argument against the cases being related, don't you think?"

"It could, but we see it differently. The first case—the Bailey boy off the cliff—was a hands-off murder, something that might be more appealing to someone who has never killed before. No direct violence other than maybe just a shove. The second might indicate an appetite for more satisfaction, something more violent, personal. But the killer is surprised by how hard it is to kill someone, and decides that for the third —and hopefully final—victim, to use a simpler but still intimate method of killing that will let him see the fear and regret in his victim's eyes before he pulls the trigger."

As I said it, I pictured Spencer on the mountain with William Brown backed against a tree and being sentenced to death.

Joe said, "Okay, so as far as the captain goes, you're running with a theory that the three murders are related, and that the motive is what?"

"It has to be revenge for something, Joe. I can't think of anything else since we don't think it's a professional job. It's not like there are any other obvious motives: sex, financial gain, drugs . . ."

Josie said, "I think our killer's a woman."

Joe and I both snapped our heads in her direction. She defended her statement silently, looking each of us directly in the eyes, unwaveringly, one and then the other. I wondered if she wasn't fantasizing about a little revenge on the warden.

"You think a woman could crack a guy like Bellovich over the head with a club when the guy trains with those sticks every day?"

She raised her chin. "I think all three of those victims were caught flat-footed. That tells me that none of them recognized the threat. Especially with Floyd's case, the Bailey brother that went off the cliff—"

"Todd," I said.

"—how could anyone else get him out to a dangerous point like that unless he was completely unaware of the danger he was in?"

I thought about it for a moment and it made sense, but then I pictured Spencer on the mountain. "Or the killer is a person of authority."

Lieutenant Black grimaced. "That's not a good thought," he said, unaware that Josie and I also had a game warden on our minds.

I thought of updating him about our plans to go to the mountain, but I quickly abandoned the idea. I wasn't willing to take a chance of anyone shutting us down on that case. It wasn't ours to work, but Josie and I were going to work it anyway, with or without anyone's knowledge or approval. Besides, we had given Joe plenty to keep the captain happy for the week-end. He'd be hitting the sauce before long anyway, and as long as no cops were killed over the weekend, the captain would remain in his suburban home with his Crown Vic tucked away in the garage while he weeded his flowerbed in shorts and a visor, pasty white legs reflecting the sun.

"Alright, boss, that's about all we've got. Can you make sure Stover's okay with a little extra overtime this month? I'm sure we're going to work this thing through the weekend."

"It has the attention of the sheriff, Richard, work as much overtime as you'd like."

I nodded. "Thanks, boss," and Josie and I walked away.

Out of the lieutenant's earshot, Josie whispered, "Jesus, you think this could be a cop?"

I shrugged. "That or a woman, like you said."

Josie's eyes lit up. "Or both. A woman cop."

18

Jacob Spencer had readily agreed to meet us at Gorman at four. Interestingly, he didn't even ask why we wanted to talk to him.

Floyd and Mongo had gotten back at two thirty. The bureau had mostly emptied of the few who had come in today. Even the captain had left early. Farris and Marchesano sat at their desks across the squad room from where Floyd and Mongo sat. It was just the six of us, grouped in twos and spread across the vastness of our office space, the room silent except for the occasional ringing phone.

"Hey."

Josie looked up from her computer.

I glanced at my watch; it was a quarter to three. "What do you say we have a quick meeting before the tech crew gets here, make sure we're all on the same page."

"Sure," she said, pushing her chair back from her desk.

Floyd looked up as I headed his way. "Let's have a quick meeting."

"You're not the boss of me, Dickie," he said. Then to Mongo, "Come on, dude."

We gathered around Farris and Marchesano. "Lizzy, you going with me and Rich?" I asked.

"I wouldn't miss it," she said.

"Good," I said, smiling. "Okay, here's the plan—" I directed my speech to Floyd and Mongo, who stood with arms crossed while occasionally glancing toward Josie, who had perched on the edge of a desk "—we'll keep talking to Spencer up at Gorman until you guys are completely off the mountain. I have no idea how long it's going to take them up there, but we won't let Spencer leave until I get a text from one of you saying you've cleared Gorman. Once you're off the mountain, as long as we've finished with Spencer, we'll wrap it up with him and won't be far behind you."

"Should we all meet somewhere after?" Farris asked.

Floyd said, "Why don't we go to that Mexican restaurant in Santa Clarita, Dickie, the one we all went to that time after searching for—" he stopped and glanced at Josie, and didn't finish his sentence.

"We can do that," I said. "Rich, do you know where the Fiesta Cocina is in Santa Clarita, right off the Five at Magic Mountain?"

Farris nodded. "I think so."

Marchesano said, "I know it."

"Is that okay with you guys? We can debrief over cocktails, even have the tech crew come along if they'd like."

Floyd said, "They love us there."

"Okay, so that's the plan. Any questions?"

"What if you can't keep dickhead talking that long?" Floyd asked. "We may be up on the mountain for a while."

I shrugged. "I'm pretty sure Rich and Lizzy can keep him going all afternoon, maybe into the night."

"Home-slice will be lucky if I let him leave at all," Farris said, "the creepy little white boy."

"Floyd, what'd you find out about the juvie records on the Bailey brothers and their buddy, Mr. Bellovich?"

"Doesn't look good. We'll have to get a court order, which means we'll have to have substantial cause. I'm worried a judge is going to see it as a fishing expedition." He shrugged. "I mean, we can try, but I think it might be a lot of work with no payoff."

"Somebody knows what they did," said Marchesano. "We need to talk to everyone they know. That should be next on our list of shit to do. Talk to all their girlfriends."

Josie said, "And the parents."

"I'll take the naked mom," Floyd said.

"Wait a minute," I said, "there's another way around those records."

Farris said, "Microfilm."

"Exactly right, Rich. If they were detained or even just named as subjects in criminal reports when they were juveniles, their names will appear somewhere. Everything from back in those days was copied onto microfilm and that shit is stored forever. We can start by searching the Lomita and Marina del Rey records from whatever years the boys were sixteen and seventeen years old. We can go back further if need be, but my guess is whatever they got into, it was after they were driving but before they turned eighteen. Geographically, we just have to hope they were popped by sheriffs, not the boys in blue."

"Who remembers how to run those microfilm machines?" Farris asked.

"I can probably find my way around them," I said. "I remember doing quite a few as a trainee in patrol. My training officer didn't allow us to ask the secretaries to do it for us."

Lizzy said, "I know how to use them."

"Okay, so that can be a good task for the weekend when there's fewer secretaries in the station," I said. "We can split up. Lizzy and Rich, you guys can take the marina since you're working a fresh case there anyway, and likewise, Josie and I will handle Lomita. Floyd, you and Mongo get the Bailey parents. If we need to hit up the mayor again, Josie and I can do that. We'll save that for our last option. Sound good?"

Everyone seemed agreeable with the proposed direction of the case.

"We still should go back on the roommate," Lizzy added, speaking of her and Rich's case. "I still think he knows something."

I nodded. "Okay, good plan. And Josie and I need to go back on Eddie's girlfriend. Looks like we'll have a full weekend."

Floyd said, "Are they paying overtime?"

"Hello there," called a voice from across the squad room. We all turned to see Sergeant Brady coming toward us with a pair of misfits, one who looked like a librarian and the other like a parolee, one white and one black, one male and one female. Following behind the leprechaun they looked like a gang out of a Charles Bronson movie.

After greetings and introductions, we began our caravan north.

———————

I HAD OFFERED TO DRIVE, SO LIZZY AND RICH LOADED INTO MY CAR, THE latter volunteering for the back seat. We led the way, and Floyd, Mongo, and Josie stayed on our bumper. A white van trailed along behind but didn't follow the protocol of caravanning, which is to stay tight and not let others wedge into our line. When lane changes are required, the vehicle at the rear moves first and holds the opening while the others move in, starting with the vehicle farthest back and finishing with the lead one. Sergeant Brady had never learned the techniques of traveling hard and fast as a team.

I called Gorman Station while en route and told Deputy Kennedy that Spencer might be there before us, and that we were on our way to interview him.

Soon we passed through Santa Clarita, Castaic Lake on our right, then Pyramid Lake on the left. Shortly thereafter, our trailing vehicles peeled off on the 138 and we continued north toward Gorman Station. I glanced at Lizzy and then met Rich's gaze in the rearview mirror. "Well, here we go. How do you guys want to go at it?"

"We have to kill some time," Farris said, "so I say we have him walk us through the whole thing again. Tell us about the night he found Josie in the shed and killed the Watkins kid. Make him give us every detail again and see if anything's changed after six months. Then I might have more questions for him about that, depending on how it goes. After that, he's all yours."

"I might also have some questions for him about the night he found Josie, but I'll wait until you two are finished with him. Then, after I talk to him about that night, and the Watkins kid, I'm going to ask him about the Brown murder, see if I can rattle his cage a bit. The idea—beyond keeping him off the mountain for a few hours—is to make him sweat a little bit. Maybe stimulate him to visit the scene again once the cameras are in place."

From the back seat came Farris's famous chuckle. I glanced in the mirror to see his bright smile. "You want to jack homeboy up?"

"Hell yeah I do. You have some ideas?"

I glanced in the rearview mirror and saw Farris staring out the window at the mountains to the east. I could almost see the wheels turning. I waited. After a moment, he said, "It'll be close to dark by the time we finish. I say we come up with something during the interview that prompts us to talk about going back to one of those two scenes—or both—but then argue about the time of day and the weekend off and discuss among us the idea of going back up the mountain next week. Give him time to ponder it, and let's see if he goes back up to check it out." He ended with his eyes on mine in the mirror.

"I like it."

"We'll come up with something, I promise you. I've already got a few ideas."

"Like?"

"Well, one question I have for him is why he might think Watkins used that shed, and if he had ever seen him down there before. Then, among ourselves, we can ponder the answer, and one of us might say something about maybe he was using it as a stash house if he was moving dope, like Spencer alleges. Then we can talk about there being no evidence of that, and maybe someone can question how well we searched the shed and area. Someone can say, 'Shit, he might have had a stash under that floor and we never knew it.' Now, if I'm Spencer, and I want to keep Watkins as the primary suspect in Josie's kidnapping and the Brown murder, I'm going to get up there and stash some dope under that floor before we get up there to search it. How sweet would that be, catch that on the video?"

"Jesus," I said. "That would be the string that unravels the whole case —both cases. That's good, Rich. Really good."

"That's my partner right there," Lizzy said.

"I like it," I said, reinforcing my enthusiasm. "I like it a lot."

We then rode in silence for the remainder of the drive. I was mentally preparing for the interview, and likely my two partners were doing the same. I slowed and eased down the off-ramp into Gorman, made a right, and headed for the one-of-a-kind station situated along the southern stretch of the Tejon Pass.

We walked in through the front door and found Spencer sitting at the kitchen table inside the residence station. He and Deputy Steve Kennedy each had a cup of coffee on the table before them but there was no happy-conversation-in-a-coffeehouse feel to the meeting. Confirming my suspicion that an awkwardness lingered, Kennedy immediately rose, and, after briefly greeting us, excused himself, telling us to make ourselves at home. "There's a fresh pot of coffee on the counter," he said on his way out.

Before he stepped outside, Kennedy paused, and said, "Detective Jones, can I get a quick second with you?"

I walked outside with him and closed the door behind us. "Everything okay?"

"He's tripping about this interview," Kennedy said. "I just wanted you to know that. He was asking all kinds of questions about why you guys wanted to talk to him, et cetera. I just told him I had no idea—which is the truth. What's up?"

"We're just rattling his cage a little."

I knew I could trust him, but nonetheless stopped short of letting him in on our operation and revealing to him that we would be installing cameras. The fewer who knew, the better. Someday I might need him to be able to raise his hand in court and swear he never knew about any of it.

"I guess you still aren't sure about him."

I shook my head. "No, in a nutshell. But we also don't have any evidence to say he's dirty, so keep that in mind. I don't want anyone treating him any differently until we can prove something."

"Got it. No worries."

"Where's your partner?"

Kennedy smiled his boyish grin for the first time this afternoon. "Kramer's off for the weekend. We work overlapping shifts and I'm here until Monday while he's off having fun. Let me know if you need anything."

I reached for the doorknob, then stopped. "Hey, if you don't have any reason to be up there, try to avoid Liebre Mountain over the weekend, if you don't mind."

His brows crowded together, curious.

"Don't ask. Just, if you can, avoid the area—the shed and where Brown was killed for sure."

"You got it, sir."

We shook hands, and I went inside to find the three of them at the table. Farris sat next to Spencer. In my mind, I was smiling at the strategy: Farris would in no time be crowding him, getting inside his comfort zone, making him sweat and squirm. Lizzy was on the other side of him where she could offer support and comfort if Spencer started to protest the line of questioning. *Good cop, bad cop.* We would have to walk a fine line—keep him on the ropes but not have him say bullshit, I'm not putting up with this, and walking out. They all had coffee in front of them, so I helped myself to a cup before sitting down across from Spencer and Farris.

Farris looked at me. "I was just explaining to Jacob that we simply needed to go over everything again, no big deal."

I looked at Spencer and he forced an awkward smile, trying to look comfortable. But I could see he was anything but comfortable, and I didn't blame him. Farris was the master in an interview room, known to wring sweat from even the blameless. This game warden was going to lose ten pounds from his already too-thin frame. I wondered if he had lost weight since the last time I saw him, or if I just hadn't remembered how lean he was.

I said, "Yeah, low key, man, no big deal. Boss has us all jumping through hoops on this case because the old man's got his nose in it."

"The old man?" Spencer asked.

"The sheriff. You know, there's been a lot of fallout from the Watkins kid being smoked. Watkins Senior created a stir, him and his attorney."

Spencer nodded and seemed to relax a bit. I hadn't planned to use the pressure-from-above strategy, but when it came out, it made perfect sense, and I was proud of myself for the way I delivered it. I looked at Farris. He winked and then turned to his opponent.

"So, Jacob," he started, "let's walk through this whole case again, from start to finish, just to cover our asses."

I sipped my coffee and got ready for the show. There were few things I admired more than watching a master work his craft. It could be said about Farris—to quote an old southerner friend of mine—*he sho do know his onion.*

19

WE HAD BEEN AT IT FOR TWO HOURS AND SPENCER WAS READY TO GO. Twice he had started to say he was done, but both times Farris calmed him with a soft touch—a hand on his arm or shoulder—and his soothing tone. "You're cool, man, we just need to cover a few more things." Each time, Spencer would slouch back into his seat in resignation.

The planned conversation about us getting back up to the mountain came off perfectly. It provided the desired effect as well as a startling revelation of Lizzy's talent for improvising. Farris had suggested we go back and search the shed and surrounding area better, and I had agreed, adding that I'd like to have another look at the Brown murder site as well. We were checking our watches and speculating how much light we might have left if we wrapped up quickly, when Lizzy blurted out, "I've got a nail appointment and date night with hubby. It's been six damn months, can't we come back next week?" Farris and I didn't give in right away though, making her work for it. "Look, Dom had to take the night off so we could go to a play. He doesn't get weekends off very often. He'll kill me if I get hung up on this."

Farris had turned to Spencer. "His real name is Domenico; she calls him 'Dom.' Dude's straight Italian, second generation. Can you believe it? Gets himself on LAPD's Metro team and marries himself this pretty little sister. I still think he's mafia." Then Lizzy had shot him a look and I had chuckled, and Spencer had relished the conversation moving away from that night on the mountain when he killed a boy whose eyes had probably shown surprise. That had likely stayed with Spencer ever since, occupying rent-free space in the warden's head.

When the theatrics were finished and I had not yet received a text from anyone saying they were done on the mountain, I shifted gears and asked Spencer about good hunting spots in the region, telling him I hoped to find time to go hunting this year. I had only been trying to kill time, but instead found an unexpected nugget. When Spencer talked about hunting, there were two things that became crystal clear: it was something he was passionate about, and he was very reluctant to reveal the locations of deer herds. "Oh, there's not a lot left over here, hardly any. You never see nice bucks, but if you go way back on Frazier Mountain, you might find something over there." His reference was to the other side of the interstate, away from Liebre Mountain. I gained another insight as to why Brown might have been killed when caught poaching, why Josie and her boyfriend might have been run off the road when found alone on the mountain at night, and why the Watkins kid might have taken a .40 caliber slug to the chest that night at the shed. There was more to it than just the tidiness of putting Josie's kidnapping and Brown's murder on someone who wouldn't be able to defend himself.

My phone vibrated in my pocket and I looked at it under the table. It was Mongo. "Done."

I took my final stab at Spencer, knowing it might be the last. "Jacob, why do you think William Brown was murdered? Any ideas about that?"

He shook his head and averted his eyes.

"I think it's because he was caught poaching."

Spencer shrugged.

And then I took a gamble. "There was a trail cam—"

Now we had eye contact.

"—but we haven't been able to get the images enhanced, and what we had was too far away to see our suspect clearly. So we sent it off to the FBI, and you know how the feds work, it could be a year before we get it back. Anyway, just wondered what you thought about that."

The tight skin of his skinny neck showed the hard swallows he took before responding, contradicting his coolness. "No idea, man."

I slapped the table as I got up and watched him jump, and when our eyes met, I smiled. "Thanks, Jacob. We'll be seeing you around."

Steve Kennedy was seated on the tailgate of his county-issued black-and-white Ford Bronco, the contents of which appeared tidy and recently organized. The truck, sitting over a patch of wet gravel, glistened in the waning daylight. A bucket was turned over and next to it a sponge sat drying in the warm air.

"Get a lot done?" I asked, indicating the sparkling rig with its reorganized contents.

He smiled. "You bet. How about you guys?"

Farris said, "I'd say it was well worth the drive."

We all shook hands and said our farewells. I started for my Crown Vic but stopped when I saw that it, too, sat on a blanket of wet gravel. I turned back to Kennedy and smiled. "You're too kind, sir."

He waved it off as no big deal.

As I started to drive away, I saw Spencer walk out of the sheriff's office. He was headed straight for his truck, his gaze on the ground.

"Well this will be interesting," I said, turning out of the lot.

"Let's get a drink," Farris said from the back seat.

"I'm for that, and you're buying," Lizzy said. "Talking all that shit 'bout my ol' man in there."

"What'd I say that wasn't true?"

"He isn't mafia. He might run high in that hot Italian blood, and there may be some family secrets nobody talks about, but mafia is a bit of a stretch."

"Hey, man," Farris said, "it was all just entertainment, baby."

"And I ain't your baby, neither."

Farris leaned up and tugged her ear. Lizzy spun in her seat and threw a punch, though I don't think she connected. Farris was laughing, and I said, "Kids!"

Lizzy turned back in her seat. "It's gonna be a long weekend, with this crew."

We were all smiling, having fun, enjoying the evening now that the work was finished, and it was time for drinks and food. The interview had been a success and I was confident that if Spencer was the one who killed Brown, and the one who ran Josie and her boyfriend off the road and then held Josie captive in that shed, he would soon be starring in a sheriff's video, coming soon to a courtroom near you.

My phone lit up—still on silent—and a picture of Floyd appeared on the screen. Lizzy laughed at the photo that had been taken of my old partner in a hotel in Virginia on the morning after a long day's work capped with too many beers. His bloodshot eyes were only half opened and his hair a fright, as he had stared at the phone camera and flipped me the bird.

"What's up, shithead?"

There was no levity on his end, a rare and troubling sign when dealing with Floyd. "We're going to pass on drinks."

I could hear the trouble in his voice. "What's up? Everyone okay?"

"No. We'll chat later."

"Josie?"

"Yeah. We'll chat later."

"Okay, shit. It was being back up there, huh?"

"Yeah. So anyway," he said, "Josie's tired and we're going to get her back. We'll see you guys in the office tomorrow."

I knew he was trying to keep it light on his end with Josie in the car. "Is she going to be okay?"

"She's just tired. I think we'll swing by the office and grab her car, have Mongo take it to her house and I'll drive her home."

I could hear Josie's voice in the background. "What's she saying?"

Floyd chuckled, still trying to play it cool. "Oh, she's protesting, says she's fine, but we'll take care of her tonight so she's good to go tomorrow."

"Tell her to take tomorrow off. I can handle the plans we had without her."

"Yeah, good luck with that. Okay," Floyd said, "I've got to go. I'll call you later."

I hung up and my phone immediately showed a text. It was from Mongo: *She's not okay.*

"She okay?" Farris asked.

"No, I don't think she is. Floyd couldn't talk. Mongo sent a text saying she isn't okay. Floyd was trying to keep it light on the phone, but I could hear it in his voice. He'll call me as soon as they get her home."

Lizzy said, "They're taking her home, right? Not dropping her at the office?"

"They're going to swing by, and Mongo will grab her car. They'll take care of her. I'll see what Floyd has to say later before deciding what to do. Damnit! I shouldn't have sent her up there."

"It's not your fault, Dickie," Farris said. "Didn't she tell you she'd been back up there? That's what you said earlier."

"Yeah, but still. She probably didn't spend much time there. She probably just looked from the roadway and didn't go down to the shed. Tonight, she would have gone down to the shed, and probably inside it too. I shouldn't have—"

"She's a strong woman," Lizzy said, "she's going to be alright. Maybe I should go stay with her."

I told Lizzy that Josie's mother lived with her and that they were close, so she would probably be fine at home. Then I suggested we all just wait to hear what Floyd had to say before deciding how to proceed. The idea of calling a professional peer counselor even occurred to me, but I always worried that when you did, there was a stigma that followed. I didn't want the brass to know she was struggling, if she was. Unless it was bad. The question was, how bad was it? Should I risk letting it go? She had received counseling in the months following the incident, but I was fairly certain those sessions had ended. Maybe it would just be a matter of getting her back into that.

We were on the Golden State Freeway headed south, and I didn't slow down in Santa Clarita. I knew none of us would want to stop for a drink now. I was doing eighty, sailing along in the fast lane, alone with my thoughts, worried about my partner and cursing myself for allowing her to go. I should have protected her from that. There would have been nothing wrong with doing so; I'd do the same for any partner, male or female. I didn't want to lose Josie as a partner, and I sure didn't want to lose her as a friend.

Before long, we were taking the off-ramp to the office and I hadn't yet heard from Floyd. When we arrived, I pulled up near the back door. "I'm going to go in and wait until I talk to Floyd before heading home."

Farris said, "I need to mess with some stuff at my desk before I can leave."

"Me too," said Lizzy.

I knew they were both full of shit, but we pretended they weren't and the three of us went inside and straight to the break room where we made a fresh pot of coffee and waited quietly.

Finally, Floyd called.

"Okay, she's home, but she's a mess. She started shaking uncontrollably up there at the shed, and when I touched her shoulder to see if she was okay, she jerked away, violently, and cried out. Then she dropped to the ground and sobbed. It was awful, man. She is *not* okay."

"Jesus."

Rich and Lizzy watched me intently, perhaps trying to hear Floyd. I clicked off with him and looked from one to the other. "I'm going to go see her."

Lizzy said, "I'm going with you."

"Me too," said Farris.

20

It would still be relatively early by the time I got home, the earliest in a week. We had gone to Josie's, but her mother sent us away, saying she was resting and wouldn't see anyone.

I hoped a Dodgers game would be on TV and that I could relax with a cold beer, get my mind off Josie for a while, and not think about cases again until after a full night's sleep. Dodgers or no Dodgers, cold beer was a must. I pictured a box of Coors Light in the fridge, certain there was no need for a stop.

I pulled to the curb in front of my apartment and saw Red the Fed sitting on the steps that led from the first-floor apartments to a well-manicured lawn framed by planters filled with of a variety of flowers. She had a glass of wine sitting next to her and a cigarette burning in her hand. I hadn't known her to smoke, not that I knew her well at all. In total, we had probably spent four or five evenings sharing a drink—one time, a meal— and it had never gone any further than that. There was something about the voluptuous Scot—who was beautiful and single and apparently interested —that made me hold her at arm's length. Maybe it was the fact that she was a federal prosecutor. Maybe it was also the fact that one day, when I returned from a run, I found my front door ajar. I knew I had closed it behind me, though I had left it unlocked. She had been home that day and

I'd been wondering ever since if she had snooped in my apartment. Or maybe I was just doing what I do, as Floyd likes to say, looking for an excuse to destroy another potential relationship.

"I didn't know you smoked," I said quietly, as I drew near to where she sat.

She picked up her wine and scooted to one side and motioned for me to have a seat. "Good evening, Detective. You've sure been putting in some long hours."

I glanced at my watch; it was almost eight. If the Dodgers were playing, they weren't at home; I would have seen the lights from the stadium as I drove north on the I-5 from the East L.A. interchange. But there were no lights from Chavez Ravine, and I hadn't turned on the radio to see if they were playing somewhere else, my mind too cluttered with the new issues at hand. Either way, it didn't matter; I found something better to do.

"Let me go grab a beer and set my stuff down," I said, indicating my briefcase. "You want something?"

She held up her glass and examined the contents. "Sure."

"Beer or scotch?"

"Scotch sounds good. On the rocks, please."

I skipped the beer myself and returned a few minutes later in shorts and a T-shirt with two tumblers of the good stuff. Emily was extinguishing her cigarette with the bottom of a sandal. I handed her a scotch and took a seat next to her on the narrow step, our bodies only inches apart. The cigarette smoke was gone, though I could still smell it, mixed with the floral scent I had come to recognize as hers.

We toasted, and she said, "I haven't smoked for twelve years, not regularly, anyway. I have an occasional cigarette when I'm drinking, if I'm alone and feeling sorry for myself."

I was loathe to ask, fearing the possibility of taking on another woman's problems. So I didn't. "I get that."

"Rough night?" she asked.

"We've been busy. Have a case that looks like it's going to be a series of specifically targeted victims with a purpose, maybe a grudge. Then we also have some stuff cooking on an old case—I told you about my partner being kidnapped a while back—"

She nodded and took a sip of her drink.

"Well, we're running with some leads on that case too, and . . ."

She watched, waiting for me to go on, but I realized I was close to sharing intimate details of my partner that I wasn't sure the fed deserved to know. I wasn't sure I *trusted* her to know. But Josie was weighing heavily on my mind. I was concerned about her and wished I could talk to someone about it. I thought of my last relationship, the one with the shrink, Katherine. She was someone with whom I could confide. But with Emily, I wasn't so sure. Not yet.

Emily broke the awkward silence, gently patting my knee. "Something sure has you tied in knots. Do you want to talk about it?"

The question caused me to grin slightly. "You sound like my ex now, and she was a shrink."

"I'm sorry."

"No, it's okay. We both have lots on our minds, apparently. I guess we could either burden each other with our troubles, or distract one another with lighter topics."

I could feel her gaze upon me, and I turned my head slowly to face her, her soft hazel eyes glimmering in the glow of yellow street lights. After a moment, I looked away. She reached over and tugged at my arm, pulled it toward her, and then placed her hand in mine and tightened her fingers around it. She lowered her head to rest on our clutched hands, and after a long moment, she kissed my hand. She said, "I have an idea of how to perfectly distract us both."

I SAILED ALONG TO THE OFFICE THE NEXT MORNING, BEATING THE SATURDAY traffic that would soon clutter the freeways as if it were another weekday. Everyone in Southern California had somewhere to be—the beaches, the baseball fields, the soccer fields, Disneyland, Hollywood, and, for we unfortunate few, work. It was a rare Saturday where, had I not had a full day of work planned, I might have actually preferred to stay home. I smiled at the mental picture of a freckled woman curled between satin sheets, who smiled when I had kissed her goodbye a few minutes earlier. What a night it had been.

Jesus, what had I done?

It was only seven, too early to check on Josie. I hoped she had been able to sleep. I actually hoped she had taken something and slept the night away, and I prayed she hadn't had nightmares about the mountain. I'd call her on my way to Lomita after a short stop at the office.

The bureau was surprisingly active for a Saturday morning. Detectives in shirt sleeves and ties scurried around, busy and preoccupied. There were a dozen at least. Raul Martinez was one of them, and he and I met on the path to the kitchen.

"What's going on around here today, Raul?"

We rounded the corner and headed for the coffee.

"I'm not sure what everyone else is doing, probably a busy night last night. Joe and I are working on that goddam West Hollywood case, the girl off the balcony."

"That turn out to be a murder?"

He shrugged, handed me the cup he had just filled and began pouring one for himself. "I think so, but we're a long way from proving it. Plus we've got a lot of pressure from upstairs."

We didn't have an upstairs, but I knew what he meant, and it wasn't heaven. Upstairs referred to the higher ranks—the brass, administrators of our department—no matter where they were physically located.

"'Tis the season," I said.

"Did you pick up a political one?"

I blew on my coffee and took a sip, and then we both turned and started back toward the squad room. "Yeah, the son of Mayor Bellovich, Palos Verdes."

"What's the story on it?"

"I don't know yet. But I have a feeling it's a revenge deal. He and two of his best buddies—who happen to be brothers—were killed."

"You picked up a triple?"

"No, different cases. Different times and locations. We're pretty sure they are all related. Floyd and Mongo have one, Farris and Marchesano the other. We're working them together."

We had come into the squad room and stopped to finish the conversation. Raul started for his side of the room with a parting, "Good luck."

"You too, buddy."

On the way to my desk, I passed Lacy Jones, my illegitimate sister. "Hey Sis, what's going on around here? Why's it so busy?"

Lacy stopped and glanced around the office as if she hadn't noticed. "Our team had a busy night, two deputy-involved shootings, an hour apart. One in Compton, the other in Paramount. Plus the standard two or three Friday night killings. Anyway, I think everyone's just cleaning up from a busy night. What have you got going?"

I saw Farris and Marchesano come through the back door, so I gave Lacy the short version, and we parted ways. They veered toward my desk and I met them there.

Lizzy said, "Any word on Josie?"

I shook my head and glanced at my watch. "I was just going to call her."

They waited. While I rang her phone, I stared at the wall decorated with photographs of homicide detectives at various crime scenes. The call went to voicemail, so I ended it and tossed my phone on my desk. Neither of them spoke.

"I just stopped by for a file and some coffee, on my way to Lomita. You want to meet back up later this afternoon?"

Farris said, "Yeah, as a matter of fact, I was going to tell you—"

"Oh boy."

He grinned. "Nah, no big deal. I was just going to let you know that Compton gangs got a tip on the Lowe case."

"Jackie Melvin Lowe. Low Boy."

Farris said, "They popped a dude with a tail who doesn't want to go back to the joint, so he talked. Not a witness, just knows what's up in the hood."

"Parolee huh? How long's his tail?"

"Not sure, but it doesn't matter; his parole officer said he'd violate him if we wanted, cut him a break if he helped us out."

"He from Jackie's hood, this parolee?"

"He stays right there by the market where them dudes hang out, said they were talking about it the other night. Came up with two names and a gang, and Compton has the horsepower on both of them. One's a straight-up shooter, and the other's a junkie, someone we might be able to turn. Anyway, they're looking for those two dudes, and if they find them, I figured you might want to go in on the interviews with me. No big deal if you don't; I can take Lizzy. I just thought with you knowing the case better—"

"Yeah, Rich, no problem, man. Let me know."

He nodded and stepped away, and Lizzy followed. "Happy hunting," he said.

I tried Josie's phone again and it went straight to voicemail this time. She had turned her phone off. I picked up my case file and headed for the parking lot. In my car, I fiddled with the vents and got the air conditioner working before pulling away. Then I had a thought, and I sent Josie a text. *Thinking about you. Let me know if you need anything. Get some rest and call me when you feel like it.*

I drove to Lomita, continually checking my phone for a reply that never came.

21

I was surprised to run into Slocumb at Lomita Station. "What the hell's an Ops lieutenant working Saturday for?"

Deac looked behind him to clear the hallway where we stood, not far from the captain's office. "Jesus, this crazy broad has me doing all kinds of goofy shit. Today we're going to a car show—and that's not too bad—but last weekend we went to a goddam soccer tournament, if you can imagine that. Anything to support the community, she says. We hand out goddam stickers and baseball cards and shit like that and call it outreach."

I chuckled and shook my head.

"Now tell me, how the hell did you get rolled up to Lomita?"

Deac again cleared the hallway with a furtive glance while backing up to lean against the wall, a grin stretched across his face. "Well, it's not that big of a deal, but in short I threatened to kick another lieutenant's ass. He cried about it to the captain, who decided he couldn't bury it, so he wrote me up and that has to be reviewed by the chief. Well, she likes me—"

"You're talking about Chief Tanner."

He nodded. "—so she says, 'I can't sweep this under the rug, but I don't want to lose a good lieutenant either.' She tells me she's going to send me to Lomita to work for Captain Russell until they fill in that spot with a new Operations lieutenant. Tanner says, 'She's a little kooky, but she means well.' So, that's the score. I work here six months and keep my mouth shut, and I'm back in Detective Division on the next transfer."

"So you're in the penalty box."

"Exactly."

We waited until a young uniformed deputy passed by. I said, "What was the story? Why did you threaten the other lieutenant?"

Slocumb smirked. "It really was nothing major, but this lieutenant had asked about going to Santa Barbara for a training gig, and I told him no, because I was going to be out on vacation that week, so he needed to stay in town. See, one of us had to always be available, since we're always on call. Well, I'm down in San Diego, and I get a call in the middle of the night about some off-duty shit one of our detectives got involved in. I tell them, call Hall, he's got the on-call. They said, no, he's in Santa Barbara at a training class.

"To say I was a little pissed is an understatement. I don't know how bad this off-duty thing is going to be, how many days I'm going to be dealing with it, so me and the wife pack up and drive home in the middle of the night and I go into work to handle this bullshit.

"When I see Hall the next week, I confront him about it, ask why the hell he went ahead and put in for that training, when I told him I couldn't cover. He tells me he had gone to the captain and got permission. So I told him if he goes behind my back again, there's going to be a fight in the parking lot, and he'll be there." Slocumb shrugged. "That's all there was to it."

I shook my head. "Well that's bullshit."

"What have you got going?"

"I need to research some old cases on your microfilm machine. You know where it's kept?"

"I know where my office is, where the head is, and where I park my car out back." He grinned. "That answer your question?"

I chuckled. "Gotcha, boss. Don't worry about it, I'll wander around with a stupid look on my face until someone feels sorry for me and decides to help me."

We shook hands and went our separate ways. Moments later I found the secretariat, and I walked its interior perimeter until I found a small room off to one side with a copy machine and an antique microfilm machine and several cabinets full of film cartridges. "Perfect," I said, though nobody was listening. I perused the shelves until I found the two years we had decided to search, and collected several cartridges. I pulled a chair over to the machine, turned it on, and went to work.

Forty-five minutes later I pulled my phone out and hit the dial button for Floyd.

"What's up, Dickie?"

"When are you guys talking to the parents?"

"Mongo and I just left King Taco and we're on our way. Forty-five minutes, maybe. Why? What's up?"

I hit the yellow print button and the documents began stacking up in the tray, three pages of a redacted 261 report—Rape by Force. "I'm looking at a rape report from twelve years ago. Todd Bailey, seventeen, is the named subject, then there are two other white male subjects, both unknown. I think this is it."

"No shit! What's the victim's name?"

"Unfortunately, that's the problem. It's not listed."

"How's it not listed?" Floyd asked.

"It's been redacted. Maybe because she, too, was a minor? I don't know. We need that name though, if you can get it from the parents. See what mama can tell you while you're rubbing suntan lotion on her shoulders."

"Alright, we'll see what we can do. How's Josie?"

I sighed. "Haven't talked to her. Tried a couple of times to call and sent her a text. Nada."

"Okay, well keep me posted. I'll let you know what we get from the parents."

I hung up with Floyd and called Farris to give him the news.

"That's outstanding," he said, "because we've got nothing here at the marina. We're just finishing up."

"Okay, I'm going to go talk to Bellovich's old man, Mister Mayor, and see what I can get out of him. Floyd and Mongo have the information about the rape and are on the way to your victim's parents' home. I'll call or shoot you a text when I'm done and heading back to the office."

"Okay, man. Any word on your partner?"

"I haven't heard from her, Rich. I'm hoping she took a sleeping pill and zonked out."

After I hung up with Farris, I gathered the printed documents and returned the film cartridges to their rightful places, then found my way back to the kitchen via the administration office. I thought I'd say goodbye to Slocumb if I saw him, but he was nowhere to be found. I helped myself to a cup of coffee to go and walked to my car under a clear blue sky. I checked my phone again but there were no messages and no missed calls. Josie was on my mind as I drove to the coast.

A team of gardeners appeared to be finishing up at the Bellovich home. I parked across the street, because their truck and a trailer full of equipment took up all the curb space in front of the residence. Six Hispanic men in khaki-colored shirts darkened by sweat were working their way to the truck with landscaping tools while another followed behind, blowing the remnants of their efforts toward the street. I passed the group at the apron of the driveway and greeted them collectively with a nod and a "Buenos días."

I rang the bell and waited. The sultry assistant answered, wearing loose shorts and a T-shirt, and holding a cup of coffee. She wore no makeup and her hair was mussed. Her facial expression went from one of boredom—or perhaps annoyance—to one of surprise. She seemed to have expected anyone other than me to be at the mayor's doorstep.

"Detective, how may I help you?"

"I need to speak with the mayor, ma'am."

"I'm afraid he's not available."

I allowed a moment to tick by as I studied the mistress-in-disguise before me. "It's important. I just have one question for him."

She turned without speaking and left me standing on the step, pushing the door only half closed behind her. I waited, and soon the mayor appeared, barefoot in his seersucker robe, grimacing.

"What is it?" he asked.

I looked behind me to see the gardeners loading into their vehicle. "I have a question for you, sir."

"Yes?"

He obviously had no intention of inviting me in, so I got straight to it. "Todd Bailey was arrested for rape while he was still in high school."

He waited a moment. "Is that your question?"

"My question is what do you know about it?"

The mayor shrugged. "Nothing. Why?"

"Because two other boys were listed on the report. I thought maybe you'd know something about that."

His eyes narrowed and he straightened his posture as if he needed to establish who was in charge. Max Bellovich was the type to always be in charge, but that's only because he had never dealt with people like me and my colleagues.

"I don't appreciate the accusation I think you're making here, Detective. You'd best be careful before dragging my murdered son's name through the mud."

"I don't intend to drag anyone's name through the mud, but this might be a valuable lead. I need to find out who the girl was."

Bellovich let out a long sigh. "I have no idea what you're even talking about, to be honest. Maybe you should worry more about who killed my son than what his friends might have done back in third grade."

"High school, actually. Your son and his friends."

The mayor's eyes narrowed, his unshaven face twisting as he snarled, "I'll be calling your sheriff." Then he slammed the door.

"Well, that could have gone better," I said to the closed door.

As I drove away, I dialed Floyd, but the call went to voicemail. I pictured him and Mongo sipping mimosas with the missus, the three of them poolside and one of them naked. Hopefully, just one of them naked. But also working hard to get the information. *Missus Bailey, do you recall the time the boys got in trouble for nailing that one girl who had said no?*

I sent Farris a text letting him know I was headed back to the bureau and didn't get anything from Eddie's father, Mr. Mayor. Driving along, I could see sailboats meandering off the coast, yachts sailing farther out at sea, and beyond all of the recreational seagoing craft—far away on the horizon, where the blue skies faded to gray—were the ghostly outlines of two large ships skulking south, likely headed to port in San Pedro. I wondered what it might be like to board a ship and sail away from the masses. Not that I had ever wanted to be a sailor, and I was fairly certain I'd be seasick, but the idea of sailing the ocean, backpacking into the wilderness, or gliding through the skies appealed to my reclusive leanings.

I thought about my relationships and realized it was this secret desire to be alone that had sabotaged each of them.

I HADN'T NOTICED HER CAR IN THE LOT AND WAS SHOCKED TO FIND JOSIE sitting at her desk, staring at her computer screen. Her gaze drifted in my direction and then flicked away, back to business. Was she angry, or embarrassed?

"Good morning, partner."

Without looking up. "Good morning."

"I tried calling, came by to check on you. Did you get my text?"

The bureau had emptied out since earlier this morning and now it felt like a Saturday, with only a few investigators scattered about. Josie looked behind her before setting her eyes on mine. "I didn't want to see anyone. I didn't want to talk to anyone. I just needed some space, and some time. You, of all people, should understand that. I'm fine."

I started to ask what she meant by that but thought better of it. Besides, I already knew what she meant, and she wasn't wrong. We were two separate, independent people, each having been molded by our histories. Knowing this allowed me to draw back, give her that space she needed. After all, what was the difference? She showed more emotion, but I knew that I would have suffered the same trauma revisiting that scene if it had been me in the shed for four days. The only difference was that I wouldn't have allowed anyone to see my fear and anxiety, and rather than going home, I would have gone to a bar. By myself.

I took a seat at my desk and began thumbing through the Bellovich case file, avoiding eye contact with her. "I think we found a motive for the killings."

"Really?"

In my peripheral vision, I could see she had turned to face me. I continued, "There's a case on microfilm that shows Todd Bailey was arrested for rape when he was seventeen. There were two unnamed subjects whose descriptions match the general descriptions of his brother and our boy, Eddie. Ten to one that's what this is all about."

"Is she a cop now?"

I found the printed microfilm report and handed it to her, meeting and holding her gaze for a long moment. She took the papers and forced a small smile. "Thank you."

"We don't know who she is; her name is redacted from the report. I went and saw your buddy Mad Max the Mayor—you should have seen him in his seersucker robe and slippers—and he was no help either. In fact, we'll probably take a beef for me bringing it up to him; he wasn't very happy about it. 'You'd better be careful before dragging my murdered son's name through the mud.' Anyway, he isn't going to give us anything. Floyd and Mongo are hitting up the lovely Mr. and Mrs. Bailey, see if they can get anything from them."

"She's going to be our suspect," Josie said, "I can feel it. I've felt that it was a woman from the beginning, but it seemed a stretch. At first, I thought the girlfriend killed Eddie—before we talked to her. I think this makes a lot of sense. These assholes raped a young girl and she came back as a confident, vengeful woman. Good for her."

Now I was the one who glanced around the room. *Jesus Christ,* I thought, *don't ever say that aloud again!* There wasn't a cop who hadn't, at one time or another, seen a victim of revenge-motivated violence, and thought it well-deserved. But to say it—especially as the lead detectives who represent that victim until justice is served—just wasn't done. I wasn't going to mention it, though, because I knew where she was coming from. When she saw Eddie Bellovich lying on the studio mat with his broken head, she had probably imagined Spencer lying there in his place. She likely thought of the game warden again when she saw that Sean Bailey had leaked to death on the floor of his garage at his Ladera Heights home. Maybe she saw herself walking Spencer to the end of Inspiration Point, backing him to the edge for a photo, and then thrust-kicking him in the belly to send him over backward. She might have fantasized about him tumbling until he smashed onto the rocks below, the cold salty waves crashing over his lifeless body. Who didn't, on occasion, dream of revenge against evil sons of bitches?

"We have to figure out how we're going to ID her. Court records are sealed, reports on film are redacted, and we're looking at what, eleven, twelve years ago? If Floyd and Mongo can't get anything from Bailey's parents, this is going to be tough."

"What about going through their high school yearbooks, running all the girls?"

"That would be hundreds. Besides, what would we look for? How would we find her?"

Josie pondered it a moment. "Maybe we don't have to ID her that way, just find some of their classmates who are still local, and then talk to them. You know everyone had to have heard about it. Forget the class pictures and just look at the various event photos, you know, the cool kids that show up over and over in all the activity pictures in the back."

We were both leaning back in our chairs, staring into each other's eyes, contemplating. Josie was biting at the end of a pen and I was tugging at my mustache. Neither of us would make good poker players, the both of us showing we had no cards to play.

A thought struck me. "It's not going to work."

Josie frowned. "Why not? You have any better ideas?"

"No, it's not a bad idea, but I just realized something: if the rape happened to someone at their school, the other boys would have been identified. Don't you think?"

She nodded. "That's a good point."

"But maybe we could still go with your idea and get some information from classmates. I would imagine everyone heard about it. Maybe someone would say, 'Oh, they were accused of raping a girl from such-and-such school,' or whatever. I mean, we have to start somewhere."

"What about the deputies who took the report? Or the detectives who handled the case?"

"Bingo!" I exclaimed. "That's brilliant. Why didn't I think of that? They'll have notes, and those notes won't be redacted. I'd say the investigators are the way to go. Good thinking. All we have to do is find out who was handling sexual assaults out of Lomita at that time and hope they kept their notes or the original case file."

Josie smiled, pleased with herself. I smiled in return, pleased with her disposition. She was back in the game, and she was going to be okay.

22

By the time Floyd and Mongo returned from the Bailey home, Lizzy, Rich, Josie, and I had come up with a solid plan for going forward, having presumed that the Bailey parents weren't going to entertain any thoughts of dredging up *minor mishaps* from their little darlings' adventurous childhoods. The partners walked in with shades on, their ties loosened, and sleeves turned up.

"What have you two been up to? By the looks on your faces, I'd say no good."

Floyd flipped me off, and they gathered around our desks with the others. "We got dick. I fucking hate white people."

Farris nearly spit his coffee and Lizzy grinned and shook her head.

Floyd continued, "Seriously, there's that wrinkled old bitch with her morning cocktails and Valium, and her pool boy, Skip, some loser surfer boy who probably reminds her of her misspent youth—the slut—and then you've got the old man with his pickled brain, who's completely disinterested in any of it, just wants to know when the coroner's office will release Sean's body so he can bury the kid's dumb ass next to his brother. I say fuck 'em all." He flopped into a chair. "What've you idiots got going?"

"Well while you've been out making friends, Josie and I've been brainstorming—"

"Jesus," Floyd said, "that must've been a short-lived session."

"—and she came up with tracking down the handling detectives, see if they have the original file still, or at least case notes. And you are in rare form today, partner."

"Yeah, whatever," Floyd said. He looked at Farris. "Do you hate white people, Rich?"

Rich chuckled.

Floyd said, "You can be honest about it, because I'm totally with you on this."

Shaking his head and smiling, Rich said, "I mostly hate rich people, to be honest about it. I don't care what color they are. The more money they have, the bigger assholes they are. But I'll tell you something else about rich people—"

"What's that?" asked Floyd.

"You tell me how much money a man makes, and I'll tell you whether or not I'd sleep with his old lady, sight unseen. I'd maybe bed an ugly one every once in a while, but nine out of ten, I'd be striking gold, no pun intended."

"Men are pigs," Lizzy declared.

"So figuring out who handled the rape case will wait until Monday," I said. "Does anyone have anything pressing that we can work on until then?" I glanced at my watch. "I mean, we don't have to ruin the whole weekend if we've run out of leads."

I looked around to see everyone shaking their heads or shrugging as if there wasn't much else that could be done over the weekend. Floyd said, "I think since we're here anyway, and they're paying overtime, we'll dictate a supplemental report on our so-called suicide and get caught up on that."

Farris glanced at his watch. "That's not a bad idea. Couple more hours and then take the rest of the weekend off. How do you want to handle tracking down the investigators?"

"Josie and I can go down to Lomita Monday morning and handle that. Let's plan on meeting at the office after lunch and we'll figure out how to proceed from there. Hopefully we'll have a name for our primary suspect by then."

There were nods all around and everyone went their own way, leaving

Josie and me seated alone at our adjoined desks. "You okay, kiddo?"

She glanced up. "I'm fine."

"Do you have any plans for the rest of the weekend?"

She shook her head and looked away.

"Me neither. If you want to hang out or anything—you know, just need a drinking buddy or whatever—I'm free as a bird."

Josie smiled. "What about Red?"

I looked away and shrugged.

Josie said, "You dirty dog!"

"What?"

"You know what. You know *exactly* what."

I suddenly felt flushed, as if I had been caught in a lie. But I hadn't lied, I had only omitted unnecessary details. "Anyway, let me know."

"Perfect," Josie said, pushing out of her chair. "I say tomorrow we have a barbecue at your place. I'd like to meet this lady fed of yours. Plus, I have always wanted to meet Cosmo. I trust you haven't abandoned her too."

"Him. And no, I would never abandon my fine, finned friend."

"Okay, so what time?"

I chuckled. Was she serious? "I don't have a barbecue."

"No problem, we'll order out. Or better yet, we can go out for Mexican."

"Me and you."

"No, me and you and Red."

I rolled my eyes. "What is it you have up your sleeve?"

Josie opened and closed her top and middle desk drawers, likely making sure she had everything she needed, and then stood up and collected her purse, attaché case, and keys. After rolling her chair to its rightful position at the center of her desk, she paused and looked down at me. "I want to meet her, that's all. Is anything wrong with that? We're partners, right? I should know the women in your life."

What a double standard, I thought. I hadn't known about her relationship with Tommy Zimmerman until after he was killed. There was no way I was going to mention it. But with that thought came enlightenment: I had presumed her breakdown on the mountain was a result of reliving what had happened to *her*, and I hadn't even considered that she was mourning the loss of her friend, or lover, whatever Tommy had been to her. Now I felt better about Josie's episode on the mountain and her need for a period of distance. What I wasn't sure about was her motive for inviting herself over. Did she really have an interest in meeting Emily? Or was she using that as an excuse to not be alone tomorrow?

"Okay, you're on. I'll make a date with Emily and let you know what time. But whatever you do, don't call her 'Red the Fed.'"

Josie twirled her keys around her finger and smiled. "Cool. See you tomorrow."

I watched her walk out and thought I'd trade Red and ten others like her for a woman like my partner.

23

MONDAY MORNING JOSIE AND I MET AT THE OFFICE TO DROP A CAR AND ride to Lomita together. I parked mine and jumped in with her, relieved to no longer be driving in traffic. Settling into my seat, I breathed deeply to take in the fresh floral scent that I presumed to be my partner's body wash. Maybe it was her shampoo. Either way, there were worse odors with which a homicide cop could start his day.

"What'd you think?"

Josie glanced over at me as she wheeled out of the parking lot and started for the freeway. "Yesterday?"

"Yeah, yesterday."

"It was nice. I enjoyed myself."

She knew I wanted her opinion about Emily, but was either going to make me ask for it outright or lead me on for a while. I didn't want to seem overly concerned about her opinion on the matter, so I let it go.

It took us nearly an hour to get to Lomita Station in Monday morning traffic. Josie and I chatted about everything other than our personal lives—mostly department happenings and bureau gossip—when I wasn't on the phone. I had received several calls already this morning, all of them concerning various cases other than the ones I was most concerned with and interested in: the murders of Eddie Bellovich and the Bailey brothers, and the cases on the mountain, those likely involving the game warden Jacob Spencer.

One such call came from Rich Farris, who wanted to tell me about some new developments in our Compton rap artist case, the murder of Jackie Melvin Lowe, Low Boy. Farris had gotten a call from one of the Compton gang investigators who said the two dudes we had wanted picked up were both in custody. One was being held for a parole violation —meaning he wasn't going anywhere anytime soon—and the other had been charged with a chickenshit robbery case that wouldn't likely make it to court. However, he was on probation, so we needed to make sure his probation officer would put a hold on him so we would have more time to work the case.

I gave Josie the details when I got off the phone, and she asked, "What are you guys going to do with them?"

"We're going to try to work them, one against the other, I guess. See if either of them wants to give it up. Probably have to deal with that in the next day or two also, as if we don't have enough going on."

We turned off Pacific Coast Highway onto Narbonne Avenue, which turns into Palos Verdes Drive East. But we weren't going to the Rolling Hills Country Club; rather, we turned into the rear parking lot of Lomita Station which, but for the drop in elevation, and a white, country-style fence line interspersed with shrubbery and fruitless plum trees, might have at least provided a view of the third tee box, a slice of the rich man's playground.

I suggested we check in with Slocumb first, let him know what we were doing so he could keep his captain off our asses and hopefully away from our investigation. Josie agreed, so the admin office is where we began.

I told Lieutenant Slocumb what we had discovered and what we hoped to find by tracking down the case investigator. He said it made sense to him, and told us to come along, that he'd introduce us to the D.B. lieutenant and we could start there. We followed him to the detective bureau where we were introduced to a heavyset white man with a drinker's bumpy red nose, O'Neil by name. After Slocumb left us there with him, O'Neil said, "You got a case number?"

We did, and I thought maybe this could have been as easily handled by phone. But if the detective was still here, we'd want to talk to him. If he was no longer assigned here, we'd need to find out where he went. If he had retired, we'd want to get a home address and phone number for him. Just like with interviewing witnesses, it was always easier to get information from people in person than it was by phone or email.

Josie read him the case number—*slowly*—as he repeated it one digit at a time and punched at his keyboard with a fat index finger.

"I'm still trying to learn this newfangled case management program they gave us. It's pretty good, once you get used to it. Has everything in it, all the case data and who it was assigned to and all of it. No different than the paper journals we kept, but now the captain can see what we're doing without getting off her fat ass and coming back here. That's the best part of it, truthfully."

"Is it going to go back twelve years, Lieutenant?" I asked.

"Oh yeah. We've had it for at least that long, more 'n that probably."

While his bloodshot eyes roamed the screen, I wondered how long the man had until retirement, and how long he had after that. The job could wear a guy out, and some didn't help themselves much along the way. This guy hadn't done a sit-up since the academy, was my bet.

"Okay, here ya go," he announced, his words drawing out slowly. "Looks like this case was handled by Pete Hanson, who's been retired close to a decade. What else do you want to know?"

"Do you have a victim name there?"

I edged closer to his desk as he scrolled up on the screen to see additional data. "No, nothing here. This is probably back when we first started using this program, and a lot of the old-timers didn't care too much for it and they wouldn't put too much in there. Their name, case number, maybe check the box for active or inactive, and move on. It took us a few years to get the guys to put everything in here, and the new guys—and ladies—are pretty good about it. I'm not all that surprised that old Petey didn't put much information in there."

"Okay," I said, "how about the old files?"

"We don't keep the paper files that long; we've got nowhere to store them all. Everything's on the computer now."

"Well, not everything, apparently."

He noted my tone and shrugged. "We live and learn. What's your interest in this rape case? The girl end up croaking?"

I shook my head. "No, the suspects did."

O'Neil leaned back in his chair and smiled. "I'll be goddamned. You got a vigilante on your hands, huh?"

"Maybe. How about the contact info for Hanson? Maybe we'll get lucky and he kept all of his old notebooks."

The lieutenant turned his chair a quarter turn and pulled a file from the bottom drawer of his desk. I wondered if there was a bottle tucked farther back. I wasn't judging; there were still plenty of bottles in the desks of homicide detectives, even after all these years of evolving. He opened the file on his desk and ran his big finger down a column on the left, stopping at Hanson. "Here ya go."

Josie stepped over and quickly jotted the information into her notebook. She told him she got it, and he put the file away.

"Anything else?" he said, checking the watch stretched over his huge wrist.

"Did Hanson have a partner?"

"He did, but you're not going to be able to talk to her."

I had a bad feeling, but asked nonetheless. "Why's that, boss?"

"She died of cancer, just a few years back."

Josie, a pen still hovering over her open notebook, said, "Who was that, sir?"

He looked at her and ran his big fingers through his thin gray hair. "Her name was Kathy Kowalski. She was a good broad—sorry, uh, woman."

In the car, Josie handed me her notebook and started the car. She was fiddling with the air conditioner while I copied Hanson's name, address, and phone number into my notebook, along with the name Kathy Kowalski. I drew a line with an arrow after her name and wrote in larger print: *Deceased, natural causes.* I held Josie's notebook out for her, but she was checking her face in the mirror. When she finished, she snatched the notebook from me and pulled the shifter into Drive.

"Where to? You want to go see Hanson or call him?"

"Hell, he's right over here in Long Beach," I said, pointing east, "practically on our way back to the office. I say we pay him a visit."

We went east along the most non-scenic portion of Pacific Coast Highway, which took us through Harbor City and Wilmington—two unattractive districts within the City of Angels—and into Long Beach. We skirted the south border of Signal Hill, a small town with a mixed history. The city was thus named because it was once the place from which the Puva native people communicated with other tribes on Catalina Island, twenty-six miles away. Later, in the twentieth century, oil was discovered there. More recently, only a few decades ago, a black football player had been found beaten and hanged in its city jail.

At the traffic circle, we took the spur northeast and were nearly in Hawaiian Gardens—a city that, in spite of its name, was no bed of hibiscus at all—before we found the modest home of retired sheriff's detective Pete Hanson.

24

"THAT WAS ODD."

Josie agreed. We were creeping along the 605 Freeway now, headed north, back toward the office. She fiddled with the navigation system on her phone, a program that suggested best routes of travel given traffic conditions, road construction, and even the presence of cops. It did not, however, take into consideration the presence of food establishments, bars, or general scenery. She said, "It smelled like old people and cats in that house."

"His mannerisms were odd, for a cop. Didn't you think so? I never would have made him for one if we had met somewhere in public."

"He didn't look like a cop," she said.

"I know he's old now, but still… And did you see the boxes stacked in the dining room? You can't tell me those were all taxes and old bank records. I bet anything he took cases with him when he retired. Everyone does. He's probably writing a book."

The navigator told us to take the 105. "Don't do it. She doesn't know what she's talking about."

Josie shook her head. "It's data from all of the other commuters. Everyone uses it."

"You trust these people? Look around you. Me, personally? I make my own choices based on logic and experience. Besides, you go where she tells you, everyone knows where you're going. Why alert the enemy?"

"Who's everyone?"

"Zuckenberg, Mueller, all of them."

"It's Zuckerberg, and he's the CEO of Facebook, not part of the FBI or CIA."

"Still, you can't be too careful. People are putting things in their houses now that spy on you. I can't believe it. When I retire, I won't even have a cell phone anymore. That's how I feel about all of this technology."

"You're a dinosaur, Jones."

"How's that make me a dinosaur, going my own way? I'd say it makes me a pioneer. Stay right here on the 605, take the Pomona and we're there, no messing around."

She took the 105 west as instructed by her phone. "Are you hungry?"

"Yeah, I'm hungry, but there's nothing to eat this direction. We're screwed now."

"You're such a baby sometimes."

"Go where you want. I need to call Farris, see what he wants to do on our dead rapper case. Let him know we're hitting walls on identifying our rape victim. How the hell are we going to identify her?"

"There's got to be another way."

"Like?"

"How about Hanson's partner—"

"She's dead, remember."

"—I was going to say, maybe her spouse could tell us something, or maybe she left files from work behind, boxes stored in the garage."

"That's not a bad idea," I said.

"Thank you."

"But taking this freeway *was* a bad idea, so you're only on your game about half the time. I expect more from you."

She shook a fist at me. "Mister, I'm warning you."

We agreed on lunch in East L.A. since there was nothing between here and there, and while she was negotiating early afternoon traffic, I was on the phone again. Farris said we'd talk when I got back to the office, that he had an idea about the Low Boy case. I told him we were coming up with goose eggs on our venture to identify the rape victim, and I'd fill him in when we were back in the office. I said, "It may take us several hours, the way my partner drives."

Josie pulled into the office parking lot and I spotted the other four members of our newly formed, unofficial task force seated at the table on the outdoor patio. "Lookit there, we're having a meeting." I glanced at my watch. "Probably too early to be cracking out beers."

We parked and walked over to join them.

"Are we having a meeting?" I asked, walking around the table to the far side, which was fully shaded.

"Impromptu," Farris said. "But your timing is good. Tell us about your lack of success today."

I briefed the group on our efforts to identify the rape victim and lamented the frustration we were feeling, having had no success. I told them about the "new" case management system that had been in place for a dozen years or more, and how it was just our luck that the rape case had almost no information. There were no hard files stored from that far back, and the best he could do was provide us with the retired detective's name and contact information.

Josie described Hanson and his home: "He was an odd little man, rosy red cheeks and pale skin, a guy that never gets out. You never would've made him for a cop. His place reeked like the home of an old woman who collects cats and forgets to close the refrigerator door, and it hadn't been vacuumed or dusted for ages. It was gross."

I said, "There were all these file boxes stacked up in the dining room and a computer on the table. We asked about the case, and of course he had no recollection. I suggested maybe he had the file somewhere, indicating the boxes in the other room, and he says those are personal files, and no, he didn't keep any of his case files from the job."

"So what's this guy's problem?" Floyd asked. "Did he go batshit crazy when he retired, or did he leave that way?"

"No idea, but I don't like that he's clammed up over this case. I mean, yeah, it happened more than a decade ago, but how many rape cases do you think a Lomita detective handles in his career?"

Josie peeled off her suit jacket in the early afternoon heat. I had left mine in the car. She said, "We're going to try his partner next. She's deceased, but we think maybe the family would allow us access to her files, if she kept any when she left the job."

"What's her name?" Floyd asked.

"The dead girl?" Mongo asked, as if Floyd had hit a new low.

Floyd glared at him.

Josie flipped open her notebook. "Kathy Kowalski."

Lizzy said, "I knew Kathy. We worked custody together, way back when. I think she passed from cancer, if I recall."

"That is correct," Josie said. "Would you like to handle that detail then, since you have a connection to her? It might go over better with the family."

She shrugged. "Yeah, we can do it."

Farris nodded in agreement.

Nobody seemed to have anything else to add, and individual conversations broke out among the group. Farris tapped my arm and said, "Do you have some time to work on the Compton case?"

"Our rapper?"

"Yeah, man. Of the two in custody, one is supposedly the shooter, this dude they call Eight Ball, and his homie, Big Smoke, was the driver. I want to go at Big Smoke and see if we can turn him. Then, we bring them both down to Torrance Court in a couple of days and put them together in a private lockup that we'll have the tech crew wire ahead of time, see what they rap about. If we don't get Smoke to talk, he'll surely have to tell Eight Ball about the interview."

"They aren't housed together now, are they?"

Farris shook his head. "One's at Twin Towers, the other's at Wayside."

That meant they were housed in different parts of the county. Twin Towers Correctional Facility was one of our two jails located on Bauchet Street near downtown Los Angeles; the other was Men's Central Jail. Between the two, they housed approximately half of the county's 22,000 daily average of inmates. Wayside was a 2,600-acre property located near Castaic, an unincorporated town in north Los Angeles County near Santa Clarita. In 1983, the name was changed from Wayside Honor Rancho to the Peter J. Pitchess Detention Center, in honor of the twenty-eighth sheriff of Los Angeles County, and also to reflect the change of its structure. It used to be a working farm facility where much of the harvest was used to feed the county's inmates, and those in minimum security worked in the fields. There were now several facilities on the property that house nearly 8,000 minimum- to maximum-security prisoners. Those of us who had been around a while still called the place Wayside.

"Please tell me the guy we're going to interview is in Twin Towers."

Farris chuckled. "No way, man, you know you aren't that lucky. We need to go to Wayside."

I thought about it a minute. "Can it wait until Friday?"

He shrugged. "Maybe. What are you thinking?"

"We'll need to go back up on the mountain with the tech crew and retrieve those video cameras. Might as well do it all at once."

Farris stood up from the picnic table and looked up at the sun for a moment. He turned to me and said, "Let's plan it for Friday then. Do you have any ideas about how to go at our boy?"

"I do," I said. "On a similar case I had, I used a poor-boy for a prop—not the actual case file folder—where I wrote both suspects names on the file, wrote 'SOLVED' across the bottom, and made sure I had that sitting on the table during the interview. The dudes couldn't stop looking at it, and I think it had a real impact on them. Of course, the shooter on that case didn't budge, but his accomplice, when I interviewed him with the file propped on the table, was moved to give it up. I guess seeing your name on a file that says 'solved' is highly motivational. Also, I printed MURDER, 187 P.C. as bold as I could on the top. I think something like that would be good to do again."

Farris nodded. "I like it."

"I also made sure to put the victim's true name and also his moniker on the folder. I didn't want them getting their murders mixed up."

"Yeah, you know they won't have any idea who the hell Jackie Melvin Lowe is, but they'll recognize 'Low Boy' for sure."

"Oh, one more thing," I said, "let's write 'Weapon Recovered' on the file too."

He frowned. "We don't have the murder weapon."

"Right, but they're both in custody, so they're going to shit about that. In that other case I did like that, they started naming off their fellow gang members who had access to the gun, and wondered which fool got popped with it. Good stuff on the recording."

Rich Farris smiled widely. "Yessir, that is good stuff right there. Okay, we'll do it. Let me go catch up with Lizzy and find out when she wants to hit up the family of that detective, what was her name, Kemblowski?"

"Kowalski."

"Right on, man," Farris said.

As we walked toward the office, he said, "Hey man, how's Josie? She okay now?"

"She's good, brother. She's good."

2 5

THREE DAYS LATER, THURSDAY, I SAT IN THE OFFICE REVIEWING A REPORT that had been returned from a secretary. Josie and I had submitted our dictation Tuesday morning, and I was surprised it had come back so quickly. It was the first investigation report on the Edward Bellovich case, and I had to assume that the supervising secretary had known of the case and its priority status. There were few mistakes to be corrected, and I had just finished my review when Rich and Lizzy strolled over to my desk and announced they had identified our rape victim.

I saved and closed the Word document and spun my chair around to face them. "Outstanding! How'd you do it?"

Lizzy handed me a manila file folder that showed signs of wear. It had handwritten block printing on its tab: RAPE, 261 P.C., and a file number. The names Hanson and Kowalski appeared on the opposite top corner of the file.

The file was thin, and it made me think back to my days of working as a station detective. Burglary, robbery, assaults, and even rape cases seldom comprised much more than a dozen or so pages of both the patrol deputy's report and the investigator's supplemental report. Some cases had more, but many had that or less. At Homicide, it was not uncommon to produce a hundred typewritten pages of investigation reports on one case, some-

161

times many more. Those reports would be compiled with all of the reports from others involved in the case—patrol deputies, crime lab personnel, coroner's investigator, and medical examiner, to name a few—to make a murder book. Murder books were generally four inches thick and, for some cases, there would be several volumes.

By the weight and thinness of the file in my hand, I guessed there hadn't been a lot done with this case. I didn't know Kowalski, but I had met Hanson; I wouldn't be surprised to see that his efforts had been minimal.

As I pulled out the report, Lizzy began, "There's not much to it. It looks like the case was technically Hanson's—or maybe he was the primary—and Kowalski was brought in to interview the victim."

"Makes sense," I said, thumbing the pages. I had called it right, a three-page crime report, which was the same report I had obtained from the microfilm, a two-page supplemental report by Detective Hanson, and three more pages by Kowalski documenting her interview of the victim and the collection of evidence. "Interesting though, that she kept the case file, not Hanson."

"Do you want to read through it, or do you want the highlights? I read it while Rich drove us back."

I put the report down and looked at Lizzy. "Let's hear it, and then I'll probably read it too."

She glanced around the office. "Where's Josie?"

"She left early today for an appointment. I'll fill her in tomorrow on the way up to the mountain."

Farris had pulled up a chair. "She's going back up there with you?"

"I told her I'd handle it, but she insisted. She said she needs to heal, and she has something she wants to leave up there in memory of Tommy."

Lizzy said, "Good for her."

I motioned for Lizzy to have a seat also, and as she did, I pulled my notebook out and started on a new page. On the top I wrote in block letters RAPE CASE, scratched two heavy lines beneath it, and then I added the file number. Below that, the victim's name and age: Kishi Takahashi. I paused and looked at the name for a long moment before turning my attention back to Lizzy.

She began, "The victim was a first-generation Japanese American who lived in Venice with her parents and a brother. She and a friend from school went to a party at Abalone Cove in Palos Verdes—"

"I know it well," I interjected.

"—and that is where she met the suspect, Todd Bailey. The victim's friend had known Bailey before, and it isn't really clear if that's why the girls attended the party or not."

"What's the girlfriend's name?" I asked, hovering the pen over my notebook.

"Cathy something—I don't remember, it's in the report," Lizzy said, indicating the file on my desk. "Anyway, apparently Bailey took the victim for a walk down the beach and the two of them ran into two other boys who seemed to be acquaintances of Bailey. Kishi—the victim—had worn cutoff shorts and a string bikini top, and one of the boys untied her top and pulled it off her. In her interview, she said she was shocked and outraged, and she began striking the boy who had taken her top. The others grabbed her, and she said the rest became a blur. All she knew was that once she was overpowered, the remainder of her clothing was torn from her, and she was raped by Bailey while the other two held her down."

"That must be from the supplemental report," I said. "The first report —the one I was able to find at Lomita—didn't have any of that information."

Lizzy brushed her hand through her hair. "The first report has almost nothing. Kowalski did the interview and wrote it up in good detail. A rape kit was administered at Daniel Freeman and held as evidence, and that was about it. Hanson got an arrest warrant for Bailey and a court order for his DNA, and the case was filed. There aren't any other notes about court proceedings. That's about it."

"So without a court file, we don't even know who prosecuted the case. Usually, in a case like this, the prosecutor is going to have interviewed not only the victim, but her parents too."

Farris said, "Hopefully the girl is still around. Something like this, the family may have packed up and headed back to Japan."

He might have been right about that, but I hoped not. "You guys haven't run her yet?"

Lizzy shook her head. "No, we just walked in with the file."

I glanced at my watch. "I say we run her real quick through DMV, get an address, and if she's local, go have a visit. Tomorrow's going to be a busy one and I don't want to wait on this. What do you guys think?"

Farris nodded and Lizzy reached out for the file. "Let me make us each a copy of this file, and then I'm going to book it as evidence and write a report of how we came to be in possession of it."

The two of them walked away and I sat staring at my notebook, contemplating. How does a rape case get buried by the judicial system? Had Bailey even served time? I wanted to read through all the reports because the longer I pondered it, the more questions I had. What had the detectives done to try to identify the other two subjects? That's what juveniles were called, *subjects;* suspect was too harsh a word for the little darlings who raped, robbed, and murdered their fellow citizens.

As a patrol deputy, I handled a murder wherein the shooter was fourteen. He shot a woman on a dare, a hard-working young lady who was walking to the bus stop to catch her morning ride downtown where she worked long days for minimum wage to help support her family. Her hair was still wet from having showered a short time before the thug and his friends pulled their car in behind her and a gang initiation transpired. He was merely a *subject*, a subject who no doubt had remained free to kill again…and again.

Lizzy's voice snapped me out of my reverie. "Nothing, can't find her."

"What!"

She handed me some papers, photocopies of the file's contents. "I ran her by name and birth date, all we have. Nothing."

"Maybe she's married," I said, "has a different name."

"The DMV should still have her maiden name listed in the files, the name she first got licensed under."

"If she was licensed before she married," I argued. "Japanese families are often much stricter than Americans, especially first generation. What about the friend she went with?"

"Well, there's another problem. They only put a first and last name for her in the report, no date of birth, no address, and her name is Cathy Brown. Do you know how many of those there are?"

"I imagine a few," I said.

"Yeah, a few hundred," she said, "and that's for each variance of spelling. With a C, with a K, or is it Katherine, and Katherine can be with a K or a C also, and there's several ways to spell all of them. This sucks."

I pondered it a moment. "What did they list on the report for her address?"

"You mean from then, back when this happened?" she asked.

"Yes," I said. "We can go knock on the door and hope the family is still there."

She glanced at the report again. "Venice."

"Where's your partner?" I asked.

Lizzy looked around as if she had lost something. "I don't know, probably at a bar by now. He's having a rough day. On the way back, he was on the phone with his attorney. Apparently, the ex wants more money."

I shook my head. "Well there you have it. He was already wound up and ready to fight, then you tell him about three tough guys raping a young girl. It's a wonder any of us is sane around here."

Lizzy said, "If I can't track him down, me and you can go to Venice," and she turned to walk away.

I nodded, but she didn't see me. Then I looked at the name in my notebook again: Kishi Takahashi, and I pictured a pleasant young girl, soft spoken and maybe unsure of herself in social settings. A whiz in class but awkward at the high school games, or dances, or parties at the beach. I could see where a girl like this could become a victim given the circumstances described in that report, but I had a hard time seeing that same girl getting revenge on the monsters who had raped her.

And another word came to me, one from her own culture: dishonor. The three boys had *dishonored* her. Dishonor did not become her people. *Death before dishonor.* It was the way of the samurai, and maybe this was a variance thereof: death *after* dishonor, or because of it.

26

Farris was nowhere to be found, so I loaded up in Lizzy's white, county-issued Dodge Charger and we headed for Venice. Appreciating the ride, I said, "Nice, Lizzy… You must know people."

"Monica takes care of me because she loves me."

I could picture our fleet manager sitting behind her desk, smiling in spite of the whining she tolerated daily. "Monica loves everyone, Lizzy."

"Nun-uh, she don't love *everybody*."

"Fair enough," I said, as I reached over to adjust the air conditioning. "Did you figure out where your partner went?"

She turned it back down a notch. "He had shit to handle, to quote the man."

The afternoon rush hour traffic was heavy, so I made use of the time by reading through the rape reports again, making some mental notes of questions to ask if we were able to track down Miss Kishi Takahashi, or any of her family. While doing so, the samurai thought came to me again. I called Floyd.

"Hey, do samurais use those fighting sticks that we talked about?"

"Are you changing theories on this, think we have a murderous warrior whacking white boys?"

166

"No, dummy, I don't. Now can you answer my question? Where are you, anyway?"

"I'm on my way home, and no, that isn't what they're known for. Samurais are famous for their swords—that and preferring hara-kiri over being captured by their enemy. What are you up to now?"

"We've identified the rape victim, and she's Japanese. So I was just thinking—"

"Well there's your first problem, Dickie—you were thinking. But to put this dumbass idea of yours to rest, the whole idea of it is death *before* dishonor, and the death refers to one's own death, not someone else's. Besides, I don't think there was ever a woman samurai."

Lizzy leaned against the headrest, driving with one foot propped on the dash, bored as we crept along the congested Santa Monica Freeway headed toward the coast. I could see her long lashes behind her sunglasses from my side-view angle, and I could see that her eyes were heavy with boredom or fatigue. I cut it short with Floyd, telling him that we hadn't yet been able to find the young lady in question, but that Lizzy and I were on our way to Venice to look for her.

Floyd said, "Do we love Venice Beach?"

"I guess," I said, "I mean, we do enjoy the weirdness of it." I told him thanks for his help, but now he was boring me, and he should hang up on himself.

Venice Beach—for as long as Angeleños of my generation could remember—had always been a draw for the extravagant, the outrageous, and the gawkers who travel from all around the world to experience it all. Skaters, volleyballers, basketballers, musclemen—and women—artists, musicians, magicians, and all manner of entertainers could be found along the promenade. Fishermen flocked to its southern pier and surfers to its northern waters. Bars, restaurants, and shops plying diverse trade lined the streets, as did hordes of homeless, drunkards, dope fiends, gangsters, and a host of other shady characters. It was also where the legendary Rock and Roll Hall of Fame band The Doors had been formed.

On the south side of the city, south of Venice Boulevard, was a congested neighborhood of small, century-old homes alongside large, modern reconstructions, framed and interspersed with small streets and man-made canals. Locating the address once used by Kishi Takahashi was a challenge, and finding a place to park was nearly impossible. I told Lizzy to pull over at a corner where the curb was painted red and a small shop with its doors open advertised "Tattoos by Creeper." Two bikers stood in the doorway, eyeing us while puffing cigarettes and blowing smoke into the afternoon sky.

I was out of the car before Lizzy had turned it off. My suit jacket hung in the back and I didn't bother getting it out before walking up to the two bikers. "Where's Knuckles Malone?" I asked, pushing the front brim of my fedora up slightly.

Both of their postures seemed to soften as their interest piqued. Knuckles was a wannabe biker who had been stabbed to death in the marina two years earlier. I knew, because I had had the pleasure of seeing the stupid look he had on his face when he died. I also knew that the bikers had all tired of his antics, which drew resentment from the locals and unwanted attention from the cops, making the drug trade of the local bike gang dip lower than the stock market in 1931.

"Never heard of her," the bigger one said.

Their eyes shifted from the badge and gun on my belt to my partner coming up beside me. Lizzy was fit, confident, and the type of woman who drew the glances of men across all walks of life, from lawyers to cops to dirtbag bikers who sold meth out of their tattoo shops.

I stepped closer to the larger of the two, sending him a clear signal and commanding his attention. "Well here's the deal, Tiny. My partner and I are going to take a stroll around this block over here and check an old address we have for *her,* and you and your girlfriend here are going to make sure nothing happens to that super cool cop car parked in front of your shop."

He glanced at the Charger, and then his gaze quickly returned to me, squinting as he tried to decide how to handle what I had dropped on his porch.

I continued, "Now, when we get back, as long as our car is unharmed and you two dummies are still standing here, we'll leave peaceably and never return. If something goes wrong, we'll set up shop on this corner for the next six months and see how long your business survives."

"This is the city, man, you sheriffs ain't supposed to be here."

"The bear goes everywhere," I said, a reference to the symbol of the

California grizzly in the center of our badges. "And you know the sheriff doesn't play games."

A slight nod of the bearded big man's head told me we were on the same page, and that our vehicle was safe where it was parked for as long as we needed. I handed him a business card and said, "Speaking of those blue-suiters, if LAPD should come around and harass you about our car, tell them we're on the job, tracking a killer."

For the first time since we had arrived, the big man grinned. "You might be looking for the wrong man, if you think that faggot Knuckles killed anyone. In fact, I can tell you where to find him, and then we don't have to deal with the stench of your bear shit."

"Yeah, where would that be?"

"Last I knew for sure, he was at the coroner's office," he said, showing a mouth full of rotted teeth.

I smiled back. "We're going to go check for ourselves, see what we come up with."

Lizzy joined me as I turned and walked away, confident they were watching us closely as we left, and that they would watch our vehicle even more closely until we returned. It was just bad business to have the cops camped in front of your tattoo and meth shop, and even those two morons were smart enough to embrace the idea of us leaving in the near future, never to return.

We walked along a canal brimming with salty water supplied by the ocean, outlined with hedges to deter access from anywhere other than the designated points. Unmanned canoes and paddle boats sat tied afloat at points along the shore, their loose ends drifting with the current. Wooden bridges arched over the water, and we followed one to the other side. Palm trees rose high above the modern two-story homes that had decks and balconies designed to showcase the scenic views. The small enclosed areas were furnished with lounge chairs, and in many cases stored various water toys.

One home stood out from the others, as it had clearly not been renovated, updated, nor even maintained over the years. The single-story, century-old construction was an eyesore among the exquisite homes that surrounded it. The numbers displayed on the wall near the front door, one of them hanging upside down, identified it as the residence we were looking for.

The three wooden steps to the front door creaked under our feet as we slowly approached. An old rocking chair sat on the porch with a small table next to it, magazines and books scattered about. A small bowl with crusted old cat food sat on the rotted wooden planks below the table. Lizzy and I stood still on opposite sides of the door—not in front of it—and listened for a few moments before I knocked. After a minute, I could hear someone shuffling around inside, slow movements that gave me an image of an elderly person or someone with disabilities moving about. But there was no ramp near the stairs, so I eliminated the latter, and pictured an old Asian person working his or her way toward the door. Maybe that was hopeful thinking, but I wasn't disappointed when the door opened.

Looking up was a hunched, frail woman clutching a shawl that covered much of the floral-patterned dress she wore, one that could have doubled as a nightgown. She wore delicate wire-rimmed glasses and her small face was framed by short gray hair.

Lizzy displayed her six-point gold star. "Good afternoon, ma'am, we're detectives."

The woman smiled slightly. "Oh?" she said, stepping further across the threshold and looking past us, scanning the area as if she expected to see that there had been trouble.

"What is your name?" Lizzy asked.

With a heavy accent, she said, "Yasuko Takahashi."

Lizzy and I glanced at one another. A gray cat with a white patch on top of its head slipped past the frail woman and began rubbing its head on my pants while weaving in and out of my legs. I took a step back, but the cat persisted. Lizzy asked the woman if she was related to Kishi, and I looked up in time to see her shake her head and begin to retreat.

Lizzy said, "Ma'am, we just need to speak with her."

"No English," the woman said, as she began closing the door.

I reached out and stopped it, gently. "Ma'am, please, can you tell us where to find her?"

She shook her head again. "No, I don't know. I go."

The door closed softly, and Lizzy and I stood still for a moment, the gray cat butting its head against me. "What now?" I asked.

170

Lizzy shrugged. "I don't know. Harass the bikers?"

I gently pushed the cat away with my leg and stepped off the porch. "It *would* make me feel better."

We paused at the sidewalk, and I asked Lizzy if she thought we'd have any luck with the neighbors. Both of us took a moment to look over the revitalized homes before she answered. "I'd bet none of the neighbors know anything about this family."

I glanced around. "I'm sure you're right. But, we're here, and Tiny and his girlfriend are watching the car, so we might as well try."

A half hour later we were back at the car with no new leads on Kishi. The bikers watched as Lizzy went around to the driver's side, and I paused at the passenger door. I looked at the big man and said, "Did you know Knuckles got himself killed?"

The biker said, "It's what I told you," shaking his head, the smart one among us.

I popped the door open and paused before folding myself inside. Lizzy had started the motor and was ready to go. I said, "What a tragic loss of life." I smiled and the biker smiled back. As we drove away, I wondered if that murder had ever been solved, and tried to remember who had been assigned as the primary on it. Floyd and I had been called out to assist, but I couldn't recall why, much less whether or not the case was solved or why Knuckles had gotten himself killed. It occurred to me that my friend, Tiny, might know.

27

FRIDAY MORNING, I HEADED TO WAYSIDE WHERE RICH FARRIS AND I HAD agreed to meet at nine. We were going to accompany the tech crew up to the mountain to retrieve the video cameras from the shed where Josie had been held, and from the wooded area where William Brown had been shot through the heart. Afterwards, we were going to interview one of our two suspects on the Jackie Melvin Lowe case. It was the beginning of what promised to be a long day, and I hoped it would be a productive one as well.

During my drive I made several phone calls. First, I returned a call from a deputy district attorney named Moreno who had left a message about a case Floyd and I had investigated three years earlier, an infant shaken to death by the drug-addicted mother's boyfriend. I had almost forgotten about it since we had solved the case, made the arrest, and he was charged and bound over for trial within a month of the baby's death. Not always, but usually, cases that unremarkable and without media attention go to trial much sooner. Moreno said he wanted to go over the case with us since it had been handed off to him and he had never met the investigators.

The next call was to Emily, my neighbor, with whom I had crossed a line that might have been better left uncrossed. But now that I was clearly on the other side of that boundary, there were certain expectations that had to be met for civility's sake. She had left a message while I was on the phone with the prosecutor, asking if I had plans for dinner and leaving a Los Angeles area code number that I was certain would ring me through to the U.S. Attorney's Office. When she picked up, I said, "How do I file a complaint about a fed who has been sexually harassing me?"

She either recognized my voice or had caller ID, or both. "Those types of complaints are only heard in person. Would you like to schedule a time? My evening is wide open."

I smiled, looking at the traffic ahead of me but seeing Emily's hazel eyes smiling back, picturing her behind a bulky wood desk covered by court files, a cup of hot tea at hand. "I'll have to check my availability and get back to you."

"Oh really? Hold on one sec—" she said, and then her voice was farther away when she said, "No, the John Rondeau file... Yes, thank you," and then back to me, "Are you still there?"

"I am. What'd old John Rondeau get himself into now?"

"Hey," she said, "I thought we agreed no business talk between us."

Though I had mostly dismissed any notion of Emily having ulterior motives toward our relationship, I had never completely gotten over my suspicion that she'd snooped in my apartment while I was out. Over the months that followed, Floyd had convinced me I had lost my mind and that I always subconsciously undermined relationships due to my fear of commitment. The guy might have read too many Cosmos in his life, but that didn't make him wrong.

"I was kidding, anyway," I told her, "I don't know a John Rondeau. How about seven? I have a packed day but should be able to be home by then."

"Seven's fine. How about Thai? Does that sound good to you?"

"Always," I said, and we ended the call with quick goodbyes to avoid awkwardness.

Before calling Floyd to tell him about the meeting I had scheduled for us with Moreno, I pondered the conversation and wondered if it was John Rondeau, or Jean Rondeau, and since the question was due to the French origin of the surname, I wondered if it was spelled with or without an X. If I did a little bit of research to see what this Mr. Rondeau—or Rondeaux—

was up against with the United States Attorney's office, I could be certain of what types of crimes she prosecuted. From the beginning I had told her that federal prosecutors were not on my Favorites list because the only dealings I had ever had with them were when they were prosecuting cops. They had an army of prosecutors assigned to their infamous Public Corruption and Civil Rights Section, who spent all of their time and energy trying cases against local cops with the assistance of their friends in the Civil Rights section of the FBI—or, as we liked to call them, *Famous But Incompetent*. If Rondeau was a cop, then I would know that I was now sleeping with the enemy. But maybe Rondeau was a mobster and she worked their Organized Crime Section, or maybe he was a billionaire CEO and Emily worked in their Tax Division. In the latter cases, I would have to find something else with which to sabotage our budding relationship.

But I talked myself out of investigating my sexy neighbor, and moved on. I dialed my ex-partner's cell and told him about our meeting next week with Deputy D.A. Moreno.

He said, "Is that Barbara Moreno? She's hot."

"Manny Moreno, Family Crimes."

"Damn."

I then went on to tell him about the trip to Venice and the disappointment of that. He said, "Well, yeah, dumbass, she's not going to tell *you* anything. Have you looked at yourself in the mirror? You probably scared the poor little old lady to death."

"Feel free to take a shot at her," I said, "I don't know where we're going to go from here on this thing. We have to find our little friend Kishi."

"Our little killer, Kishi. Hey, I do have an idea though, in all seriousness."

"What's that?" I asked.

"How about if I get that hot little Japanese girl from the Training Bureau, Stacy Ito, to go down there with me and translate?"

It was a good idea, and I didn't hesitate to tell him so. "Yeah, great idea. Set it up, and don't waste any time doing it."

"Yeah, alright, whatever," he said, and hung up without saying goodbye.

The entry to Wayside started with a drive across a bridge over the Golden State Freeway, and then a check point with a security gate and guard shack that is manned around the clock by armed deputies. Signs were posted warning that you were entering a custody facility and that no weapons, drugs, or alcohol were allowed beyond that point. Deputies would pull up and show their credentials, and they would be waved through without delay.

Beyond the gate was a turnout—also used as a turnaround—and parked in the shade of the turnout was Lizzy's Charger. She, Rich Farris, and Josie were standing beside it, waiting. Farris was in shirt sleeves and a tie—as was I—but the girls were dressed in jeans.

There wasn't enough shade for both of us, so I pulled in behind Lizzy's car and left mine running with the air conditioner turned up high. I lifted my hat and wiped at the sweat on my forehead as I settled in near my partner. I was pleased to see that Josie showed no signs of stress or worry this morning, though we would be headed back to the mountain.

"Good morning, kids."

Lizzy said, "Josie and I are going to handle the mountain detail while you and Rich take care of your interview. That way we don't make an all-day deal of this."

I looked at Josie. "You sure? I mean, we won't be long here, and we can all go together."

"It was my idea," Josie said. "We even called the tech crew and asked them to bump it up an hour." She glanced at her watch. "They should be here any minute."

"Do you want us to head up there when we're done?" I asked.

"There's no reason for it," Josie said. She put her hand on my arm and said, "We'll be fine. You boys handle your interview, and then head on back to the office and we'll meet you there later this afternoon. Oh, I notified Kennedy and Kramer that we'd be headed up there also. Kramer is off but Kennedy said he'll drive up if nothing else is going on."

I nodded solemnly. Though I had my concerns, I knew Josie wanted and needed to do this. She and Lizzy were capable, but nonetheless, I would always be more protective of her than I would of any male partner. I guess that's just the way it would always be for me and men like me. "Okay. Be careful."

She smiled, patting my arm before retreating to Lizzy's vehicle.

Farris went to Lizzy's car and retrieved his suit jacket, the mock case file we would be using during the interview, and his briefcase. He went to the passenger's side of my vehicle and placed his belongings in the back seat. He then joined me as I stood watching the lady cops load up in their vehicle.

"That's a helluva crew right there, my brother."

I didn't respond.

He said, "Don't worry about them, Dickie; they'll be fine."

The tech crew pulled through the checkpoint. We said our goodbyes and the girls drove off in the Charger, flipping a U-turn and waiting for the van to follow.

"Yeah, I guess," I said, and once again I lifted my hat and wiped at the sweat beading on my forehead. "Well, let's go see your boy."

Rich and I loaded up and headed to Supermax, Wayside's maximum-security compound officially known as the North County Correctional Facility, or NCCF. We secured our weapons in gun lockers in the lobby area outside of security, and we traded our sheriff's ID cards for visitor passes. Once we had signed in, a young, chiseled deputy in a tightly-tailored uniform led us to a private interview room that would allow us an unrestricted visit. Farris plopped the file folder on the table and rearranged the seating so that he and the suspect would be knee-to-knee without the table coming between them. We each took a seat and waited in the cool, dim room, where only muted sounds of movement and chatter could be heard beyond the steel door and concrete walls. Farris looked over at me and held my gaze for a long moment.

"What? I can see the wheels turning."

"Nah, man, I was just thinking, it's too bad you and I have never hooked up as partners. Whenever we've caught a case together, I've enjoyed working it with you."

I smiled. Farris was a solid investigator and a good man, one well respected by all. "Thanks, Rich. Maybe someday."

He shrugged. "Don't know how much longer I'm going to go, Dickie. Two years, tops. Maybe less."

I could see something in his eyes I hadn't seen before: worry, distress, uncertainty. It wasn't the Compton gang case; of that, I was certain. We could solve that murder or walk away from it, neither of us losing a moment's sleep. That was just the way it was when you handled fifteen to twenty murders every year. The truth was, some victims really did matter more than others. When a hardcore gangster—a known shooter—got himself killed one week, and the next week you picked up a murdered child case, that's when you grasped the reality of homicide work. You came to terms with choosing one victim over another, and you accepted the fact that not all cases were equal.

"What's bothering you, Rich?"

His gaze drifted toward the ground. "Nothing, man."

I got up from my seat on the other side of the table and sat where our suspect would soon be sitting, me and Farris face to face, two heavyweights in the interrogation room. Now what?

"Don't bullshit me, Rich. You've got something on your mind, or something heavy in your heart. What is it? You know I love and respect you and it will stay between us. I know you have something you need to tell someone."

"But I promised—"

I heard footsteps coming and the sound of keys jangling; our suspect was being escorted in, finally. "Rich, it's too heavy to hold. Share it with a friend you can trust."

Keys rattled in the door. Farris looked at me, nearly choked up. He glanced at the door that we both knew was about to open. I saw him swallow, and his gaze came back to me. "Lizzy's got the big C."

"Here's your guy," a deputy said, pushing the door wide open.

I stood up and moved away from the inmate's chair but kept my gaze on Farris, who had scooted his chair back slightly and motioned for the inmate to have a seat in front of him. The deputy said, "Tap on the door when you're done; I'll be out in the hallway."

The door closed and the three of us sat silently for a long moment in the heaviness that hung in the room. Farris kept his gaze on the inmate, I kept mine on Farris. The inmate, Mr. Johnny Burns, was focused on the folder that sat displayed on the table and bore his and Dewayne Lewis's names beneath the caption: "MURDER, 187 P.C. – JACKIE MELVIN LOWE, A.K.A. LOW BOY."

2 8

THE INTERVIEW OF JOHNNY BURNS, A.K.A. BIG SMOKE, DIDN'T GO AS well as I had hoped. Farris was off his game, no doubt Lizzy heavy on his mind. I wondered when he had learned of her cancer diagnosis. When had it been revealed to him? How long had he been holding onto it? Only a short time, I reasoned, given the effect it clearly had on him today. I thought about when he disappeared from the office yesterday afternoon, after the two of them had returned with the information about Kishi Taka-hashi. I wondered if it was during the day while they were in the field that she revealed it to him. They had been at the home of Kathy Kowalski, a deputy who had died of cancer herself. That could have been the primer for a heavy conversation, maybe even a breakdown.

Farris would be a captive audience for the hour drive from Wayside to the office, and I looked forward to our conversation. I watched as a deputy led Johnny Burns from the interview room to take him back to his cell. Though we hadn't got from him what we had hoped, this was only a small battle in our war. The stage was set for a recording session at the Torrance Courthouse the following Monday, starring Big Smoke and his shooter buddy, Dewayne Lewis, a.k.a. Eight Ball.

We signed out, traded visitor badges for our IDs, and stepped over to the gun lockers. As we retrieved our weapons and extra magazines and were securing all of it on our belts, Farris said, "I blew that one, Dickie. I'm sorry, man."

"He wasn't going to give up his homie, Rich. It's okay, he couldn't keep his eyes off that folder. He and Eight Ball will have plenty to talk about in the lockup Monday morning, and that's what counts."

"Yeah, I guess," he said, and started for the door. I followed.

I drove us through the security checkpoint and again had to show our IDs before being allowed to depart. I checked my phone and saw there were no messages.

"Do you have anything from the girls?" I asked, indicating his phone.

He pushed a button to unlock the screen. "Nothing. I would imagine they're still up there."

We rode in silence for a few minutes, southbound on the Golden State, before I pressed him. "So what's the story on Lizzy?"

Farris drew in a deep breath and let it out slowly. "I just found out yesterday. I guess she's known for a couple of weeks. They found something during a checkup, ran some tests, and she's got some type of blood cancer—I don't remember what she said it was. My head felt like I'd been punched by Tyson when she said it; I had this fuzzy, hollow feel, and the rest of her words were unclear to me. They seemed to echo like I was on the other side of a canyon, though we were sitting next to each other in her car."

He turned his head to check his side-view mirror and kept his gaze there for a long moment. I checked my mirrors and saw there was nothing to see, and then waited in the heavy silence.

"They haven't decided on a course of action yet, but she plans to work until she can't. I told her to take time off, relax—she doesn't need the stress of this job on top of all that."

I nodded, certain he didn't see me, his head turned as if he was taking in the sights through the passenger's window. I waited but he didn't seem to have more to say, or maybe he couldn't talk. I could see his neck was drawn tight, his jaw clenched. I said, "If they found it during an exam, that's probably a good thing, don't you think? Probably caught it early if she hadn't had any symptoms yet. Right?"

Farris shrugged and held his gaze out the window. I imagined his eyes were red and watering and he was probably embarrassed about it. I decided to change the subject. "What's our plan for Monday?"

He was silent for a long moment before answering, still not turning his head to face me. His voice was melancholy. "It's all set up. tech crew will wire the holding cell over the weekend. I've got them ordered out for court, so they'll pick up the early morning buses out, and the deputies at Torrance know to put Big Smoke and Eight Ball in that one cell—and nobody else. It's a hard cell away from the others that they use for special handles, so there shouldn't be a lot of background noise. That's it. I figure we'll get down there early and make sure everything goes according to Hoyle, and then after they're in there together for an hour or so, we can do something to stimulate conversation, just to make sure it pays off. Maybe we'll pull Big Smoke out and sweat him again, put him back inside after a while and watch his homie sweat him about why he was talking to the po-po."

"Like maybe he gave them up," I said.

Rich Farris looked confident again, now back in his groove, the awful things in life we can't control set aside for a moment. "Yeah, because he'll be wondering how else they're being charged on that murder. Nobody's ever talked to him, and now he's called out for an arraignment. By the time they get bused back to their jails later in the day, without having been arraigned, they might start figuring out that something's up, maybe even figure out they've been had."

"Maybe when we pull Smoke out, we give him the impression his homie already talked. Then when he goes back in and Eight Ball starts with him about talking to the cops, Smoke might come right back at him, accuse *him* of talking to the cops."

Farris swiped at his eye, trying to do so inconspicuously, and chuckled. "Shit, we might want to make sure nobody gets killed in there."

I shrugged and smirked. "Oh well. It wouldn't be any loss to society."

The silence came on quickly again when we ran out of Low Boy topics to cover. I tried to think of something else but couldn't. I remembered that it was Friday, and that Emily and I had made plans for the evening. I started to say something about it, just to talk, and decided against it. To mention something good in my life felt wrong at the moment. I thought about the three cases we were working together with Floyd and Mongo, and I tried to come up with something to say about any of those. Again, nothing sounded right in my head. I knew if I forced conversation it would be awkward, so I chose to let it be.

For the next half hour, we rode through L.A. in a shroud of weighty silence.

———

FLOYD BURST THROUGH THE BACK DOOR OF THE OFFICE WITH MONGO IN tow. It may have been my survival instinct, or it might have been intuition, but I found myself spinning in my chair to watch him beeline toward me. He pulled a seat from the unoccupied-at-the-moment desk next to mine and plopped down in it, slapping his notebook and a can of Copenhagen down among the scattered files of one of my teammates. He pushed his sunglasses up on his head and said, "How do you like me now?"

"About the same as I did before you got here, to be honest about it— not very much."

"Well, you're going to like me a whole lot better when I tell you what we've discovered."

"You found our girl, Kishi."

Mongo had settled behind him, positioned like a bouncer at the front door of a nudie bar, his eyes appraising the most threatening parties in the joint—currently, me and Floyd. It was said the easiest job in the world was being a bouncer at a bar full of working-class men. The hardest was having the same job at the same bar on ladies' night. Mongo fit the profile of the latter. Tired, impatient, ready to pounce.

Floyd said, "Sort of," and flipped his notebook open.

I waited, looked up at Mongo who stared back unblinkingly.

Floyd said, "She had a legal name change a year after the rape." He held up his notebook and read from it. "Sunako Hisakawa."

"Easy for you to say," I said.

"It's spelled with an H, but it sounds like a K. *Khee-sa-ka-wa.*"

"Is there any relevance to the name?"

"Funny you should ask—"

"I figured you would have already looked it up," I said, "searching for a hidden meaning."

"Hisakawa means a long time ago. But Sunako, that's what's interesting—and then you put them together—"

"Yeah?"

"Sunako means dark side. A dark side a long time ago."

I knew that couldn't have been a coincidence. "I wonder what Kishi means," I said, not expecting an answer.

"Funny you should ask," said Floyd. "Kishi means a happy and long life. She apparently didn't want that name after our dead assholes had their way with her on the beach, stole her innocence."

"Her life."

Floyd said, "Right, Dickie."

After a moment, I said, "How'd you get the information? From Grandma?"

"Yeah, Mongo and I stole Stacy Ito from the Training Bureau and hauled her cute little ass to Venice. That, by the way, is how I know the meanings of those names. Anyway, it worked out really well, because Stacy, being smarter than all of us put together, said we needed to stop and buy her a gift. Apparently, gift-giving is a big part of their culture, and Grandma, being from the old country and all—"

"That's cool," I said.

Mongo stood guard, silently appraising the room.

"What'd you guys get her?" I asked.

"A nice little sake set, a beaker and two cups, dark green with two tones of brown. Really nice, honestly, and it only cost me about…a hundred bucks."

I looked at Mongo. Strangely, he seemed to smile with no change to his stoic face. It confirmed what I knew, that Floyd was bullshitting me.

"Yeah, whatever, dude," I said to him.

"It was close to that, with the sake."

"It came with sake?"

"No, dummy," Floyd said. "But we weren't going to give her a sake set without having something to pour into it. So we bought the set and two bottles of sake. A hundred bucks total."

"And she needed two bottles?"

Floyd smiled. "We didn't know how much it was going to take to get her talking."

I grinned.

He said, "And there's another custom about gifting things in fours—you don't do it. Apparently, four is an unlucky number in their culture. The word for 'death' is pronounced the same as the word for 'four.' So we added two bottles to make it a five item gift. Make sense, Dickie?"

"I'm about ready for five shots of something myself, to be honest."

"Why, what's wrong? I bring you good news and you're not happy. See what an asshole you can be?" He turned to Mongo. "See?"

Mongo moved his head up a centimeter. I took it as a nod. Floyd stood waiting for me to defend myself. I couldn't tell him everything that was *wrong*. I couldn't tell anyone about Lizzy. Maybe Emily, since she was removed from the circle and wouldn't know anyone and would be a good person with whom I could lament about it. But not Floyd—not yet.

"Nothing," I said, "just one of those days. Thanks for getting this done. Did you happen to find out where she lives, too?"

He shook his head. "Grandma said nobody has seen her for years. They were apparently very close, and Grandma got pretty teary at times when she talked about her. The sake helped some with that, but still... Anyway, she gets a card from Kishi—*Sunako*—every year, with a return address to a PO box in Hollywood."

"Hollywood, huh?"

"Hollywood, Dickie. They love us there."

I considered the information about the PO box. "Did you already try DMV?"

"Way ahead of you, Dickie; same thing, comes back to a box in Hollywood."

"I thought it was illegal to use a PO box for an address on a DL."

"They don't catch it when it's at one of those UPS stores, a hard address with a box number. Her DMV has 'Unit 1196,' so it looks like an apartment building on paper. But it's not; it's a UPS store."

"Great. I guess we write a warrant and see what information we can get from the UPS store, huh?"

Floyd nodded and pushed out of his chair. "Yeah, me and Mongo can handle that since we have all the information. I mean, we might as well, we're practically working this case by ourselves anyway."

I forced a grin.

The two started to leave and Floyd turned back to me. "Also, you should know something else about that culture. When you give a gift, you use both hands no matter what it is, and when you receive a gift, you do the same. So I could hand you a pen, or a grenade, and I would offer it to you with both hands. You would accept it by also reaching out with two hands. Important stuff to know, Dickie, just in case you dump the Irish fed and find yourself a nice little Japanese girl—which I would highly recommend."

"She's a Scot, thank you."

"Whatever," he said, and walked away.

2 9

My cell phone buzzed on the desk, still on silent from the interview. It was Josie. I grabbed it quickly. "Hey, how'd it go?"

"Good. We just came off the mountain, going to stop in Santa Clarita and grab a bite to eat—we're all starving—and then on to STARS."

"Did we get anything on video?" I asked.

"We don't know yet. That's why we're going to STARS with the tech crew after we stop and eat. They don't do anything with evidence videos until they download the original onto a server that is backed up on two offsite servers. Then they'll burn a copy for us. Lizzy and I will bring that back to the bureau, and if you make us some popcorn, we can have Friday night movies in the conference room."

I thought about my date with Emily and checked my watch. It was nearly three now, so it would be at least six or seven before the two of them were back at the bureau. It would probably take us several hours or more to review a week's worth of video footage. Even though the cameras were motion-activated, I expected there would be plenty of motion from various mountain critters activating them during a week's time. But I was also anxious to see if we scored on the operation, and I knew Josie was too —far more than I.

I glanced at my watch again and had a thought. "I promised Emily dinner tonight—"

"Oh *really*?" she teased.

"Yeah, but maybe if we planned on movie night starting at eight, I could take her to dinner, and then, I don't know—"

"Do you want to bring her with you?"

That idea had already occurred to me, but when I started to propose it, something felt wrong. "No, I don't think—I don't know. What do you think?"

"Bring her along. I'm sure she'd enjoy seeing where you work."

"I'm not sure I'm ready for that."

Josie chuckled. "Yeah, right. Okay, eight it is, and I'll expect to see Red the Fed with you."

"Her name is Emily. Whatever you do, don't—"

"Goodbye, Dickie."

I sat, alone with my thoughts, surrounded by empty desks and chairs, the squad room nearly empty on a Friday afternoon, nothing new. I looked around and thought about bringing Emily in, showing her around the place that felt more like home to me than my apartment did. I amused myself with the thought of relocating Cosmo to the office so we'd see more of each other, moving a set of shelves holding case files away from the wall so I'd have a place to put the larger-than-necessary tank. But Cosmo might get bad vibes being here, surrounded by men and women who carried with them the memories and restless spirits of those whose lives had ended violently. This was no place for an uncorrupted fish.

I started to call Emily but changed my mind, deciding to send her a text instead. Then I deleted the text and retreated from my phone, the source of my anxiety. Though truthfully, it was the idea of advancing a relationship that caused my apprehension, a trademark Dickie phobia. I had only to look in the rearview mirror of my love life to see the path of destruction, like remnants of tornados or war, casualties littering the trail —some smoldering, others in full rigor.

At 7:30 Josie arrived at the office and frowned when she saw me sitting at my desk, still dressed in the clothes I had worn all day.

"You haven't been home."

"I got busy."

She rolled her eyes and set an armload of files down. "You're impossible. What did you tell the fed? Same old excuse, hung up at work?"

"Where's Lizzy?"

"She dropped me off and headed home, so I guess it's just me and you. You ready?"

I pushed my chair back and stood up. "Let me get a fresh pot of coffee brewed and I'll meet you in the conference room."

"Deal. Bring me a cup too, please. Cream and sugar."

"So you want pudding, not coffee."

She waved me off, took a seat at her desk, and opened her laptop.

We met in the conference room and settled in for a lengthy viewing of mountain life as seen by a tree. I assumed there would be critters: deer, bear, a variety of birds, squirrels and chipmunks scurrying about through the leaves, up and down the trees, and over logs. It would be Animal World until it wasn't, until the cameras were activated by the presence of humans. There might be a variety of those as well: hunters, hikers, game wardens worried about spending their lives in prison. I had high hopes for the latter but was prepared for disappointment.

The animal kingdom came to life, the camera showing the area where William Lance Brown was shot through the heart. When the video first began, I couldn't see what had triggered the motion detector. I studied the screen, but nothing was visible. Then a slight movement on the ground caught my eye. "What is that?" I asked, pointing at the TV.

Josie leaned forward but had no answer. Then it moved again, dashing several feet before stopping and again blending into the forest floor, nearly invisible. I said, "That's a badger!"

"I've never seen one," Josie said. "It's cute."

This was Part I of our movie night spectacular. We had saved the best for last, video shot from the shed where Josie had been held hostage and where Junior Watkins had died at the hands of Warden Jacob Spencer. The badger moved and stopped again, providing more entertainment than I had expected. I said, "Those fat little bastards are mean as hell."

"I think it's cute."

The next frame showed a doe grazing past, taking her time, moving one step at a time without looking up, her tail twitching like a puppy's, giving the impression she was happy. *Why wouldn't she be,* I thought. It seemed peaceful in the soundless video, the whining of distant motorcycles and four-wheelers, the cracks of rifle shots absent from the scene. The deer faced away from the camera's view at first, and Josie said, "Oh, it's a whitetail."

I told her it was a mule deer and explained the difference, but she argued that the white rump is how the species got its name.

"No, the white rump is just that, a white rump. There's no such thing as white rump deer. Its tail is sort of an off-white with a black tip, see? That's a muley. There are no whitetail deer in California, as far as I know. But once you see one, you'll understand how they got their name. Their tails are large, almost pyramid shaped, and the undersides of them are bright white and furry. When it lifts its tail, you can see it a mile away. They're beautiful."

Josie picked up her phone and began thumbing the screen.

"Looking for pictures of them?"

She didn't reply.

I said, "I'm surprised she doesn't have a baby with her," and then I wondered if she hadn't been bred, or if the baby had been harvested by a hungry coyote, or worse yet, a poacher.

"Ah," Josie said, looking up from her phone to the screen just as the doe stepped out of view. "I see now."

The next frame showed a bear in very low light. I noticed the time stamp indicated the following morning, the Saturday after the cameras were installed. The black, medium-sized bear lumbered across the screen and was gone.

Josie said, "Oh my gosh!"

But that was the extent of our big game entertainment, as the next hour or so of viewing showed only small, rodent-type critters scuttling about and the yellow eyes of an unidentified creature in the black of night, a dog-like animal I assumed was either a fox or a coyote. The last scene showed a leprechaun-looking man with two foxes behind him. It was the tech crew sergeant Paul Brady, followed by Josie and Lizzy, the latter two swiveling their heads in all directions as if they were lost. Brady came right at the camera and gave us a close-up of a wiry brow over his intense eye before the screen turned black.

We took a break before starting Part II, and we both went for fresh coffee. As I poured us each a cup, Josie said, "Well, that was entertaining, though disappointing too."

"I didn't expect much there, to be honest. But I have a feeling something might happen at the shed. There were two cameras, right?"

She nodded, gently blowing her coffee.

"I think we're going to have something there, to be honest. The Brown site, I bullshitted him about finding a trail cam. Well, that was a mistake. I wanted to make him nervous—and I did—but, in hindsight, it would have been better to have mentioned that there could be something like that up there that we might have missed. That might have gotten him to go look."

Josie shrugged. "I still sort of expected him to show up there, if for nothing else than to relive his kill."

My head bobbed in agreement.

There were fewer animals to entertain us in Part II, though passing birds provided plenty of footage that had to be reviewed. It occurred to me that if somehow they could have adjusted the sensitivity of the motion detector, they might have dialed it back some.

Part II was actually divided into two parts as well, the first being the view outside of the shed, a wide angle from twenty or so feet away, showing three sides of the dilapidated structure and a perimeter of about thirty feet. The second half would be footage recorded inside the shed. Hopefully, the motion of rats wouldn't activate the cameras, or we'd be here watching until Monday.

Josie watched intently, but her gaze seemed far beyond what was shown on the screen. This probably wasn't the best thing for her, I thought, but it was too late to reconsider her involvement. I would rather have battled the bear we saw in Part I than argue with her about whether or not she should be this involved in the case. Josie had made up her mind the day that Jacob Spencer came and visited her in the hospital and gave her the creeps. It was his demeanor and responses that caused her to consider him a suspect, and that feeling had only gained momentum as the months ticked by.

It was nearly an hour later that we were rewarded for our time and effort. The camera had come to life as Jacob Spencer slid down the mountainside in his tan and green uniform, a rifle in his hand. "What the hell is he doing?"

Josie didn't answer. She leaned in toward the screen, her body rigid, her pulse beating visibly in the veins of her neck.

Spencer stopped at the bottom and brushed himself off while looking around, concern on his face. I had been down that mountainside and I knew from the way he came into view that he must have slipped on his way down. What I didn't know was why he would bring a rifle with him. Maybe he was expecting trouble. He looked around as if somewhere, in the back of his mind, he expected a setup. But apparently cameras weren't something he had considered.

The time stamp showed it was early Sunday morning, 7:10 to be exact. I wondered if the timing was relevant, and concluded he likely took a day to consider his options. I had interviewed him at length Friday night, planting the seed as I mentioned we should go back to the mountain and look around more carefully, more thoroughly. We had also provided him a window of opportunity, Lizzy arguing that she couldn't do it that evening, me saying I didn't want to ruin my weekend plans, and whatever we did could wait until next week. After all, I had said, six months had passed since the ordeal. So it made sense that Spencer had considered his options the rest of Friday night and into Saturday. He must have decided he only had one chance to make sure he hadn't overlooked anything that could tie him to Josie's kidnapping or William Brown's murder, or any detail that would make his case against Junior Watkins as the suspect in both of those crimes that much stronger.

Whatever was about to happen on the screen we were glued to had actually happened five days earlier, but it felt as if we were experiencing it live. It occurred to me that we had taken a big chance not returning for the equipment until today, but then we had no idea for sure when—or even if —Spencer would take the bait. I was grateful that we now had footage of this action on the mountain, our case unfolding in front of our eyes. Josie and I sat glued to the TV and at the edge of our seats, not a sound in the room but occasional deep breaths.

Spencer approached the shed tentatively, rifle in hand, his head working on a swivel.

"Come on, asshole," I whispered, "come on."

"Why did he come down the mountainside rather than riding his four-wheeler around the long way and coming in on the flat?"

It was a good question. "I don't know. Maybe to not leave tracks? What's he wearing, cowboy boots? Shit! That's why he slipped. That son of a bitch is wearing cowboy boots to throw us off. I wouldn't be surprised to find out they didn't even fit him, that he was smart enough to wear a different size."

"You think he's that clever?"

"I think he's stupid like a fox."

Spencer was at the threshold now. Josie said, "What's he doing?"

He looked around again before pushing the door open and stepping inside, the rifle leading the way.

"Jesus Christ, you don't think he has someone else—"

It hadn't occurred to me. "No… No way. Could he?"

He was out of view now, but the footage from inside would have to wait until we viewed everything from the outside camera first.

Josie said, "We need to fast forward, see what he's doing."

It was tempting. "Remember, all this happened five days ago. Let's take it slow and methodical."

She huffed, keeping her gaze glued to the screen.

The next scene showed Spencer exit the shack, without his rifle. I frowned at the TV. "Now what the hell's he doing? He forgot his rifle, probably set it down to do something. He'll be going back in."

Josie didn't say anything, and she didn't move an inch.

Spencer moved back toward the mountain, looking left and right as he walked.

"Your rifle, dumbass," I said.

Then he was out of our view and the footage moved to a new frame, the time stamp showing it was much later in the day. Two deer sauntered by, a doe and her fawn, picking at the ground and moving slowly, relaxed. I said, "What the hell?"

"More deer."

191

"No, I mean, look at the time stamp; that's almost eight hours later, after Spencer left. He never went back for his rifle."

"He will realize he forgot it and come back for it, don't you think?"

I didn't know what to think. My brows crowded together, and I squinted at the new scene. This frame showed the onset of darkness, and I noted the time: 7:35 p.m., dusk. A covey of quail joined two on the ground, and I realized they were what had triggered the camera. The next frame showed daylight. It was the next day; Mr. Coyote late for dinner, the quail no longer there. He sniffed at the ground and paused at the sight of the shed before moving along.

It took us another forty minutes to finish with the week of outside footage, and Spencer never came back for his rifle.

"Interesting," I said.

Josie looked at me, the TV screen no longer a point of focus. "What?"

"Why would he leave that rifle there?"

Her brown eyes grew bigger. "Because it's the murder weapon. That's what he killed Brown with."

"And he's going to leave it there now, like we missed it somehow? That doesn't make sense."

"The floor in there is rotted and some of the boards are warped enough you could pull them up with your hands. Trust me, I studied every inch of that place. Maybe, since you mentioned going back up and seeing if anything was missed, he's banking on us tearing the place apart. If that's the case, he puts the rifle under the floor and voila, we find the murder weapon in the same place where Watkins allegedly stashed things."

I pictured Josie tied to the floor inside the dingy shed but said nothing. This was tough on her, I knew, but it seemed now she had been right about Spencer and that the pieces were coming together. For cops, there was one way to heal an open wound, and that was to toss the offending party behind bars and let the gate slam shut behind him. She needed this.

"Well," I said, "let's go see the conclusion then. If you're right—if that prick hides that rifle in the shed—I'm buying the cocktails tonight."

"If I'm right, we're heading north."

I shook my head. "Too risky. It won't go anywhere; he'll see to it. He wants us to find that, *if* you're right. We'll go tomorrow morning. I'll get ahold of Floyd, see if he wants to come with us."

Josie said, "You don't think we should wait and see what's on the rest of the video?"

"Either way, we know that rifle's in there. We're going tomorrow morning for sure."

"And you think we need backup."

I was texting Floyd and didn't look up when I answered, because I was about to lie to her, and I wasn't going to look her in the eyes when I did. I knew that she was probably thinking that if it were me and Floyd, or me and Farris, we would have just gone; but since it's me and Josie, I thought it best to have Floyd come along. With my eyes still on my phone, I said, "No, but we can always use the entertainment." Then I hit send: *I need you to go with us back up to the mountain in the morning. Be at the office at seven.*

Three dots raced back and forth for a moment before his reply popped up. It was a middle finger emoji. I answered, *thanks,* and told Josie he was looking forward to it.

30

At 6:45 a.m. Floyd came through the back door of the station in boots and a Homicide Bureau polo tucked into his jeans. He wore his gun and badge on one side of his belt and an extra magazine on the other. I was dressed similarly. He beelined to my desk and said, "What'd you come up with? It better be good."

The door flew open and Josie hurried in, also wearing jeans and boots, but her ensemble was topped with a red flannel shirt, untucked and with the sleeves turned up. Oversized sunglasses covering her face.

"I'll fill you in on the way up," I told him. "Let's go."

I pushed out of my chair as Josie drew near. "You ready?"

"Let's go," she said.

"How are you feeling this morning?"

Floyd said, "Oh, did you two go out last night? I noticed you were working late, given the time you texted me."

"I'm fine," Josie said. "Anxious."

I gathered my briefcase in one hand, keys and ball cap in the other. Casual attire required downgraded headwear. As we headed for the door, I told Floyd, "Yeah, we had a few indeed. We had cause for celebration."

Floyd pushed the door open and waited until Josie and I passed through it. Crossing the parking lot, he said, "You're driving, right?"

"Yep."

"So what's the cause for celebration?" he asked, moving toward the passenger side.

Josie said, "You can sit up front with your sister."

"You sure?" Floyd said, as he joined me up front. "Let's hear it, Dickie."

"We've got footage of Spencer at the shed," I said, pulling out of the parking lot and gunning it toward the freeway. The traffic was light early on Saturday morning. "And he planted a rifle inside. Josie's convinced it's our murder weapon from the William Brown case, and I think she might be right."

He frowned. "Why the hell would he do that?"

"He pulled a board up from the floor and tucked it underneath. When interviewing Spencer last week, I said to Farris that we needed to get back up there and search the place better, hoping to plant the seed. He apparently took the bait. He obviously wants us to find the rifle and match it to the Brown murder, and then all the pieces fit together just the way he's been saying all along. Watkins killed Brown. Watkins ran Josie and Tommy off the road, and held Josie captive in the shed until Spencer found them and saved her. See, he thinks this puts a bow on it. He's going to shit when he finds out we have video of him planting the murder weapon."

Floyd looked over his shoulder. "Good work, Josie."

"Hey, this has been a team effort," she said. "I'm just glad it's panning out."

He said, "It might be a team effort now, but it was nothing until you spurred it on. Dickie here thought that douchebag Spencer was a cool dude, and a hero. I never liked him."

It was always fun to argue with Floyd, but he was right, I had been blinded by the game warden angle and it was Josie's great instinct that had put Spencer in our sights and driven the case forward. I glanced in my rearview mirror. Though her eyes were concealed behind the shades, I could see she had met my gaze. "He's right, Josie, this is all yours. I honestly couldn't be prouder to have you as a partner."

She cracked a slight smile. I looked away, back to the business ahead of me, and we started north in silence.

We were fifteen minutes from the office, sailing north, our progress unimpeded by traffic as the sun quickly rose from the east, lighting a crystal-blue spring day. The forecast called for highs in the eighties, the thought of which made me sweat. Floyd turned in his seat again and glanced over his shoulder. "Hey, did you guys hear about Lizzy?"

I glanced over but didn't respond. How could Floyd have already known? And how was he not sworn to secrecy by whoever told him?

Josie said, "Yes. How did you know? She was keeping it quiet."

I frowned, staring straight ahead. How did everybody know? I guessed: "Farris."

Floyd shook his head. "Nope. I have sources; you know that, Dickie. Nothing happens at the bureau without me knowing about it. Speaking of, did you guys hear about Lieutenant Roberts getting popped for domestic violence?"

"Wait," I said, "how did you guys hear about Lizzy? Farris told me and I was sworn to secrecy."

"Lizzy told me yesterday," Josie said. "We spent all day together, and she needed to talk about it. I think it was good for her. We had a good cry together and then we were able to laugh a little and she knows we all have her back. Also, she knows Farris told you."

I shook my head. "This place is worse than a hair salon. What about you?" I asked Floyd.

"I am not able to reveal my sources," he said.

"He's full of shit—everyone knows." Josie said.

"How's everyone know?" I begged. "I mean, why do I get the secret-squirrel-don't-say-anything shit, and everyone else already knows?"

Josie said, "Because you got it from Farris, and he's probably the only one in the whole place who hasn't told ten people. When did he tell you?"

"Yesterday," I said. "I think it was a similar situation to you and Lizzy spending the day together—he needed to talk about it to someone. Anyway, what's the prognosis? I didn't ask him for any details. Is it some type of girl thing, breast cancer or something?"

Floyd was shaking his head as Josie said, "No, it's leukemia."

"Ugh. That's bad, right?"

"It's not good," Josie said, "but she's young and strong, and she can beat it. We all need to rally around her. It's all about staying focused like with any other fight for your life. There will be ups and downs, good days and bad ones, and really bad ones too; that's when she'll really need us. All of us."

Floyd turned his head and gazed through the window. Josie continued looking straight ahead, her eyes always there when I checked the mirror. The mood was dark now, the tension thick. I drew a deep breath and let it out slowly. "So what's the deal with Roberts? Domestic violence, huh?"

He turned to face me again. "Yeah, apparently him and his old lady don't get along very well—haven't for ages but have stayed together for the kids. Anyway, I guess he was home on his day off last weekend, drinking beer, avoiding her, and she started in on him about his drinking. It was like ten in the morning, and he was cleaning the pool. I guess he basically told her to get off his jock, go inside, leave him be. I mean, the guy just wants to be left alone outside with his pool and a beer, but she's all over his shit. At some point, they start arguing, and she ends up getting thrown in the pool. She called nine-one-one and Chino took him to jail. They hate L.A. cops out there."

"They booked him?"

"Yep."

"Jesus. I guess that's why I haven't seen him around. Never heard anything about it though. Is the department going to can him?"

"He's suspended but I heard he's filing his papers. He was only a couple years from topping out anyway."

Josie said, "That's too bad, but you can't put your hands on your spouse. He should've known better."

"But did she allege he hit her, or what? I mean, ending up in the pool doesn't sound like much. Shit, she might have tried to grab his beer and lost her balance."

Floyd chuckled. "He should have used his one phone call to get your advice."

I shook my head. "Well, that's too bad, but I'm more concerned with Lizzy right now than anything else. Farris is taking it hard." I almost said he had hinted about us being partners but realized that would open a whole other can of worms. Josie still had plenty to contend with from her ordeal, and the last thing she needed was to worry about losing her partner. Besides, as much as I liked Farris, I wouldn't trade Josie for him; not if I could help it, anyway.

We continued on in silence for a while and were nearly to Santa Clarita when I spoke again. "Anyone want anything to eat or drink, need a potty break?"

"I'm good," said Floyd.

"No, let's get up there," added Josie.

"Okay, let's do it then. Oh, I almost forgot to tell you, Kennedy from Gorman's going to meet us up there and bring two four-wheelers with him. He said he can drop the trailer up above and drive his Bronco in from the bottom, and we can follow on the four-wheelers."

"Why wouldn't we just ride with him in his Bronco?" Josie asked. "That's what we did to retrieve the cameras."

I glanced at her in the mirror. "Phil Gentry and Doc Provost are coming from the lab. They'll meet us at the pullout just off the freeway where we had the command post before."

"No shit? What's Doc coming along for? She's so hot."

"Gentry's going to handle photos and evidence—that rifle when we recover it, for one—and I guess Doc is coming along in the event we need to lift shoe impressions. She loves all that casting shit, though honestly I think more than anything she just wanted the overtime."

"She loves us," Floyd said.

"Anyway, they'll have a shitload of equipment to bring with them, so we figured they can ride in the Bronco with Kennedy."

"That's cool," Floyd said, "though if Doc changes her mind, I'd be happy to have her double up with me on the four-wheeler. I'd even ride bitch for her."

Josie said, "Same."

Floyd whipped his head around to look at her, excitement, hope, and joy written all over his face.

I chuckled and held her gaze in the mirror. "You learn something new about your partner almost every day."

"So it seems," she said.

A HALF HOUR LATER WE WERE GATHERED WITH KENNEDY AND THE CRIME lab crew on a turnout at the bottom of the mountain. From there we started the slow drive up to the ridge above Josie's shed, which is how I referred to it outside of her presence. Kennedy led the way and we brought up the rear, sandwiching the white crime lab van between us. At the top, we pulled our vehicles to the side of the road where—if you were on the passenger side, and you strained to see deep into the ravine below—you could see the old miner's shed that held bad memories, dark secrets, and now, hopefully, evidence of murder. My blood was pumping with anticipation and excitement.

We unloaded from the car and Josie paused at the edge, looking down. I stepped over to her side. "You okay?"

She nodded, and then turned away from the view below. "Yeah, let's do this."

I went over and offered to help Kennedy offload the four-wheelers. Floyd continued past us and beelined to Doc Provost, and I could hear his cheerful greeting as he turned on the charm. Phil Gentry, always serious about his work, was piling equipment bags over each shoulder at the side of his van. I called out to Floyd, "Hey, when you get done flirting with Doc, how about giving Phil a hand?"

He flipped me the bird and Josie started toward Phil. "I've got it," she said.

Soon we were caravanning down a long, winding dirt road that would take us a couple of miles beyond the shed before we would be able to drive up to it from the bottom. I rode behind Floyd and kept my head down to avoid the dust from Kennedy's Bronco ahead of us. Josie rode solo on her four-wheeler; for some reason I had felt it was more appropriate to double up with Floyd than to be nuzzled that close to Josie, though I would have preferred it the other way.

At the bottom, we stopped a hundred feet shy of the shed and assembled on foot near the front of Kennedy's Bronco. Gentry went to work snapping pictures. I pointed toward the embankment behind the shed, the steep hillside that, if you climbed straight up, would take you back to our vehicles. "Over there's where Spencer came down."

Gentry and Provost followed me in an arching half-circle to the point where Spencer was first seen coming down the mountain on foot. This allowed us to see all we needed without disturbing any potential evidence, such as his tracks from there to the shed and back. Once there, we all began scanning the ground as we moved slowly in the direction of the shed. Whenever a shoe impression was located, an evidence marker was placed on the ground next to it, and we continued forward. It was a long, slow process, but one that we all knew was necessary; you never relied on any one piece of evidence in a murder case. Though we had video of Spencer going into the shed with the rifle we hoped to recover, we wanted to strengthen our case against him with physical evidence.

We stopped at the front of the shed, each of us studying the path we had just covered. There were eleven markers showing the trail, each displaying a unique number, one through eleven. Every impression would be photographed and referenced by its assigned number, and then careful consideration would be given as to which—if any—of the impressions were worthy of casting. We knew from the video that Spencer had worn cowboy-style boots, and he likely did so to minimize the evidence of shoe impressions. However, he had unknowingly made our job easier because any other shoe impressions in the vicinity were those of hiking-style boots, impressions left from hunters or hikers or members of the Watkins clan who perhaps visited the site on occasion to mourn the death of Junior.

There seemed to be a level of hesitation, the anticipation mixed with doubt that each of us likely carried. All too often these efforts didn't turn out the way we would have hoped. Nothing was certain. According to the video, there would be a rifle under the floor inside that shed. If our instincts hadn't betrayed us, that rifle would soon be identified as the weapon used in the William Lance Brown murder. There was a lot riding on the next few moments, and the buildup was similar to the kind felt before one jumped into a pool of icy water.

Josie said, "Let's do this," and started for the door.

31

Early Monday morning, Rich Farris and I met at the office and took his car to the Torrance courthouse. He looked tired, his eyes were bloodshot, and he reeked of booze. Other than solemn greetings and idle chat, little was discussed until I offered a recap of the weekend. I told him about the video and how Friday night Josie and I had sat in the conference room watching Jacob Spencer plant a rifle beneath the floor of the shed on Liebre Mountain, and how, early the next day, we went up to get it, us and Floyd and Gentry and Provost from the lab. I told him that a couple of boards were left loose—obviously loose, Spencer making sure we wouldn't miss it—and that the rifle was found beneath the floor.

"It was a Ruger Mini-14, their Ranch model. Two-two-three, same caliber we pulled out of the tree, the bullet that killed William Brown."

Farris slouched in his seat behind the wheel, his shoulder braced against the door. He didn't glance over during the conversation, his red eyes straight ahead on the road. He said, "No shit, huh?"

"Gentry was going to walk it down to Firearms first thing this morning. We're betting it's going to be the murder weapon; why else would he put it there?"

"Who's the gun come back to?"

"Serial number's been removed, which is interesting."

Farris sipped at the coffee he had brought along. "Does Fish and Game carry Mini-14s? Maybe it's a department gun, previously issued to him. I'm sure you've already run him through ATF to see if he's ever owned one."

"Yeah, he hasn't. That's a good thought on the department gun. But you would think he would have to report his as missing or stolen."

Farris looked over. "There you go. See if that completes the circle, a report where he claims the rifle was stolen from his truck, probably up there on the mountain where that kid and his family lived."

"Watkins."

"Yeah, the compound."

Getting Farris into the hunt seemed to have awakened him; maybe it took his mind off the heavy issues he was likely pondering. I had little doubt Lizzy was on his mind. I said, "That's a good thought, Rich; I'll be sure to check it out."

"What about prints on the gun?"

"Gentry was going to handle that before taking it to Firearms, but I expect it will have been wiped clean."

Farris seemed to ponder it a moment. "The problem is—or maybe the brilliance of it is—if Spencer has reported his gun stolen, his prints on it won't do you any good."

"Yeah, I thought about that too, Rich. The thing is, if there aren't any prints on it at all, or if Watkins's prints aren't on it, that's pretty suspicious too."

He took another sip of coffee. "True, circumstantial evidence."

"Guess what else we found?"

Farris looked over, drooping eyelids lazily blinking over bloodshot eyes. "Bigfoot."

"Well, yeah, but I mean in the shed, under the floor."

He shrugged. "Tell me."

"Six kilos of meth."

His eyes popped wide. "What's that about? Do you think Spencer planted that too, make the kid look like a dope dealer?"

I shook my head. "No, I don't. Spencer didn't have the idea to plant anything until we put the thought in his head. And of course, we don't have any video of him or anyone else taking the dope into that shed during that week."

"So what do you think?" he asked.

"I think he popped a couple of loose boards and had the surprise of his life. He might have even felt like he struck gold, because now we'll see that Watkins was a no-good dirty little dope dealer and a killer."

"So you think the dope was Watkins's?"

"Yeah, Rich, I do. And if we didn't have video of Spencer planting that rifle, we'd be screwed trying to put a case on him. But what this does for me is it answers a question that's been nagging at me for six months, making me continually question the Spencer angle we were working with, and that is how and why Watkins knew that Josie was in that shed unless he put her there. Well, it looks like Watkins *was* dealing dope after all, and that the shed was his stash pad. I think he stumbled upon Josie when he was going for his dope. And I think Spencer didn't know what to do with her once he had put her in there, but then maybe decided to just let her die there, because he should have killed her but didn't have the balls."

"The same guy that executed your dude against the tree? He didn't have the balls?"

"I don't know, Rich...maybe he just couldn't pull the trigger on a woman. Who knows?"

"And your boy on the tree, you think he was dealing dope too?"

I shook my head. "Nope, I think he was poaching. For Spencer, I'm pretty sure that's what this is all about. I think he hates poachers and felt some sort of godlike authority on *his* mountain to enforce the laws as he saw fit. It reminds me of that story about the deputy who shot the unarmed burglar back in the seventies, the dude who had a hard-on for thieves and had said they should all be shot—and then he shot one."

"And he went to prison for murder, too," Farris added.

"Yeah, he did. Maybe him and Spencer can be cellies someday soon."

We were off the freeway now and just a few miles from the courthouse. Farris glanced at his watch, and said, "I hope this goes well this morning. I'd like to get this case off my desk before—"

I waited, and after a long moment, he glanced at me and continued. "I talked to Lizzy last night. She's coming in today to tell Stover she's going out on medical leave. They're going to start treatment on her this week, and I guess the doctor warned her that they're going to go at it aggressively, and it's going to take a toll on her."

I pictured Farris hanging up the phone last night and gravitating toward the liquor cabinet.

He said, "I don't know what they're going to do with me, leave me as an extra, or put me with someone else. I'm not going to take a new guy, I can tell you that. I'll tell Stover that in no uncertain terms. Put me back in Unsolveds if you have to, but I'm not taking any more new kids. Hell, I don't care if they put me in Missing Persons."

"How much longer are you planning to go, Rich?"

We were at a red light, waiting, a block from the courthouse. He glanced over. "I was thinking I'd do another three or four, but now I'm not so sure. Maybe I'm just tired, need a vacation."

"Take some time off, Rich, let your batteries recharge. All this shit will still be here when you get back."

He nodded, and then the light turned green. As we pulled into the lot, he said, "Where are we on the surfer boys' murders?"

I knew he was talking about Bellovich and the Bailey brothers, though none of us had ever referred to them as the surfer boys. "Floyd and Mongo are running down leads to find the rape victim. They've discovered she changed her name, and now it's just a matter of finding her. So far everything's coming back to a PO box in Hollywood."

He parked in the far north parking lot among other cop cars and courthouse employees reluctantly arriving to start their weeks. As we walked across the lot, I said, "I'm going to pop in and see Judge Arnesen and have him sign my warrant return for the Bellovich case, the crime scene warrant."

"I'll meet you down in lockup," he said.

We approached the front and skirted the line of people being screened for weapons and contraband, flashed our badges and went separate directions inside without further conversation. Riding the elevator to the third floor, my thoughts were on Rich Farris and Lizzy Marchesano. It was funny how one could be going through life swimmingly and suddenly something shoots up from the murky waters and takes a giant bite of you.

The doors slid open and I stepped into the hall, my wingtips clacking against the tile as I made my way to Department M, the words of a favorite sergeant ringing in my ears: *Tough times don't last, tough people do.*

After Judge Arnesen put his John Hancock on the bottom of my Return to Search, I filed it and the original warrant at the clerk's office and obtained a warrant number. I had intentionally not filed it when it was issued in order to avoid publicity before the next of kin were notified. It was old news now—*Mayor's kid found murdered in his home*, the papers had said, *found by the girlfriend*—and ever since then, everyone had been speculating about the killer loose in Rancho Palos Verdes, few outside our bureau knowing it was one of a series.

I found Farris in the break room next to lockup where buses were arriving with inmates who had appearances in the various departments of Torrance Court. Dewayne Lewis and Johnny Burns had already arrived, according to Farris, and were enjoying a reunion down the hall from where we waited, in a quiet room away from the masses of inmates.

"I wish we could listen in live," I said, helping myself to a cup of coffee before joining Farris, who sat at a round table looking at his phone.

"I say we give them one hour, go rattle their cages, and then give them another hour," Farris said, and glanced at his watch. "Be done and out of here before the noon break."

"When do we get the recording?"

"Tech crew is going to collect their equipment as soon as we're done, and they'll have a copy of it ready for us by tomorrow."

"So we have to wait. I hate waiting."

Farris shrugged, set his phone on the table and leaned back in his plastic chair. "I've got nothing but time, my brother, until I run out of it." He forced a smile, stretched his legs out in front of him and clasped his hands behind his head, closing his eyes.

An hour later we popped open the heavy door and stepped into the cold, windowless concrete room. Burns and Lewis sat together on the only bench, each wearing cotton L.A. County Jail–issued pants and shirts. Burns, having come from Wayside, was dressed in orange, and Lewis was representing Men's Central Jail in blue. Being Blood gang members, neither of them would ever wear blue—the color of their rival Crips—of their own accord.

Farris nodded to Big Smoke, Johnny Burns. It was subtle, but no doubt picked up by his homie, Dewayne Lewis. Then, pointing a finger directly at Lewis, Farris said, "Alright Eight Ball, let's have a little chat."

Lewis glared at Burns as he slowly stood up from the bench and shuffled toward us. Burns averted his eyes, focusing on the concrete floor. We escorted Mr. Lewis—the suspected shooter of Jackie Melvin Lowe—to another room down the hall where three chairs had been placed in the center of an otherwise empty chamber. Farris pointed toward one of the chairs and said, "Sit."

Once we were all seated, Farris handed me the mock case file whereon Lewis and Burns were listed as suspects. Notations on the file indicated the weapon used, and that it been recovered, though it hadn't. Farris began with the basics: *name, birth date, where do you stay when you're on the streets? That's a* very different question than asking where they live, a question to which the answer is always their mama's house regardless of how many years ago they stopped living there. *What do they call you? What set are you claiming?* Because every gang has sets or cliques, and to know somebody was a Blood was as non-specific as knowing someone was a cop. And finally, *So tell us about how your big homie Low Boy got himself killed.*

Lewis sputtered the answers, licking his lips and continually looking at the case file I had propped on my lap with the written details comfortably displayed for his viewing pleasure. After a half hour of receiving mostly lies in response to Farris's questions, we took him back to the bugged room and left him and his homie alone to work things out.

On the way back to the office, Floyd called and said the PO box in Hollywood was a dead end as far as finding an address for Kishi Takahashi, a.k.a. Sunako Hisakawa, because apparently, they didn't require a hard address from their customers who rent mailboxes. "There is a phone number listed though, so maybe we can track her down with the number."

"Yeah, maybe give it to Tyrone, have him see what he can come up with without our having to write another warrant."

He said it sounded like a plan and they would see us at the office a while later.

Farris had gotten quiet again once the work was finished and we were headed back to the office, where he would find himself partner-less and where his future was uncertain for the time being. I felt for him, being similar in nature, the type to resist change. When I returned to work after being shot, only to find Floyd was no longer my partner and that the chances of us being back together were slim, I had slipped into a depression. Fortunately, I had picked up an interesting case with Ray Cortez, who turned out to be a perfect fit for me at the time. Before long, I was back to feeling good about my position in the Homicide Bureau. Then Ray was sent to Unsolveds and Josie came to me with baggage and a reputation and I thought that was going to be the end of me. Similar to how Rich Farris felt now, I had had thoughts of being a loner in Unsolveds or Missing Persons or anywhere other than working the floor with a new partner who I just knew would never work out. Boy, had I been wrong about Josie.

"Everything happens for a reason," I finally said, breaking the heavy silence in the car.

Farris never took his eyes from the road, and after a long moment, he said, "Yeah, well, that doesn't make it any better, or any easier to accept."

32

My day began at STARS, where I picked up a USB flash drive that contained the audio recording of our arranged meeting between Dewayne Lewis and Johnny Burns at the Torrance courthouse. I was excited to listen to it but had no way to play it during my drive to the office, so instead I thought about Kishi Takahashi and wondered how we were going to find her. So far, she was the best lead in our Bellovich case. She was the *only* lead in our Bellovich case.

I called Floyd. "You on your way in?"

"Yeah, sitting in traffic; what about you?"

"Same. Just picked up my recording from yesterday's deal in Torrance, looking forward to hearing what's on it. It'd be nice to have clear audio of those two assholes talking about whacking Low Boy; I could use a break in a case."

"What did you find out about the rifle?"

"I'm hoping we hear back from Firearms today. And I was hoping *you'd* come up with something on Kishi Takahashi."

"Yeah, well, those leads keep slamming into walls, Dickie. I've got a call in to a connection who can get employment, maybe track her down to a job. Everybody's got to earn a living."

The idea of her living in Hollywood, under a name other than that of her family, caused me to wonder just how she might have been making that living. "Hey, you said you've checked criminal history under the new name, right?"

"Yeah, Dickie, I did. There was nothing."

"What about checking with LAPD Hollywood, see if they know her?"

"Why would they know her if she has no record? This isn't Mayberry RFD, dipshit."

I had an image of a petite Japanese girl in heels wearing a tight skirt and sequined blouse, peddling her goods on the Boulevard. "Maybe she's been F.I.'d on the strip. If there's one thing LAPD does well, it's their field interviews. Those assholes write down the names and horsepower on every single person they contact who doesn't earn a citation or a trip to the pokey. Then, their secretaries put all of that information into a database, which can be a wealth of information. I'd say we try that, see if something pops."

"You think she's a hooker."

"I'm just suggesting they might've contacted her. Or, I guess, wait and see if anything pops for employment. If there's nothing there, though, I say there's a chance LAPD's made contact with her. *A chance.*"

Floyd sounded unenthusiastic about it. "Yeah, I don't know, Dickie... It seems to me if she's working the streets, she'd have some arrests."

My image of the girl shifted from the streets to a hotel lobby. "Maybe she's a call girl."

"You know, Dickie, there are ways for a girl to make a living other than working as a hooker."

"Like what? I'm not talking about all girls—I'm talking about a girl who changed her name, who lives in Hollywood, who severed ties with her own family, and who lost her virginity to three assholes on a beach, all of whom have suddenly become victims of murder. I say that screams hooker."

"Maybe she's in a band, or she's a tattoo artist, or an actress."

"I'm at the office now. Let me know when you get the results of that employment search and then we'll talk."

"Yeah, I'm at East L.A., gassing up. Think I'll get the trustees to wash my car while I'm here. I'll see you in a few, dickhead."

I disconnected, backed into a spot behind the bureau, and locked it up.

I had nowhere to be today and I was glad of it. Sometimes the commuting around the county was the worst part of the job. There were times when the number of miles I put on my county car in one day equaled a trip to Vegas.

Inside, the bureau hummed with activity, investigators busy on phones and computers and talking murder among themselves. I set my briefcase and hat on my desk and started on my usual arrival loop: the head, the kitchen for coffee, and then the front desk to check my mailbox and look at the board. I was always curious to see how many murders had come in overnight and if there was anything interesting. I was two-thirds through the route when Joe Castro joined me in the hallway on the way to the front desk.

"What's happening, Joe?"

Castro was one of the veterans in the bureau, a former narcotics detective whose appearance had transformed from that of a heroin-addicted *vato* in long baggy shorts and oversized button-up shirts, to a distinguished executive who wore fashionable suits and ties and kept his full head of gray hair and matching mustache neatly trimmed. His speech belied his new appearance, a mix of street and hip with an occasional bit of Spanish flair: "Nada, man, what's happening? Where's your sexy partner?"

I looked around as if I had lost her. "I haven't seen her. How's your West Hollywood balcony case going? The sheriff still up your ass on that one?"

We had stopped at the wall of mail slots, and each of us was tending to whatever contents we found. I had a note handwritten on a sheet from one of the message pads used by the front desk personnel; Mr. Bellovich's personal assistant was inquiring as to the progress we were making on the investigation. I also had a stack of subpoenas. As the investigating officer, the D.A.'s office would routinely expect us to serve our witnesses and prepare them for court. Their office had its own investigators, but they were spread thin, shared by nearly a thousand prosecutors across the county. But also, homicide cases were different: the relationships between investigators and their witnesses were generally bound tighter than those in other cases, and, at least with the sheriff's department, the investigators were very hands-on, involved in every aspect of the judicial process.

Castro looked up from the handful of papers he had pulled from his slot. "We're done with it. Suicide. All the hullabaloo for nothing, as it turns out. It was fun making some politicians sweat in the meantime though."

"I bet. What, married councilmen having cocktails with their young, sexy constituents at the hotel bars?"

"Or hookers."

"No shit?"

He shrugged. "I think so, at least a high likelihood. And of course, none of the statesmen remembers our victim, though a bartender and a waitress both put her in the bar, mingling, just a few hours before she took the plunge."

"How'd you figure out it was a suicide?"

Joe's partner, Raul Martinez—Joe's polar opposite: short, overweight, sloppy, cheap dresser—rounded the corner. "Partner, we've got to roll. Officer-involved shooting in El Monte, we've got the assist."

Joe clapped me on the shoulder. "See ya, Dickie," and started back toward the squad room, his partner trailing behind him.

I followed behind, working my way toward my desk, subpoenas and message in hand, thankful I wasn't rolling out on the officer-involved shooting case. I hoped no cops had been injured and that was all the thought I gave it. Our bureau had anywhere from three hundred to five hundred cases come through each year; you couldn't concern yourself with all the cases assigned to others. I arrived at my desk to see Josie had snuck in during my tour of the office.

"What's up, kiddo?"

"Nothing, pops. What's up with you?"

"Pops, huh?" I chuckled. "I've got the audio from yesterday—was looking around for Farris to see if he wanted to listen to it with me."

She glanced over both shoulders. "I haven't seen him. I'd like to listen to it though."

"Let's do it in the conference room where it's quiet and we won't be disturbed."

I started in that direction and Josie grabbed her coffee from her desk and followed. "Have you heard from Firearms?"

I glanced over my shoulder and paused, waiting for her to come alongside me. "No, not yet. I'm hoping by the end of the day."

The look on her face revealed her anxiety about the situation; we were on the verge of breaking her case and the William Brown case wide open, and we both felt it. But she had more of a personal investment than me, and she was clearly more on edge about the results of the rifle examination.

In the conference room, I placed my laptop at the end of a long table and inserted the USB drive. I opened up the audio file and hit play, and we both leaned back and waited. The muted sounds of keys jangling, doors opening and closing, and the rustling of movement was all there was to hear for the first ten minutes. I could picture one of the two inmates waiting alone in the bleak cell, and I wished we had been able to have video to watch as well. My eyes grew heavy and I had started to drift off when the sound of a door jolted me. After it closed, the conversation began.

Wassup?

Tell me.

Shee-it, I can't call it. You got all the money.

(laughs)

Man, they got me up in here for arraignment. I ain't got no mother-fuckin' cases down here, Torrance.

Check it out, dawg, they came at me on that shit with yo' boy—

Who came atchya, man?

Homicide, nigga, who else? Some brutha in threads and a white dude with a hat, like muthafuckin' Bogart, Dick-fuckin'-Tracy.

Gaw-awd-dam.

Mmhmm. Put it to me, man, like, yeah, we know you were there—some shit—like, you know, like they got some nigga puttin' it out there.

Someone snitchin'?

I paused it. "The dude with the high-pitched voice, sounds like Eddie Murphy when he gets excited, that's the driver, Johnny Burns, a.k.a. Big Smoke. The other one's our shooter, Dewayne Lewis, a.k.a. Eight Ball. That's according to Farris's source."

"Eight Ball, huh?" said Josie. "They call him that because he's a junkie, or because he's a smalltime dealer?"

"Maybe both."

I pushed the play button.

Must be, man. How else they come up with yo' name and mines?

They brought me up?

Nigga it right on the folder, yo' name, mines, the fool, and then it say they got the gat.

What! How they got the gat? Who you leave it wit'? I tole you get it gone when you dropped me at Shanay's pad.

I made a note: *Shanay—shooter went to her house after 187.*

I left it with T-Loc, and that little nigga he got runnin' 'round wit' him, that little cockeyed nigga be lookin' at you and lookin' at another mutha-fucka too.

(laughing)

You mean, uh, what dat nigga name? Uh, hang on, hang on... Don't they call 'im Lil' Roo, or some shit?

More notes: *Gun to T-Loc and Lil' Roo—cockeyed Male Black.*

Yeah, dat's it. Damn, nigga, how they get the gat? You better check wit' yo' lil' homie and say wassup, find out if that muthafucka be the snitch, have that shit handled, man, and I don't mean after a while, neither. Gawdam, man.

The sound of rattling keys stopped the conversation, and then a door was opened.

Eight Ball, out here.

"That was Farris," I said.

Josie nodded.

The door slammed closed and there was nothing but the occasional groan and sounds of rustling for the next half hour. Then more sounds of keys and the door and shuffling about. When the door closed again, the conversation started but abruptly stopped.

What they want wit'—

I waited, listening intently while watching the time move on the audio player. I turned up the volume and turned my ear to my laptop. Josie scooted closer and watched, cocking her head as well. After several moments, I retreated.

"They quit talking," I said.

"Eight Ball's smarter than he looks," Josie replied.

"He'd almost have to be."

33

As Josie and I walked through the office, returning to our desks, I spotted Rich Farris coming out of the captain's office looking none too happy. He saw us and came over.

"Everything okay?"

He shrugged. "He wanted to talk to me about Lizzy. What's up?"

"Nothing, just finished listening to those two knuckleheads." I held up the USB drive. "You want to hear it before it goes to the secretaries?"

He shook his head. "Nah, I'll catch the transcript. What's the take-away? Anything good?"

"I think so. They definitely talked about the case. They took the bait about the gun being recovered, and that had them plenty worried. They dropped a couple names that might lead us to it."

He nodded, signaling me to continue. I referenced my notebook: "T-Loc, Lil' Roo, and some hoochie mama named Shanay-nay. I'll run them through CalGangs and get them ID'd. See if any of them are on probation or parole, and if not, maybe we can write a warrant to go after the gun."

"Sounds good, man," Farris said, though his tone indicated no enthusiasm. "I'm going to head out of here for now, take the rest of the day off. Give me a call if you need anything."

With that, Rich Farris turned and left. Josie looked at me and said, "He's not doing well."

I thought of how I might be handling it if...*if.* "No, I suppose he isn't."

Josie and I returned to our desks and we both automatically checked our voicemails, each of us hoping for a message from Firearms.

"Did you hear from the crime lab?" she asked.

"No, you?"

She shook her head and opened her laptop. I did the same, going through my mail for the next ten minutes. The situation with Lizzy and the effect it was having on Rich Farris weighed heavily on my mind. Josie likely shared that burden, while also fretting about the report we were awaiting from Firearms. To top it off, there had been an officer-involved shooting, and although those of us who were not involved in its investigation appeared to carry on business as usual, the idea that one of *us* had just been involved in a potentially deadly encounter was an additional, unspoken heaviness.

I pushed my chair back from my desk and spun it a quarter turn to face Josie. "I'm going to go check with the desk about that officer-involved, see what the status is and ask if they need any help out there."

"I think I'll put a call in to Firearms," Josie said, "make sure they haven't forgotten us."

Just as I began to step away, her desk phone rang. I paused and listened to her side of a conversation: "Detective Sanchez... Yes... Oh, great, thank you, yes, we've been hoping to hear from you... Okay... umm...yeah. Okay." She looked up at me and tucked the phone beneath her chin. "We need to run up to the crime lab."

I retrieved my hat and keys from my desk.

Josie said into the phone, "Fifteen minutes."

She hung up and looked at me for a long, silent moment.

"What is it?" I asked.

"It doesn't sound like good news. They want to show us the results, apparently."

She was right, that didn't sound good. The report should be like the results of a pregnancy test: you either are or are not pregnant. The bullet that passed through William Lance Brown's heart was either fired from Spencer's rifle, or it wasn't. The exception to that simplification would occur if there were not sufficient markings on the projectile for comparison. But that was not the case. We had known for months that the evidence-held projectile recovered from the tree did, in fact, have adequate rifling characteristics to determine the type of weapon it had been fired from, and also to match it to the murder weapon if it was ever recovered. I tried to stay positive. "If it was no match, they'd just say so."

Josie shot me a glance but didn't respond. She gathered her belongings, and we pushed through the back door and walked to my car under the bright afternoon sun. My tires squealed against the blacktop as I raced out of the parking lot, apprehension and anxiety building inside me. Neither of us spoke as I rushed through traffic as if I were on my way to a hot call. I wasn't, of course, and there truly was no urgency to the situation. The truth of it was I, too, had a personal investment about the case against Spencer. Josie was more than just a partner to me. As with any good partner, a strong bond had developed between us and I cared deeply for her. I dreaded the idea of bad news from the crime lab.

In the Firearms section of the lab we met with Forensic Firearms examiner Tori Givens, a short, robust woman with long brown hair. She was a transplant from Texas who had both the drawl and charm of her native land. She moved from her desk to greet us as we arrived. "Y'all must have flown," she said, checking her watch, "or been nearby."

"We were at the office when you called," I said, "and traffic wasn't too bad."

She turned and started toward a table against the far wall, and we followed. A man in short sleeves and a wide tie, sporting a wiry blond mustache, walked out of the supervisor's office and passed by us without a greeting. I figured he was the new supervisor I had heard about, one who had not been well received by the examiners. There had been a lot of changes at the crime lab lately, and although I was unable to keep up with them all, rumors of discontent had spread from their bureau to ours.

I glanced around to see all of the desks and work areas empty, and thought it was odd. "Where is everyone?"

Givens glanced back at me. "You guys called us out for an officer-involved. Downey, I think."

I nodded. "El Monte. We don't know anything about it though; another team is handling it."

She stopped at a table where the rifle we had recovered from the shed was displayed, along with a small evidence envelope and several hand tools, a borescope among them. She pulled a pair of gloves from her lab coat and stretched them over her hands.

"Your suspect went to great lengths to destroy this evidence," she said, her hands now outstretched, exhibiting the rifle before her. "Not only did he take a file or grinder to the serial number, but he mostly obliterated the rifling in the barrel."

"Great," I said, my irritation clear in my tone.

She glanced over her shoulder. "Here, y'all, come around to the other side and have a look-see for yourself."

Josie and I stepped around to the other side of the table and positioned ourselves across from the Texan in her lab coat. She opened a laptop and turned it so that we could also see the screen. Then she retrieved the borescope from its case and began working with it. Before proceeding, she paused, said, "Wait, let me show you something else, first," and stepped away, returning in a moment with another rifle, an AR-15.

"First, I want to show you what the barrel should look like when we run the scope through there. Y'all might have already seen this?"

Josie shook her head.

The expert continued, "This little gem here, called a borescope, will get us inside that barrel with light and magnification, and we'll see it all here on the computer. It's a camera that allows me to video or take still photographs of the inside, which I've already done with your rifle."

There were no cords connecting the device to the computer, so I asked, "Does that feed through Wi-Fi?"

"It does," she said, as she began feeding the tiny camera in through the chamber of the AR-15.

I watched the live feed displayed on her laptop, a full-screen view of a dark tunnel with spiraling cuts that I knew to be the lands and grooves, or "rifling." There were areas that were shiny and others that were dull. There were blemishes and pitting. The camera went deeper into the tunnel, the rifling making it appear to twirl.

Givens said, "This one looks pretty good as far as the rifling goes. The barrel's not in the best of shape—you can see all of that pitting from rust—but the rifling is definitive, the lands and grooves unmolested. Yours doesn't look like this one here, and I'll show you that in a minute."

She backed the camera out and moved the AR-15 to the side. Josie drew in a deep breath. I said, "This doesn't sound good."

Givens glanced up and then began feeding the camera end of the borescope into the rifle that had been recovered from the shed and attributed to Jacob Spencer. "The bad news is that your rifle—this one here—has gone through a series of efforts to alter identification. The serial number has been obliterated and the bore has been acid etched and"—she stopped feeding the camera and pointed to the video on her computer —"somehow rasped down, like it has almost been bored out, but roughly. Maybe a Dremel tool or something similar."

The screen showed a similar dark tunnel that was the inside of the barrel, but the characteristics differed significantly from the first barrel she showed us. There were no lands and grooves, more like deep striations throughout an otherwise smooth bore.

"See how there's no rust, no pitting, nothing—including no lands and grooves?"

"Uh-huh."

"Yeah."

"Okay, so that's like a freshly bored smooth barrel. I don't think acid etching alone would have removed all of the lands and grooves, and it does appear that some type of tool was used to bore through here."

She pulled the camera out of the barrel and exited the video on her screen. Referencing the small evidence envelope that lay to the side, she said, "We haven't bothered to test fire the rifle, nor to unseal your projectile here. There's no sense in it; there's nothing in the barrel that's going to allow us to make a comparison. What about a casing?"

I shook my head. "We didn't recover one."

"Well, that's too bad. That'd be the one way to identify this as your murder weapon."

Josie said, "You said, 'The bad news is'… Was there any good news to go with this?"

Givens stepped a few feet away and placed the AR-15 on a rack that held dozens of other rifles. She returned and flipped Spencer's rifle over and ran a gloved finger over the nearly-obliterated serial number. "I think we'll be able to raise that serial number."

"Yeah?" I said, hopeful. "How's that done? I've heard of it, but never knew anyone who's had any success doing it."

"There are two methods: magnetic particle inspection and chemical restoration. I'll do the magnetic particle first because it is non-destructive. We get one shot with the chemical restoration."

I looked at Josie, who shrugged. "It doesn't prove this rifle killed Brown."

"True," I said, "but it is powerful circumstantial evidence. What other reason would he have to plant the rifle, other than he believes it would link Watkins to the Brown murder?"

She dropped her head and sighed.

"Josie, this is only a small setback. We're going to nail him."

She didn't look up. Givens said, "Sounds like you guys are invested in this one. I wish I could have been more help."

"I don't even know that the serial number's going to help," Josie said, and wiped the back of her hand at the corner of an eye. "This just really sucks."

Givens shot me a puzzled look. I turned back to Josie. "Let's get out of here."

Josie started for the door. I thanked Givens for her work and whispered to her, "It's personal, sorry."

She nodded and turned back to her work.

On the way back to the office, Josie sat quietly staring out her window. My mind had been processing the information we had just received, and I began working it out verbally, hoping to cheer her up.

"So if he obliterated the serial number, he did so to prevent us from knowing the gun belonged to the Department of Fish and Game. He doesn't have one registered to him. But why would he disassociate himself from a gun that can't be determined to be the murder weapon?"

"He probably figures we have the casing," Josie reasoned.

"No, I don't think he does," I argued. "I think he picked that casing up and knows damn well we don't have it."

"Then, what?"

I thought about it for a moment while negotiating traffic on the Long

Beach Freeway. "I think the barrel job was done first. Maybe he was going to keep the rifle, turn it back in, whatever, and wanted to make sure it could never be matched to the bullet that killed Brown. Maybe he figured nobody would notice, or maybe it was meant to buy him enough time to find another barrel for it on the black market, somewhere he wouldn't leave a trail. Then we do the interview a couple weeks ago and I put it in his head that we're going back up to the mountain. He decides planting the murder weapon would be his best bet at having this case permanently wrapped up, so then he removes the serial number."

Josie glanced over, her face expressionless.

"But here's the thing, this is all good circumstantial evidence. We have him on video planting the gun. We can articulate a motive for him to do so with other circumstantial evidence: he killed Watkins quickly and claimed the boy raised a knife toward him, yet Watkins was armed with a pistol. We know Brown and Watkins were both poachers and that Spencer is obsessed with enforcing the laws against any illegal hunting. There was no reason for Spencer to have gone back to the mountain that night—much less to the shed—following an extensive search led by our department, without good cause. For that matter, why hadn't he told us at the debriefing if he had concerns or ideas about checking that shed?"

"Okay, that's all true, but do you really think a jury is going to convict him of murder without any physical evidence whatsoever?"

"I'm not worried about a jury just yet," I said. "I'm talking about probable cause for a search warrant. We have enough to search his home and vehicles, his office, desk, and locker, his state-issued pickup truck, his four-wheeler. And you know what I think we'll find?"

Josie tilted her head slightly and I could see her brows raised behind her sunglasses. "What? Tell me."

"A souvenir, for one—the expended cartridge case from the Brown murder scene, the one he was careful to not leave behind."

"And two?"

I smiled. "Tools and acid. Maybe even metal shavings on the floor in his garage that could be matched to the metal of that barrel. Even if that isn't enough to file on him for Brown's murder, or your and Tommy's thing," I said, avoiding the words *murder* and *kidnap* when talking about what had happened to Josie and her friend and fellow deputy sheriff,

Tommy Zimmerman "it's enough to file felony weapons charges against him. That would at the least get him fired from Fish and Game, and it would give us something to beat his balls over. I'm telling you, Josie, we may have to work hard at this, but we're going to nail that son of a bitch. I promise you."

She was looking straight ahead through the windshield. I glanced back and forth from her to the road, waiting for something. I imagined the wheels were turning, and I was hoping she would start seeing the potential of the case and get past the significant impediments we had just suffered.

Finally, she smiled. "Buy me lunch before we get back to the office. It's going to be a long day, partner."

34

IF THE DAY SO FAR WAS ANY INDICATION OF HOW THE REST OF IT MIGHT GO, it was one of those rare times when the idea of leaving early and turning off the cell phone seemed like the thing to do. I seldom did that, but occasionally the thought would cross my mind. Leave it all behind and go golfing, fishing, collapse on the couch and take a long nap. Have a late cocktail lunch and stay through the happy hour. There were options that trumped the daily grind.

Floyd said, "You're going to love me when I tell you where Mongo and I are headed next. And then you're going to owe me a steak and beers. Plural, as in multiple. Why do you look like shit?"

We were back at the office. Moments before, I had collapsed into my chair, tossed my hat on my desk, and somehow lost all forward momentum, mentally and physically. I had been staring at the closed laptop mindlessly. When I first sat down, I had begun thinking about the affidavit I needed to write in order to have a search warrant issued for Spencer's home, office, and vehicles. Josie had volunteered to write it, but I had insisted that I handle it. She was a victim in the case, and it would be best to minimize her involvement, at least on paper.

I turned to see Floyd had struck his pose, the part-fighter-part-GQmodel stance, a smile stretched across his face. "What could you possibly do to make me love you?"

He pulled up an empty seat. "Dickie, I've got an address for your girl, Kishi, a West Hollywood apartment with active utilities in her new name and old social security number."

I nodded to show my appreciation.

"And that's not all. We've located the name change court records, and all we have to do is swing by the clerk's office and get copies of the file."

"Where's the file?"

"Downtown. Right on our way to West Hollywood. Do you want to go, or shall we haul her in if she's home? We were thinking if she was willing and able, we'd get her to go to West Hollywood and we could interview her there."

"That would be good," I said, my mind now racing to think of the options. "I'd sure like to be there for the interview. I mean, you're more than welcome to talk to her first—you and Mongo—but I'd like to be at the station, watching and listening while you do. Maybe I'd have some questions for her once you've finished."

Floyd shrugged. "You can talk to her first if you'd like, Dickie; it doesn't matter to me. We can pick her up and drag her ass down there and let her cool until you and Josie are there. Should we get ahold of Rich and Lizzy too?"

"I say we leave them be; they've got enough on their plates right now. In fact, both of them are off now, Farris for the rest of the day, Lizzy for a while, apparently."

Floyd shook his head sorrowfully.

"But you guys take the first crack at Kishi. You've got the first case of the series, and your victim was without question involved in her rape. So let's do it like that. You and Mongo talk to her first, Josie and I will monitor and take the next crack at her."

He glanced around the office. "Where's Josie?"

I shrugged. "Not sure. We had some bad luck with that rifle, and she's not in a great mood. She might be in the girls' room powdering her nose."

"So that's why you look like shit."

I frowned at him.

"Dude, you look like someone stole your puppy."

"Nah, just disappointed maybe. You know, this shit isn't like the movies where all the pieces fall together, the good guys win and get the girl, and everyone lives happily ever after except those who were killed."

"Yeah, they were even less happy."

I shook my head, not even humored by Floyd today.

"I'll let you know when we've got your girl in hand, and you and Josie can put on your happy faces and meet us at the station—West Hollywood."

"Good luck," I said.

He began walking away.

"Give me a call when you pick up that file," I said, "if there's anything interesting in it."

He waved a hand. "Will do."

I watched him walk away, messing with other detectives he passed, shadowboxing with one and hugging another, exchanging jovial greetings with both. I thought back to the day we met at a police rodeo. We were introduced by a mutual friend—another deputy who fought bulls when he wasn't clowning around—and quickly found that we had a lot in common: We both liked rodeo—I was a fan; Floyd rode bulls. He was hoping to transfer to Firestone Station for his patrol training; I had trained at Firestone and was still assigned there. We both liked Coors Light. He liked my Jeep. I liked my Jeep. His wife liked my Jeep, so I had tossed her my keys and told her to take it for a spin. Floyd had fished a wrinkled twenty from his jeans and said, "And while you're out—" and she had cut him off, acknowledging we needed more beer. It had been an eventful twenty years since that dusty day in Salinas, California—two decades of being partners and friends, surviving deadly encounters side by side, and working a variety of assignments together, including patrol, plainclothes detectives, and finally, Homicide. We had traveled the country together on the county dime, chasing bad guys and solving crimes, and occasionally even having fun. Okay, truthfully, almost all of it had been fun; Floyd always insisted on that.

Josie came around the corner as Floyd faded away, and I realized I'd had a good run of luck when it came to partners. I turned back to my desk and started writing an affidavit for the Spencer search warrant, suddenly reinvigorated.

"Do you want me to do anything?"

It was Josie settling into her chair next to mine.

"You can start on the ops plan while I type up the affidavit, if you'd like. I have a feeling the LT is going to make us run this up the ladder before we can do anything with it, but we might as well have everything ready."

"How far up do you think it will go?"

"Paper on another cop, a murder rap? I'd say all the way to the top. And now that I'm thinking about it, we might as well go for broke; let's write a Ramey warrant also, use the same probable cause statement for both."

"You think there's enough for an arrest warrant?"

"Yeah, I think so. But that doesn't really matter, does it? We'll have to convince a judge, but only after we get the blessing from the sheriff, most likely."

I looked down the end of our row of desks and confirmed Lt. Joe Black was gone. I glanced at my watch: 4:27. Joe was the type to get in early and try to beat the traffic out of downtown, so I hadn't expected him to still be in the office since our team wasn't up for murders. That reminded me, though, that we would be back in the rotation come the weekend. There was no rest for the weary, no light at the end of the tunnel, but, as Floyd had pointed out, the dead were less happy than those of us who had not yet joined them. Which was one thing we had going for us.

We worked silently side by side, clicking away at our keyboards. We wouldn't be able to finalize the affidavit until Firearms finished their examination. If they were able to restore the serial number, and if that serial number came back to the Department of Fish and Game, that would be icing on the cake. We already knew it wouldn't come back to him, because we had searched ATF records and found he had no such rifle registered to him.

Josie grabbed her desk phone before I realized it had rung. "Sanchez," she said, dropping the more formal greeting that included her title. "Sheriff's Homicide, Jones," was my standard greeting. I watched her and listened, wondering if it would be the lab already with a report on the serial number. Her face went slack, and she leaned back in her chair. Either it was bad news, or no news on the Spencer front. She began speaking in Spanish. I deciphered enough to know she was speaking to her mother, and that she was less than pleased with the conversation.

It was the perfect time for a cup of coffee.

When I returned, Josie was off the phone, back to typing on her computer.

"Everything okay?" I asked.

She turned to me and rolled her eyes. "My mother, sometimes."

I chuckled. "I bet."

"She's leaving for Reno with her friend, Irma. Neither of them speaks English—shit, I don't even think Irma's legal. They're taking a bus, two little old women from the old country. Can you believe it? 'We're in a slots tournament. It'll be so much fun, *mi hija*.' What could go wrong, right? Anyway, she wanted to let me know she'll be back Saturday night, and not to worry."

The phone on her desk rang again and I grinned. She snatched the handset from its cradle. "Yes? ... Oh, yes, this is Detective Sanchez, I'm sorry, I—"

I watched while she flipped the pages of her William Brown notebook to a blank page and readied a pen.

"Uh-huh... Okay, yes, go."

She jotted some notes, thanked the caller, and hung up. She whirled in her chair and was off toward a bank of computers along the wall, computers we used to access law enforcement applications that were not available on our individual computers. "We've got a serial number," she said, the cadence of her voice matching the quick steps she took.

I waited at my desk, leaning back in my seat and staring at the back of my partner's head. Her long, flowing black hair brushed her shoulders as her head turned back and forth from her notebook to the computer screen.

After a moment, she pushed out of her chair and pumped her fist. "We've got the fucker!"

3 5

WHEN THE DICE WERE HOT, IT SEEMED YOU COULDN'T LOSE; THE NUMBERS kept turning up sixes and eights and everyone around the table cheered and drank and raked in their chips.

And then, suddenly, two white-dotted red cubes would sail from an outstretched hand, tumble across a field of chips, bounce against the cushioned rail at the far end, and then, as if the world slowed, breathless gamblers gawk as a dice rolls to a stop, five dots facing up. The other, still in motion, turns slowly, teetering, threatening a two but teasing the prospect of one more turn. It falls dead with its two beady white eyes fixed toward the ceiling. The gamblers withdraw, hushed mutterings and sudden thirsts as they wait for the stickman to sweep the dice—a five and a two, *craps*—into the center of the table.

A similar bitterness washed over me when the next call came in. It was Floyd, and he was in West Hollywood where he had just crapped out at the apartment of Kishi Takahashi, also known as Sunako Hisakawa—*a dark time long ago.*

"She's dead."

"What do you mean, 'she's dead'? Like, you found her dead in her apartment, or she died a long time ago and someone there told you about it?"

Josie spun her chair, eyes fixed on me, and began biting at her pen. I mouthed "Kishi" to her, and she mouthed the second F-bomb of the afternoon. They were rare coming from Josie, but it was an F-bomb sort of day.

Floyd said, "The manager filled us in. Apparently, she's the girl who took a plunge off that hotel balcony a couple weeks ago, the case Martinez and Castro are handling—"

"Are you shitting me?"

"Not even a little bit. Hey, wasn't that thought to be a murder for a while?"

"Yeah, that's how they were looking at it, but I just talked to Joe this morning and he said it's been ruled a suicide."

"They're sure?" Floyd asked.

Josie frowned. "What case is a suicide?"

I held a finger up, asking her to wait. Into the phone, I said, "I didn't get the details, but Joe seemed confident of it. He also implied that she was a hooker."

"I'll be damned," Floyd said.

"You probably will," I agreed. "Listen, let me see if I can get ahold of Joe or Raul. They were rolling out on the officer-involved so I'm not sure they'll be available to chat much, but I want to make sure we're good to go through her apartment."

"I'm sure they've already done that," Floyd said. "The manager said the apartment was sealed for a couple weeks, and now he's got the okay to clear it out."

"Okay, well, let me try nonetheless. Also, I don't want to take any chances. They might have been through it already, but not with an eye toward what we'd be looking for."

"Let me know, Dickie. Me and Mongo will stand down until I hear back from you. But make it snappy; I'm getting thirsty."

I hung up with Floyd, lamented with Josie, and sent a text to Joe Castro telling him I knew he was tied up on an OIS, but could he please call at his first convenience. Five minutes later my cell rang. It was Joe. I quickly told him the situation with his jumper in West Hollywood and how it might be related to our cases, and asked if we could search her apartment.

"We're done with it, have at it."

"Thanks, Joe. Hey, how did you confirm it was a suicide?"

"A note. I'll show it to you later. Actually, I'll put a copy on your desk when I get back to the office tonight, assuming you'll be gone."

I thanked him and hung up, and then gave Josie the thumbs up while calling Floyd.

"The apartment's all yours," I said. "We'll hang out here until you finish, just in case you come up with anything." Before I let him go, I asked, "Was there anything interesting about the name change court file?"

"Nothing that I can see. I'll show you later or put a copy on your desk before we go home tonight."

At this rate, my desk was going to see more traffic than the Harbor Freeway. I hung up with Floyd and said to Josie, "It's going to be a long night. What do you say we go grab something to eat?"

WE CHOSE A LOCAL MEXICAN JOINT. AS WE SLID ACROSS RED VINYL benches in the high-backed booth, it occurred to me to be grateful for the privacy the arrangement afforded us. We knew from previous visits that the food was okay, and the margaritas were good, but it was always busy and loud. It was happy hour, which suited us fine; it was nearly customary that homicide dicks drank while on the job. We placed our orders but didn't wait for cocktails to arrive before digging into the warmed chips and hot salsa that were placed between us. Josie chewed her chip and waved a hand at her mouth, then took a long drink of her iced water.

"This salsa is hot!"

I laughed and took another big bite. "Maybe for a watered-down Latina it is... Just right for this gringo."

She rolled her eyes, took another sip of water, and said, "Have you realized yet that this suicide deal blows our entire theory on the Bailey brothers and Bellovich case?"

"That sounds like a circus."

She cocked her head, insisting on a straight answer.

"How so? We don't know anything yet. Let's see what Floyd comes up with and we'll roundtable it and go from there."

A waitress, clad in a red and black ruffled skirt and white shirt, put two margaritas down and disappeared.

Josie said, "Eyes here, Jones."

I grinned, caught red-handed.

She said, "There's nothing to roundtable. She couldn't have been our killer."

"Why not?" I asked, frowning. I had already surmised that Kishi must have jumped to her death due to the guilt of committing the murders, and now I was only hoping we would be able to prove that she had.

"Do you remember the night we picked up the Bellovich case?"

"Mm-hmm," I hummed around another bite.

"We were bumped up in the rotation because Castro and Martinez had a meeting with the sheriff that same morning—on their West Hollywood balcony case."

I sat with a half-eaten chip hovering between my mouth and the salsa. She was right, and I hadn't yet considered the timeline of those three cases relative to the suicide. I'd been too excited over the prospect of having homed in on our suspect to even make that leap. In my defense, I was also running hard on the Spencer case as well as the Jackie Melvin Lowe case. Overload caused fatigue, which led to missteps and oversights, neither of which were acceptable when investigating murder. I reached to dip my chip and Josie grabbed my wrist.

"No double-dipping!"

"Huh?"

She indicated the half-eaten chip dangling from my grip. "Don't dip a chip you've already bitten in to. Gross."

I stuck it in my mouth with no salsa, frowning at my partner while chewing slowly. After a sip of my drink, I said, "Well, shit. She was already dead when Bellovich and Sean Bailey were killed. Son of a bitch. But what about Todd Bailey? Was she still alive when that happened?"

"So you think she killed one of the three. What, the other two are coincidences?"

She was right, that didn't make sense. There was no doubt in my mind that the three cases were related—but related to what? The revenge of a rape case had made perfect sense, and it had seemed as if all of the pieces would fit together once we found Kishi Takahashi. I never imagined we'd find her dead.

Where would we go now? I wondered. A lot of time and effort had been expended chasing the wrong lead. Back to square one: Who had motive to kill the three boys? What had they done to get themselves killed? I still dismissed the idea that the murders were professional hits, the result of a drug deal gone awry or some other crime-related business blunder.

Our food came with warnings of hot plates, and I asked for another round of drinks before the waitress was able to wiggle away. The sight of her in that ruffled skirt was one I believed I could never get over. I was still pondering the new information and back-tracing our steps to see where we had gone wrong when Josie finished her first bite, set the fork down, and said, "Maybe she killed Todd and someone else did the other two for her, after she died."

It was an interesting thought. "Finished the job for her."

Josie nodded.

"But who? It would have to be someone she loved dearly or paid handsomely."

She worked her fork into a salsa-smothered green chili relleno and paused. "A lover? A brother? Her father?"

"So she kills Todd, lures him out to the cliff somehow and sends him off the edge, and then the guilt of it causes her to commit hara-kiri off the hotel balcony. Your theory is she told someone about what she had done, and why, and after she killed herself, that someone was motivated to kill the other two of the three who raped her, who ruined her life and brought all of this on."

"Exactly. Except hara-kiri is technically suicide by knife or sword, not leaping off a building."

I set my fork down, took my cell phone out and sent Floyd a text. *Have you found anything that would indicate a lover?*

My phone rang. It was Floyd. "Hey," I said as a way of greeting him. "We're eating now but I just wondered if you had any names we can follow up with."

"Yeah, I knew what you meant. I'm calling to tell you we're on the wrong path. If you haven't figured it out yet, two of our three murders happened after she offed herself."

"Right, we were just discussing that. What if she did Todd, and someone did the other two for her?"

"Like who?"

"That's what I'm asking you, asshole."

Josie shot me a look and glanced around, reminding me we weren't in the office. I lowered my voice. "Did she have a boyfriend?"

"Nothing we've come up with, Dickie. We're on our way back to the bureau. When you and your girlfriend finish dining, why don't you meet us there."

I glanced at my watch. "Okay, give us a half hour or so."

We finished our meals in silence, each of us alone in our thoughts. For me, I had serious doubts now that Kishi Takahashi was involved in the murders in any way. But we hadn't discovered any other possible motive for the killings, so for the time being, I was working through the unlikely scenario that Josie had posed, one wherein someone came in and batted cleanup for our little samurai. It did make sense that she could have killed Todd Bailey and then, overwhelmed with the guilt of it, taken her own life. But it also made sense that she killed herself to end a life of drugs and prostitution, after having lost her innocence one dark night on the damp sands of Abalone Cove.

On our way back to the office, I hadn't a profound thing to say. "We're missing something."

36

THE SIGNATURE READ PETE HANSON. WHEN I SAW IT, MY MIND WENT blank for a minute as I worked to recall the familiar name and where I had first heard it. It was obviously related to the case, since I was now looking at it on the bottom of a court document detailing the name change of Kishi Takahashi.

I leaned against an unoccupied desk next to Floyd's. Josie sat in the chair that belonged to the desk I had borrowed. Mongo and Floyd, who were turned from their desks, leaning back in their chairs, told us about the apartment search, and discussed with Josie her theory about Kishi having committed the first murder and a loved one doing the other two. They went back and forth, but their words escaped me as I stared at a copy of the court document Floyd had provided, trying to recall the name Hanson.

Finally, I interrupted. "Who the hell is Pete Hanson?"

The three of them looked at me. Josie said, "The weirdo Lomita detective."

"Jesus Christ," I said, "you've got to be shitting me."

"What?" Floyd asked.

I held the document up for display. "He was her witness in the name change proceedings. How the hell does he get involved in something like that?"

We all exchanged glances, each of us seemingly searching the others for an answer to the puzzling question: How does the detective assigned to the rape case of a teenager become a witness to her name change? That was a civil court process that had nothing to do with law enforcement.

I tapped the photocopied document. "Right here on the petition, Peter Hanson, witness, and then notarized, stamped, and submitted. Why? How—"

"We need to pay Hanson another visit," Josie said. "This is really interesting. What's the date on that, anyway?"

I searched the form until I found the date it had been submitted to the court. "This was more than two years after the rape. There's no reason Hanson should have been involved with her after that much time. Not on a rape case."

"Was he still on the job then?" Floyd asked.

Mongo shrugged, having no answer.

I also shrugged. "I guess we should find out. I don't know that it matters though; either way, this is bizarre-o at best, criminally creepy at worst."

We adjourned the informal meeting, and Josie and I wandered over to our desks. "Hey look, Castro dropped off a copy of the suicide note." I looked around to see if he was anywhere to be found in the bureau. He wasn't, at least not that I could see.

Josie walked over and leaned into me to see it. There was a sticky note on the front: *It's more of a poem, but it's obviously a precursor to her suicide.*

Side by side, Josie and I silently read the words attributed to Kishi:
Solely through death
may life be defined
in the darkness of night
brightness does blind
substantial the price
of a night in the cove
paid with a life
but not mine alone
bittersweet the taste

of vengeance
served cold

When I finished reading, I looked at Josie and saw her eyes track back to the top. She was reading it again, this beautifully penned, cunning calligraphy, intimations offered to those who sought answers. For Castro and Martinez—who lacked the knowledge we now had—it was only a presentation of self-pity, a predecessor to the vile act of taking one's *own* life. They didn't know about *the night in the cove* or *vengeance served cold*, so the hint that someone else would also be paying *with a life* had apparently eluded them both.

Josie reached for the paper, her gaze glued to the message it contained. I released my grip, and she backed blindly to her chair. When her legs touched it, she felt for the seat with one hand and lowered herself without breaking her gaze. I waited, watching Josie's eye scan back and forth, a computer analyzing every last detail. I could have clapped a pair of cymbals together near her head and not jolted her from her deliberation.

"I get this," she finally said, lowering the paper and meeting my gaze. "I *feel* this."

"How so?" I asked.

Her eyes drifted away and slowly came back. "I'm with her on this, the vengeance served cold. I'm glad she killed that son of a bitch, and I'm thankful that someone finished the job for her, killing the other two. I only wish she hadn't jumped afterward. This is sad, Richard."

There was pain in her eyes, but I didn't know if it was borrowed or her own.

"Well," I said, trying to lighten the mood, "let's not say that to anyone else. I don't want you to end up on the suspect list for the second and third cases."

It didn't lighten the mood at all. Her eyes darkened as she said, "You're missing my point."

I pondered it a moment before arguing that I hadn't.

She said, "If I can feel that way, why couldn't any other cop?"

"Hanson," I said.

She nodded.

"But why?" I mused aloud. "Why would he be able to relate to this the way you can? I mean, I get where you're coming from. You're seeing Spencer at the edge of that cliff and relishing the age-old concept of vengeance—an eye for an eye. But I also know that you wouldn't actually do that—"

"Don't be so sure," she said.

"—and I can't imagine any cops risking their lives, throwing away everything they'd worked for throughout their lives and were finally enjoying."

"Did it appear to you that Hanson was enjoying his retirement? He looked like a miserable, beaten-down old man on his final approach in life. Maybe this was his last hurrah."

I drew in a deep breath and let it out slowly. "I don't know, maybe. We should have had them make us a batch of margaritas to go."

Josie looked around the office and then pushed out of her chair. "Let's go."

I too scanned our surroundings as if I had missed something she had just discovered. There was nothing. It was late on a Tuesday night and the office was nearly empty. Floyd and Mongo were on the other side of the squad room at their desks, and there was certainly someone at the front counter manning the phones, but there was no one else stirring. I wondered if she was thinking of going to see Hanson, and I was preparing myself to argue against it. *Not yet. Settle down, Josie, let's take this slow.* It had already occurred to me that we needed to know everything about him so that we could see what made him tick. There had to be *something*, if he were in fact involved. Josie had been kidnapped, tied to a filthy wooden floor inside a rat-infested shed and left there to die after her boyfriend was killed. It was easy to understand her ideological flirtation with vengeance. I had been a victim before as well—several times. I had been shot, I had been badly beaten, I had been bitten by a vicious dog— well, as vicious as a chihuahua could be. I, too, had relished the idea of vengeance at times. What victim of violence hadn't? I didn't know. I imagined some would not. Maybe Gandhi, Mother Teresa, John Lennon… But most people would be inclined, ideologically, toward exacting revenge. What was the justice system? Revenge. If you kill someone, we, the state, will kill you back. Theoretically speaking. Who hadn't cheered watching Dirty Harry blow away a child molester with his .44 magnum? Whatever had made Hanson snap—*if he had*—needed to be discovered before any further contact was made.

I said, "Where are you wanting to go, Hanson's?"

She frowned. "Hell no, not yet. Let's go get drunk."

3 7

On Wednesday mornings, the captain held bureau meetings, boring to death weary detectives with announcements of administrative twaddle before investigators briefed on their recent cases. The meetings were mandatory, which meant nearly three-quarters of the eighty investigators assigned to Homicide Bureau attended on any given week. My attendance trumped that of my high school attendance record, which is to say I didn't *always* miss the "mandatory" Wednesday meetings.

A microphone was necessary for those speaking to be heard in the far corners of the squad room, a warehouse-sized carpeted room with six columns of desks, one for each team of fourteen investigators and their lieutenant. Team Five was in the back, far from the podium, and oftentimes I worked on my computer or even spoke softly into my phone, handling business during the festivities. Today, I leaned back in my chair, eyelids heavy, sipping coffee. I had been kept out late by my partner—the same partner whose desk sat next to mine, vacant. I imagined her waking in worse shape than had I, and assumed that a woman required far more grooming to make herself appear presentable with no evidence of overindulgence.

Captain Stover finished with the announcements and complaints— which I had noticed were considerably fewer as he neared his retirement—

and passed the mic to Joe Castro who had worked his way to the front, ready to brief his case.

"Good morning," he started. "Martinez and I handled an OIS for El Monte PD yesterday, occurring at Rush and Merced in South El Monte. The suspect, Jose Luis Torres, a.k.a. Demon, from El Monte Flores, was wanted for a drive-by shooting that occurred over the weekend in Rosemead. It resulted in a bystander's death, a thirteen-year-old girl—I think Fines and Cooper handled that. Anyway, Demon was on the hot sheet—"

Someone said, "Hey Castro, 1970 called, and they want their word back."

He smiled and continued, "—and two of El Monte's gang cops spotted him driving out of a liquor store parking lot, so they went in pursuit of him. Demon blew through a solid red and t-boned a furniture delivery truck, pretty much totaling his piece of shit. When he bailed out of the hoop, he had a gun in his hand, and the rest is history, as they say. Both officers fired and the suspect was dead at the scene."

"Shall we have a moment of silence?" someone asked.

Castro smiled again and continued, telling members of the bureau what type of weapon was carried by Demon, and that he had been active in the area, doing collections for the Mexican mafia and "putting in work"—shooting rival gang members. He encouraged anyone with open cases in the area to have their Firearms evidence compared to the recovered weapon in Demon's case.

There were a few questions for Castro, but I didn't pay attention. I was texting my partner to see where she was and when she would be in, reminding her we needed to brief our lieutenant and probably the captain on the Spencer case so we could go forward with the search and arrest warrants we had prepared for him.

Before Castro finished, he updated the status of the balcony case, telling everyone it had turned out to be a case of suicide. He handed the mic to the next detective who was waiting to brief his case, and I slipped out the back door with my phone to my ear, a ploy I used frequently to leave the meetings early. Josie had just arrived and told me so in her text.

We stood outside in the shade of the building, talking about our strategies for the busy day ahead of us: We were first going to bring Joe Black up to speed on the Spencer case, and he would no doubt tell us we needed to run it by the captain. The three of us would join Stover in his office and close the door. We would tell him about our evidence and that we were going to arrest the game warden. The old Stover would have hemmed and hawed and come up with other ideas for going forward on such a controversial case, likely suggesting it be run up the flag pole to the man upstairs before anything was done. But the Stover of late might say good job, go get him, and no more time or effort would be wasted. I was trying to think positively.

Then we'd brief him on our case involving the mayor's son, the two sons of a wealthy businessman and his slutty wife, along with a former hooker—*oh, did we mention this is the same girl that caused all of the commotion in West Hollywood by jumping off a balcony?*—and, well, there's just one more teensy little thing: we think a retired Lomita Station detective might be involved.

Maybe, just to confuse him, I would mention the Jackie Melvin Lowe case also, and he would frown and say, "Who?" and I would tell him, "Exactly."

Soon the parking lot was busy with detectives loading up in their cars and heading out to fight crime throughout the County of Los Angeles. Josie and I filed in and went directly to the head of our row of desks where Joe Black sat gazing at his computer screen. I quickly briefed him on the two cases that mattered, and the three of us went to see the captain.

As I briefed the Jacob Spencer case, Captain Stover chewed at his thumb, carefully measuring every word I spoke. Occasionally, his gaze would dart toward Josie who sat next to me. He hardly looked at Joe Black, who sat on the other side of Josie. When I finished, he took his time to respond, clearly thinking it through.

After a moment, his eyes shifted toward our lieutenant. "Joe, do some research and get me a contact with Fish and Game, a commanding officer of whatever they have in the way of internal affairs." Back to me, he said, "I've got no problem with any of it, but I don't want us to end up killing a game warden. I want to set this up in a controlled environment and make sure it goes down without a hitch."

"You're thinking of having their internal affairs pull him in?"

"Do you have a better idea?"

I combed my mustache with my hand while considering it. "I'm not willing to trust that evidence won't get destroyed if he is called in to I.A. He's going to panic. For that matter, he might flee. I've been thinking about it, and I have an idea. Kennedy and Kramer are the two resident deputies in Gorman. Their shifts overlap, and there are days where each of them works alone. I say we have one of them request Spencer's assistance with an arrest, and we use Major Crimes to not only provide an under-cover—who will be the person arrested—but to then follow them to the station. See, Kennedy, or whichever one it is we use, will ask Spencer to assist him in the booking process. Maybe get Kelly, that big biker-looking asshole from the surveillance team, someone whose appearance alone would make it a reasonable request for assistance. They take him to Santa Clarita for booking, and after they check their guns into the lockers and enter the booking area, we come in and break the news to Spencer, tell him he's under arrest. He will be unarmed and significantly outnumbered. I don't think he'd try anything stupid."

Stover said, "Fine. What else?"

"We book him, have Floyd and Mongo coordinate the search warrant executions at his home and office, his county vehicle, et cetera, while me and Farris take him on."

"Why you and Farris?"

"Josie needs to stay out of all of it. She's a victim in one of the two cases we're going after him on. Floyd and Mongo are up to speed on the case and I'm confident in their abilities to handle the warrants without oversight. Farris is the best we have in an interview room, and he's not only familiar with the case, but he's also already interviewed Spencer. He saw right through him, even when I didn't."

"Okay. Now what about another case? What are you trying to do here, Jones, milk me for more overtime?"

"We've got a sticky one, Skipper, and it might involve a retired deputy sheriff."

I broke it down for him in excruciating detail as the case was, thus far, complicated and circumstantial. I first laid out the timeline and the murders, provided details about the victims and their families, how we came to know about Kishi Takahashi and suspected she might be involved in the murders, how we now knew that she most likely had only committed the first—and that, too, was circumstantial—and how the detective in her rape case seemed to have remained a part of her life for at least several years, having been a witness to her legal name change.

"What is the guy, a weirdo? What do we know about him?"

That was the Stover I appreciated. Josie said, "I can answer that. Yes, he's a weirdo. What we can tell you is that he lied about remembering any such case or having kept the file. He appears to live alone, just him and his cats, a dirty old man who probably looks at school girls."

I was surprised by the leap she had made, but I didn't argue.

"And you think he had a relationship with this girl?"

"He couldn't have a normal relationship, so maybe, yeah. She turned hooker, so she'd sell her body or soul to get what she needed. Who knows what he promised he could do for her? Maybe he was supporting her financially."

"At least once or twice a week," I added, a reference to her mode of income. I continued, "Look, boss, we aren't anywhere near ready to move on this yet. We need to dig through this guy's background, find out everything on him. We'll need access to his personnel files, and somehow, without tipping our hand, we're going to need to talk to people who worked around him, see what made him tick. Our theory is that he had to have something more than a young Asian girl rubbing his crotch to push him to murder. There's something there with him, we can feel it. We just need to uncover it and the pieces will fall together."

"Well, he's retired, so as far as I'm concerned," Stover said, "he's fair game like any other suspect. We don't have to notify I.A. or anyone else. I say stay your course and keep me posted every step of the way."

Lieutenant Black said, "We will, Captain. Thank you."

On the way out the door I paused and turned back. "Oh, I almost forgot to mention it, but me and Farris are about to solve the Jackie Lowe case with two in custody."

He frowned. "Who is she?"

AFTER BRIEFING THE CAPTAIN, JOSIE AND I GRABBED OUR FILES AND OUR suit jackets and loaded into her car for a drive downtown. The traffic was about usual for late morning on a Wednesday in L.A. We were headed to the Hall of Justice, where we would review the personnel file of retired deputy sheriff Peter Hanson. From the Hall, as it was commonly called, we would walk across the street to CCB—now called the Criminal Justice Center. Most of us who had been around since the late twentieth century still thought of it as the Criminal Courts Building. There, we would find a judge to issue the warrants for Jacob Spencer. Back at the office, Lieutenant Black was going to be researching the Fish and Game information for the captain. Everything seemed to be coming together, and the mood in the car was light but energetic, hopeful.

Built in 1925, the Hall of Justice was the first construction of what would become the Los Angeles Civic Center. Bounded by Temple Street, Spring Street, and North Broadway, the site had been a lumber yard and corral, and the location of shootouts, murders, and hangings. Opened in 1926, the Hall featured fourteen floors, the top two of which had comprised a seven-hundred-cell county jail known as HOJJ—the Hall of Justice Jail. Over the years it would boast the involuntary guest appearances of famous mobster Bugsy Siegel, cult leader Charlie Manson, and daredevil Evel Knievel, among others. Other floors were occupied by courtrooms, the district attorney's office, sheriff's offices, and a morgue. The latter had been located in the basement, and shared in the history of legendary guests, including Marilyn Monroe and Senator Robert F. Kennedy. While the senator underwent his postmortem medical examination, his killer, Sirhan Sirhan, occupied one of the cells fourteen floors above him.

The 1994 Northridge Earthquake forced its doors to close. Sheriff's Department operations were relocated throughout the county, some to STARS Center in Whittier, others to nearby Monterey Park. Homicide was sent to Commerce for "temporary placement" in a leased building in an industrial park area. In 2015, the Hall of Justice was reopened after having undergone a complete restoration. That same year, more than two decades after being displaced to its temporary home on Rickenbacker Road in the City of Commerce, Homicide was relocated. But not back to the Hall where it would be within walking distance of the Criminal Justice Center, City Hall, and the United States District Court where my neighbor and current *plus one,* Emily Bruce, worked as a federal prosecutor. Homicide was moved to Monterey Park, ten miles east of its original downtown location.

With a sense of nostalgia, Josie and I crossed the polished tile floors through a gold-marbled foyer with shining brass rails and high gilded ceilings. After checking in with security, we entered one of the four century-old elevators that were now of modern, automatic design. Gone were the days of white-gloved operators garbed in black slacks and red vests over white shirtsleeves, cheerful men and women who sat on stools offering greetings and friendly smiles. "I guess we have to drive these things ourselves now," I said, pushing the button that would take us to the third floor, where we hoped to have unrestricted access to Hanson's personnel files.

At the front counter of Personnel, Josie and I signed in but didn't note the requested reason for our visit. The lady at the counter poked a red fingernail at the empty space and said, "You have to indicate the purpose of your visit."

"Our captain has spoken with yours," I said, "and for reasons of case sensitivity, we are not going to indicate on your sign-in log which files we wish to view. You can check with her if you'd like."

She appraised me for a moment and then looked at Josie, who nodded, apparently conveying through some type of female code that it was okay, *he's telling the truth.* I pictured the two of them making eye contact across a bar, one giving the *good-to-go* signal to the other, a nonchalant nod to say *he's not a serial killer.* The woman, dressed in stretchy gray slacks and a loose-fitting turquoise blouse, indicated a row of chairs against the wall behind us. "If you want to have a seat," she said, and then abruptly turned and disappeared beyond the counter area.

I didn't want to have a seat against the wall, but I also knew better than to say so. We all worked for the same department, and few things aggravated me more than when I was treated as an outsider, a common man. What part of "Sheriff's Homicide" had escaped this woman?

Josie elbowed me and led the way to the seats. I settled next to her and asked why she had jabbed my ribs.

"Because you're doing that thing you do."

I rolled my eyes. She had gotten that from Floyd, I knew, this amateur-hour psychoanalysis that purported to know my thoughts and motivations, and—like thermometers, seismographs, and depth finders on ships—use this knowledge in the prevention of catastrophes. They both—Josie *and* Floyd—were suddenly my immediate source of irritation, maybe more so than the lady at the counter.

The counterwoman returned and placed a thick file on the countertop and looked at Josie. "Here ya go, ma'am."

Josie popped out of her seat and started for the counter. "Excuse me, but could we use an office, or a break room? Someplace with chairs and a table?"

She smiled at Josie. "Well of course, honey. Follow me." Her smile vanished as her gaze washed over me and she turned away.

I fell in behind them as the man-hating counterwoman led us to an interview room and told us to take our time. She closed the door behind her, and I paused to take in the small space. I wondered if this was the place where today's applicants were grilled during the background phase of their process. In my day, it had been a terrifying experience: *Have you ever stolen from an employer? Lied on an application? Used drugs? Used alcohol to excess? Cheated on your spouse or girlfriend? Have you had sex with barnyard animals?* Sweat would roll off your brows as they pounded you with accusations of moral corruption and general ineptitude. I speculated how those interviews might differ now: *If you are currently using any illegal narcotics, you will be required to have stopped using said drugs before your appointment to the sheriff's department.* Or, *Have you been involved in gang activity within the last six months? You will need to cease any such activity...* It probably hadn't deteriorated to that point, but times had certainly changed since I was hired. That said, change was part of life; my predecessors would have been disqualified for infidelity or cohabitation, both of which most of my colleagues and I could be found guilty.

Josie cracked the file open and I took a seat next to her. "I don't know how much of this is of interest to you," she said, pushing the file between us after I sat down next to her, "but I say we start with discipline."

"Discipline is a fine place to start."

We read through two pages of discipline over a thirty-year career; it wasn't much—a couple of written reprimands for minor infractions of department rules, and two occasions where Hanson had received suspension days related to "preventable" traffic accidents. There were no founded citizen complaints or use of force complaints. The guy was squeaky clean, compared to most of us. I probably had half a dozen founded discipline actions in my file: excessive use of force, unauthorized pursuit, unauthorized discharging of a firearm, failure to report an off-duty incident...

Next, we thumbed through the chronological units of assignment. After completing academy training, Hanson had worked at Men's Central Jail for just under two years. He transferred to Lomita Station and remained there until he retired, working patrol for eight years, then station detective bureau for the remainder of his career.

There were photographs attached to his file: one from the day he was sworn in as a deputy sheriff, and another some ten years later when station photos were taken. Like many of us, he looked much different in the photographs than he had when we met him decades after they were taken. As a rookie, and even later as a veteran deputy, Hanson appeared squared away, sharp, healthy, and physically fit. At his home, he lacked energy and confidence. His eyes were beady and skeptical. He almost seemed concerned about us contacting him—or was that an opinion I had formed since learning about his participation in the name changing of Kishi Takahashi? He had, in fact, lied about that case, telling us he had no recollection of it. But was he guilty of more than lying? That was the question, and it was one we weren't going to find the answer to in a personnel file.

Josie flipped through the remaining documents and slapped the folder closed. "Nothing."

I shook my head and then stood up. "Nothing *here*. Let's see what we can get from Lomita."

Josie had stood and was collecting the file folder and her notebook when she paused, seeming to contemplate what I had just said. After a moment, she said, "Do you really think that's a good idea?"

I shrugged. "I have no idea. What are you thinking?"

"I think someone there will have loyalty to him. I don't think it's worth the risk talking to people he's worked with. I really don't trust that lieutenant."

"Slocumb?"

"No, the D.B. lieutenant, whatshisname?"

"O'Neil."

"Right," she said.

We returned the file and signed out, and then we signed out again in the lobby before walking through the front doors into the midday heat and swelling pedestrian traffic. I checked my watch and realized it was noon. "Lunch break. We'll have trouble finding a judge now. Why don't we head toward Lomita, go by and see Judge Arnesen at Torrance—he'll have no trouble signing these warrants—and then we'll go see Slocumb. He can get us any station records on Hanson, and he isn't going to say a word to anyone. Plus, he might be able to steer us toward someone to talk to, someone he knows he can trust."

"Buy me lunch along the way?"

"You got it."

39

WE ARRIVED BACK AT THE OFFICE LATE WEDNESDAY AFTERNOON WITH AN arrest warrant for Jacob Spencer in hand. We also had a signed search warrant for his residence and areas under his control at his place of employment—his vehicle, locker, and desk.

While Josie drove us around half the county during the day, I was on the phone setting up tomorrow's operation. I had called Lieutenant Black first and made sure we were good to go as far as the administrative end; he said we were. I called Steve Kennedy at the Gorman station and told him about the warrants and of our plan to dupe Spencer into the booking area of Santa Clarita so that he could be arrested without incident—hopefully. At least if there were an incident, it wouldn't be an armed one. I called Sgt. Dwight Campbell and asked if his surveillance team was available for tomorrow, and told him what we had planned. He said they would be happy to help out but warned that they would be out of hours early in the day and that Homicide would have to pay the overtime. They worked a forty-hour flex schedule, meaning that they could technically be finished with their work week by Tuesday or Wednesday if they were working long hours on a case. Somehow, they were always out of hours when we needed them, and Homicide never said no to paying overtime for their services. I called Farris and asked if he would be available for the interview of Spencer, and he said "sure," but hadn't sounded very enthusiastic about it. I knew he was out of sorts about his partner, and I completely understood that. I also knew the best thing for him right now was for him to climb out of his bottle and get his head back in the game. My last call had been to Floyd. He and Mongo were on board, but it would cost me beers at the end of the day, he said. I had assured him that Josie and I would be happy to cover a tab if all went well.

Josie typed up the operations plan and titled it Operation Payback. I suggested we come up with something that wouldn't be Exhibit One in a civil suit against us and the county if something were to go wrong and we had to beat or kill Spencer. She changed it to Operation Canary, and when I asked why, she said, "Because he's going to sing like a little bitch when he realizes he's going to prison."

"You mean, he's going to sing like a canary."

"No, he's going to sing like a little bitch, but I can't call it Operation Little Bitch."

Fair enough.

She printed the ops plan and I double-checked it before making copies of it and of the warrants for the various people who would be involved in tomorrow's operation. I left a copy on Black's desk, and another on Stover's. When I got back to my desk there was a fresh coffee waiting for me, along with Josie, looking like the cat who had swallowed the canary. I thanked her for the cup and plopped into my seat, suddenly exhausted from the long day.

"If all goes well tomorrow, we'll finally get some closure for everything that happened on the mountain," I said, again avoiding specific references to her ordeal. We still hadn't spoken in depth about it and I guessed we never would. And the moment I said it, I regretted doing so. Josie had been bright and energetic, hopeful and resolved. When I inadvertently took her back to that time and place, her eyes darkened, and her jaw tightened. I said, "Now all we need to do is figure out who killed Bellovich and the Bailey boys."

Without answering, she turned to look at her computer. I could see she was going through emails, but only as a way to avoid conversation. I had to pull her back.

"Are you ready to go see Hanson?"

She looked at me and frowned. "Now?"

I glanced at my watch. "We either do it tonight, or we take the chance of it being pushed to a back burner. Tomorrow's shot, and Friday we're up for murders again. You know how that goes."

I could see the conversation drew her thoughts away from the mountain. She said, "But we haven't figured anything out about him. The personnel file was a bust. Lomita was a bust. All we have is that he was a witness to a name change; what is that? Nothing. Or at least, not much."

Josie was generally a very positive-minded person. She wouldn't have been arguing against going forward under normal circumstances. There had been an instant mood swing when I screwed up and mentioned the mountain. She was likely thinking of Tommy, and reliving those cold, lonely, fearful nights she had spent tethered to the floor of an old miner's shed. I hadn't planned to go at Hanson without having more information, but I also didn't know what else to do after coming up with nothing from our efforts thus far. I did know that I needed to pull Josie out of her dark place, and I only knew of one way to do it: get her head back in the game.

"I don't expect much from him," I said, "but we can at least give it a try with what we have. Maybe he will panic and do something stupid if he thinks we're looking at him for the murders."

Josie sat up, her eyes widened. "You know what we haven't done?"

I shrugged.

"We haven't checked his name through our database here."

No, we hadn't, and it had never occurred to me to do so. She had a point. When a deputy is involved in a shooting, Homicide investigates the case. There wouldn't necessarily be any information about such an event in personnel files or his station file. But the case would be stored in the Homicide library, and a quick search of our in-house database would allow us to see if he had ever been part of one of our investigations.

"No, we haven't," I said. "You mean to see if he's been involved in any other shootings?"

"Yep. You know how that goes, the first time is the hardest. It seems a stretch to think the man we saw in that house could beat one man to death, then shoot another in cold blood. But what do we really know about him, other than that he was a detective?"

"A detective who apparently got too close to one of his victims."

"Yeah," she said, "which is a whole other level of creepiness."

I nodded slowly, and Josie watched me for a moment. Then she pushed out of her chair and said, "Come on, let's go up to the desk and run his name."

She took off and I followed. Josie said hello to the civilian manning the desk, took a seat next to him, and logged in on a computer. She typed Hanson's name and hit enter, and waited while it processed the request. Nothing came up. She typed it in again, this time spelling his name with an E rather than an O, wisely knowing that one minor typo could make the difference. Still nothing. Exasperated, she leaned back in her chair and stared at the monitor.

I came up with another idea. "Hey, run his name in the Event Index." This was the same program we had queried to see if Bellovich or the Bailey boys had ever been listed on any sheriff's reports as suspects, victims, witnesses, or informants. The names of deputies who write the reports are not entered into the index, so we wouldn't be flooded with information about every report Hanson had written in his thirty-year career. However, if he had ever been listed as the victim on any report, that information would be indicated.

"What are you thinking?" Josie asked.

"I'm not sure. Let's just see if anything comes up."

She closed out of the Homicide case tracker and opened up the Event Index, typing Hanson, Peter on the top line. "Do we know his DOB?"

I hadn't brought my notebook. "Yeah, but I don't have it with me. Try it without, see what comes up."

"Bingo!"

"What is it?" I asked, leaning over her shoulder.

She put her finger on the screen to indicate the third result on the first page. "Right there, a Lakewood file number with a rape stat code. He was an informant on the case."

I grabbed a phone message pad and copied the file number. "Let's go back to our desks."

Josie followed me from the front desk and down the hall. As we turned in to the squad room, where few investigators still remained late in the day, she said, "Are you going to call Lakewood?"

"Yeah, get a copy of that report sent over, if they have it. Should be on microfilm if nothing else." I held up the piece of paper with the file number. "Four years before Kishi was raped."

"And he never worked Lakewood."

"No," I said, "But he lives there."

"Yep."

I picked up my desk phone and ran my finger down a phone list until I found the number for Lakewood. I punched it in and waited, and when the operator picked up, I asked for the secretaries.

Fifteen minutes later I received an email with the report as an attachment. I printed it out, and Josie and I huddled at my desk to read it together. The first page listed details of the incident: date, time, location, classification of the crime. This was a report of a rape that had occurred in Hawaiian Gardens on a Saturday night in June, fifteen years ago. Next on the report were the names of informants, victims, and witnesses. Hanson was listed as the informant with Lomita Station's address and phone number indicated for his contact information. The victim was listed next, but the name and contact information had been redacted. *Here we go again,* I thought. The next area of a crime report is where suspects are listed. There were two on this report, both described as "Unknown" male Hispanic adults, eighteen to twenty-one years of age, black hair, brown eyes, five eight to five ten, one hundred thirty to one hundred fifty pounds. They could have been any two of many thousands—but they weren't any of the three boys who had raped Kishi Takahashi.

I flipped to the second page where evidence is listed. Evidence Item 1: Rape Kit from Victim (redacted). 2: Photographs of injuries to Victim (redacted). 3: Clothing belonging to Victim (redacted).

On the third page, the narrative began:

On the indicated date and time, I (Deputy Johnson) contacted the informant at Lakewood Regional Medical Center where the victim was being treated. The informant stated that he is the father of the victim—

"Jesus," I said.

"Oh my," said Josie.

"Well," I said, "I think we have plenty to speak with him about now."

We finished reading the report, shoulder to shoulder, Josie finishing each page before I did and waiting for me to flip to the next. The information of the assault was vague and would be detailed in a supplemental report taken by a female deputy. That report hadn't been included with the first report. But the details were not as important to us as was the fact that Hanson's daughter had been raped a couple of years prior to the rape of Kishi Takahashi, a case to which Hanson had been assigned as the primary investigator. This information allowed us to better understand how he might have developed a relationship with Takahashi that clearly exceeded professional boundaries. But to what degree? That was a question we would pose to him.

"And what ever happened with his daughter?" Josie asked, rhetorically. "That will be interesting to find out."

I knew she was taking the leap that we both had taken since Hanson's name was discovered on the name change document, considering that Hanson might have been involved in the murders. It had seemed like a stretch before, but it now seemed plausible. No matter, he was our only lead at this point. More than believing he could have been involved in the murders, I hoped he would be able to shed some light on what had happened. He had lied to us about remembering the Takahashi rape case, and there had to be a reason for it.

"Let's go," I said. "This could turn into a long night and we have an early start tomorrow, a day that is sure to be a long one."

Josie grinned. "And then we're up for murders again."

"And then we are up for murders."

40

HANSON OPENED THE DOOR AND TURNED AWAY, LEAVING IT OPEN AS AN indication to follow him in. I went ahead of Josie, not what I normally would do given my inclination toward chivalry, but his demeanor had put me on heightened alert. I watched him carefully, searching for weapons within his grasp. His loose-fitting, soiled sweatpants didn't allow for a gun in his waistband, and the T-shirt he wore was a size too small, making it easy to see there were no bulges on his person other than those that were natural, the growth around the waist experienced by inactive, elderly men and women. The room was dirty and cluttered, which made my visual inspection of the tabletops a difficult one. A TV remote partially covered by a crossword puzzle book drew and held my gaze for a long moment. The pile of clothes on the sofa next to where he sat could have concealed a bazooka, but I wasn't comfortable asking to search the area for weapons before we began. If he hadn't been a retired deputy sheriff, I would have. I was taking a chance I didn't want to take—but I did so, nonetheless. The end table to his left held a sweating plastic cup, the contents of which were a mystery.

Josie stayed near the door. I saw her eyes scanning the area, and I knew she would keep an eye on the hallway and entry into the kitchen. My back would be to both because of where I was forced to sit, next to the disheveled retiree.

"You obviously remember us," I said, as I perched on the edge of a chair next to the couch.

He rubbed the gray stubble on his face and then smoothed his hair, what was left of it. A double wash and rinse and a good brushing was what it needed, but I wasn't going to mention it. He said, "Sure, Homicide. You've got some case involving some rapists or something."

Keeping my gaze on his right hand that now rested atop of the pile of clothing next to him, I fumbled with my notebook and flipped it to a page I had marked on the way down. "Kishi Takahashi," I said, "was the case we asked you about the other day."

His gaze shifted to beyond my shoulder where I knew Josie stood.

"Yeah, that sounds about right," he finally said.

"You told us you didn't remember it."

"It was a long time ago."

"But it was the type of case you'd remember, is it not?"

He cocked his head. "Why is that, Detective?"

"You tell me, Mr. Hanson."

"Please, call me 'Pete.' Mr. Hanson was my father, and I no longer have a title."

I nodded. "Is it as hard as they say, hanging up the badge and gun?"

He reached over and picked up the sweaty cup, and as he took a long drink the smell of whiskey reached me. It was a welcome relief from the stagnant odor of body and filth that hung in the air like a dark cloud. He lowered the cup a few inches from his mouth, and said, "It's a lonely, boring goddam path to the end."

"I bet," I said, recognizing that he was a man who wouldn't be making much of a dent in our pension fund. If I were to *actually* bet, I'd put a C-note on a bullet through the roof of his mouth—two years tops. Give me two-to-one, I'd make it a year. Depending on how the rest of this interview went, I'd maybe have to modify either the life expectancy or the manner of death. If we left him here under a cloud of suspicion, I'd give him twenty-four hours. If he left with us, wearing stainless steel bracelets, I'd go with forty-eight hours and change the manner of death to hanging by county-issued bedding.

He took another drink, lowered the cup, and stared at it.

I said, "It wasn't the truth, was it, Pete?"

He shook his head slowly, his gaze remaining fixed on the liquid relief in his hands.

"You knew her well, didn't you? Miss Takahashi."

He shrugged, took another sip.

"In fact," I said, "you maintained a relationship with her over the years; isn't that right?"

He didn't shrug or nod, and he didn't look up from his cup. A long moment passed before he took a gulp. I watched him tilt the cup back, and I could see him swallowing large gulps of the liquid pain killer. I felt we had him, that we were sitting with a former lawman who had crossed the line, that he knew it was the end of the road for him. I wondered if Josie felt it too. I pictured her behind me—I didn't dare take my eyes off Hanson—and I knew she would be watching closely and analyzing his every word. She must've felt as I did by now, that he was our man. He had avenged the horrific crimes committed against one young woman, perhaps while thinking of a second one, one even nearer and dearer to his heart. Maybe one that he had failed and left vulnerable. I wondered where she was and made a mental note to ask him about her.

He looked me directly in the eyes. "It isn't what you're thinking, Detective. I'm not a goddam pervert." He looked away again, and said, "She was just a little girl, the age of—"

I waited, but it didn't seem he planned to finish. "Your daughter," I said.

His eyes came back to me, darker than before, a hint of anger mixed with sadness—or was it regret?

I said, "Tell us about your daughter, Pete."

He jiggled the ice in his cup. "I need a refill," he said, pushing out of the worn cushions.

I quickly rose, and I felt Josie move behind me.

Hanson made an effort to smile as he said, "You two are a bit jumpy."

I followed him into the kitchen and watched him empty the contents of a Coke can into the cup and top it off with cheap bourbon. He gestured with the bottle in my direction, and I shook my head to answer his question. He picked up his cup and took a sip, then looked around the adjacent dining room for a moment. "All these," he said, waving his cup toward the boxes piled up along the walls, "are old cases. You were right about me having that file, though I don't have it anymore. I didn't think it would be smart to keep it around after—"

He pushed by me and went back to the couch.

"I gotta hand it to you though, Homicide's still the best. You guys don't miss anything, that's for sure. To the Bulldogs," he said, lifting his cup.

"After what, Pete?"

He fixed his gaze on the cup again. "Well, you guys aren't here on accident; I know that."

"After the boys were killed."

"That's right," he said, matter-of-factly.

"What do you know about that, Pete?"

He looked at me and grinned. "Well now, that's where you're gonna have trouble. I know enough about the game to know when to shut the hell up."

"Tell me about your daughter, Pete. What happened to her, back when she was a kid, about the same age as Kishi?"

He took a long pull. "You know what happened to her."

"Fair enough," I said. "I'm not going to bullshit you. I owe you that respect. Yes, we know what happened to your daughter, and we know that you must've taken a special interest in Kishi when the same thing happened to her. You stayed in touch with her, you had a relationship with her—"

"Not like that," he insisted.

"A friendship," I corrected. "Maybe you were a father figure to her."

He didn't speak.

"We know you helped her get a new start in life, with a new identity. Helped her get a place in Hollywood," I bluffed, hoping I was right that he had.

He nodded slightly, not surprised at all that we had discovered it.

I said, "She killed Todd Bailey because he raped her."

He shrugged, took another drink.

"She took him out to the point, maybe lured him out there. He wouldn't have recognized her all these years later, I'm sure. So maybe she gets him out there with the idea he could score, and then what? Pushes him over? Points a gun at him and tells him to jump?"

Hanson glanced at me and then away.

"Were you there with her?"

He sat motionless, his head down, not even contemplating a drink now. I had struck gold. I saw him out there with her, that's how it happened. He gave Bailey an option and Bailey thought maybe he could survive a jump into the ocean. He would have seen the darkness in Hanson's eyes as Hanson told him why he was going to die that evening. Why he *had* to die that evening, and Bailey took his chances going over.

"You *were* there with her," I said, an edge to my tone. "In fact, you set it all up. She wouldn't have thought of doing it that way. You planned it, you set it all in motion, and you saw it through—maybe in spite of her objections. And then she killed herself, disgusted by the dishonorable act she had been a part of. Ashamed more for the revenge than she had been for being victimized. She died because of you!"

He dropped the cup of Coke and bourbon, which distracted me for a second before I realized his right hand had dug beneath the pile of clothes. I lunged toward him, grabbing his right arm with both hands. But why hadn't I drawn on him, ordered him to freeze and prepared to shoot him if necessary? These thoughts flashed through my mind as I gripped his clammy wrist, committed now to stopping him from reaching his gun. I drove my shoulder into his face while pushing his arm down, hoping to contain the shot if he pulled the trigger. Time slowed, and I became aware of the dampness of his pungent breath, the wiry hair of his forearm, the thickness of his wrists, stronger than I could have imagined.

My grip slipped against his sweaty arm, and he reached farther into the pile of clothes. I feared losing control of his arm and allowing him to take a shot. Though I hadn't seen a weapon, I imagined his hand was wrapped around one now, or that he was still reaching for it. Yet I rejected the thought of shooting him; he had been one of us. A cop.

Josie came over the top of me. "Drop the gun! Drop it!"

Had she seen the gun? Was she going to shoot him?

My grip slipped again.

Josie yelled, "I'll shoot! I'm going to shoot you! Let go of the gun!"

I waited for the gunshot in the stench of bourbon and body odor. His whiskers rubbed my side, reminding me that he was mostly beneath me, and I wondered if Josie even had a shot. I was growing tired, my grip of his sweaty arm slowly slipping, slipping, slipping. My heartbeat pounded in my head, harder and harder. How long could I hold on?

She needed to take the shot. We were there, at the juncture of life and death. The idea that I would soon be sprayed with blood and brain matter didn't deter me from willing her to take the shot—a carefully placed one.

I couldn't hold on much longer, my arms burning with fatigue. I thought of yelling for Josie to shoot. Maybe she wasn't sure she should, not knowing if it was justified at this point or if I had the situation under control. I knew of similar shootings—I had interviewed deputies and officers who had been involved in just this type of situation, where one cop was struggling with an armed suspect, and the other cop took the bad guy out with a contact shot to the head. I thought about those interviews and remembered that in many of those cases, the struggling officer was the one who gave the command to take the shot. It occurred to me that her situation was worse than mine; she had to make a decision about taking a man's life—a former deputy sheriff no less—but was unsure of how dire the situation was. I needed to communicate my fears, let her know the situation was indeed a grim one. The man was stronger than he looked, and I was losing my grip. If his arm broke loose, one of us could be killed.

I blinked at the sweat that burned in my eyes, drew a breath, and yelled, "Take the shot!"

And a mighty blast echoed through the room.

41

Josie shouted, "Drop the gun!"

How was he going to *drop the gun? Her command made no sense to me. My hands gripped his sweaty wrists, controlling his arms. He was immobile beneath me, and no longer resisting. Had* Josie taken him out with that gunshot? I slowly released my grip of Hanson's wrist, and his arm fell limp.

Josie shouted again. "I said drop it, bitch."

I spun around to see Josie facing the hallway, her arms outstretched, her pistol leveled at a figure beyond her. I glanced at Hanson. He was alive, watching me, his eyes wide open, intent. I brushed aside the clothes and saw there was no weapon where his hand had reached, and I was momentarily paralyzed with confusion.

Josie said, "Don't make me shoot you. You don't want this. Drop the gun right now, and we can work all of this out."

For the first time, I saw her. A thin, pale girl with delicate features and inky black hair, short and spiky. She wore a black T-shirt with some type of satanic-looking design on the front. Her short sleeves revealed colorful blobs of ink covering both arms, and she had piercings all over her face. Everything about her screamed Hollywood, gothic, troubled. The fact that she held a gun to her own head now made that crystal clear.

I wondered if the first shot had been a hesitation shot—something not unheard of in cases of suicide—or if she had fired a shot to get our attention. I knew now that Josie hadn't fired; if she had, someone would be bleeding.

"He didn't do any of it," the girl said. "Leave him alone; he only has a few months left to live anyway. I did it. I did it all. I killed all three of them and yes, Kishi helped me with the first. But she apparently has a soul, something I haven't had since I was fifteen years old."

Hanson sat up, slowly. My gun was out and pointed in the direction of the girl with a gun to her head. My gaze flicked back and forth to Hanson, my free hand held toward him, signaling him to be still.

He said, "Honey—"

"No, Dad," the girl said, her gaze dashing toward him and then back to Josie. "It's over. I'm okay with this. You—you will not destroy your reputation to protect me. It's all you have left, and I won't let you go to the grave without it."

"Ashley—"

"Dad, no—shut up! Just—"

Josie had gained department notoriety when she shot and killed a bad man who had grabbed a hostage, and she had done so without hesitation. I knew she wouldn't hesitate to take the shot now, if for some reason the girl pointed her gun toward us. But I also knew the girl wasn't going to do that. I was certain that this was going to end with her blowing her own brains out, or by her giving in and dropping the gun. She was certainly teetering toward pulling the trigger at this point.

I lowered my gun but kept it in my hand. I quickly searched my mind for her name, having heard her dad just say it. *Ashley.* I said, "Ashley, you don't want your dad to see that, do you? You wouldn't do that to him."

Her watery eyes flicked toward her father on the couch. "I don't want to spend my life in prison. Daddy—"

"*Honey*—" Hanson pled.

I took a step toward her, now smelling burned gunpowder in the room. I glanced toward the ceiling but didn't see a hole in it. I took another small step, lowered my voice more and said, "I'd spend two lives in prison before I'd put a loved one through seeing what you're thinking of doing."

A tear rolled down her cheek, a streak of black showing its trail. She raised her elbow and pressed the muzzle of her gun tighter against her temple, reaffirming her resolve to check out in front of us all.

I shuffled another couple of inches toward her. "It isn't like the movies," I said. "It's a real messy thing, Ashley, something your father *will* take to the grave with him. The image of your head exploding, your brain flying across the living room, blood splattering all over the wall and soaking into the carpet as you lay there in your final moments. You will be aware of your death; I've seen it in the eyes of many. It will be excruciatingly painful during those final few minutes before you die." I moved closer, raised my voice to give it an edge, but not too much. "And that's hoping you don't survive, because then you'd live the rest of your life blowing into a straw to drive your fucking wheelchair."

Her elbow dropped an inch and her nostrils flared. Her eyes popped, anger surging through her, and then her gaze flicked once more toward her father. I leaped at her and grabbed the gun by its cylinder with one hand, her wrist with the other, and pushed both toward the ceiling before she could react. It was a double-action revolver, and the hammer wasn't cocked; she wouldn't be able to pull the trigger as long as my grip was tight enough to keep the cylinder from turning.

She stumbled backward and I yanked the gun from her hand just as Josie lunged past me and tackled her. Seconds later, Josie had the killer's hands cuffed behind her back.

I turned to look at Hanson. He was folded on the couch, weeping.

"I TAKE IT YOU'VE NEVER HAD ANY HOSTAGE NEGOTIATION TRAINING."

We were sitting in the conference room at the bureau, waiting for the captain. Lieutenant Black sat next to Josie, across from me at the cherry-wood table. He smiled and turned to Josie. "Are you telling me that Richard was less than diplomatic?"

"Jesus, Joe, I thought the psycho bitch was going to shoot us both, the things he was saying to her. I started squeezing the trigger, certain she was going to turn the gun on us. I was thinking, Okay, Dickie, I see what you're doing here, but I don't think the best way to stop a suicide is by turning her homicidal."

I chuckled, took a sip of my coffee, and said, "I wish this were scotch. I really could use a drink right now."

Lieutenant Black, his brows furrowed, said, "What did he say to her?"

Josie shook her head and rolled her eyes. "You don't want to know, Joe. It was bad. He was telling her shit like her brain would fly across the room and her head would explode and she might not even die, but that it takes several minutes to die from a headshot—"

"It could happen," I said, in my defense.

"Then he tells her she might survive and would be bound to a wheel-chair the rest of her life, a vegetable—and not in a very nice way."

"That's actually what set her off," I said. "I could see she was so goddam mad at me at that second, that she wasn't thinking about pulling the trigger."

"She was thinking about pointing the gun at you and *then* pulling the trigger."

I shrugged. "I was never one to play the 'good cop' role. Hey, why does the captain want to see us, anyway? We didn't kill anyone or even break anything."

Lieutenant Black said, "Richard, this is now a very delicate situation, one that the captain is going to have to first explain to the sheriff, and then smooth out for the press. You've got a mayor's son and two other boys who were killed by the daughter of a deputy sheriff. That's going to send the media into a frenzy."

"Hanson told us his daughter turned to drugs not long after she was raped. It's sad, really," I said. "You'd like to think she might have turned out differently, if not for what she went through. Same with Kishi, I guess, and the rest of them."

"It is sad," he agreed. "How did the two of them come together, this deputy's daughter, and Kishi?"

"Ashley's the daughter's name," I said. "She and Kishi became friends through Hanson, who was a divorcee by then. Ashley had lived with her mother when her parents first split up, but her mother couldn't deal with her so she went to live with dad. She was sort of lost, had turned to drugs and alcohol, and Hanson's doing the best he can as a single father. Then he gets this rape case assigned to him at work, the Kishi Takahashi case, and he tries to rescue Kishi, keep her from going down the same path as his daughter had. After his work on the rape case is finished, he stays in touch with Kishi, just trying to help her. He's smart enough to know he's walking a thin line, so he tries to protect himself from allegations of sexual misconduct by taking his daughter with him whenever he goes to see her. So the two of them, Ashley and Kishi, became friends, and that might have been the worst thing that could have ever happened to Kishi. Ashley was already a lost cause, an angry, vengeful young woman who was filled with hate."

"Who could blame her?" Josie said.

Lieutenant Black and I both looked at Josie. She met our gazes unapologetically and pushed her hair back behind her ear.

"What?" she said. "There's no doubt Ashley was unhinged, and I feel sorry for her. But I also get it. I can see where that rage came from. I saw the result of that pent-up anger in Eddie's studio."

As my partner spoke of this anger and rage, her eyes grew dark, her stare distant. I knew the origin of her passion, and I understood it, though at times it made me uneasy. She still had a long way to go toward healing from her own traumatic experiences.

"I feel horrible for her father," I said. "I think his heart was in the right place, but he made some bad decisions. He should never have allowed himself to become involved with that young girl, in any capacity. I'm not blaming him, but look at all the damage that's been done. I hate to say it's all on him—it isn't —but had he done his job and moved on, none of this would have happened."

It was quiet in the room. Josie's fist, clenched and white knuckled, covered her mouth. Lieutenant Black leaned on the table, his fingertips pressed together to make a steeple.

"And now he's crawled into a bottle," I said, "numb as he lives out his final days."

Lieutenant Black shook his head. "That's a shame."

"During the standoff," I continued, "the daughter said he was dying. But Hanson dismissed it later during our interview with him. He said he's having some trouble with his liver but denied that it was killing him."

"But he's drinking like a fish," Josie added. "There were booze bottles everywhere."

Lieutenant Black seemed to consider all of the information for a long moment, then asked, "You're sure the girl did the murders?"

I knew what he was thinking: Was it actually her, or had it been her father? We had gone to his home with the idea that he could be our suspect, but I left there knowing that it wasn't Hanson who had committed the murders, but his daughter, just as she confessed.

"Joe, I have no doubt she was the killer. Not only did she sponta-neously confess to killing them all, but I saw it in her eyes, heard it in her voice. She wasn't covering for anyone. If anything, it would make more sense that Hanson would cover for her, since he's dying. But he didn't."

Josie said, "She's more capable, in my opinion."

"How so?" the lieutenant asked.

Josie shrugged. "She just is. She's the type who'd kill without hesitation."

"The old man is worn out, tired, and drunk," I said, "just waiting it out. Ashley, on the other hand, is a twisted knot of rage, dark and unhinged, a real powder keg."

Lieutenant Black nodded, seeming to consider all of the information. He said, "But other than what she blurted out during the situation with her father, she hasn't confessed."

"She wouldn't talk to us in an interview," Josie said, "but she did chat with me a bit when I was booking her at Lakewood. She didn't exactly confess again, but she made it clear she wasn't sorry for what she had done."

I glanced at my watch and saw it was nearly midnight. I wasn't tired; I was jacked up, full of energy, on an adrenaline high as I relived those moments when it could have gone any direction but ended the best way possible. I kept running it through my mind, seeing it end in the other ways: Ashley pulling the trigger and blowing a hole in her head. Contrary to what I had told her, she would have been dead before she hit the ground. I pictured her turning the gun on us, and me and Josie slinging lead at her until she crumpled against the wall and slid down to the carpet where she died slowly, blood gurgling out of her mouth, a swath of crimson painting the wall behind her.

"Speaking of drinking," I said, "I'm going to have a cocktail after we talk to the captain. Who's joining me?"

Joe said, "Not I, sir. It is already hours past my bedtime, and we *all* have a long day tomorrow."

Josie said, "You know I'm with you. Shit, that was one hell of a night. There's no way I could go home and go to sleep, not until I get a few drinks in me."

I smiled. "Atta girl."

43

Early Thursday morning I raced north on the Golden State Freeway—running late, hung over, and hungry. The briefing was set for seven o'clock at Santa Clarita and I was hoping to be there by a quarter after. I called Floyd to let everyone know, and then I filled him in on the events of the night before. When he finished cursing me for not letting him know we were going to go confront the suspect on the three related murders, I said, "Dude, we had no idea it was going to go to shit."

After the briefing, we broke up and went our separate ways. Floyd and Mongo were going to drive to Palmdale to keep an eye on Spencer's home until given the word that he was in custody. At that time, they would serve the search warrant on the house with the assistance of a couple of Palmdale Station detectives. Steve Kennedy was going to drive to Gorman, where he would call Spencer from the station desk radio and ask if he was free to assist him on an arrest. He would tell the game warden to meet him at the station and they would drive out together. The surveillance team would follow Kennedy to Gorman and then split off and head to nearby Frazier Park, where they would set the stage for the action. There was a deputy who was living in a camp trailer at a small trailer park while building a cabin further up Frazier Mountain. The trailer looked like a place you'd buy meth, and Kennedy had given the deputy a hard time about it. When we came up with the plan, Kennedy had said he would see if we could use the trailer for the operation. I was going to hang out at Santa Clarita and wait for the show to go down in the booking cage, if all went according to plan. Josie was at the bureau with Lt. Joe Black, where they would monitor the activity by radio, keep the captain apprised of all activity, and make the appropriate notifications when the time came to do so. Lieutenant Black would be making the call to the administrative offices of Fish and Game to tell them that we had arrested one of their wardens.

At half past eight, Detective Steve Kelly crushed a cigarette with the toe of his boot and stepped into a trailer parked in Space #3 of Friendly RV, located on Frazier Mountain Road. The trailer rocked as the big man moved through it, finding the closet-size bathroom toward the rear. He relieved himself with little concern about accuracy, and then pondered for a long moment how to flush the camper-style toilet. He shrugged. Turning to face the mirror, Kelly pulled a small brush from his back pocket and clamped it between his teeth while removing a rubber band from his ponytail. He brushed out his hair, pulled it back into a tight ponytail, and then groomed his beard. The big man squeezed from the bathroom, walked to the front and peeked through the clouded window. He could see his sergeant's Tahoe across the street, tucked into a market parking lot. Kelly's outlaw biker look was completely appropriate for the area; Dwight Campbell, on the other hand, not so much. He had told the crew, "When we start rolling, I'll bring up the rear. Don't none of these rednecks around here wanna see no brutha cruising in a Tahoe." Kelly glanced the other way and saw the rest of the crew, each of them blending in as best they could, considering they still had all their teeth. Satisfied, Kelly wedged himself into the table seat, lit a cigarette, and pulled his pocket watch from his vest. It had stopped sometime during the night. He placed it back where it belonged and adjusted the chain that held it there.

TWO HOURS LATER, KENNEDY WHEELED INTO SANTA CLARITA STATION with Spencer riding shotgun, undercover detective Steve Kelly riding in the back seat. Along the way, Kelly was working toward his SAG card, calling the two of them motherfuckers and threatening all manner of things that might happen when they removed his cuffs. I had listened to it on the wire, and now Farris and I sat in the station parking lot, low in my car as we watched Kennedy and Spencer unload the undercover from Kennedy's black-and-white Bronco. As they led him to the back door of Santa Clarita, I saw they had used two sets of cuffs to restrain Kelly's arms behind his back. Only once or twice in my career had I found it necessary to use two sets of handcuffs to get a man secured due to excessive muscle and mass.

Kennedy keyed open the back door that led directly into the booking area, and the three lawmen—one of whom was also a criminal, and it wasn't the one in handcuffs—stepped onto the stage for the final act.

Farris and I hurried inside through an adjacent door that would allow us to catch all of the action. The three of them were already inside the secured area where firearms were not allowed. Deputies would check their guns into any available gun locker on the wall outside of the secured area, and then once inside, they would remove the arrestee's handcuffs and continue the booking process. I saw that the holsters of both Kennedy and Spencer were empty. Kelly, the biker-looking faux arrestee, stood facing the wall. Spencer stood behind his right shoulder, Kennedy his left. Kennedy said, "Okay man, I'm going to take the handcuffs off, and I don't want any trouble with you. Got it?"

Kelly said, "I'm cool, man." Ninety percent of arrestees who made threats on the way to jail changed their tunes when the moment came. Kelly played it perfectly.

The cuffs came off one hand at a time, and Kelly was told to put his hands on the wall as each was freed. He did, the model prisoner.

I tapped on the booking cage screen. Spencer looked back and I waved, smiling widely. "Hey Spence, how're you doing?"

He half smiled in return. "Okay. How are you?"

"Couldn't be better. Hey, I think you and I should have a chat."

"Oh?" he said, tentatively.

I waved a hand, no big deal. "When you're done there. No hurry."

"What are you doing up here?" he asked. Spencer knew enough of our operations to know I wouldn't be there unless I was investigating a homicide.

Farris stood next to me, and I indicated him with a nod of my head. "We're going to be making an arrest today."

"Oh," the game warden replied.

"Yeah, it's on the Brown case."

His face went pale, and he took a small step toward the cage. I saw Kelly turn from the wall, prepared. Kennedy nodded to give me the go-ahead. They were ready.

I said, "Yeah, it's been real interesting putting it all together, the Brown murder, my partner's kidnapping, Deputy Sheriff Tommy Lee Zimmerman's murder. Funny how it all just came together here the last week or so. Yeah, I can hardly wait to tell the son of a bitch that I've come for him, that he's never again going to see freedom, that he's going to spend the rest of his days being someone's bitch up at the big house, probably have his name changed to 'Peaches.'"

Jacob Spencer swallowed hard, his Adam's apple jumping in his skinny throat. He tried to force a smile as he said, "So, uh, who did it?"

Kelly had stepped up close behind him and Kennedy had moved to his side. Spencer didn't seem to notice.

I plastered the arrest warrant against the cage, and he leaned over to have a closer look. I said, "It's you, asshole. You're under arrest for murder."

His jaw went slack. He began to step backward, shaking his head, his mouth parted as if he had something to say, but couldn't find the words.

I indicated over his shoulder. "Watch behind you."

He turned to his left and Kelly stepped into him with a thundering overhand right. Spencer folded and hit the ground.

"Oh shit!" I exclaimed.

Farris chuckled.

Kennedy knelt down and began handcuffing the semi-conscious Jacob Spencer as the watch sergeant appeared by our side. He must have heard the sound of Spencer hitting the floor. He stepped closer to the cage and peered down at the game warden.

"He must've made a furtive move," said the sergeant. "I'll call for paramedics." He turned and started back toward his office, moving slowly while whistling softly, a walk in the park.

"That's how I saw it," I said.

"Yep," said Farris, "the old furtive movement."

Kennedy shrugged—*no big deal.*

Kelly, stone-faced, said, "Tommy was my friend."

4 4

I HAD BEEN A STRANGER TO CHINATOWN DURING THE LAST YEAR OR SO, AS the shootout in Yee Mee Loo's had changed the feel of the place. It was, for me, no longer the quiet getaway, the place for friendly conversations with complete strangers who shared an affection for the hole-in-the-wall, no-nonsense, drinking-man's bar. I had missed the jukebox full of golden oldies and the gentleman bartender, but I hadn't been able to bring myself to go back until now. Its central location was ideal for the cast of characters who agreed that a debriefing was in order.

Though we beat the evening crowd, the daytime regulars were strewn along the long stretch of the bar where normal people would naturally choose to sit. This worked out perfectly for us cops who preferred the far corner where our backs were to a wall and we could see both points of entry. It was there that Floyd, Mongo, Josie, Rich Farris, Steve Kelly, Dwight Campbell, and I gathered to revel in a successful day of police work.

Floyd, Josie, and Dwight sat on the three available stools, while the rest of us huddled behind them. Zhong, a small man with thick black hair plastered to his head, took our orders and began filling mugs of beer and shots of whiskey. He wasn't the talkative type, but with an exchange of smiles I knew he was as pleased as always to see us. I hadn't been so sure he would be; Zhong was keeping bar the night a professional came through the doors to fulfill a contract that had been placed upon my head. Dwight, Steve Kelly, and Floyd were there watching my back, and we lit the killer up like a Christmas tree on the floor of Zhong's otherwise peaceful bar.

Floyd and Mongo were recapping the successful warrant service at Jacob Spencer's home; they had collected tools, acid, and shards of shaved metal in the garage, metal believed to have been filed from the rifle Spencer had planted in the shed. A pair of cowboy boots that would likely be matched to the shoe impressions taken from around the miner's shed. There was also a collection of deer heads, more than a dozen of them, in varying stages of do-it-yourself taxidermy. Some heads boasted fully mature antlers; others were newly sprouted, a few yet in velvet. The varying stages signified that some of the deer had been taken out of season, evidence that Spencer was himself a poacher. That would help us establish motive for the Brown murder, which of course led to the events that took Tommy Zimmerman's life and resulted in the horrific ordeal Josie had survived when she was held captive in the miner's shed. Floyd said, "And he's a weird dude, too; there had to be a hundred bottles of piss scattered around the house."

"What?" Josie asked, her nose wrinkled.

"You think I'm kidding, ask Mongo."

Mongo snarled, showing disgust.

Floyd said, "Beer bottles, Coke bottles, Gatorade—you name it."

Dwight said, "Did you check the toilet? Maybe homie ain't got no plumbing. You know how you fuckin' rednecks are."

Floyd laughed and took a swig of beer.

I said, "You guys missed Kelly knocking Spencer on his ass. One punch, and homeboy folded like a cheap lawn chair."

Josie said, "I would've given anything to have been there for that."

Floyd set an empty glass on the bar. "I believe you were buying tonight, Dickie."

I smiled at him. "The tab's open, partner."

Floyd nodded and then turned to Farris. "How'd the interview go, anyway?"

Farris shook his head. "He lied and denied, and when that didn't work, he cried."

"He knew better than to cop out to us," I said. "I mean, really, who tells the cops they committed murder?"

"Enough of them do," Farris said, and raised his glass to toast dumb criminals.

"But we have enough to file on him, right?" Josie asked.

"No doubt," I said, pushing my hat up slightly in front. "I think he'll end up copping a plea in the long run, which might be best for us all." Of course, I was only thinking about Josie's welfare when I said it, and I saw the relief in her eyes at the mention of it.

"Man, what a week," Floyd said. And we drank to that as well.

At Farris's urging, I recapped the incident at Pete Hanson's house and told how the whole thing came together to solve three murders. "We solved the goddam mayor's kid," I finished, glancing at Josie with a smile stretched across my face.

She smiled back, remembering those exact words she had spoken two weeks earlier. She filled in the rest of her line: "Because that's how badass we are."

We bumped fists, both of us grinning widely.

I said, "And if I recall, you predicted it as a woman killer early on."

Josie just smiled to confirm it.

I took a long pull from a cold beer and then glanced toward the front door again.

Floyd noticed me looking. "Relax, Dickie, Leonard isn't coming back."

"It's not that," I said. But the mention of Leonard flung the door to that dark room wide open, and I paused at the image of that night: muzzle flashes, smoke hanging in the air, the subdued popping of gunfire and people screaming while Frank Sinatra serenaded and a killer bled out on the floor.

Josie said, "Are you expecting someone?"

It took a moment for me to come back from the memory. But when I did, I thought of *her*, and I smiled. Because I couldn't help but smile when I thought of Emily Bruce. *Red the Fed*. It had been a big step for me to send the text, but I had. We were blocks from the courthouse where she worked, and I hadn't seen her much in the last week. To bring her here was, in my mind, a risk in and of itself. This was a gathering of cops celebrating the successful conclusion of a couple of tough cases, and there would be reflections on how those cases were resolved that some outside of our profession might find appalling. Especially a federal prosecutor. But for all of my initial paranoia, I was beginning to see that she was a simple woman whose passion for her profession had been diminished over the years. It occurred to me that I might have been using this opportunity as a test. If she fit in with this group, she was a keeper.

She said, "It's the fed, right? What's-her-ass."

"Emily," I said.

"She's coming?"

I nodded toward the door. "She's here."

The door closed behind her, the beam of sunlight disappearing, a reminder that it was not yet nighttime. Emily pushed her sunglasses up on her head and looked around, probably waiting for her eyes to adjust to the darkness. I pushed through the crowd and went to her. "Hey," I said, when her gaze met mine.

She smiled. "Hey yourself."

I offered my hand and she took it, so I led her along the silk-paneled bar, past red velvet lanterns and statues of the eight immortals of Chinese lore. We joined the gathering of contented cops, and I made the introductions. Floyd got up and offered her his seat at the bar, and Emily took it. His back was to her when he looked at me with dancing eyebrows, a wide grin on his face. Floyd was letting me know that he unequivocally approved of the Scottish lass.

The conversations continued. Steve Kelly was arguing to his sergeant, Dwight Campbell, that the spectacular punch to the face of Jacob Spencer was indeed necessary and justified. Dwight didn't truly care that it had happened; he was just annoyed that along with every use of force came reams of paperwork, a thing the salty sergeant despised. Floyd was getting the details about Lizzy from her partner, Rich Farris, whose thirst seemed unquenchable and all of us knew why. Mongo was a spectator in that conversation. I propped an elbow on the bar and listened while Josie and Emily chatted happily—two roses gracing a cactus bed. They talked wine, they talked music, they talked hairstyles and manicures and summer fashions and exotic vacations. They talked about everything other than the job; women were different that way.

My stomach was growling, and I suggested to the ladies that the three of us slip away for dinner. Emily beamed and said it was a lovely idea.

Josie declined. "I have a hot bath and early bedtime in mind. I'm exhausted, and I have a feeling I'll sleep better tonight than I have in a very long time."

I imagined she would as well, and I pictured her tucked comfortably between scented sheets, a fan twirling slowly above her, a smile on her face as she welcomed darkness for the first time in months.

"Okay," I said, "but you have to buy out."

"What? I have to buy a round to leave?"

"No, the buyout for you is the hooker story."

Emily, sipping her drink, raised her brows.

A grin crept onto Josie's face. "It wasn't really that big of a deal."

"I want to hear it," I assured her.

She stood, shrugged her purse onto her shoulder, and finished the rest of her drink. She set it down, resolutely, and pushed it toward the well. "Okay, Slocumb used me as a decoy on a prostitution sting. It was my first time—"

"So you say."

She backhanded my shoulder. "We're wired for sound, and these things are recorded, and we are reminded to be very careful of what we say, because those tapes have to be submitted in court, unedited. Well, he sets me up. He had some dude from Narco cruise by and hit me up. This is broad daylight, not far from the station, and I'm sauntering around on the sidewalk in a miniskirt and pumps, for God's sake"—she turned to Emily —"in South Central.

"Anyway, the Narco dude rides up and I hit him up at the passenger's window. He leans over from the driver's side, lifts his shades and makes it real obvious he's looking me over. I ask if he likes what he sees, and the asshole says, 'Do they have anyone younger out here?'"

I laughed. Emily shook her head. Josie said, "And I let loose on him, calling him every unchristian thing you could imagine as he peeled away from the curb. I pulled off a shoe and launched it at his car, bounced it off the back window. I'm just lucky—or maybe he is—that I wasn't armed."

"And it's all on tape," I said.

Josie sighed. "It's all on tape, thanks to your buddy, Slocumb."

"Nice."

"I'm sorry," Emily said, "but that is hilarious. You cops know how to have a good time."

Josie smiled at Emily and then turned her attention to me. "Speaking of having a good time, we're up for murders in the morning. I'm out of here."

"You can relax," I assured her, as I had during our last on-call period. It had been a cool and drizzly Wednesday morning, the type of day you could count on to be slow in the blood business. It had been the type of situation that offered the hope of a rare on-call period where none of the teams was sent out. This time, our on-call would begin at six tomorrow morning, a Friday, and last until ten o'clock Saturday night. The news cautioned of a sudden rise in temperatures, and there would be a full moon tomorrow night. "What could go wrong?"

***

Stay tuned for a sneak preview of UNWRITTEN RULES…

But first:

I love staying connected with my readers through social media and email. If you would like to connect, find me on BookBub, Amazon, Goodreads, Facebook, Instagram, and Twitter. You can also sign up for my newsletter and receive bonus material, such as the action-packed short story, Harder Times.

As a newsletter subscriber, you will receive special offers, updates, book releases, and blog posts. I promise to never sell or spam your email.

Danny R. Smith

Dickie Floyd Novels

UNWRITTEN RULES
Book 6 in the Dickie Floyd Detective Series

A crowd had gathered across the street, impeding the flow of commuters arriving at the civic center for another day of American justice, Compton style. Cops, lawyers, witnesses. Dutiful civilians responding to their juror summonses. Defendants out on bail, free to live their lives of crime while the wheels of justice crept along. Each of them likely speculating as to what had happened here, correctly assuming that someone had died. Suddenly. Violently. The telltale signs their clues: yellow tape strung from an apartment building to the center of the street, a highway patrol car sitting ominously in the center of the cordoned area, its front end pointed at the apartment. Pointed at me, in fact—the detective in the window.

Focused on the crowd but speaking to my partner, I said, "Did you know that the first highway patrolman killed in Compton was shot by a deputy sheriff?"

From somewhere in the apartment behind me, she said, "How have I never heard that?"

I turned and looked at her. If anyone could rock disposable blue gloves and paper booties, it was Josie, a veteran detective whose dark blue pinstripe suit and cream-colored blouse blended nicely with the usual accessories one wears at a murder scene. Her dark hair hung loosely at her shoulders, offsetting the otherwise professional look of a lady cop. She appraised me as if I were a suspect in an interrogation, clearly skeptical about what I had said.

"You never heard that story?"

Her eyelashes fluttered, but not in a come-hither way. "No, Dickie, I never heard it."

I continued, "What happened, the deputy was trying to shoot this horse—"

"A *horse!* Why would he shoot a horse? And why was there a horse in Compton?"

The uniformed deputy at the door, stationed there to protect the integrity of our crime scene, turned and looked at me, his eyebrows raised. I smiled at him and turned back to my partner. "Back then—this was in the early seventies—there were several riding stables around here. Black cowboys were a thing, and let me tell you, nobody messed with them. Anyway, there had been an accident and a horse inside a trailer was badly injured. Chippies had the handle because the accident happened in the county, just outside city limits."

Looking back at the crowd outside, I visualized a dead horse in *our* scene, seeing it as it might have appeared on the news that day. There would be a crowd of course—there was always a crowd. Shaggy haired men wearing bellbottoms, Elvis sideburns and shades. The women, well, they might have taken more care with their hair and clothing than the ones who were here today. I grinned at the thought of women with their Farrah Faucet feather-cut hair and brightly-colored dresses that fell well above the knee. The newscaster, a man—almost always a man then—solemn while speculating about the horse. *Why would deputies shoot a horse?*

I said to Josie, "The deputy pulled his thirty-eight and shot the poor bastard in the head—*BAM!*"

"The horse," she clarified.

I turned to face her again. "Yes, the horse. He was trying to put it out of its misery, but the bullet ricocheted off the trailer and hit the chippie in the chest. There were no vests back then, so the bullet ripped through his ribcage and lodged in his heart. He was D-R-T."

"D-R-T?"

"Dead right there."

Josie rolled her eyes and moved away, scanning the scene.

I lifted my fedora and wiped sweat from my forehead with the palm of my hand, while eyeing the fan that stood next to me at the open window. It was off when we arrived, and it would remain so while we conducted our investigation. That was the first rule of homicide work: never alter a crime scene.

I left the window and returned to the body that lay facedown near the doorway. Staring at the dead highway patrolman, I did the math. It had been fifty years since the chippie was killed by the deputy's errant bullet. That was 1972. Two years earlier, in 1970, four chippies were killed during a shootout in Newhall, a place that was then, and remains, a world away from Compton. My gaze fixed on the dead man at my feet, I uttered, "Almost fifty years."

Josie appeared at my side, her fresh, floral scent washing over me. She said, "And that's the only other time a chippie's been killed in Compton?"

"There've been other cops killed here over the years: MacDonald and Burrell, the two Compton coppers killed over near Rosecrans and Dwight, back in the early nineties—"

"I remember."

"And others. But the chippie, the one who was killed by the deputy, he was the first and only CHP killed in Compton, to my knowledge."

"Until now," she said.

"Until now."

Josie continued making some notes for an affidavit. At this point, we didn't know anything about the dead highway patrol officer who lay prone on the floor of the modestly furnished apartment, which was otherwise unoccupied. We didn't even know how he had died. There were no obvious signs of trauma and no indication that he had encountered violence here—at least nothing we could yet see. It appeared as if he had walked—or more likely, run—into the apartment and keeled over. Nonetheless, we would investigate it as a homicide until the manner of death was established. We would need judicial blessing to seize the private residence as a crime scene. If this turned out to be a murder, we had to consider that his killer might have lived here and could have legal standing inside the apartment, meaning he would be protected against unwarranted searches of his residence. There were no *dead cop* exceptions, which was the essence of Mincey vs. Arizona, and the genesis of the crime scene search warrant. Simply, a Mincey warrant.

Josie, meandering through the kitchen, said, "The tenants are Hispanic."

I glanced around at the various pictures on the walls: Jesus on the cross, Jesus at The Last Supper, Our Lady of Guadalupe with her head bowed. There were figurines and candles adorning shelves, and a small shrine on a table in the corner. "Ya think?"

She slapped her notebook closed and slid it into her pocket. "Are you ready?"

I retrieved my phone from my pocket and tapped the button that would call the main line to Homicide. It was first on my Favorites list, programmed as '187,' the California penal code for murder. While waiting

283

for the call to connect, I tucked the phone beneath my chin and said to Josie, "I'm going to have the office put a hold on the coroner while we get a warrant signed."

Josie scanned the small apartment once more, likely making sure she had everything noted for the affidavit.

After finishing the call, I followed Josie through the doorway, pausing to address the deputy whose name tag identified him as Parker. "Nobody in or out while we're gone."

"Got it, sir."

"If the crime lab shows up, tell them we've gone to get a warrant. Also, make sure you leave the door open just as you found it, but keep the looky-loos at bay. If the landlord happens by, see if you can get some information on the tenants."

"Yes sir."

Josie and I walked down the driveway, past the CHP car where a second deputy stood. We ducked under the yellow tape and got into Josie's Charger. She started the engine and I got the air conditioner going and adjusted my vents. The plan was to go one block over to the Compton sheriff's station where we could type a search warrant and affidavit and print it out before walking next door to the courthouse.

An hour later, we returned with a signed warrant and saw that Phil Gentry had arrived from the crime lab. He was snapping photos of the outside while awaiting our return.

We signed back in on the crime scene log, gloved up, and went to work. Phil took scene photos and then dusted for latent prints. Josie and I searched through drawers and cabinets, in the closet, and under the bed in an attempt to identify the tenants or their landlord.

After a short while, I met Josie near the small kitchen and held up a black book. "This is all I came up with, some names and numbers, everything in Spanish."

She traded me the black book for a handful of mail. "Utility bills in the name of Maria Guadalupe Gomez Hernandez. By the looks of it, I'd say Maria is an elderly woman."

I looked around again and couldn't disagree with her. *Old* was the first word that came to mind. *Orderly* yet another. But who was she, and why was there a dead chippie on her floor?

Josie said, "Should we call for the coroner?"

"Sure," I said.

As Josie made the call, I stepped over to the window again. The number of onlookers had doubled, and I wondered how many of them were supposed to be inside the courthouse by now, handling their business. Two news crews had arrived and were aiming their cameras toward us.

Josie ended her call and said the coroner would be here in thirty minutes.

I said, "I'm going to canvas the neighbors. Why don't you try calling a few of those numbers, see if you can find out who Maria Guadalupe is and why she isn't home."

Josie took a seat at the dining area, which consisted of a card table under a plastic cover and two folding chairs. I walked out.

Twenty minutes later I was back with an announcement. "Coroner's ninety-seven," I said, using the radio code that indicates a unit or person's arrival at a particular location.

Josie set her phone down. "No luck with the phone numbers. Did you get anything from the neighbors?"

I shook my head. "Nobody's home next door. One of the two upstairs apartments is vacant, the other is occupied by an elderly man who said he hasn't seen or heard anything all day. Then again, he just got out of bed."

"Great. What about a landlord? Did he at least give you that?"

I held up my notebook. "He gave me the name of a property manager and the address where he sends his check, but no phone number. That can be one of our next stops. We also need to talk to court security before we leave today."

"The parking lot guards?"

"And the guys inside, see if there's any cameras that pick up the apartment."

Coroner's Investigator Nick Stewart appeared in the doorway and signed in on the deputy's log. Stewart, all business beneath his blond flattop and furrowed brow, stared at the body of the deceased traffic officer while stretching a pair of disposable gloves over his hands. "What's the story on this?"

Josie said, "Compton got a nine-one-one call, a female reporting that a

CHP officer had jumped out of his car and run toward the apartment building across from the courthouse parking structure. Deputies responded and found the patrol car as it sits with its driver's door open."

Stewart didn't look up. He was busy tucking his tie into his shirt, a habit of men who wear business attire and hover over dead people.

Josie continued: "The deputies searched the area and found the door to this apartment open, just as it is now. They saw the chippie down, so they cleared the apartment for suspects, checked his vitals, and called for paramedics. He was pronounced at zero-eight-forty-six."

Stewart scanned the small room, as if something seemed amiss.

I said, "Window was open, as it is now."

He nodded and returned his gaze to the fallen officer. "Let's have a look."

Josie said, "There were half a dozen deputies here within minutes, and none of them found anything that would give us a clue about what happened."

Stewart ran his gloved hand over the officer's head, probing for evidence of trauma beneath the thick black hair. He then turned the dead man's head both directions, gently, while inspecting all areas of the head and neck. Stewart lowered the head to the floor and retreated to the briefcase he had set behind him. He made a few notes on a coroner's investigation report, then went back to the body. Keeping his eyes on it, he said, "I'm going to roll him, guys."

Josie and I both stepped up for a closer look. I would have expected to see blood oozing from beneath the body had he been shot or stabbed. The absence of any obvious trauma had me puzzled. Maybe he had been struck in the head or knocked out by a punch to the jaw. Neither of those things would necessarily cause bleeding. But would that have killed him? It was possible. The more I saw of death, the less I was surprised by the peculiarity of it. Death could be strange business.

As Stewart tried to roll the officer's body, it hung up on the pistol holstered on his hip. I wondered what might have caused an officer to run into a building that hadn't also raised concerns for his safety. But chippies were wired differently than deputies. The bulk of their contacts with the public were traffic related, and the majority of those contacts resulted in citations. Deputies, on the other hand, had at the forefront of their minds the notion that every contact had the potential to turn deadly. It would be rare to see a deputy chase a man into a building without having drawn his weapon. Especially in this neighborhood.

But had this officer actually chased someone into the building? This was only an assumption on my part, which was a violation of Rule Two in homicide work: never assume anything. I reflected on the briefing as it had been told to us by the handling unit when we arrived. The officer had jumped out of his car and run into the building. No mention of him chasing anyone. I wondered who might have made the call, and what they had seen that caused them to call 9-1-1.

I tapped Josie's elbow and said, "Let's make sure we get a copy of the nine-one-one."

The deputy at the door said, "I'll have the watch deputy take care of that for you, sir."

I looked over at him. "Thank you, sir."

Stewart had lowered the officer's torso to the floor and released his grip on the dead man's shoulder. "No sign of any significant trauma, just a small contusion on his forehead." He stood up and took one step backward while peeling off his gloves, staring at the chippie.

I knew Stewart would forgo probing the officer's liver to document the body temperature relative to the ambient temperature. It was unnecessary to do so when the circumstances of the case removed any question of the approximate time of death. Some coroner's investigators might have been inclined to do so anyway, in order to check off each box on the crime scene procedures list. Stewart was a seasoned professional who had the confidence to allow common sense to guide him, and he was also one who would handle a dead officer with great reverence.

"Did you see his name tag, by chance?" Josie asked, her pen posed over her notebook.

"Officer Gomez," Stewart answered, his voice low and melancholy. "Let's see if he's got his ID with him."

I waited while Stewart went through the dead officer's pockets one by one. This was a task that, by law, police officers and detectives were not allowed to perform. The body belongs to the coroner. Until a representative of the coroner's office was there to do it himself or available to give a detective permission to do so, we were not allowed to move the body or search through any clothing or belongings that were worn by or attached to the decedent.

The license was in a breast pocket. Stewart held it at arm's length to read it. "Antonio Carrera Gomez."

I turned to meet Josie's gaze. "Gomez. That was the name on the utility bill, right?"

She nodded. "Could be a coincidence though. It's a common name."

"How's that work again, with the two last names?"

"So, traditionally, the two last names are the first last names of one's parents. In this case, you would have Carrera as the first last name of his father, and Gomez as the first last name of his mother. Does that make sense?"

"You're saying that Maria Guadalupe could be his mother, right?"

"Technically, yes. But again, it's a very common name."

"But here he is, dead on her floor."

Stewart reconfigured his tie while saying, "You think he's related to someone here?"

"We don't know," I said. "We'll find out though."

Stewart looked at me. "If you identify the next of kin and make notification, let me know."

"You bet," I said.

Josie asked, "What do you think, Nick? I mean, with such little trauma, what might have killed him?"

He shrugged. "We'll see what they find during the post. Could be a natural."

The thought that it might have been a natural death had crossed my mind. Though the officer appeared fit, it didn't mean he couldn't have dropped dead from a heart attack after running from his car into the building. When it's your time to go, it's your time to go.

From the hallway, the patrol deputy said, "Sir, CHP brass is ninety-seven."

I nodded and looked at Stewart. "Are you ready to take him downtown?"

"Transport's outside waiting, and I've done all I can here. Are you guys finished?"

"I think so," I said, moving back to take a glance through the window.

There were half a dozen CHP cars out front now, men and women in their tan uniforms with blue leg stripes standing together. Several deputies stood scattered not far from them, set apart in their tan uniform shirts with dark green pants. One of them waved his hand from the CHP car toward the building, perhaps hypothesizing what may have happened. I turned from the window. "Would you mind if we gave the CHP brass a walk-through before we move him, Nick?"

Stewart shrugged. "I've got no problem with it."

Gentry had packed up his equipment. "I'm out of here, Dickie. Are you going to want aerials? I could probably go up in a bird this afternoon if I don't get another callout."

I thought about it briefly. "Yeah, why not. It's a dead cop."

He gave me a thumbs up and walked out, his gear slung over his shoulder.

I went outside and addressed the CHP brass that had arrived, telling them we didn't yet know what caused their officer's death. I said, "There are no obvious signs of significant trauma, so at this point, it's anyone's guess. He may have had a heart attack."

A heavyset man, gray hair matching his neatly trimmed mustache, said, "But we have no idea *why* he was here in Compton."

The two bars on his collar told me this man was a captain, and I assumed he would be the commander of their South Los Angeles office, located not far from where we stood.

"Could he have had court?" I asked, turning to glance at the court-house behind me.

The captain shook his head. "Not down here. Officer Gomez was assigned to the Newhall office, and he was on duty since zero-six-hundred. We had no knowledge of his departure from his assigned beat this morning."

Available on Amazon

289

Independent authors count on word-of-mouth and paid advertising to find new readers and sell more books. Reviews can help shoppers decide about taking a chance on authors who are new to them.

I would be grateful if you took a moment to write a review on Amazon.

Thank you!

Danny R. Smith

THE DICKIE FLOYD SERIES

- A Good Bunch of Men
- Door to a Dark Room
- Echo Killers
- The Color Dead
- Death after dishonor
- Unwritten Rules

SHORT STORIES

- In the City of Crosses - A Dickie Floyd Detective Short Story
- Exhuming Her Honor - A Dickie Floyd Detective Short Story
- Harder Times: A Cop Goes to Prison - Not a Dickie Floyd Story

AVAILABLE ON AUDIBLE

- A Good Bunch of Men
- Door to a Dark Room

ABOUT THE AUTHOR

Danny R. Smith spent 21 years with the Los Angeles County Sheriff's Department, the last seven as a homicide detective. He now lives in Idaho where he works as a private investigator and consultant. He is blessed with a beautiful wife and two wonderful daughters. He is passionate about his dogs and horses, whom he counts among his friends.

Danny is the author of the *Dickie Floyd Detective Novel* series, and he has written articles for various trade publications. He publishes a weekly blog called The Murder Memo, which can be found at dickiefloydnovels.com.

He is a member of the Idaho Writers Guild and the Public Safety Writers Association.

Made in the USA
Coppell, TX
11 November 2020